STEPHANIE ROWE

HUNT THE DARKNESS

HUNT THE DARKNESS (*Order of the Blade, #11*)
Copyright © 2017 by Stephanie Rowe.
Cover design © 2017 by Kelli Ann Morgan
www.inspirecreativeservices.com

ISBN-10: 1-940968-50-X
ISBN-13: 978-1-94968-50-6

For further information, please contact:
Stephanie@stephanierowe.com

Dedication

To Malinda Davis Diehl, Donna Bossert, and Nikki Pearce, for all their help and their passionate support of authors and books. I love you guys!

Acknowledgements

Special thanks to my beta readers and the Rockstars. You guys are the best! There are so many to thank by name, more than I could count, but here are those who I want to called out specially for all they did to help this book come to life: Malinda Davis Diehl, Leslie Barnes, Kayla Bartley, Alencia Bates Salters, Alyssa Bird, Donna Bossert, Jean Bowden, Shell Bryce, Kelley Daley Curry, Ashley Cuesta, Denise Fluhr, Valerie Glass, Heidi Hoffman, Jeanne Stone, Dottie Jones, Guinevere Jones, Janet Juengling-Snell, Deb Julienne, Bridget Koan, Felicia Low, Phyllis Marshall, Suzanne Mayer, Jodi Moore, Ashlee Murphy, Elizabeth Neal, Judi Pflughoeft, Carol Pretorius, Kasey Richardson, Caryn Santee, Amber Ellison Shriver, Summer Steelman, Regina Thomas, and Linda Watson. Special thanks to my family, who I love with every fiber of my heart and soul. And to AER, who is my world. Love you so much, baby girl!

HUNT THE DARKNESS

Chapter One

VLADIMIR HAWKINGS WASN'T a real sunshiny kind of guy.

Flawless blue skies weren't high on his list either.

And laughter? That infectious, bubbling mirth that was so contagious that it could turn an entire battlefield of bitter, bleeding warriors into giggling idiots? He could honestly say he absolutely hated laughter.

Not because he was a bitter, miserable, anti-social bastard (well, okay, he was, but that was beside the point). He despised those things because every single one of them reminded him of Sophie Flanagan, the most irritating, sassy, unapologetic, irreverent female he'd ever met.

Sophie was also the only person he'd ever fallen completely, madly, hopelessly, and eternally in love with.

She'd been his best friend. His only friend really, due to his not-so-endearing antisocial bastard tendencies.

She'd been his partner in crime since they were small enough to crawl through the slats in his kingdom's main gate and sneak out into the woods.

And, most significantly, she was the girl he'd married in a secret ceremony when they were sixteen, binding her to him in a magical, unbreakable promise to always protect her...which he had then failed to do.

She'd died twelve hours later because he'd failed her.

Even after two hundred years, every time he thought of her, a dark cesspool churned inside him. Since her death drove his actions and thoughts pretty much every second, of every minute, of every day, that meant he was basically one rotting pile of darkness these days. Which was good. It drove him relentlessly, turning him into a merciless hunter who never abandoned what he took on.

He never stopped to think.

He never stopped to feel.

He just kept going, head down, trying to stay ahead of the ghosts haunting him so ruthlessly. Usually, he succeeded. Usually, he was an automaton, swooping in to rescue a missing or kidnapped kid here or there, and depositing them back where they belonged to the waiting families who actually *cared* if their kid was dead or alive. Usually, he was a machine.

Except when he slowed down, looked around, and noticed that life was real. When he heard someone laugh. When the sun's warmth managed to penetrate the cold shield he kept wrapped around him and began to thaw the icy barrier encasing his soul.

Like today, when he had nothing else to do. No one to save. Nothing to distract him.

That's when life got shitty.

Vlad slouched lower in the battered wooden chair, watching the scene in the street through half-closed eyes. A man and his wife were arguing about something. Nothing, probably. People argued about such dumbass things. The fools didn't get it. They never got it, not until they'd been to hell and back. It was then that they'd sometimes finally realize how much time and energy they'd wasted on stupid shit that didn't matter. But since most people didn't survive hell, it was a lesson few people learned in time to find meaning in life, including him.

He knew it now, but it was too fucking late.

Scowling, he leaned back in his chair, glaring at the other diners to make sure no one was crowding his space, but everyone was keeping their distance.

As he liked it.

He took a sip of his beer. It was warm, close to hot even, stripped of its chill by the humid heat swirling through the brutal Midwest summer weather. He stretched out his legs, his heavy, black motorcycle boots thudding on the old wooden deck of the weather-beaten cafe he'd graced with his presence for lunch. As he moved, the chains that wrapped around the boots clunked against each other, a dull sound of metal against metal. It was too hot for his leather jacket, but he didn't care. He liked having it on. The battered leather, creased and shiny from so many years of gruesome living, made people avert their eyes and scurry to the other side of the street. As if a few yards gave them any hope of survival if he ever decided to go after them.

People's delusions of safety were a crock, and sometimes he wanted to shake them down and bellow at them for being so stupid as to think that their measly precautions actually ensured their safety. Why weren't they ready for the knife to stab them in the back? Why weren't they looking over their shoulders? Why did they trust that life wasn't going to rip their foundation out from under them? Why the hell did they trust the people they loved?

He used to try to warn people. He used to try to help. He didn't anymore. People saw the world they wanted to see, and that was it.

"Is this seat open?"

Vlad looked up slowly, his trademark scowl in place. An old man with grizzled, gray hair was standing next to him, holding a bottle of the same beer Vlad was drinking. His hair hung in tangled mats down his back, and his beard was the same, reaching almost to his waist. His blue eyes were vivid, sunk deep into pits in his heavily wrinkled skin. He was wearing a black wool cape pulled tight around him, obscuring all but the tips of what appeared to be battered cowboy boots.

Vlad was kind of impressed that the old man had dared to speak to him. Not many people did these days. Sophie had always had a soft spot for old people, so he sighed and decided that practicing courtesy once a century wouldn't be a bad thing. Vlad responded, lifting one shoulder in a shrug, granting the old man permission to take the chair to another table that was overcrowded with pompous self-absorbed bastards pretending to be friends.

"Great." The man pulled out the chair and sat down beside him.

He sat down.

At Vlad's table.

Beside Vlad.

What the hell? Clearly, Vlad had made a strategic error by showering this morning. Apparently, he smelled too good. Or maybe it was his hair. It always got shiny when he washed it. He had to stop doing that. Shiny hair wasn't antisocial enough.

The old man set his beer on the table with a solid thud.

Vlad couldn't remember the last time anyone had sat next to him. It was irritating to have someone so close, but at the same time, the boldness of the old man was mildly interesting.

Not many people surprised him, and he found he was intrigued by the old man who'd ignored every sign Vlad had sent to stay away. "Seat's taken," he said, testing the old man, but weirdly, not really caring if the guy stayed. "Move."

The old man grinned at him and wiggled his bony ass more deeply into the chair, flashing yellowed teeth that hadn't had a close enough relationship with basic hygiene over the years. "Nice day, isn't it?"

"Nice day?" Vlad repeated in disbelief. Was this guy actually making idle conversation with him? "*Nice day?*"

"Yep. Sure is." The old man took a long sip of his still-frosty beer. "What's going on? Anything good?"

Vlad's head began to pound. He wasn't sure he could recall the last time someone tried to make small talk with him. Or even spoken to him voluntarily. Yeah, he got emails with names, descriptions, and info about missing kids from people who'd heard about him in whispered conversation in dark alleys, but he never actually *spoke* to anyone, other than the kids he'd rescued. Even then, he did only what was necessary to get them to go with him. He worked hard to make it that way, and now he remembered why. Conversation made him think, and

4

he didn't like to think anymore. His mild curiosity retreated, replaced by annoyance. He wanted his space.

So, he didn't answer, turning away to check out the progress of the street fight. The husband and wife who had been gearing up for a throw-down fight were now standing close together, their heads bent toward each other in earnest discussion. As Vlad watched, the man took his wife's hand and squeezed it gently. It was a moment of perfect harmony, a triumph over an argument, and it made Vlad even more pissed off than he'd already been. "It's a lie," he said aloud, muttering to himself.

The old man raised his bushy eyebrows. "What is?"

Vlad jerked his chin toward the couple. "That. They act like they care, but one day, they'll betray each other. Why do they lie like that? Why don't they just lay it out there and say, 'look, you're hot, and I know that I promised to love you forever, but I'm going to fuck you over in a major way at some point, so all this shit is just a lie.' That way, everyone knows what to expect and you can prepare yourself."

His tablemate tilted his head. "Two reasons."

"It was a hypothetical question."

"There's no such thing. Every hypothetical question is a thinly veiled cry for illumination. I am happy to provide."

Vlad raised one eyebrow. "Yeah, that was definitely a thinly veiled cry. I do that a lot, you know. Cry, beg for philosophical clarity, and shit like that."

The old man was undaunted. "So, you have no theories about why humans offer love and support to each other, even if the future could be bleak?"

Vlad snorted. "I know all I need to know about how pathetic human nature is." But he had to admit he was mildly curious what this old man had to say. It had been a long, damned time since anyone had offered an opinion to him. It felt strange to be in an actual conversation, but at the same time, something about it felt familiar, like he'd been here before with this guy, waiting for an answer. Weird, but he'd seen enough not to be surprised by anything. "Do I know you?"

The old man ignored his question. "The first reason people

declare their love and make promises is because not everyone fucks their loved ones over. Some people actually fulfill their promises."

"Seriously?" Vlad snorted in disdain. "You've lived as long as you have, and you still think that? What kind of fairyland did you grow up in?"

"I've lived for over three hundred years," the man said. "I've seen far more than you have, young man."

Three hundred years? So he wasn't entirely human? Vlad narrowed his eyes, not sure what he thought of the fact he wasn't the only immortal at the table. "I've seen plenty in two hundred years. Not sure another hundred makes that much of a difference." His mind flashed back to a day long ago, the one that had changed his life forever. *Sophie.* For a split second, grief washed over him, a ruthless, overwhelming grief laced with guilt so sharp he couldn't take a breath. Swearing silently, he shoved his emotions aside and glared at the old man. "I learned enough about human nature in my first sixteen years. Didn't need any more than that."

The old man spun his beer between his hands, his blue eyes focused on Vlad. "Would you like to know the second reason people open themselves up to love, even if there is no guarantee of a happy ending?" he asked conversationally.

Vlad sighed, and took a sip of his near-to-boiling beer, almost grateful for the distraction from his memories. If this old man's inane conversation gave him even a tiny respite from them, then he'd take it. "Yeah, sure. Lay it on me."

"Because being ready for someone you love to betray you doesn't make it any easier to face when it happens." The old man tapped his beer against Vlad's, as if he were toasting his brilliant words, then took a long drink.

"Huh." Vlad contemplated that statement for a moment, then shook his head. He knew damn well what it was like to be sucker punched by someone he trusted. "No way. If you're prepared, then you can be ready when they screw you over, instead of letting it paralyze you until it's too late." *Too late. Too late. Too late.* He'd been too late for Sophie, because he hadn't been ready. He'd believed in the wrong people, and she had paid the price. He should have been smarter. He should have somehow realized what was going on. But he hadn't. "No one can get to me now, and I like it that way."

"Do you?" There was disbelief in the old man's voice that rankled Vlad. "Is it really so fantastic to live in isolation, decade after decade, with no one noticing or caring whether you take your next breath? Having no one that matters to you? Having no reason to wake up and face another day? Is that really the life that burns in your veins to be lived?"

"Enough." Vlad glowered at him, all amusement gone. "Nothing burns in my veins, and I like it that way, so—"

A child's shout caught his attention, and Vlad instinctively looked across the road for the source of the noise. Three boys were skateboarding, and a fourth had fallen behind. He was smaller, younger, maybe a kid brother, and he couldn't keep up.

"I make no promises I can't keep." Not anymore, at least. He never responded to the emails asking for his help. He just took off in the middle of the night to see what he could do. Sometimes the parents woke up to find their kid crawling into their bed. Sometimes, they didn't. But he never promised *anything*.

Vlad watched the smaller boy approach a divot in the sidewalk that the other kids had jumped. It was almost a foot wide, a hazard that would send the younger one flying. "No one gets disappointed, and I don't owe anyone anything. It's the way it should be."

"You don't want to be a hero?"

"I'm no hero." Vlad leaned forward, watching the scene more closely. The kid was getting closer to the broken sidewalk, but he wasn't slowing down. He was looking ahead, yelling at his brother to wait up.

"You're supposed to be a hero," the old man said. "It's your birthright."

"My birthright?" Vlad glanced at his tablemate. There was something in his eyes, something knowing, something Vlad was sure he'd seen before. "I do know you." It wasn't a question this time. "From a long time ago." But he couldn't place him.

A pleased smile stretched across the weathered face. "Yes."

He offered no more explanation, but before Vlad could ask, another shout jerked his attention back to the street. He turned sharply, and he saw the kid's wheels hit the broken sidewalk. The skateboard flipped, and the youth went careening through the air, heading straight into the street, into the path of an oncoming garbage truck. "Stupid kid." Vlad jerked his index finger at the boy. The youth stopped in midair, and then tumbled backwards, landing softly on the sidewalk next to his board while the truck rumbled past, oblivious.

"You're not a hero?" the old man said, nodding at Vlad's extended finger.

He closed his hand into a fist. "What do you want?"

The man leaned forward. "Prince Vladimir, your time has come."

Vlad stared at him, shocked by the use of the title he'd abandoned so long ago, by the reminder of the world that had betrayed him on so many levels. "What did you just call me?"

"Prince Vladimir." The old man leaned forward. "Surely you remember your kingdom's magi?" He held out his hands. "Sir Anton Nikolov, at your service."

For a split second, Vlad was too stunned to react. Pain struck deep and hard as he stared into the eyes of the magi who had magically bound him to Sophie when they were married. The magi had been younger then, still spry and agile, not the old man he'd become. For a split second, Vlad was back in that moment. He could see the freckles on Sophie's cheeks, her blue eyes gazing at him with such hope and trust, and her trademark sparkle. He could feel the power swelling through him as he'd sworn his life to her, to his friend, to a girl he'd never kissed romantically in his life, but was still willing to promise forever to.

"You remember." Sir Anton smiled, but Vlad felt like he was free-falling into the past, into hell, into the horrors he'd worked so hard to survive.

Images of the childhood he'd worked so hard to forget

tumbled through his mind. Of Sophie. Of his parents. Of hers. Of the crown Vlad had destroyed after that God-forsaken night. Of Sir Anton, Vlad's magical tutor and mentor, who Vlad had seen riding into the mountains on his horse the night all hell had broken loose. "You could have helped," Vlad snapped. "You could have used your magic to save her, but you left. You *walked away*."

Sir Anton raised his grizzled eyebrows. "She was your responsibility, not mine."

"What the fuck? Seriously? I was sixteen, and I had no idea how to use my powers. Your *job* was to train me—" At Sir Anton's serene expression, Vlad slammed his mouth shut against the rage that wanted to spew out of him. Fuck yelling at the old man. He'd hated him for so many years, he didn't have the energy to hate him to his face, not now that he was just an old, withered man. Regrets and blame wouldn't change the past. He took a deep breath. "I have nothing to say to you."

He tossed a twenty on the table to pay for his beer, then he stood up and strode away, emotions raging through him so violently he could barely make it across the deck. He fisted his hands, fighting to blank his mind, to shove aside the emotions that haunted him every second of his life.

His boots thudded on the steps, and he strode over to his Harley, which was parked illegally right in front of the cafe. He swung his leg over the seat, then froze when he saw Sir Anton standing in front of him, blocking his path.

"Get out of my way," Vlad snarled, not even caring how the old man had beaten him to the bike.

Sir Anton put his hands on Vlad's handlebars. "She needs your help."

Vlad didn't care who Sir Anton was talking about. There was no way he was in the mood right now to go save some kid that Sir Anton wanted rescued, someone the old man had decided not to save himself. "I don't help anyone. Ever."

"Look at your finger."

Vlad didn't even acknowledge the command. He just punched the ignition button on his bike...but nothing happened. His bike, which he kept in meticulous condition, didn't start. Anger fermented through him, and he glared at the man gripping his handlebars. "Get your magic out of my bike," he snapped.

"Look at your finger," Sir Anton repeated.

Scowling, Vlad held up his index finger, the one he used for magic. "Looks fine."

"Not that one."

For a moment, Vlad had no idea what the old geezer meant, and then, suddenly, awareness dawned on him. The old man was staring at Vlad's left hand, at his wedding band from his marriage to Sophie. Vlad gritted his teeth, refusing to look down at the ring he'd never taken off.

The day they'd been married, his wedding band had been a glistening gold. She'd gone back to her kingdom that night, to pack her belongings so they could run away together...and she'd never returned, because that was the night her parents had murdered her.

The moment Sophie had died; his wedding ring had turned from gold to black. Over the years, it had faded to a dull gray. He was afraid if he stopped thinking about her, the ring would disappear completely, and he'd lose what little connection he still had to her. The ring was *his* connection to her, and he wasn't about to let Sir Anton threaten it. "Fuck off."

Sir Anton leaned forward, his blue gaze piercing. "Look at the ring. *Now.*"

The command seemed to reach inside Vlad, jerking him from his stubbornness. Instinctively, his gaze slid downwards to his hand. It looked the same as always. Dull gray. "So what?"

"Wait."

Vlad gritted his teeth in irritation, but just as he was taking his gaze off it...it changed. For a split second, he was too stunned to register what he was seeing. The ring was no longer a dull gray. It was a turbulent purplish-black, like the oceans of hell had come to life on his finger. Pain surged through his hand, and he realized it was burning him, searing his flesh as if it was melting through his skin. In the hours before Sophie had died, when death had been looming, the ring had turned that color and burned his hand.

Just like this.

He jerked his gaze off the ring and looked at Sir Anton. "That's why you're here. You know why my ring is doing that. Tell me."

"Princess Sophie isn't dead. She's in grave danger. She needs your help."

Chapter Two

FOR A SPLIT second, hope leapt through Vlad, a violent, almost unbearable hope that Sophie was still alive, that he would see her, that he could have a second chance—

Fuck. No. It was a lie.

Sophie was dead. He knew it. He'd seen her die.

The old man was playing a trick on him. Anger churned through Vlad, and he leaned forward, putting his face right up to the old man's. "Listen to me," he said, his voice dark and ominous. "Sophie's dead. I know she's dead, because after my parents tried to kill me, I went to find her. I arrived in time to see her parents hurl her into that pit of demon hell to try to save their precious kingdom. I heard her screams. I watched her slip out of my hands into that abyss. I watched my ring turn to black as she died." He would never forget watching Sophie plummet to her death, screaming for him, her hand outstretched for his.

His name had been the last word she'd ever spoken. In the face of death, she'd called to *him*...and he'd failed her.

Sir Anton began to laugh, a pitying, cynical laugh. "Is that what you thought all these years? That your black ring meant Sophie was dead?" He slapped Vlad's face, his palm stinging with surprising force. "You stupid punk. The black meant she was suffering. The gray meant her suffering had lessened somewhat. If she were dead, the ring would have disappeared."

Vlad felt himself blanch. "*What*?"

"Yes, you fool. The purple and black colors mean terrible, terrible things are happening to her. She's in trouble, Prince Vladimir, and you're the one who is supposed to help her. You were bound to her by magic, by a ring that connects you both *until* you die."

Until death do you part. He remembered the words. But he hadn't realized...he hadn't understood... "The ring..." He could barely say the words. "It would have vanished if she were dead?"

"Yes. The bond was until *death*. If you've still got a ring, you've still got life."

"*Jesus.*" Vlad was paralyzed by the news. "Sophie's alive? She's been alive this whole time? *She's been suffering?*" The world began to spin, a thousand stabs of guilt and horror hurtling through his body. He felt sick, almost violently ill at the depths of his betrayal. He'd been carrying her call for help on his hand all this time, and he'd ignored it? He'd run around hating everyone on the fucking planet, while she'd been in hell?

He'd seen her fall into the pit. He'd watched the chasm slam shut, cutting him off from her. He'd felt his connection to her die, severed by death, leaving behind nothing but a gaping emptiness that she had once filled.

But she hadn't died? She'd survived? But how? Where? He grabbed the front of the old man's cape. "Where is she? Don't tell me she's been with the demons this whole time." His entire body tensed as the words left his mouth, as the possibility loomed before him. No, it was impossible. *Impossible.*

Sir Anton raised his eyebrows. "She's been with the demons this whole time."

"*What*?" Vlad felt like he'd been sucker punched in the gut, and he gripped the magi's cape more tightly. "You knew? All this time, *you knew*? Why didn't you tell me?"

Sir Anton shimmered slightly, and suddenly Vlad wasn't holding onto his cape anymore. The old man had moved six inches backward, just out of Vlad's reach. "You weren't ready."

"I wasn't *ready?* What the fuck?" Sweat beaded on Vlad's brow and he gripped his handlebars, struggling to grasp the enormity of the situation. He bowed his head, fighting to regain his composure, to think, to stay in control of the situation. All the self-recrimination hammered at him, but he fought it off, knowing he had to stay focused. He had to find solutions, not self-hate. The time for hating himself would come later, after Sophie was safe. "Where is she? How do I find her?"

There was no answer.

He looked up.

Sir Anton was gone.

Swearing, Vlad jerked around in his seat, searching the crowds, but he was gone. "Hey!" He leapt off the bike and started running. "Come back! How do I find her?" He shoved his way through the crowds, searching for a black cape, but all he saw were shorts and tank tops, people dressed appropriately for the heat. "Anton!" He reached the end of the street, and his heart sank when he saw empty sidewalk stretching ahead of him. "Come back!" he bellowed.

But the magi had vanished.

Vlad looked down at his hand. The ring was churning violently, the purple and black now mixed with scarlet red droplets that looked like blood. Strength seemed to drain from his body, and he collapsed to his knees. "Sophie," he whispered, his voice raw with anguish. "I'm so sorry." The weight of his guilt was so heavy he could barely breathe. How had he not known she was still alive? How—

No.

No.

No.

He didn't have time for that. He had to find her, and he had to do it fast. But how the hell was he supposed to find her?

He shoved himself to his feet, struggling to find his balance as he stumbled over to his bike and swung his leg over the seat. He didn't turn it on, though. He just sat there, the hot leather seat burning through his jeans while he fought to find answers about a world he hadn't thought of in centuries. His parents were long dead. He had no idea if his kingdom was still there. Was that the place to start? To the abyss that had opened up and taken her?

He let out his breath, replaying everything he could remember about that night. The demons. The smoke. The acrid stench of suffering and taint. The stoic expression on his mother's face as she'd thrown him into a steaming pit of hell that he'd escaped only because of his magic. The same cold look on the visages of Sophie's parents as they did the same thing to their daughter. The way that abyss had sealed itself, vanishing from sight as soon as Sophie had fallen into it.

No, that wasn't the place to start the search. That had been two hundred years ago, and the abyss had closed instantly. He'd clawed at the earth until his fingers were raw, trying to pry open the earth that had claimed Sophie. There had been no way in. The demons were long gone from there.

But where were they now? Who knew demons? Who *really* knew demons? He didn't have time for fake practitioners. He needed the real deal. He'd been so far removed from that world for so long, he didn't even know where to start.

Gritting his teeth, he closed his mind, his thoughts leaping across years as he scanned everything he knew, everyone he'd met, every experience he'd had. They flooded his mind like a movie in fast forward, tumbling through in perfect clarity—

A face flashed through his mind, and he stopped, drilling down his focus. He recalled a man who had come to visit the kingdom just before the demon attack. He'd warned the royal family of the impending demon assault. He'd known it was coming, and he'd told Vlad's parents how to protect themselves, not that they'd listened. Instead, they'd chosen to make a deal with the demons, to sacrifice their son for their kingdom's safety. Who was the man who'd warned them? Who was the man who'd known about the demons?

Vlad quieted his mind further, struggling to recall the man's name, his face. He saw a shadowed brand on the man's forearm in the shape of a spear. A Calydon, one of the immortal warriors created from demon blood thousands of years ago.

The name flashed in his mind, and his memory flooded back. The man had been named Dante Sinclair.

Vlad's eyes flew open, stunned by the memory he'd shut out for so long. He'd run into Dante again recently, less than a decade ago, but hadn't recognized him from his youth. He'd helped Dante track some rogue Calydon warriors in the Oregon high desert...until the rest of Dante's team had showed up, and Vlad had learned what they were all about.

Dante hadn't simply been a badass warrior. He'd been the leader of the Order of the Blade, a band of elite Calydon warriors who protected innocents from rogue Calydons. The Order was a group of self-proclaimed heroes who were willing to fuck over the innocent in the name of duty, just like his parents, and Sophie's.

The moment Vlad had learned that Dante and his crew believed in sacrificing one to save thousands, he'd withdrawn his aid. After the betrayal by his parents, Vlad had zero tolerance for pretentious self-proclaimed heroes who used their mantle to hide the fact that they sought only glory and power at the expense of the weak.

He'd rescued the rogue from the Order, and then trapped the team in a mountain of boulders that he'd known would take them days to dig out from under. He'd abandoned them, once again reminded of the bitter nature of humanity. Glory in the name of sacrifice was all a bunch of crap.

He hadn't bothered to waste energy remembering them...until now. Calydons had demon heritage, and Dante Sinclair was rumored to have a mansion in Oregon, over two thousand miles away.

They probably hadn't forgotten that he'd sabotaged their mission, and he was shitty at apologies, especially when he didn't actually mean them, but he'd deal with that when he got there. He needed their help, and he'd figure out how to get it.

This time, when he punched the ignition button, his engine roared to life. He glanced down at his finger, and brushed his thumb over the churning ring. *I'm coming, Sophie. I swear on my life I'll be there. Hang on.* He thought of her face, of her voice, of her laughter, and something turned over in his chest, something he hadn't felt in so long. Hope? Connection? A fissure in the constant loneliness that consumed his existence?

He might see her again. He might hear her voice again. He might have to block one of her punches when she got annoyed with him. He bowed his head, fighting off the surge of emotions, emotions so different from the hate that had beat at him for so long.

After a long moment, Vlad lifted his head. His face was hard. His mouth tight. His gaze steely and focused. The face of the warrior he hadn't bothered to be for a very long time.

He hit the gas. The bike leapt forward, the engine roaring as he sped north, hurtling ruthlessly toward a team of warriors who were his only chance to save the one person who mattered to him.

How long did he have? When his ring had turned purple two hundred years ago, she'd been in the demon crevasse within two hours.

Son of a bitch.

Was that all the time he had?

He couldn't fail her twice.

BEING HUNTED BY demons was never convenient, but there were definitely times that were less convenient than others.

Like now.

Now was a very inconvenient time to be hunted by a demon.

Especially when the demon in pursuit was an enraged demon king, who was incredibly pissed that Sophie Flanagan had just kidnapped his current concubine and was trying to get her to safety.

On her best day, Sophie was no match for even an underachieving runt of a demon, so the odds of her winning a face-to-face showdown with Lucien were pretty much nil. The fact that she was handicapped by the unconscious woman in her arms, whose fate depended on Sophie's ability to win, made the situation all that much more...challenging? High pressure? So insanely stressful that she could barely think clearly?

Yeah, that last one. That was a pretty accurate description of how she was feeling at the moment.

Her arms trembling with fatigue, Sophie pressed herself against the wall of the cavern, trying desperately not to gasp for breath as she listened to Lucien's heavy footsteps thud along the adjacent tunnel.

His footsteps paused, and she heard him inhale, as if he were sniffing the air, tracking them. Sophie grimaced, sweat trickling down her temple. Lucien was a thug who ruled with brutality instead of finesse, but he would be able to sense them if he slowed down enough to try, which it appeared he was doing.

She couldn't stay any longer, but if she moved, he would hear her.

If she didn't have Ashlynn in her arms, she could dissolve into mist and escape on her own, but there was no way she was leaving Ashlynn alone where Lucien could find her. Panic hammered at her, but she fought to stay focused, to think, to figure out something she could do.

Lucien let out a growl of frustration and slammed the wall she was leaning against, making her jump. Rock crumbled down around her from the force of the impact, even though the wall was several feet thick. What had he hit it with? His fist? His wings? His horns? Was he just pissed, or had he found her?

Not that any of that mattered if he broke through. She had to distract him long enough to get away. Now.

Desperate, she crouched down and gently set Ashlynn on the floor. Then she spun around and pressed her hands against the wall of the cavern, pouring energy into the rock. She knew Lucien would sense the power rush, and he'd know it was her. It would take him only a few seconds to pinpoint where it was coming from.

He froze, and she knew he'd felt her.

Frantically, she opened her psychic connection to the rock, thrusting energy through the underground rock walls. Her energy shot past Lucien, hurtling through the rocks toward the end of a distant tunnel. She held on as long as she could, trying to reach as far past Lucien as she could, knowing she had only a fraction of a second left before he pinpointed her location.

At the last moment, she took a deep breath, gathered the energy she'd sent through the wall, then released it in a violent burst. It exploded through the distant rock wall with a loud, echoing crash.

Lucien crowed with victory, and his feet thundered away from her, racing down the tunnel toward the explosion, and away from her.

She quickly crouched down, pulled Ashlynn into her fatigued arms, and then stood up, staggering as she tried to keep her balance. She looped her friend's arm around her neck, and then broke into a stumbling run, eschewing stealth for speed.

Lucien would be back quickly, and he would be furious.

She had to have vanished by then, or Ashlynn would be dead.

Which meant she had a minute, maybe two.

Chapter Three

S OPHIE REACHED THE hidden door in the rock with only seconds to spare. She leaned against it, pouring her energy into the rock. The rock responded immediately, welcoming her. A five-foot-high, three-foot-wide section of rock dissolved, and she quickly stepped through into the adjacent tunnel, taking Ashlynn with her, hoping the shortcut would save her as it had so many times in the past.

The moment they were through, the door reformed behind her. Sophie carefully checked the hallway, but it was empty. Relief rushed through her, and she willed her exhausted legs toward the doorway of her best friend's home. She reached the door and kicked it lightly. "Maria! Open up!" she whispered.

No one answered.

Sudden fear gripped Sophie. Where was Maria? She was always home this late at night. If she wasn't there, Ashlynn would die. She had so little time left.

Ashlynn's eyes flickered open. "Too late," she whispered. "Maria's not home. Too late this time."

Sophie tightened her grip on Ashlynn. "No," she said fiercely. "Don't give up. It's not over." She kicked the door. "Maria! Open up!"

The door opened, and Sophie's best friend, Maria Souvaine, poked her head out. Maria's gaze landed on Ashlynn, and she swore. "I just treated her yesterday. She can't keep this up." She quickly stepped back, pulling the door open wide, not needing to ask what had happened. "The toxicity from Lucien's semen is building up in her too much. I can't clear it enough."

"I know, but you know she can't say no to him. No female can deny a demon once they've mated." Sophie hurried inside, frowning when she saw how pale Maria was. Demons like Lucien didn't need to rape women. All they needed to do was draw them into their spell, and the women were theirs forever. "Are you okay?"

"Fine." Maria shut the door and threw the deadbolt. "I know demon sex is addictive, but dammit. I hate this. These women were stolen. They don't belong here."

"I know they don't." Sophie sighed. "Trust me, I know."

Maria's gaze flicked to hers, and grimaced. "Sorry, Sophie. I didn't mean to remind you about your old home—"

"It's all good." There was no point in bothering with the "what ifs" about her life. Sophie looked around the small one-room home. "Where do you want her?"

"In the back," Maria said.

Shifting Ashlynn in her arms, Sophie hurried across the room to a door tucked in the corner. A tattered black cloth hung across the door, and Sophie ducked inside. One of the cots was already occupied by a woman she didn't recognize. The woman was unconscious, her skin grayish blue, on the edge of death. The streaks of pink on her cheeks showed that Maria had saved her, and her body was starting to heal. She knew instantly that Maria hadn't answered the door because she'd been in back, healing her.

She glanced back at Maria as she eased Ashlynn onto one of the cots. Maria pulled the curtain closed, and then turned to hurry over to Ashlynn. Sophie could see now that Maria's face was almost as pale as her patient's, with streaks of gray. Her wild, black hair was disheveled, and her eyes were tired. As she knelt beside Ashlynn, Sophie saw Maria's hands were shaking.

She put her hand on Maria's arm, and grimaced when she

felt how cold her skin was. "You took too much of the poison from the other woman. You're in trouble."

Maria shrugged as she put her hands on Ashlynn's cheeks. "It had to be done. She was in bad shape." But even as Maria spoke, she swayed dangerously, and Sophie had to grab her to keep her from falling over.

Sophie frowned as she steadied Maria. "How much poison did you take in? Maybe you shouldn't heal again right away. You don't look so good—"

"Ashlynn doesn't have time for me to take a break. We both know she's dying."

Tears filled Sophie's eyes, but she quickly blinked them away. Too many women died here. Granted, it was always in the throes of ecstasy with their demon lovers, but great sex didn't seem to be a worthwhile payoff for death. "You don't do anyone any good if you die, either, Maria. You're not completely immune. If you poison yourself too much—"

"I won't die." Maria's steely glaze glittered even as she sat down on the floor and leaned against the cot, as if she could barely hold herself upright. "But there's no chance in hell that I'm going to let Ashlynn die of demon poisoning if I can do something." She looked at Sophie. "You have my back, right?"

"Of course." If Maria pushed herself so far that she passed out, it was Sophie's job to protect her until she was conscious again, no matter what the cost. Maria was the only one who could heal the women that the demons brought to the underworld as lovers, and if she died, every woman in the kingdom would eventually die as well. Maria and Sophie were the only ones who weren't bound to a demon male, so it was up to them to save the others, or at least keep them alive for as long as possible. "I'll stop you if you push too far."

Maria pointed to a small table by the other cot. "Get the dagger, Soph." She rested her forearms on the cot, sagging wearily as she glanced across the room. "Please."

"Of course." Sophie hurried over to grab the jeweled knife Maria used for healing, then handed it to Maria. "I wish I could do this for you."

"Trust me, I'd be thrilled to delegate the poison ingestion to you, but it's a job for demon princesses, and you, my friend, are sadly devoid of any demon blood." Maria swiftly dragged the blade across her palm, making a small cut in her palm. Ashlynn was unconscious again, unaware when Maria made the same slice across her hand.

Maria immediately pressed their hands together, mixing her half-demon blood with Ashlynn's, dragging the toxins out of Ashlynn's body and into her own.

"You're playing the demon princess card again?" Sophie sank down on the cot, exhaustion suddenly overtaking her. It had taken almost two hours to get from Lucien's quarters to Maria's, carrying Ashlynn. She needed to crash, but she knew how weary Maria was, so she kept the conversation going to distract Maria and keep her mind focused. "You're only half-demon, and you're not actually a princess," she teased.

Maria leaned her head against the metal bar on the edge of the cot, grimacing as her body began to drag the demon poison into her already compromised body. "In this realm, I'm considered a demon princess, so that's good enough for me. Just because you think you might have *actually* been a princess before you wound up here doesn't make you the expert on all things royalty." As the transfer of blood occurred, Sophie saw Ashlynn's chest move in a deep inhale, and a faint streak of pink appeared on her cheek.

Relief rushed through Sophie. "It's working." This time. They couldn't look further ahead than that.

Maria grinned, even as her eyelids fluttered closed. "Because I rock."

Sophie grinned. "You're such a badass," she agreed.

"Badass?" Maria snorted. "I'm a gentle, nurturing healer."

"Gentle?" Sophie eyed Maria's black leather pants, thigh-high boots, and scarlet red bodice. "Sorry, girl, but gentle is never going to describe you."

"I know." Maria sighed, grimacing as a wave of pain hit her. "I'm a demon. A stupid, cursed demon, just like all the bastards killing these women."

"Don't." Sophie cut her off. "You're not like them. You

use your demon blood to save lives."

"There's nothing good about demons. We both know it." Maria opened her eyes, and looked at Sophie. "You have to see me for the demon I am, Soph, or you're never going to be able to kill me when the time comes."

Sophie grimaced at the reminder of the promise she'd given her best friend. "You're not going to become an evil demon, so I'm never going to have to kill you."

"Your naïveté is so endearing." Maria closed her eyes again, her skin becoming more ashen. "For hell's sake, you're a two-hundred-year-old virgin. What do you know about evil?"

Sophie rolled her eyes at Maria's familiar refrain. "Give me a break. I'm not naïve. I'm a virgin because I dissolve whenever a demon tries to touch me, not because I'm some sheltered, innocent maiden." In her two hundred years in the demon world, she'd seen enough to haunt her for eternity.

Maria opened her eyes a tiny bit. "Are you even curious what sex is like?"

"Sex with a demon isn't sex. It's a way for them to trap you and slowly kill you. No, thanks, not really feeling like I'm missing much." Not that she could have sex even if she did want to. Dissolving when any male tried to touch her was automatic. She instinctively ran her thumb over the ring that encircled her fourth finger. Every time she dissolved, it started at the ring, and spread throughout her body. Whenever she felt a tingle in that finger, she knew she was going to start checking out—

She frowned suddenly, realizing that the ring felt hot to the touch. She glanced down, startled when she saw it had turned purple and black, the River Styxx had come to life on her hand. The last time it had been like that had been right when she'd first arrived in the demon world. Over the years it had gone gray, but now, it was seething again.

Sudden foreboding pulsed through her, a paralyzing fear deep in her belly. Why had it changed? She didn't know, but something deep inside her told her it was bad. Very bad.

She didn't remember where she'd gotten the ring. She knew only that she'd had it when she arrived in the demon realm, her memories of her life in the earth realm were faded and distant. She'd never taken it off. It connected her to the life she'd once had, the person she'd once been, a past she couldn't recall, but that she clung to anyway. Additionally, since the ring was where her dissolving always started, it was the source of her defense against the demons, almost as if it were protecting her.

And now it was an ugly black and purple, and it was burning her skin, almost as if it were made of acid. She swallowed at the sudden fear clogging her throat, and she instinctively looked around, half expecting to see death looming in the walls to claim her.

"Soph? What's wrong?"

"Nothing." Sophie fisted her hand and jerked her gaze off the ring. Maria was frowning at her, her skin so pale that she looked almost translucent. Sophie's fear increased at the sight of Maria's pallor. "You should stop healing Ashlynn."

"Another minute." Maria closed her eyes again. "It's sort of ironic, you know," she mused. "You've never had sex, and I've had sex so many times that I can't even remember my first time. So many mindless, faceless fucks that it doesn't even matter anymore."

Sophie's heart softened at the vulnerability Maria had never shared. "I thought it didn't bother you."

"Of course it doesn't bother me." Maria shrugged, her eyes still closed. "It's great. Lots of fucking, can't remember most of them. What a way to live."

Sophie laughed softly. "As spoken by a lust demon."

"Half lust demon," Maria sighed. "Half. The other half is human female. I do have a heart you know."

Sophie smiled gently. "Trust me, I know you have a heart."

Maria opened her eyes and Sophie saw a vulnerability in them that her friend rarely showed. "I try," Maria said softly. She held up her hand, and they both watched the black blood fall from her palm. Her blood had never run red, not once. "But all my power comes from my demon side. It's just a matter of time until it wins."

"Stop it," Sophie interrupted, hating it when Maria talked about losing what remained of her humanity. "You know damn well that you use your demon power for amazing stuff, like saving the women who wind up here as sex slaves for your brother—" She cut herself off at the look of pain in Maria's eyes.

"He's a good guy," Maria protested.

"He's full lust demon," Sophie said. "He has sex with women until they die."

Pain flicked across Maria's face. "He can't help it—"

"I know. I know." This was a no-win conversation. Maria would never give up believing in her brother, because if she did, by transference, it meant that she had to truly accept her own demon nature, which she would never do, and shouldn't do. "Listen, you need to get some sleep, healer girl. Let Ashlynn be. She can heal the rest on her own."

"I can feel her aura. She's really weak. She needs time to recover." Maria's eyes closed and she rested her cheek against the settee as she continued to fuse her blood with Ashlynn's. "She'll never survive more demon semen right now, especially the king's. We have to hide her."

"I know." They were deep within the boundaries of the premier demon kingdom. There was nowhere to go that a demon couldn't find them...except one place. It was far, but it would work. "I have a place I could take her." She gently pulled Maria's hand away from Ashlynn's, cutting off the healing. "No more."

"I feel fine," Maria protested, her eyes still closed. Her skin had turned a pale shade of gray, and her cheeks were sunken.

"Liar." Sophie realized grimly that she'd have to protect Maria from herself. There could be no more healing for several days—

The door suddenly crashed open, and Sophie and Maria jumped as a huge shadow loomed in the doorway. Her stomach dropped as the massive demon strode into the room.

The demon king had found them.

Chapter Four

L UCIEN'S ARMS WERE huge pistons of muscle, and
black tattoos covered his skin. His chest was bare, and
a black mantle of fur cascaded across his shoulder and
down his back. Massive black horns curved from his
head, and his bitter, black gaze bore down on them. His tight
black pants stretched across his massive thighs, and leather
boots hugged his calves. He was pure menace, and Sophie
froze.

Too late. She'd waited too long. She couldn't hide Ashlynn
now. Damn.

He was so close she could smell his rancid breath and feel
her skin curdle from the sheer force of his taint. Dear God,
how had these women withstood sex with him? Her ring
burned, and she felt her hand begin to dissolve, instinctively
fleeing. She fought it, unwilling to leave the weakened women
alone without protection.

His black eyes bore down onto Ashlynn, who had begun
to tremble. He'd come for her, wanting to finish what he'd begun. Dear God, how would she stop him from taking Ashlynn?

"Get up," he snapped at Ashlynn.

She groaned under her breath, and rolled onto her side,
fighting to get upright, but her arms gave out, and she collapsed on the cot, her breath coming in desperate gasps.

Lucien's coal black eyes narrowed, and he inhaled deeply, scenting the air. "She is done," he said with disgust. "No heir, and a body wasted." He growled, a menacing sound that was thick and dirty in the air.

All the women stayed utterly still, willing him not to notice them. Sophie held her breath, hoping that he'd realize it was time to turn his focus elsewhere. If he selected a new concubine, it would give them the time they needed for Maria to recover before she had to heal his next woman. The first month with a demon ignited a woman's libido, driving her into a hyper-energetic state. The poison didn't start to hurt her until later.

Lucien glanced at the bed, and sniffed at the woman Maria had been healing when Sophie had arrived. He shook his head, immediately rejecting the woman who had been used by another one of his demons. Fresh blood is what he wanted, a female who could produce the heir he'd been trying to create for centuries.

His gaze rolled back to them, and it settled on Maria.

Sophie's heart jumped in fear as interest ignited in his eyes. "The demon princess," he said softly, lust drifting so thickly over Sophie's skin that she again started to dissolve. But when Maria gripped her arm, her friend's fear pulled her back into her body.

Maria pulled herself to her feet and stepped forward. Her hands were on her hips, her shoulders back, her feet spread as she lifted her chin. With her black leggings, and blood red bodice, she looked as menacing as Lucien, but Sophie could see the sweat trickling down between her shoulder blades, the only indication of exactly how much effort Maria was expending to stay vertical and not collapse. "I'm off limits," Maria snapped. "You don't get to have me. No one does." Her voice was steady and sharp, but her fingernails were digging into her palms so hard that Sophie could see droplets of blood on her skin.

Lucien had tried to take Maria a number of times in the past, but she'd always fought him off. He was afraid to hurt her because of her value, and as a demon half-breed, she was the only woman in the kingdom who could actually defend herself against him.

But right now, she was deathly weak, and Lucien had figured that out.

Maria glanced at Sophie, her eyes filled with worry for the first time since Sophie had known her. They all knew what happened to the women Lucien selected. They died. Even Maria wouldn't be able to withstand the poison of his semen. If Maria became contaminated, there would be no one to save her, and without her, there would be no light left for the women dragged into this hell.

There would also be no light left for Sophie either. She didn't need Maria for healing. She needed Maria's friendship. Maria was all she had in this bleak, rotting world.

Lucien strode forward, and Maria stood taller as he neared. He caught her chin in his hand, his twisted fingernail curving into her flesh as he lifted her face toward his. Sophie steadied Ashlynn, all three women waiting in silent anticipation of his next move.

"A lust demon," he said thoughtfully.

Maria slapped his hand away. "Don't touch me," she snapped. "I'm the vessel."

"Are you?" He leaned forward. "Here's what I'm thinking. I think that if our prophesied demon queen was planning to use your body to come back to life, she would have done it by now. I think you're not the half-human, half-demon vessel in the prophecy. I think maybe, it's time to see exactly what a female lust demon can do for me."

Maria jerked back as he reached for her, and lost her balance, her body so weak she couldn't stand. Sophie's heart was racing as she leapt forward to catch her before she fell. "She's too important," she snapped as she pulled Maria behind her.

"I'll make that decision." Lucien's wings suddenly exploded from his back, massive, skeletal wings that slammed into the walls of the small room, knocking debris from the rock walls. He knocked the women aside with one stroke of his wings, and Sophie yelped as the women were flung against hit the far wall. Her heart thundered as Lucien grabbed Maria and dragged her over to him. "Mine," he snarled.

Sophie saw Maria's hand move toward the dagger in the small of her back, and she knew her friend was summoning her power to fight him. But what was the point? She wasn't strong enough to win, and the battle would sap what little reserves she had left. There was no way to stop him from taking what he wanted, and he wanted the one thing he'd never been able to take until now: Maria.

"No!" Ashlynn leapt to her feet, and then fell. "Don't take her," she shouted. "Take me."

"You're worthless." He gripped Maria's hair and dragged her over to him, his gaze pinned on her mouth. "One kiss and you won't fight me anymore," he whispered. "They never do."

He lowered his mouth toward Maria's, and Sophie realized that he was right. The first kiss always incited such lust in the women that they were under his spell for the duration until the pain set in. Tears filled her eyes at the thought of Maria losing who she was for the bastard. "No—"

Maria struck. Her moves were lightning fast, her fist sinking into his chest—

He slammed her with his wing, and she crumbled to the floor, inert. Lucien laughed softly, then reached down to drag her to her feet. As his fingernails brushed Maria's arm, she flinched and tried to crawl away. Tears filled Sophie's eyes at the sight of Maria so weakened. She'd left herself defenseless to Lucien because she'd healed all the other women. Damn him! He couldn't do this!

Determination flooded Sophie. There was no way she could let Maria die. She was too important. "Take me!" she blurted out, leaping forward. "Take me."

Lucien went still, his gaze snapping to hers, as he gripped Maria's arm. "You are not for taking," he said, but there was no mistaking the gleam of interest in his eyes.

"No," Maria snapped. "Don't be an idiot, Sophie. He'll kill you, too."

Lucien and Sophie stared at each other. "You dissolve," he said. His gaze flicked over her breasts, but Sophie knew he wasn't really seeing them. All he was seeing was a chance at the woman no demon had ever been able to even touch, let alone bed.

"I can stop." That was, of course, a complete lie, which is why it was a safe offer. He couldn't touch her, but if he thought he could, maybe he'd leave Maria alone.

"Can you?" He released Maria and walked over to Sophie, ignoring Maria's protests as Ashlynn hurried over to drag her away. He reached up toward her face, and Sophie felt her finger tingle where the ring encircled her finger. His fingers brushed her chin, but her skin dissolved a fraction of a second before he made contact.

He snorted. "Liar." He spun away toward Maria, and Sophie's heart dropped.

"Teach me," she shouted at him. "Teach me what it's like. Teach me how to be there for sex." Even if she couldn't learn to stay corporeal, if she convinced him to try with her, it would give Maria the time she needed to recover enough to be able to fight him off.

Lucien turned back toward her, his gaze raking over her again. Slowly, he strode toward her until he stood right before her. The stench from his body was rancid, as if a thousand animals had died in his flesh and been left there to rot, but his muscles rippled in a body that was the ultimate physical specimen.

He leaned forward, studying her intently.

She lifted her chin, facing him. Her finger was burning, her body screaming at her to dissolve, but she fought desperately to hold her form. Slowly, ever so slowly, he raised his hand. She flinched, but he didn't try to touch her face. Instead, he extended his index finger toward her shoulder, his eyes gleaming. "Tresses of gold," he said softly.

She realized he wanted to touch her hair. Clenching her jaw, she focused all her energy onto her hair, but she felt it begin to dissolve even before he reached it.

"If I don't feel your hair," he said, "I will have sex with the half-breed right here, right now, and I will hurt her."

Fear tore through her and she snapped her gaze to his just

as his fingers reached her hair. She froze, her heart hammering in fear, as she felt her hair move under his touch. He sucked in his breath, and she froze.

Dear God. *She'd felt that.*

Her hair dissolved, but it was too late. They both knew he'd succeeded in touching her. If it could happen once, it could happen again, and again, and again. Suddenly, too late, she realized what she'd done. She'd offered herself up as the ultimate challenge, and Lucien would not stop until he'd won, and he'd do *anything* to gain her compliance, including hurting Maria.

"I accept the substitution," he said. "You will come to my rooms at midnight, when you complete tonight's Graveyard Hunt. I claim you."

And then, he spun on his heel and swept out of the room, retracting his wings a split second before they tore out of the walls.

"Sophie," Maria said, her voice breaking in anguish. "What have you done?"

She turned toward her friend, shoving her trembling hands into her pockets. Her ring finger was burning so badly she could barely keep the tears at bay. She felt as though the ring was tightening on her finger, digging through her flesh to her very bone. "I've bought us time," she said.

"No," Maria said, leaning weakly against the wall. "You've bought yourself death of the very worst kind."

Sophie managed a smile as she pulled her hand out of her pocket to rub her finger. The pain was increasing, getting worse by the minute. What was going on with that ring? Not that she'd take it off, no matter how much it hurt. The ring was the only thing she had from her past, and she treasured it. So, she just grimaced, and tried to massage the skin to take the sting out. "We'll find a way out of it. We always do." But as she said the brave words that had gotten them through so much, she saw the look on Maria's face, and she knew that this time, it was different.

This time, they were up against Lucien, the demon who had fought his way to the throne, acquiring his title through the sheer force of his power, his hate, and his evil. And now, she belonged to him.

Chapter Five

"WE'RE DOWN TO seven," Ryland Samuels announced, striding right in front of Gabe Watson's weapon.

Gabe averted his blade, frowning at Ryland's interruption of the training session with their newest recruit. Gabe had been working out for over four hours with Drew Cartland, the son of their deceased leader Dante Sinclair. He'd been trying to get Drew's skills refined enough to get him into active duty as an Order of the Blade warrior as soon as possible. Once a team of hundreds spread throughout the world, there were only nine left. Nine elite fighters to manage all the Calydons who went rogue and went on sprees of deadly violence.

They needed muscle, and Gabe felt that Drew's skills could be an asset. It was his temperament everyone was concerned about: too quick to trigger, and prone to use violence as a first option. Despite the hesitations about Drew, however, they were in need of warriors, so Gabe was trying to fast-track the youth.

He held up his hand to signal Drew to wait, as he turned his attention to Ryland. "Seven what?"

"Thano and Zach just resigned from the Order."

"What?" Gabe lowered his hook sword, staring in shock at Ryland, who was wearing the same black leather pants, heavy boots, and black tee shirt he always wore. He looked like a badass who would deliver death to anyone who breathed on him, which was almost true on some days. "They would never resign. No one resigns. The Order is for life."

The Order of the Blade was the elite group of Calydon warriors who protected innocents from rogue Calydons who had succumbed to their demon heritage. Very few beings were strong enough to stop a Calydon who had descended into the killing rage, so that was the Order's job. Kill friends. Kill sons. Kill fathers. Do whatever it took to save innocents, no matter how much you cared about the Calydon you had to kill.

It sucked, and at the same time, it was the greatest honor possible.

No one left the Order. *No one.* And yet...Thano Savakis and Zach Roderick had left? What the hell? "Why?"

Ryland's jaw was tense. "Zach feels that his time is better spent protecting Rhiannon's jungle."

Gabe ground his jaw at the mention of Zach's new woman. "He's leaving us for a *woman?* She's not even his soulmate. She's just...a woman." What the hell? That made no sense at all. He couldn't even comprehend that value system. He was all-in as a warrior, and there was nothing else in his life. How the hell did Zach justify abdicating to help a *woman?*

Ryland raised his brows. "When you meet the right woman, you'll understand."

"No chance." Gabe had designed his life to ensure he never connected with his *sheva*, his destined soulmate. No casual women either. Ever. A lifetime of celibacy had been an easy choice, once he'd realized how dangerous women were to the Calydons who were destined to be their mates. He would never sacrifice his mission for a woman. Ever. "No woman's getting to me."

Ryland just grinned, that same smug grin he'd been sporting since he'd found his own *sheva* and fought off the Calydon destiny that doomed every bonded couple to a fate worse than hell. Somehow Ryland, and seven other Order members had defeated that destiny...for now. Gabe wasn't convinced that fate was finished with them yet, but even he had to admit that the bonded Order members had managed to keep from going rogue, despite the Calydon destiny to do the opposite upon bonding with his *sheva.* "Once you meet your *sheva,* all that will change for you. It's different once you meet her, Gabe. Better. So much better."

"Better?" Gabe stared blankly at Ryland, barely even able to comprehend the fact that his teammate was *smiling* when all the shit was crashing down around them. "You're talking about me finding a *sheva?* Don't you even care that Zach and Thano bailed?"

Ryland's smile dropped off his face. "The Order saved my life. I care." The steely edge to his voice told Gabe all he needed to know. Ryland was still committed.

He nodded in acknowledgement, and then returned the conversation to the topic that mattered. "Why did Thano bail?"

Ryland shrugged. "He said he had another mission."

"Another mission? What the hell does that mean?" Gabe ran his hand through his hair, tension sliding through him at the thought of losing Thano and Zach. They needed them. Badly. "The Order is critical to the protection of innocents." There was nothing more important than the Order's mission. "Without us, innocents *die.*"

As hard as he'd worked for the last two centuries, there had been times when Gabe hadn't been able to save everyone. The souls of every innocent he'd buried still clung to him, driving him forward. He worked relentlessly, trying to save everyone, but there were too many rogues, too many innocents, too many lives that slipped between his calloused fingers.

Ryland nodded. "He knows that."

"Fuck." Barely even noticing that Drew was listening avidly, Gabe turned away and pulled out his phone. He called Thano, and the warrior picked up immediately.

"Hey, hot stuff," Thano said, with his typical irreverent demeanor. "Did I forget your birthday or something?"

"You're leaving the Order?"

Silence. Then. "Yeah."

"Why?"

39

"I need to be somewhere else."

Gabe's fingers tightened around his phone. "You know damn well you're one of our best warriors. We need you."

Thano laughed, sounding too damned relaxed for a guy who'd just broken his oath to the Order. "I know you guys are all going to be getting arthritis soon, but you'll just have to pop some aspirin and invest in some ice packs for after battle. I need to do this."

Thano's familiar ribbing about how he was so much younger than the rest of them almost made Gabe laugh, forcing him to pause for a second to regroup. It had been so long since he'd seen Thano, and hearing his irreverent sense of humor made Gabe realize how much Thano's absence had left a darkness over the rest of the team. Thano's light-hearted sense of humor was often the only thing that kept the team loose when things were tense. He'd always thought that Thano was going to be the one to eventually take over the team and bring them out of the darkness. They needed Thano back in a major way. "What exactly do you need to do that's so important? We can help, and then you can get back here—"

"I'm not coming back." Thano's humorous tone vanished. "The Pacific Northwest isn't my job anymore."

Gabe looked at Ryland, whose face was grim. Thano was as dedicated to the Order as the rest of them, and something in his voice told Gabe that Thano wasn't leaving on a whim. Something had happened. Something critical. "Thano, whatever it is that's going on, we've got your back. We always do—"

"Not this time. Hang on." There was muffled conversation, and then Thano came back online. "I gotta go."

"No! Don't hang up—" But Thano had already disconnected. *Shit.*

"The Order's in trouble," Drew said, looking back and forth between them. "Except for Gabe, everyone has either compromised themselves for a woman or bailed completely. It's been fragmenting since my dad died. We need my dad back."

Gabe ground his jaw, well aware that Drew spoke the

truth. Dante was the only one with the wisdom, strength, and vision to unite a band of volatile alpha warriors. Quinn Masters had been chosen as the interim leader, and he was as good an option as they had: experienced, level-headed, and skilled. But even he hadn't been able to stop the fragmenting of the Order. "I know we do."

Pain flickered through Ryland's eyes, grief that he kept hidden. Dante had been Ryland's savior, and the bond between the men had been deep and powerful. "Dante's with us in spirit. That's all we get now."

In spirit. Gabe thought about Ryland's comment, and suddenly something occurred to him. "You spoke to Dante when you were in the underworld, right? You guys encountered his spirit, right? So, he's still alive in some way, right?"

Ryland nodded. "His spirit still lives, yeah, but he's not corporeal. His physical body disintegrated and went back to the demons we are descended from when he died. Somehow, he managed to separate from his physical body so he didn't return to the demon realm with his body, but without it, his soul has nowhere to land. In the underworld, our connection was strong because of where we were, but out here?" Deep grief flashed in Ryland's eyes again, but he shoved it aside as quickly as it appeared. "He's gone. His job with us is finished. It's up to us to step up."

"Step up?" Drew broke in, his voice tight with anger. "We're failing! How many rogues have killed innocents this week alone? They're getting stronger, and we can't keep up."

"Enough." Gabe understood the youth's reaction, but irrational anger wasn't going to get them anywhere. "Listen, Drew, this isn't your problem. You just need to keep practicing." He looked at Ryland. "Do the others know Zach and Thano quit?"

Ryland nodded. "Yes—"

"Not my problem?" Drew interrupted, his hand tightening around his spear, one of the twenty-one weapons he was able to call to serve him. All Calydons had one weapon. Ever since Drew had been possessed by the ancient Calydon who'd tried to destroy the Order a year ago, he'd had twenty-one weapons to call. It made him a formidable warrior, but at the same time, there was now an edge to Drew that made Gabe wary. "The Order is my father's legacy," Drew snapped. "The mission my father stood for doesn't exist, and someone has to start it over." Anger glittered in his eyes. "I'll do it, if none of you will."

"Hey." Ryland walked over to him, the dragon scales on his arms sliding in and out of view, indicating just how on edge Ryland was. "You will *not* lead the Order. You may be Dante's son, but you have nothing of his talent or skill. You're just a kid." He looked at Gabe. "Team meeting tonight. Be there." He glared at Drew again, then turned away. He shifted into his dragon form and took off over the trees, his massive wings beating with a lazy, but powerful rhythm.

"Bastard." Drew watched Ryland fly away, and then looked over at Gabe. "No one else gets it, but you do. What are we going to do to rebuild the Order?"

Gabe slowly shook his head. "You're doing nothing. I'm going to the team meeting—"

There was a sudden roar of an engine, explosively loud. Both Calydons whirled toward the twelve-foot stone wall at the back of Dante's property just as a massive, gleaming Harley crested the top of the wall. It landed easily on the grass, churning up dirt as it raced across the manicured lawn toward them.

The brands on Gabe's arms burned, and he immediately called forth his weapons with a crack and a flash of black light. Instantly, a steel hook sword appeared in each hand, exact replicas of the brands on his arms. Drew might have twenty-one brands on his forearms and twenty-one weapons to call, but Gabe needed only his hook swords.

He was brilliant with them, and he knew it.

Gabe's fingers tightened around his weapons as the motorcycle skidded to a stop inches from him. He didn't bother to flinch, but Drew leapt back several feet. The rider's face was hidden behind a black helmet with a shadowed face shield, but his shoulders were huge and muscled. Black leather gloves encased his fingers where they were wrapped around the handlebars. He gave off an aura of pure menace, the kind of intelligent, ruthless menace that meant the intruder wasn't rogue.

As the rider pulled off the helmet, Gabe raised his weapons, the brands on his arms burning with the need to attack.

He didn't. One of Dante's rules was to never strike prematurely, a lesson Gabe had learned long, long ago, the hard way.

So, he waited.

But he was ready.

Chapter Six

I T WAS ALMOST midnight.

Less than an hour until Sophie had to report to Lucien's quarters.

And she still hadn't figured out how to save herself. Every option she thought of resulted in him using Maria to force Sophie's compliance. Their only chance was escape...but leaving the demon realm was impossible. Over the last two hundred years, they'd tried. Many, many times. There were only ways in, not out.

They were trapped.

Nowhere to go.

No way to defend themselves.

At the mercy of a creature that had none.

"Hey." Rikker, the foreman of the night's hunt in the Graveyard of the Damned snapped at her, jerking her attention back to the present. "Focus."

"Sorry." Sophie braced her palms on one of the large, blackened rocks that littered the Graveyard of the Damned, pausing to take a deep breath and try to calm her nerves. Her feet were hot from walking over the steaming lava rock, and her lungs were seared from inhaling the heat.

Every night for two hundred years, when the lava receded enough to navigate, she had been brought down here to tap into her magical affinity for jewels to search for the legendary stone that would free the demons from their realm.

Working with jewels was her respite. Despite the creepiness of the graveyard and the extreme heat, being here grounded her and strengthened her, even though a part of her always feared she would find the jewel that would turn the demons loose in the earth realm. For that reason, she always counted the minutes until each hunt was over and she could walk away, knowing the earth was still safe for another day.

Tonight was different.

Tonight, she wanted to stay down here in the heat forever, because when she left, she was out of time.

When she left, Lucien would begin the process of figuring out how to make her stay corporeal when he touched her. What would he come up with? She knew there was no limit to what the depraved leader of the demons would do, not just to her, but to anyone he thought would motivate her. With each passing moment, her fear was growing. Maria wasn't safe. He would use her to force Sophie's compliance. And what if he *did* succeed in keeping her corporeal? What if the moment with the hair wasn't a fluke? What if he succeeded in being able to have sex with her?

Dear God. Her stomach lurched and real fear thudded deep in her belly. For the centuries she'd been trapped here, she'd worked hard to protect others, but she'd never had to worry about her own safety. Now, everything had changed. For the first time since those days of her early arrival, she was scared. Really scared.

She looked up at the purple roof of the cavern. It stretched above her like an endless sky of clouds and sunlight...which, of course, was a lie. No sun had ever made it down here. The roof was getting lighter now, almost lavender, indicating that the lava would start to flow soon, forcing her and the demon excavators to retreat until the next recession.

"Keep moving."

She glanced over her shoulder at Rikker. His horns weren't as large as Lucien's, but the way they curved back from his head into razor sharp points of blackness was daunting enough. His muscles were huge, and his face was lean and angular. Unlike Lucien, who always dressed to dominate, Rikker was wearing leather pants and black boots. His only claim to his demonhood was the leather vest that adorned his naked torso, showcasing the scars that crisscrossed his flesh, the results of the battles he'd fought to surge to the top of the food chain. He wanted no one to forget what he'd earned, to forget how deadly he was. There was no softness in his face, no humanity in his voice. He was an iron-muscled machine, focused only on forcing her to track down the jewel that was responsible for the invisible net that kept the demons from crossing over into the earth realm.

Legend spoke of a spurned woman thousands of years past who had been brought to the demon realm by their leader at the time. Apparently, she'd loved him, but he'd betrayed her by making her his sex slave while he shared his bed with dozens of other women. Furious and bitter, the woman had cast a curse upon the demon realm, severing them from the human world so they could never again cross over and tempt women into their hell. She'd anchored the invisible net in a jewel that she'd buried deep in the Graveyard of the Damned. Demons had been searching the fields for the centuries since then, and found nothing, which is why they'd wanted Sophie so long ago, hoping her natural affinity for jewels would give them the break they'd wanted.

So far, she hadn't delivered, but there was nothing anyone could do about it, since they couldn't touch her...until now.

Rikker moved closer, and she stiffened, stepping away from his unexpected approach. He never bothered to come close to her. Like all demons, he was driven by lust, and since she couldn't satisfy that, he endured her presence only because she was their best hope to find the jewels that had bound them to their world so many thousands of years ago.

"I'm moving," she said, hopping over a pool of swirling melted rock. Across the plains were thousands of graves, the eternal resting place of those who had been possessed by the demons and dragged into demon hell, their bodies and souls forever trapped even after the demons had moved on.

She felt something pulse under her foot, indicating a possible jewel. She knelt down, running her hands over the spot. Her fingers tingled, and her heart started to rush with excitement. As much as she didn't want to free the demons, she could never contain her excitement about jewels. She craved them so deeply in her soul that she suspected that she needed them simply to live. She never felt as alive as she did when she found a new stone and her fingers closed around its hard, beautiful surface.

Rikker was beside her in a moment, jamming his staff into the ground. The dirt cracked in a violent snap, revealing a six-inch crevice. She immediately dissolved, slipping into the opening as she hunted for the jewel. She tumbled through the pores in the rocks, until she found it. It was black and rough, an ugly stone to the uninformed, but she sensed its beauty immediately. She swept around it, encircling it in her being, sliding through its porous gaps. The stone immediately dissolved, each particle latching into a part of her. Cradling it with warmth and love, she sped toward the surface.

She burst free, reclaiming her human form as she escaped, her hands taking shape first as the stone solidified in her palms. She knelt, oblivious to the hot lava steaming beneath her knees, watching with pure joy as the precious rock hardened.

"What is it?" Rikker knelt beside her, peering at the stone he didn't dare touch, knowing all too well that she would dissolve it instinctively if she felt it was in danger. Her first moments of connection with a stone were so close that it became a part of her, taking on her same attributes of dissolving when a demon tried to make physical contact.

"I don't know." She rubbed her thumbs over the outside edge, asking to be granted access. She felt the stone warm in her palms, and then it gently cracked open, the two halves sliding apart to reveal a kingdom of faint purple and silver crystals. "Oh..." she whispered. "Thank you. You're so beautiful."

The stone pulsed with life, and she smiled, her heart aching for the beauty of what she held in her hand. She knew that Rikker would take it shortly, claiming it as one of the resources of the kingdom, but for this first moment, it was simply hers. She filled her heart with love and poured it out through her palms, infusing the stone with the warmth and strength it would need to protect itself once the demons took ownership.

"Is that it?" Rikker asked, his eagerness obvious.

"No." She didn't need to ask the stone. She could feel its energy was pure and untainted. It was not holding the magic of a spell that held the demons captive. It was pure beauty on its own, formed by centuries of abuse by the lava fields and the decay and rot of this graveyard. She held it up, letting it sparkle. "Can you feel the beauty in it, Rikker?" she whispered reverently. "I wish that just one time, you could feel beauty in your soul instead of all the darkness that haunts you."

He didn't answer, and after a moment, she glanced over at him. He wasn't watching the stone. He was watching her face, and he had an expression she'd never seen before. It was raw and unmasked, a yearning so powerful that her heart stopped. For a split second, she felt an answering yearning, a deep, relentless desire for a man, not him, but for another man, to look at her that way, as if she were his world, and he saw only beauty in her soul, and that he would stop the world from spinning, if it would help her.

Then Rikker's face shifted from raw wonder back to his customary haunted and lethal visage. His shift jerked her back into the present, and the reality that the man beside her was a demon, a creature of the night who cared about nothing but satisfying his own need for lust, death, and freedom. The creature beside her might resemble a man, but there was nothing humane about him, no softness that would fill her heart with the kind of warmth that she craved so badly, the kind of connection that she found only with the jewels for those brief moments.

Disappointment flooded her, and she bit her lip, startled by the depth of sudden longing for a man who would stand by her side, a man she could trust. She had vague memories of a bond she'd had like that once before, of a boy she'd loved, but the memories of her earth life were faint, distant, and faded, as if they'd been stolen from her along with the life she'd once had. She had brief flashes of people she thought might be her parents, of betrayal, of loss, of fear, but they were unclear, drifting through her mind like an elusive wisp she could never quite pin down. She wasn't sure she'd even had a bond like that with a boy. Maybe it was just her imagination.

Not that it mattered what had once been.

This was her life now, and she had to figure out how to survive it. Resolutely, she lifted her chin, summoning the same fierce strength that had kept her going all these years.

Then, to her surprise, Rikker reached toward her, and she realized he was trying to touch her. Her ring finger tingled, and her cheek dissolved before he could make contact.

He froze, his fingers hovering where her jaw had been. "Why do you hide from me?"

Her heart started to pound. "What do you mean?"

"Lucien touched you. He touched your hair." The wonder on his face was long gone, replaced by a dark, hateful scowl. "I spend day after day with you in this hellhole, and I never get to touch you." He moved closer. "I watch the sway of your hips as you leap across the rivers. I imagine what your breasts would feel like in my hands when you lean over and they sway. I fantasize about what your lips taste like, and I jerk off every fucking night at the thought of what it would be like to be inside you."

Sophie froze, her heart hammering in her chest. Rikker had always been a safe zone. He'd never tried to touch her. Ever. Her stomach churned at the idea of him masturbating to the thought of her. "Why are you saying this?"

He reached for her hair, and it dissolved before he could touch it. "Because Lucien touched you. He touched your hair. That means it's possible. I want to be the man who does it." As he spoke, he lunged for her.

She yelped and dissolved, startled by how fast he'd moved. She didn't usually contemplate what a predator he was, but his sudden attack was a visceral reminder of how vulnerable she could be to him if she couldn't dissolve. She reformed several feet away, but she hadn't even finished taking shape when he moved again, lunging for her so quickly she didn't even see his hands move. She just felt their energy directed toward her. "Stop it!"

This time, she reformed further away, as far as she could manage to go, but she had just taken shape when she felt something move at her from behind. She looked down as her chest dissolved and a clawed hand pushed through the hole, fingers grasping the empty space where her breast had been only moments ago.

She spun around to see one of the other excavation demons standing behind her. He was a digger, a laborer, one she didn't even know by name, but he was looking at her as if his only mission in life was to consume her very soul. "Stop it!" She backed up, holding out her hands, as if that could stop him, then felt her hip dissolve as another hand tried to grope her.

She whirled around and saw that she was surrounded on all sides. Eleven demons, their horns twisted and sharp curving from their head, their long, blackened fingernails turning human-shaped hands into grotesque abominations. Their faces, though in the visage of men, were dark with venom and the utter void of humanity. The scent of putrid waste and sulfur filled the air, a smell she recognized from the times when she'd retrieved an exhausted woman from a demon's bedchamber after a marathon session of sex. It was the odor of demon lust, and rancid sex, of wanting so intense that it awoke in their bodies the ancient rituals of mating.

Never in her life had it been directed toward her, and now she was surrounded on all sides. "Nothing has changed," she said, trying to keep her voice even. "You can't have me. No one can."

"Lucien touched you," one of the demons said. "He touched your hair."

"I heard it was as soft as it looks. Softer. Spun gold," another said, his eyes dark and scary as he fixated on her hair.

Rikker held up his hand, and the demons fell silent. "Mine," he said softly. "I've been waiting for you for years, Sophie. Mine."

She met his gaze, and fear trapped thick in her throat. His expression was that of a man who'd claimed his woman, a predator who had identified his prey in a hunt that would never end. Suddenly, the protective shield that had kept her safe all these years was gone. She was in more danger than the new arrivals, who were selected by only one demon and claimed by him. Some of the demons even treated their women decently, and no female had ever complained about the quality of the sex, even if it did get a little rough sometimes.

But this was different. She'd been a temptation for so long, and she'd never realized how her presence had been such a tease. She'd been a temptation to their most base desires, a lure dangling before them that they could never have, creating a driving want that had been building all this time, amassing its force with greater and greater urgency...and now they believed they had a chance to take what they'd been deprived of for so long. She could see in the eyes of all the ones around her that not a single one would stop until they had her, until they'd found a way to force her to stay corporeal, the way Lucien had done.

The terrifying thing was that Lucien's momentary success meant that it was actually possible that these demons could force her to stay corporeal long enough for them to do whatever they wanted. She wasn't safe. Lucien knew it, and now, so did every single demon in the kingdom. They would try everything until they found out what the secret was, until they figured out how to take her, and then, they would unleash years and years of pent-up lust onto her.

She met Rikker's gaze. "He didn't touch me," she lied. "The rumor is wrong." She held out her hand to him, in an invitation, as if she had nothing to hide. "Try it. Everything is still the same." She managed to keep her voice steady, fighting to hide the fear that demons were so good at sensing.

Rikker broke free from the circle that ringed her and strode forward, his muscles rippling as the other demons shifted position to close the empty space he'd left behind. She lifted her chin as he came to a stop in front of her. His black eyes bore down on her, brimming with lust so thick that her skin tingled with the need to escape.

She didn't bother to try to hold her form, letting him see how his want triggered her defenses.

But this time, instead of a stoic, reserved mask, his face twisted in anger. "No," he snapped, lunging for her wrist, which dissolved before he could reach it. "I won't play this game anymore."

"It's not a game," she said. "It's who I am. I can't stop it."

"You can." He leaned forward, closer and closer until his face was a fraction of an inch from hers, no longer trying to touch her, but pressing the fullness of his threat into her. "You will pay for your deception, Sophie. You will be mine, and we both know it."

And with that, he snatched the stone from her hands, tearing it out of her grasp. Her fingers dissolved as his hand brushed through where her palm had been, but she felt the heat of his touch. His eyebrows went up in shock, and she knew that he'd felt the heat of her body as well. He hadn't touched flesh, but he'd sensed her presence.

Dear God. Why was this happening?

Shock ripped across his face, and lust flared in his eyes, a gleaming triumph that he had breached her defenses for that split second.

"Did you touch her?" One of the demons shouted the question, and as a unit, they all moved closer, tightening the circle. She could feel their desperation and lust thickening, and knew they were moments from a full-on attack.

Rikker's gaze slithered to the side, rapidly assessing the growing threat of the demons around him, closing in like bloodthirsty scavengers in a feeding frenzy. He met her gaze. "You bitch," he said softly, but loud enough for all the demons to hear him. "You lied to our leader. You never were corporeal with him, were you?"

"What?" Had she been wrong? Had he not sensed her flesh? Then she saw the knowing look in his eyes, and realized that he definitely had been fully aware of what had happened between them.

"I ask again," he said, again loudly enough for all to hear, "did you, or did you not, deceive our leader to save your friend?"

She stared at him, confused by his apparent effort to convince the other demons that she hadn't ever gone corporeal. Was he on her side? Hope leapt through her, and then she saw the muscle ticking in his cheek, and she realized the extreme effort he was expending not to attack her right then and follow up on the sliver of opportunity she'd given him.

With a sinking feeling, she realized that his efforts to deter the other demons hadn't been to protect her. It was because he'd decided he wasn't going to share her. He was going to claim her for himself, and he didn't want to have to kill ten demons to do it. There was a challenge in his voice, and she knew that he was giving her a choice. Give him a chance to breach her defenses, and he'd protect her from the others. If not, he'd tell everyone around them what had just happened, and then there would be no stopping the assault until they got what they wanted.

They would attack right now. All of them. And they wouldn't stop. Ever. If it took a thousand years, they wouldn't stop for those thousand years.

Her mouth opened, and Rikker's eyebrows went up. He reached for her chin, daring her to give him a chance.

Tears welled in her eyes, but she forced herself not to retreat. Her chin dissolved beneath his touch, but they both knew that she'd at least given him the opportunity. He nodded his approval, and she wanted to cry. "Of course I wasn't corporeal," she said aloud, to the ring of vulturous demons surrounding them. "I tricked him."

There were murmurings from the demons, and she knew she was in trouble. If Lucien believed she'd tricked him, he would punish her severely. If he didn't, he would continue his seduction. If he kept her as his concubine, everyone would believe that she was accessible, and she would never be safe. Either way, Rikker was going to haunt her every minute she was in the graveyard with him from now on because he *knew*. He would be relentless in his attempts to break down her barriers. He wouldn't stop until he figured how to overcome her one defense mechanism, so he could claim her as only a man could do.

Her oasis in the land of hell was over now, and the only question was which demons were going to destroy her, and how long it would take.

Chapter Seven

A
S HIS MOTORCYCLE skidded to a stop, Vlad knew that he'd come to the right place.

He was equally certain he might die because of it.

The two warriors stood ready, their deadly weapons angled toward Vlad with a precision that told him exactly how skilled they were. The taller one was older, and Vlad recognized him from the battle he'd interfered in several years back. Gabe Watson. He was wearing blue jeans that were splattered with blood, and his white tee shirt was equally adorned. He had a gaping wound in his shoulder that was already beginning to heal, and his hip and right thigh had been similarly assaulted.

The shorter one was younger, maybe early twenties at most. Curiosity was evident on his young face. He was also wearing jeans, and the only marks he sported were a few bruises and a small hole in his shoulder, as if a narrow sword had been cleanly plunged through it and removed. His hair was blond and messy, but beneath the youthful features rumbled a weighty darkness more fitting for an ancient warrior with a thousand years of suffering behind him.

His muscles were relaxed and ready, and his sword was angled toward Vlad's throat, but there was a lack of aggression that suggested he was less interested in killing Vlad than finding out who he was. The youth was a rebel, a warrior who had his own agenda, he was sure. Vlad liked him instantly.

But he knew who was in charge. Vlad's gaze flicked back to the older warrior. "Gabe, right?"

Gabe's face went impassive, giving away nothing. "Do I know you?"

"I came by to apologize." Shit. That sounded like the lie it was. He was a crappy liar, especially when he didn't want to do it. But his ring finger was burning, "Yeah, well, that's a lie. I need to talk to Dante."

Gabe didn't move. "I remember now. You buried us under a thousand boulders after fighting alongside us for hours to get us to trust you."

"I didn't fight with you to manipulate you. I fought with you because I thought you were the good guys. When I realized you weren't, I changed sides."

Gabe's eyes narrowed. "We are the good guys."

"Yeah." The younger warrior looked offended. "The Order of the Blade is legendary. They protect innocents at all costs."

"Yeah, I know all about that," Vlad snapped. "I know that you're willing to sacrifice one to save many. I think it's a crappy life philosophy myself. I always thought that heroes were supposed to save all the innocents, not just the important ones."

"We save everyone we can," Gabe snapped.

"Yeah, I know, I know. Heroes and all that." He didn't have time to argue semantics. Instead, Vlad looked past him at the stone mansion stretching up high toward the blue sky. "I need to talk to your boss."

"He's dead."

Vlad looked sharply at Gabe, and he saw the regret in the warrior's hardened gaze. The rawness of Gabe's emotion hit deep, raking across the shield Vlad kept sealed tightly inside him. For a second, he was catapulted back to that moment when he'd lost Sophie. That feeling of impotence and horror when he saw the flames ignite over Sophie's kingdom after he'd dragged himself out of the demon pit. How desperately he'd raced across the rocky terrain, screaming her name, praying that her parents weren't doing what his had just done. He'd never pushed his body so hard, past pain he'd never thought he could endure, and still, he'd arrived just in time to see his best friend disappearing into the smoking abyss. Dead. Because he'd failed. An immense wave of guilt rocked him, but he immediately shoved it ruthlessly away. He had no time to wallow in the guilt of failures long past. By some unfathomable miracle, Sophie had survived both the fall, and all these years in the demon realm. That was all that mattered. He had a chance to make at least one thing right, and he wasn't going to fail.

He lifted his chin, meeting Gabe's eyes. "I'm sorry to hear that. He was a great warrior," he said honestly. No lie there. He'd been impressed as hell with Dante's prowess. He still had a suspicion that Dante had allowed Vlad to bury him and save the rogue, though he'd never been able to figure out why he'd done it.

Gabe inclined his head, apparently accepting the truth of Vlad's offering. "That he was. What did you want to talk to him about?"

"Demons."

The younger warrior moved up beside Gabe, his blue eyes fixated on Vlad. "Why do you want to know about demons?"

Vlad focused his gaze on the younger warrior, giving him the recognition the kid so clearly wanted. He'd been young once, fighting for that same respect. "Someone I know was taken by them. She needs my help."

Both Calydons simply stared at him for so long that Vlad wondered whether all that black light shit had fried their brains. Impatiently, he scowled at them. "Where do the demons live? Where's the entrance to their realm? I need to get in there."

Gabe narrowed his eyes. "There are many places where the veil between the worlds is thin, but it's protected. There's no way to cross the border. That's why they're always trying to find a way across. No living person can cross into their realm unless they are brought across by a demon. Even if you were able to get across, which you can't, you wouldn't be able to bring her back to the earth realm. You'd be stuck there with her."

Vlad shrugged, unconcerned about logistics. He'd find a way. "I got that covered. I just need to know where the entrance is. Do you know?"

Sudden interest gleamed in Gabe's eyes. "How exactly do you have that covered?"

Vlad studied the Calydon, debating on how much to tell him. He generally operated on the premise that no one needed to know anything about him, but he needed Gabe's help, and he sensed a gleam of interest in Gabe's question, the kind of interest that said he might have something Gabe wanted. "I can animate living matter. I can move it anywhere I want."

"And you think you can use that to cross the border?"

"Yeah, I can figure it out, but I need to go now. Sophie needs me."

Gabe glanced at Drew, and he saw them confer silently. After a moment, Gabe turned back to him. "Can you animate a body? If a soul had left a body, could you bring the body out of the demon realm into the earth realm, so it could reconnect with its soul?"

Vlad raised his brows. "No one fucks with death."

Gabe didn't look away. "You could, couldn't you?" he challenged. "Dante's body is in the demon realm, and his spirit is in the earth realm. If we reunite them, he will live. We need him. Can you do that?"

Vlad gritted his jaw. He knew the cost of challenging death. He knew it all too well. "Where there was once death, there always has to be death." He didn't add the rest.

Gabe nodded. "Drew's a pain in the ass. We'll sacrifice him."

"Hey!" Drew's face darkened, but Gabe just clapped him in the side of the head. "Chill, kid, we'll put a demon in his place."

Hope began to hum through Vlad as he listened to the exchange. "You know where to go? You know how to find the demons?"

Gabe grinned at him, the first smile he'd ever seen on a Calydon's face. "Yeah, I got an idea. But we'll be breaking a lot of rules if we go."

A slow smile spread over Vlad's face. "Now, you're talking. When can we leave?"

"Now."

Drew looked back and forth between them. "Now? What about the meeting?"

Gabe was already sheathing his weapons. "Fuck it. We're going to get Dante."

"We are?" Drew's face lit up. "That's awesome!"

Hesitation flickered across Gabe's face, and Vlad suddenly realized where Gabe's wounds had come from. The kid was a loose cannon, a liability. He didn't need one of those, not right now. "Sorry kid. I got space for only one."

He swung his leg over his bike, and Gabe leapt on behind him without hesitation.

Before he could start the bike, Drew stepped in front of them, blocking their path. "I want to come. He's my dad."

Gabe leaned past Vlad. "What do you think Quinn's going to do when he realizes I've gone to cross over into the demon realm to help the bastard who buried us find a woman, and to bring back Dante's body? What do you think Ry's going to do?"

Drew met his gaze. "They'll stop you."

"So, you stop them." Gabe held up his hand. "Not by force. They're on your team, regardless of whether you respect their choices. The reason you aren't on the Order of the Blade yet is because you rely on force too heavily. You have to learn loyalty and restraint. Stop them from following me, but don't shed a drop of blood. You do that, and I'll recommend you to become an Order member. If you so much as scratch any of them, I'll have you blackballed."

Vlad saw the frustration warring on the youth's face, the need to be on the battle lines, and the burning desire to be called into duty as an Order member. Finally, he gave a quick, succinct nod. "I'm in."

"Good man." Gabe slugged the kid in the shoulder, then wrapped his arms around Vlad's waist. "Head south."

As Vlad gunned the engine, he heard Gabe shout over the

roar. "We aren't going over that wall again, are we?"

Vlad grinned. "Shit, yeah," he said. "Hold tight. I can lift us. We need to raise the bike ourselves." Then he hit the ignition and launched them straight at the twelve-foot stone wall.

He waited until the last second to raise them up, and he grinned at Gabe's bellowed curse as he cut it just a little too close.

As he crested the top of the wall, however, his amusement faded, replaced by a driving sense of purpose. "I'm coming, Sophie," he said under his breath. "Just hang on until I get there. I swear I won't fail you again."

But as his tires hit the ground on the other side, there was a sharp stab of pain from the ring. He glanced down and saw a drop of blood slither over his finger. Had it come out of the ring? If so...there was only one explanation.

It was Sophie's blood.

Swearing, he gunned the engine. There was no time to waste.

"HAVE A GLASS of wine," Lucien said, his voice rolling through Sophie like a silken seduction. He held up a sparkling crystal goblet, encrusted with a dozen glittering jewels.

Sophie's heart was pounding as she stood near the door, still wearing her jeans and boots from the hunt. Her ring finger was burning violently, hurting so much. She rubbed it, trying to take away the sting, but it didn't help. "No thank you."

"See these emeralds?" He turned the glass, letting the light from the dozens of candles in the room sparkle through it. "Aren't they riveting?" He was wearing a pair of soft leather pants that clung to his body like a second skin, and nothing else. His body was a sculpture of perfection, his abs carved from steel and his biceps taut. His wings had receded to tattoos across his muscular back, his horns were no longer visible, and his jaw was clean-shaven. He even smelled good. He was pure sex and seduction, complete charm that he'd turned on just for her. He'd submerged everything menacing about himself, showcasing only the raw sensuality of a man who wanted nothing more than to deliver the utmost pleasure to his woman until she was satisfied.

She could feel her body responding to what he offered her, the woman deep inside her awakening for the first time in her life. She'd never thought about sex, let alone craved it. But with Lucien focusing his entire attention on her, she could feel something inside her shifting and coming to life...but at the same time, it felt wrong, so desperately wrong, to be looking at him as a man.

She didn't want him to look at her like she was a woman.

She didn't want him to be the one to touch her.

She didn't want any of this to be with *him*.

But for the first time in her life, a part of her did want to be touched, to be kissed, to be connected with a man, which was unsettling given that she was alone in a room with *him*.

He smiled, a devastatingly beautiful smile that made her belly jump in response. "My dear, Sophie," he said, striding across the plush silvery carpet toward her. "These are the finest jewels in the kingdom. I know you, more than anyone, will appreciate them. You do not need to drink the wine. Just enjoy the jewels."

She stiffened as he neared, but he didn't try to touch her. He stopped a yard away and extended the goblet toward her. Her attention was instinctively drawn toward the jewels decorating the crystal. The only time she was ever able to touch jewels was on the hunt, and then it was only for a brief moment. Her soul began to cry with longing, and she felt herself reaching for the glass, need burning through her.

Lucien didn't move, forcing her to take two steps toward him to reach the wineglass. When her fingers closed around the glass, he didn't release it. "Touch them," he said, his voice slicing through her like a dark temptation.

She knew his strategy then. He was using the jewels to

force her to stay near him, to force voluntary proximity, and gradually break down the barriers. For a moment, hope leapt through her. He wasn't going to start with force. He was so confident in his skill as a lothario that he was going that route first. Relief rushed through her. No violence? No torment of Maria? She had time.

With a deep breath of relief, she managed a smile. If she could convince him it might work, then she could buy time. He smiled back at her, and held up the wineglass. "Touch them," he whispered, his voice almost a compulsion as it rippled through her.

She didn't bother to fight it. She wanted to touch the stones, and doing so wouldn't hurt her. So, she extended her finger and brushed the pad of it over a glittering emerald. Her body clenched with excitement the moment she felt the vibration of its energy wash over her. The energy was cool and pure, almost cleansing as it rushed through her, stripping away the fear and poison that had been building inside her. She grinned, unable to hide her delight as she touched a ruby. "So beautiful."

"These are ancient stones," Lucien said, his voice so soft it was barely an echo in the back of her mind as she lifted her other hand and clasped the bowl of the goblet between her hands. She was barely aware of his fingers clasping the stem inches from her hands as she traced each stone, listening to its story and breathing in its energy. Her muscles seemed to vibrate with strength, and her heart steadied into a strong beat.

She looked up at Lucien in shock. "I've never felt like this. It's amazing."

He smiled, a smile so beautiful she felt as if the sun had suddenly lit up her world. "I'm glad I can offer you this," he said.

She moved closer, her body literally calling her to the stones. She wanted to cradle them to her heart and envelope them in her energy. She closed her eyes, letting their power wash over her. The uncut ones were powerful, but these were something more. "They aren't from the graveyard, are they?"

"I don't know." His voice was a whisper against her ear. "You tell me. Reach into them and tell me where they are from."

Instinctively, she obeyed, broadening her connection with the stones, diving deep into their core, searching out their histories. "I feel grass," she said. "Fresh air. I think they're from the earth realm."

"Where?" His voice was distant, barely penetrating the magic of the stones that wrapped around her. "Where are they from?"

In her mind, she saw a towering majestic mountain topped with glistening snow and ice. A radiant blue sky sang its glories, and a golden sun was stretching across the earth. The mountain looked familiar, and her heart gave a tug. "I know that mountain," she said. "I've seen it." Home. It felt like home. The jewels felt like home...no, not home exactly. Something more. Something deeper. At the base of the mountain, she saw an old, stone castle, resplendent in its beauty as it rose above a humble town. Her heart leapt with longing, and she knew she'd been there. It felt right. Somehow, right.

A face flashed before her eyes. A boy. Dark hair. Blue eyes. A devilish smile. He held out his hand to her, as if tempting her to break rules he didn't believe in. Instinctively, she reached toward him, needing to touch him, trusting him—

Something ice cold hit her fingers, and she jerked her eyes open.

Her fingers were touching Lucien's bare shoulder. "Oh, God!" Her entire body dissolved instantly, and she sped toward the door. She tried to go under it, but it was closed so tightly, there wasn't a gap big enough even for the particles of her body. She realized suddenly that his room was lined with something other than the stone that it had been carved from. It was lined with a substance she couldn't penetrate. She was *trapped*.

She reformed against the door, crushed against it, staring in horror at Lucien.

He was smiling, a satisfied gleam in his eyes. "Your touch is like the silken caress of an angel," he said.

She clutched her left hand to her chest. Her ring finger hurt so much that tears swam in her eyes. What had she done? She'd touched him? On her own?

Still holding the wineglass, Lucien walked toward her. She shrank against the door, but there was no exit. The image of the boy was still radiating in her mind, but she forced it away. Instead, she focused on Lucien's face. She forced herself to think of how he'd thrown Maria to the ground. She pictured Ashlynn's beleaguered body as she'd tried to crawl from his bedchambers when Sophie had found her. She flooded herself with every reminder possible of Lucien's true nature until her body was pulsing with fear.

He reached for her cheek, and she dissolved instantly, before he'd even gotten near her.

He dropped his hand, his brow creased in thoughtfulness. "Interesting," was all he said. He reached toward her belly, and she dissolved, but all he did was turn the doorknob that she was standing in front of. "You're dismissed for the evening."

She stared at him, startled by the sudden reprieve. "I am?"

"Yes." He was studying her so intently she could practically hear his thoughts reverberating through his mind. "I have to assemble some items for tomorrow. Be here as soon as the hunt is over." He drained the glass, then tossed the empty goblet at her. She caught it instinctively, her fingers cradling the precious vessel. "Take those with you, my darling, for tomorrow, I shall have more. So much more."

He bowed low, but this time, her heart didn't leap at the gallantry. All she felt was fear, because she knew what he was going to do. He was going to use the jewels to get to her. It had worked tonight, both in his room and with Rikker. How many would he have tomorrow? His chambers would be resplendent with them, she was certain. Just the idea of it, made her soul burn with yearning, a betrayal of the worst kind.

The jewels were her weakness, and he was going to exploit it. And...it was going to work.

He raised his head, his dark gaze boring into her. "Tomorrow, Sophie, you will be mine. I promise."

"Never," she hissed, as the image of the dark-haired boy flashed through her mind again, still reaching for her as if he were entreating her to come to him. "I'm not yours." She just threw the goblet at him and fled, racing down the hallway and away from the jewels that had just betrayed her.

68

Chapter Eight

VLAD SLOWED THE motorcycle as they bumped over the tree roots. They were deep in the southern Oregon forest now, and he could feel the taint of darkness over his skin. Gabe was relaxed on the back of the bike, his balance so precise that he was no longer holding on.

They'd passed a small village a short time ago, one that looked like it had once been thriving, but now was mostly empty, except for a few people moving about. One old lady had saluted Gabe as they'd ridden by, and he'd shouted a greeting.

The engine was too loud for Vlad to ask questions, and he wasn't going to stop until they'd reached their destination. They'd been on the road for sixteen hours, and he was tired and hungry as hell, but he'd refused to stop, except for gas.

"Up here," Gabe shouted over the roar of the engine, pointing ahead.

The bike shot over the crest of a hill, and then Vlad skidded to a stop, just barely stopping on the edge of a massive crater that felt like it was leaching evil. "What's this?"

Gabe swung his leg off the bike and walked over to the edge of the pit. "Kane Santiago, one of the Order members, is from here. His father was a demon, and he came from here." Gabe crouched on the edge, extending his hand over the pit.

"This somehow connects to the demon realm."

"Excellent." Vlad toed his kickstand into place and joined Gabe on the edge. The rocky slope extended downward, straight into darkness. There was a thick taint in the air, almost a repellent, making him want to leave. But at the same time, there was an unnatural compulsion to go closer, a compulsion that came from the very pit itself. "Does the pit go to the demon realm?"

"No, but we're close, somehow." Gabe looked up, scanning the woods. "It's around here."

Vlad glanced around, but the woods all looked the same. Swearing, he fisted his hand. He didn't have time for a random search. He looked down at his hand, and saw the band on his ring finger was churning violently, almost as if it were trying to leap off his hand.

Gabe was studying it, too. "What's that?"

"A ring that binds me to a woman in the demon realm. She's calling to me through the ring. That's why it looks like that. She's in trouble."

Gabe whistled softly. "Like the *sheva* bond."

Vlad raised his brows. "What's a *sheva* bond?"

Gabe rose to his feet, shoving up his sleeve to show Vlad the weapon branded on his arm. "Every Calydon is bound to meet his soulmate, called a *sheva*. As their bond tightens, she begins to develop markings on her arm that match his. With each additional mark, she's more able to connect with him, including calling his weapon to save herself."

Vlad considered that. "That's good shit." If Sophie had been able to call him or use his powers to protect herself, that would have been a much better situation.

"No, because fate determines that he goes rogue and murders a bunch of innocents until she kills him." Gabe jerked his sleeve back down. "Several of the Order members have bonded with their *shevas,* but it's not going to hold. Fate is going to demand her due, and we need Dante back before that happens, or we're all fucked."

Vlad contemplated the magnitude of Gabe's task. "How are you going to find a soulless body in the demon realm? It could be anywhere."

"I have a blood bond with him. I'll track him through that." Gabe paced the rim of the crater. "Once we're inside, we split up. I'm going after Dante, and you can get your girl. We meet back at the entrance point to get out."

Vlad nodded. "Works for me." He thought about the blood bond. "How does the blood bond work?"

Gabe glanced over at him, and then his eyebrows went up. "You don't know how to find her?" he said, far too astutely.

"No." He didn't have time to randomly search the demon realm when he got in, and he sure as hell didn't have time to search the woods for the entrance. The state of his ring told him exactly how fast he had to find her. "How does it work?"

Gabe narrowed his eyes. "Are you blood bonded with her?"

"No." He held up his hand. "We're connected through the ring, though."

Gabe studied the ring thoughtfully. "It might work. Try focusing on it. Close your eyes and feel it. That kind of connection is powerful. See if it can guide you."

"Connection? Shit." Vlad hadn't connected with anything in a couple hundred years. He wasn't sure he even knew how. But it made sense that it might work that way. He took a deep breath and closed his eyes, focusing on the pain in his hand...but he got nothing. He started to shake his head, and then he felt Gabe's hand on his shoulder.

"Picture what she looks like," Gabe said quietly. "Picture the sound of her voice. The color of her eyes. What she smells like."

Vlad took a deep breath, trying to slow his mind back to a past of long ago. He remembered her golden locks tumbling around her shoulders as he coaxed her to jump off the forbidden rock. Her blue eyes were the color of a sky just before sunset, with almost a hint of lavender. He could hear her laughter, the sheer, pure laughter of someone who hadn't yet learned that laughter was more optimistic than the world deserved. He remembered climbing out his bedroom window to meet her by the river, where he taught her how to throw a dagger and shoot a bow and arrow.

The scene shifted, and he saw her eyes again, this time wide with terror as she fell. Once again, he was reaching for her, but this time, he couldn't catch her. No laughter this time, just her scream, tearing apart his soul. *Sophie.* He felt his hand reach out, stretching for her, and for a split second, he thought he felt the smoothness of her skin, the warmth of her touch.

And then it was gone, drifting out of his reach, sliding further and further...

He began to walk, following the image in his mind. It got further from him, and he began to jog, moving faster and faster until he was sprinting through the woods, fighting desperately not to lose the image in his mind. He was getting closer and closer, and he lunged for her, his hands outstretched—

Cold water closed over his head, sucking the oxygen from his lungs as he plunged into a mountain pool. Swearing, he kicked to the surface, his boots heavy with water. He stroked to the side of the pond, hauling himself out of the water just as Gabe appeared, only moments behind him. "Yeah, that worked," Vlad said sarcastically as he coughed, trying to clear the water from his lungs.

Gabe was down on his knees, staring into the water. "Calydons were originally created by drinking water from a natural spring tainted with demon magic," he said. "Water carries their taint. Water. Of course, *water.*"

Vlad froze and whirled around, staring into the water. It was shimmering and clear, with visibility reaching twenty or thirty feet...but still he couldn't see the bottom. "You think that's it?"

"It makes sense." Gabe looked up at him, his face eager. "How do we use it? Can you get us across the border?"

Vlad ignored the water dripping from his clothes as he studied the mountain pool. "Sophie was taken across the border into the demon realm, which means it's possible. They pulled her across." He braced his hands on the rocky ledge by the water, his mind working as he thought. "We need to get pulled across," he said. "The power needs to come from the other side."

Gabe looked at him expectantly. "Can you make that happen?"

"I might." He looked at Gabe. "You want to go for a swim?"

"Hell, yeah, I do." Gabe grinned, his face vibrant and alive. "Just give me one second." He paused, and Vlad felt the pulse of psychic energy coming from him. There was a brief wait, and then Gabe grinned. "I just contacted the team and told them where I was, and what we're doing. It's too late for them to stop me, but they're going to haul ass here to try." He grinned. "We might need their help later, so I'm giving them a heads up—"

There was a sudden burst of energy, and Vlad looked up as six Calydon warriors shimmered into existence on the other side of the pond.

"Oh, shit." Gabe blanched. "I didn't think Kane was around to teleport them. We gotta go."

The tallest Calydon shouted, and Vlad saw a dark-haired warrior begin to fade, as if he were going to teleport right to where they were. *Fuck that.* He wasn't going to be stopped! He grabbed Gabe's arm and they both dove right into the water.

The water churned above them, and he felt the rush of waves as the other warrior leapt in after them. Vlad swore when the teleporting warrior appeared beside them, reaching for Gabe. Vlad flicked his finger at him, and the warrior flew backwards, slamming into the rocky side of the pool. At the same time, Vlad increased their speed, hurtling them toward the bottom with dangerous speed.

Behind them, he heard the others swimming, but the teleporting one didn't catch up. Down they went, faster and faster and faster until—-

Crash!

They slammed against something so hard that for a moment, Vlad couldn't breathe. His entire body shouted in protest, and even Gabe clutched his shoulder, grimacing at the pain. Still holding his breath, Vlad spun around to see what they'd crashed into.

It appeared to be the stone floor of the lake. Both men began to feel quickly across the stones, searching for a gap, knowing that the others were closing in fast behind them. Every rock felt the same, and Vlad was running out of oxygen. They had no time—

His ring was burning again, jerking his attention to his hand. He immediately closed his eyes and pictured Sophie again, focusing on that moment when she'd fallen into the abyss. This time, he felt the response in the ring, and he consciously followed it across the bottom to a crevice in the rocks. He pressed his hand to the crevice and reached out with his mind past it.

He felt life. Something was alive on the other side of the rock.

He waved at Gabe, who swam over to him. The men locked wrists in silent understanding, and then Vlad turned his attention to the living matter on the other side. He swept into its cells, taking control of them with well-practiced speed. He turned it toward them, and forced it to reach out toward him and Gabe, forcing the living energy on the other side to summon them.

Vlad felt the moment that the life force on the other side of the rock began to pull on him. He tightened his grip on Gabe, and then drilled his focus down on the other side, forcing it to pull on him, to suck his soul and his body across the border. The pressure grew and grew, until his body bowed with pain. He heard Gabe's grunt of pain, and then he felt the water pressure shift, indicating that their pursuers were closing in.

He looked up as the teleporting Calydon appeared above them. He reached for Gabe—-

"No!" Vlad thrust all his energy into the living matter on the other side. He felt its roar of protest at being controlled, and then he was sucked right through the rock, dragging Gabe with him.

He felt like his body was being torn into pieces, shredded into bits, and then suddenly, he crashed to the hard ground, landing so violently that his breath was torn from his body.

Gabe fell on top of him, his body weight nearly crushing Vlad.

Swearing, Vlad shoved him aside, and leapt to his feet.

Standing ten feet from them was a man with black horns, a heavily muscled body, and massive wings that stretched twenty feet in either direction.

And he looked kinda pissed.

"MARIA!" SOPHIE FLUNG open the door to her friend's lodgings, breathless from having run so far.

Maria had apparently fully recovered from the healing. She was wearing black leather leggings, a black bodice, and she had seventeen weapons strapped to her body. She whirled toward the door when Sophie shoved it open, a dagger aimed at Sophie's forehead. "Sophie!" She lowered the dagger and leaned against the dresser, all the strength dissipating from her body.

The sudden and complete slump of Maria's body made it clear that her friend wasn't actually recovered at all. "Maria!" She raced over to her friend, and the two women hugged briefly, until Maria pushed her back and studied her.

Relief rushed across her face. "You're still coherent and sane. You didn't have sex with him, did you?"

Sophie shivered. "No, but he used jewels to tempt me. It's going to work."

Maria swore. "This is it. It's over. We have to get you out."

"Out of where?"

"The demon realm, of course. That's the only place Lucien won't be able to reach you."

For a split second, Sophie was too stunned to respond. "What? There's a way out?"

"There has to be." Maria sighed and sat down. "My brother pulls women across the boundary every day. There has to be a way to go the other way."

Hope faded as quickly as it had flared. "We've been over this a thousand times, Maria. It's always a dead end. Why would this be different?"

Maria met her gaze. "Because this time, if we don't do it, my best friend is going to die. That's what is different." Sudden tears shimmered in her eyes. "I'd never survive your death," Maria whispered. "You're all I have."

"I know. Me too." Sophie hugged her, and the two women clung to each other. For two hundred years, they'd survived in the hostile demon kingdom. "I can't believe we're out of time," she said. "I thought we had it managed."

"They're demons. You can't manage them." Maria pulled back, and then swayed to the side.

Sophie caught her arm to stabilize her, surprised at how cold her skin was. She frowned at how weak Maria still was. "Have you recovered at all since healing Ashlynn?"

"Yeah, I'm fine." Maria turned away, not meeting her gaze. "Grab some weapons. We're going hunting."

Sophie didn't move. "Why aren't you healing?"

Maria shrugged "It doesn't matter." She strapped another knife to her waist. "When are you going back to Lucien's chambers?"

"Tonight."

Maria looked at her sharply. "Really?"

She nodded.

"Okay. Then we have eighteen hours to get you out of here."

Eighteen hours? Sophie closed her eyes at the fear that sliced through her, but she shook her head. "Even if there was a way out, I wouldn't leave without you, and the other women. You have to come as well."

"Don't be a fool." Maria shoved a dart gun into her bodice. "We can't get everyone—"

Sophie folded her arms over her chest. "Then I'm not leaving. You think I can survive the earth realm, knowing that you and the others are still down here, suffering?"

Maria swore and turned toward her. "You're from the earth realm, Soph. You belong there."

"You're half human—"

"I'm also half-demon. Every woman down here has been so infected with demon semen that their blood is barely distinguishable from demon blood. You're the only one still human enough to break through the barrier."

"But—"

"Once you get out, you can figure out how to save us, but if you stay, if you become Lucien's concubine, you'll die." Determination filled Maria's face. "I'm not going to let you die," she snapped. "So don't even try."

Sophie bit her lip, knowing that Maria had a point. The invisible net that kept the demons trapped would apply to all the others. "Then I'll find that jewel and break the spell."

"And what? Let Lucien out into the human realm? Screw that, Soph. You're smarter than that. I know you are." Maria's eyes glistened. "You're going. Do you understand? It's the way it has to be."

Sophie sighed. "Fine." She was lying. She'd never leave without Maria, and from the look in Maria's eyes, her friend knew it, but didn't care. Maria was planning to make her leave if they found a way. Sophie was going to find a way to stay, or get Maria across. But neither woman was going to admit it.

"Good." Maria jammed one more dagger into the waistband of her pants. "Then let's go. My brother is hunting this morning. We'll find him." She turned away, heading toward the door. "Get some weapons. We're about to go where we're not supposed to go."

Sophie couldn't help but grin. It had been a long time since they'd mounted an out and out assault on the barrier. Even with Maria temporarily weakened, they were both more powerful than they had ever been. Determination flooded her. Maybe this was the time it was finally going to work.

It had to.

If it didn't, and she had to face Lucien tonight, she would die.

Time was up.

Gritting her teeth, she grabbed an assortment of weapons from Maria's cache. By the time she'd strapped them to various parts of her body and walked out, Maria was pacing restlessly in the hall. "Ready?"

Sophie tightened her grip on the dagger. In the past, she'd used her weapons only to protect other women, because no demon could touch her. Now...it was different. Now, her own life could be at stake. She took a deep breath, trying to steady herself for the battle she had no idea how to fight. "Let's do this."

Maria nodded, and the two women strode down the hall, side by side, to take on a battle they'd fought and lost countless times before, and they both knew it.

Chapter Nine

F OR A SPLIT second, Gabe was too shocked by the horned warrior to react. They'd crossed over to the demon realm? That was impossible. *Impossible.* And yet Vlad had dragged them across. He immediately reached out with his mind. They were here....in the realm where Dante's body was.

Dante.

Gabe immediately dismissed the demon warrior and concentrated on his leader. *Dante. Can you hear me?* He sent the pulses of energy in all directions, letting it bounce off the cavern walls and ceiling, hurtling the energy through the tunnels. As his energy sped through the halls, a virtual map of the area formed in his mind, created by the millions of messages sent back to him, like bat sonar. Within seconds, he knew every tunnel for five miles...and Dante wasn't in any of them.

Swearing, he lurched to his feet, preparing to run, when he felt something slam into his shoulder. Pain shot through him, and he stumbled, gripping his shoulder as blood cascaded down his arm. He whirled around. The demon was attacking Vlad, who was already bloody. Vlad flicked his finger, and the demon flew backward, crashing into the stone wall. "There's not enough living matter down here for me to use against him," Vlad shouted at Gabe. "Some help would be nice."

Son of a bitch. He'd landed in a hostile situation and not even paid attention? What kind of focus was that? Dante would be disgusted. Gabe called out his hook swords. The flash of black light lit up the cavern, and the crack as the weapons leapt into his palms reverberated through the halls. Gabe hurtled a sword as the demon launched himself at Vlad. The blade sank deep, spinning the demon off to the right. His wings smashed into both warriors, and Gabe was slammed against the wall over the cavern. Vlad hit right next to him, against a sharp rock outcropping that went through his torso, impaling him.

"Hey! I need him alive!" Gabe called his hook sword back as he hurled the other one. The demon slapped it aside with his wing, and his weapon clattered uselessly against the side of the cavern. Gabe lunged forward, striking fast and hard with his remaining weapon while he called back the other one. The demon blocked every blow effortlessly with his wings, and Gabe's sword didn't even penetrate the thickness of the scales that covered it.

The demon moved closer, and Gabe saw its claws elongate, blackened and twisting. Shit! He blocked one blow from the demon, but as he did so, the demon's other claw sank deep into his side. Searing pain tore through him, and Gabe gasped, gripping his side as the demon lifted him up, holding him above his head like a trophy.

"Back off!" Vlad's shout bounced off the walls, and then Gabe felt himself lifted off the end of the claw and dragged backward through the air away from the demon by Vlad's psychic energy. Vlad dumped him behind an outcropping and shoved the demon back against the wall, both at the same time.

Gripping his side against the pain surging through him, Gabe pulled himself back around the rock toward the battle. Vlad had managed to get himself off the outcropping, but he was on his side, slumped against the wall. He was pointing at the demon, and Gabe could feel the waves of energy pulsing off him, pinning the demon against the far wall. The demon was fighting hard, and Gabe could see he was already loosening Vlad's grip on him.

Vlad's face was ashen, and his jeans were soaked with blood. "I can't hold him much longer," Vlad gritted out. "Do something."

"Right." Gabe tried to stand, but his legs gave out. He could feel his muscles weakening throughout his body, and he realized that the demon had injected some sort of poison into him. Shit. He had no time to stop and heal. He slithered down to his stomach, and then rolled onto his side to free his right arm. "Keep his wings trapped," he commanded Vlad.

"Yeah, no problem." The strain was evident in Vlad's voice, but he flicked his finger again, and the demon's wings slammed back against the wall.

In the same instant, Gabe summoned the last of his strength and then hurled his hook sword at the demon. His aim was dead on, and the blade pierced the demon's chest, right over his heart and jammed into the wall behind him, pinning the demon to the wall.

No blood ran from his chest, but smoke began to rise from the weapon, as if acid was eating right through it.

Shit. "It's eating my sword. Don't demons have hearts?"

"I don't know." Vlad slumped lower. "Got another plan?"

Gabe gripped his other weapon. "His head? They must have brains, right?"

"I'm a demon, you stupid humans," the demon snapped. "We can't be killed. I have a brain and a heart, for hell's sake, but stop—"

Gabe threw the hook sword, and it went straight through the demon's forehead.

"Nice shot," Vlad said.

"Thanks." Gabe managed to drag himself to his knees as the demon howled in outrage. "It didn't shut him up, though."

"No, but it might hold him for a sec." Vlad was still on his side, apparently using his reserves to pin the demon against the wall. "You know, I think he poisoned me."

"Me too. You good at healing?"

"Most things." Vlad's face paled even more. "Not this, apparently."

"Shit." Gabe looked toward the doorway that led to the rest of the demon realm. He was so close to Dante. He couldn't die now. "Can you bring the rest of my team through? They could contain him."

Vlad looked over at him with a look that said that was one of the stupidest questions he'd ever heard. "Does it look like I'm a little busy? Because I feel like I'm a little busy."

"Well, if you brought them over, you could be less busy."

"If I take my energy off him to bring your pals over, he'll kill us while I'm distracted. Your pals will be here, but then I'll be really not busy because I'll be *dead*. Sophie will have no one to save her." Vlad looked pissed. "So shut the hell up and let me think."

All good points. Gabe wasn't too high on dying right now either. But what the hell options did they have? The demon's howls of outrage increased, and Gabe glanced over at him. "Oh, shit."

Vlad followed his gaze, and swore.

Black blood was pouring down the demon's head from the wound in his skull. It was slithering over his body, and across the floor toward Gabe and Vlad, moving with rapid speed. "Holy shit." Gabe lunged to his feet, staggered over to Vlad and hauled him off the ground. He dragged Vlad onto a higher outcropping and leapt up beside him. The move took the last of his energy, and he collapsed beside Vlad, his chest heaving with the effort of breathing.

Vlad's eyes were focused on the demon, and he was muttering something silently, his lips moving with rapid speed as if he were summoning more magic.

The demon was disintegrating Gabe's sword, and he knew it would be only seconds until the demon had broken free of that restraint. Once he could focus all his energy on fighting Vlad, he would defeat them within moments.

Shit! There had to be something—

"What the hell are you doing to my brother?" A woman's voice broke through the battle, and Gabe looked up just as a woman in black leather appeared in the doorway to the cave. She exuded sensuality, even with her dark eyes flashing with anger, and her breasts were barely contained by her top, but he quickly dismissed the eye candy part as an attempt to distract him from being focused on the battle.

Her strategy didn't work, because he didn't care about her breasts. What he noticed were the number of weapons she had strapped to her body, all of them strategically placed for access no matter what position she was in or what direction a threat might be coming.

She wasn't simply a female demon.

She was the x-factor that was going to tip the scales in the wrong damn direction.

VLAD FELT LIKE every cell in his body was on fire, and he knew the poison was working fast. His mind was reeling, and he could barely think. He was vaguely aware of someone shouting, but he could barely process it, could barely even hear it. His hearing was fading, his vision was blurring, and he felt his muscles begin to go limp, as his body began shutting down non-critical functions in order to focus on holding the demon in place and fighting off the poison.

Swearing, he managed to raise his head enough to look toward the demon. He could barely make him out, and his image appeared to be undulating. He met the creature's black gaze, and felt it penetrate his mind, building a bridge between them until he could feel the beat of the demon's heart mirror his own.

The rest of the world ceased to exist, and he could see nothing but the demon's eyes, and feel nothing but his heartbeat.

"Let me go." The demon's voice rolled through him, a heavy, thick compulsion.

For a split second, Vlad's mind wanted to obey, but he swore, fresh fury raging through him as Sophie's face appeared in his mind again. He saw the same blue eyes and blond hair, but her face was older and more angular, but he knew it was her. "No," he shouted into an abyss of silence that even his own voice couldn't penetrate. His throat hurt from the force of his scream, but he heard no sound coming from his own mouth. "I will not abandon Sophie again. You're in my damn way, so back the fuck off!"

With a roar of fury, he lunged to his feet, hurling pulse after pulse at the demon, screaming about Sophie, using every last bit of energy he had to attack the demon, at the same time his mind was whirling at high speed, processing everything. The demon couldn't be killed. Only vanquished. How to debilitate a demon? *How the fuck did he shut him down?*

The demon was living matter. What if he pulled the cells apart? What if he dismantled him? Still living, but in a billion pieces. *Yes.* His legs gave out, and he gave up trying to stand. He fell to his knees before the demon, and held out both hands, pointing all his fingers at him. He felt his magic connect to all the cells of the demon, and he began to move his hands apart.

The demon screamed in agony, a sound he couldn't hear, but that filled him with the agony of suffering, and Vlad knew his attack was working. For a split second, he hesitated, almost choked by the demon's pain. "Stand down and I'll stop," he shouted at the demon. "You don't have to make me do it!"

The demon howled in outrage, and Vlad felt him throw off part of his grip. "Fine, you stubborn bastard, if that's how you want it to be, that's how it is." He closed his eyes, and hurled all his magic into the demon. He felt the howl as the demon was pulled apart, and victory rushed through him. "Sophie," he bellowed. "I'm coming!" He had almost reached the point of no return with the demon, when pain exploded in his head and everything went blank.

HE KNEW HER.

Sophie knelt beside the man in the leather jacket as he slumped, unconscious, on the ground, studying him intently. His aura had too much power for him to be human, but it wasn't nearly black enough to be a demon. He had no horns, but his shoulders and muscles were as cut and large as any demon. His hair was a tiny bit too long as it curled against his neck. His leather jacket with the metal spikes on the shoulders was battered, worn, and smelled amazing, like earth, sunshine, and years of hard living, memories of a past she couldn't grasp anymore, but that seemed to come to life when she was near him.

She knew she should be wary of this stranger who wielded so much power that he would have killed Damon, if Maria hadn't knocked him out, but *he'd called her name.* A complete stranger, a non-demon, was in the demon realm, and *he knew her.*

His voice was still burning through her. The way he'd bellowed her name with such anguish and force had been almost terrifying, but at the same time, she'd wanted to rush over to him and shout that she was there. What did he want with her? Who was he? She studied the spikes on his shoulders. She wanted to touch them, to see if they were sharp. Her gaze slid along his shoulder to his chin, where dark whiskers lined his strong jaw.

Something turned over inside her, something deep and powerful, a yearning to touch him that was so strong that she had to fist her hand to keep from reaching for him. "Who are you?" she whispered.

There was no answer, of course, since he was unconscious. Frowning, she brushed her fingers over the spikes on his jacket, startled when she could actually touch it. The metal was sharp and cold, not of this world at all. Excitement jolted through her. "I think he's from the earth realm," she whispered in awe. "How is that possible?"

"Sophie! For God's sake, this isn't the time for gawking." Maria was dragging her brother down from his perch where the man who knew Sophie had pinned him against the wall with some sort of invisible force. Damon was unconscious, knocked out by whatever the man had been doing when he'd pointed his fingers at the lust demon. "Check the other one!" Maria ordered. "See if he's alive."

Sophie glanced across the cavern to the other intruder. He was writhing on the rocky ledge, his skin streaked with black. Oh, *crap*. "Damon poisoned him. He's dying." Fear sliced through her, and she looked down at the man beside her again, inspecting his skin more closely. For a moment, it looked normal, and then she saw faint streaks of black weaving its way through the tattoo on his neck. Alarm leapt through her. "So is this one!"

"Let them die." Maria had Damon's arm over her shoulder, and she was dragging him toward the door. "They're too dangerous. Anyone who can take down Damon is extremely powerful—"

"No! Don't you see?" Sophie lunged to her feet and raced over to her friend. She grabbed Maria's arm, and swung her friend back to face her. "Didn't you hear him? He came here for me. He broke into the demon realm *for me*. I need to know who he is."

Maria shook her head. "No. It's too dangerous. How do we know they aren't here to hurt us? You saw how powerful they are—"

"No! Don't you get it? I've lived here my whole life. I barely remember anything from before I was taken, but this man knows me. I want answers from him. Why am I the way I am with jewels? Why was did the demons bring me here? He might know!"

Maria hesitated. "I don't like it—"

"Didn't you hear the way he screamed my name? He was desperate for me. *Desperate*." Chills raced down her spine at the memory of the anguish in his voice as he charged Damon. She had no doubt that in that moment, he was acting in defense of her. Her throat tightened unexpectedly. "Please, Maria. We can kill them later. We know that demon poison works on them. Right?" She glanced back at the man on the rock ledge. He'd gone still, the only sign of life his rasping chest as he tried to breathe. "I saw you look at him, Maria. I know he caught the interest of your lust demon. It's been a long time since you've accepted a man. If you fed your demon side, your power would be stronger, maybe enough to defeat Lucien."

"I'll never be strong enough to defeat Lucien," Maria said, but her gaze flicked back to the rocky ledge. "They did manage to breach the barrier," she said thoughtfully. "Maybe they have information that will help us get you across."

"Us across." Sophie folded her arms. "I'm not leaving without you and all the other women."

Maria met her gaze. "Not all the women want to leave. Some of them have decent situations."

"Until they die of poison—" The man on the ground groaned, and she whirled around. She gasped when she saw his face was almost completely black. "Maria! You have to save them now!"

"Dammit." Maria eased Damon down to the floor. "This is going to sap me. I'll have no defenses." She met her gaze. "We won't be able to get you out of here before tonight."

Sophie bit her lip, glancing around. "Okay, then, we'll hide out here." She hurried over to the door and placed her hands on the walls, reaching out with her body. Instantly, she found a number of jewels buried in the walls of this rich soil. She disintegrated, reaching out in all directions to merge with the stones. Within moments, she reformed, and a pile of stones appeared in front of her. She piled them up quickly in the doorway, strategically placing them so their energy created a shield. Within moments, an invisible barrier was formed. She passed her hand over it, and grinned when it hummed. "That will block our energy from being traceable," she said as she whirled around. "No one will find us unless they come here specifically looking for us."

Maria met her gaze. "You better cross your fingers, girlfriend. This is going to get ugly. You're going to be the only conscious one for a while."

Sophie nodded. "I can do it." She hurried over to the leather jacketed man, and knelt beside him. "Hurry."

Maria took one last glance at the man on the rock ledge, and then she knelt beside the man on the ground. "I don't know why I listen to you," she muttered. "This sounds like a bad idea on every level."

"Except for all the ones you just mentioned a minute ago."

Maria glanced at her as she set her hands on his chest. "Yeah, true." She winked. "If we don't survive this, I just want you to know that you're my best friend, and I would have given up a long time ago if it hadn't been for you."

Tears filled Sophie's eyes. "Me, too, Maria."

"Okay, let's do this." Maria closed her eyes, and she began to work her magic.

Chapter Ten

VLAD AWOKE IN a sudden rush of consciousness. His entire body went on alert, but he didn't move even a fraction of an inch. He didn't change his breathing, or even his heart rate. Nothing gave away the fact he was conscious. He lay utterly still, reaching out with his senses to determine the situation.

The first thing he became aware of was the faint scent of primroses. Recognition slammed into him at the scent he hadn't smelled since boyhood. His kingdom had been surrounded by fields of primroses, fields that he and Sophie had spent hours roaming around in. *Primroses.*

Then, he noticed that the air around him was moving, undulating softly against his flesh like the first tentative breeze of summer. The current brushed over his shoulder, and then down his arm. Another rippled across his forehead, and through his hair. The air was warm, sliding over his skin like an invisible caress of silk. Chills popped up on his skin, and he couldn't stop his sharp intake of breath.

The air went still, and the scent of primroses disappeared.

Shit. He'd just revealed he was conscious. Swearing at his mistake, he opened his eyes immediately, then froze in shock. Leaning over him, her blue eyes just as vivid and electric as he remembered, was Sophie.

Holy shit. It was her. *She was alive.*

Except she wasn't the Sophie he remembered. He'd lived with the image of a teenage girl with rosy cheeks and white blond hair. This Sophie was a woman, with an angular face and dark blond hair that tumbled past her shoulders. She had seven earrings in each ear, each a different, glittering stone. She had all the curves of a woman, and her eyes carried the depth of a lifetime of struggle, courage, and grit.

Gone was the innocent girl. In its place was a strong, confident, sexy-as-hell woman.

She narrowed her eyes. "Hello?" she said. "Can you hear me?"

Her voice rammed straight into his gut like a sledgehammer. It ripped right through his soul on a thousand different levels, sucking the breath out of his lungs so fiercely he couldn't even speak. He thought he'd never hear her voice again, and yet, he was here, with her, the sound of her voice filling him with a hope he hadn't felt in centuries. His throat suddenly became clogged, and for a moment, he had to close his eyes to fight off the emotion rushing through him.

"Hello?" she said again.

He opened his eyes again to see Sophie frowning at him. *Sophie*. Her cheeks were flushed, and instinctively, he reached toward her, needing to touch her, to feel she was real.

She pulled back quickly, fear flashing across her face as her hand went to the handle of a dagger tucked in her waistband.

Vlad gritted his jaw, but he dropped his hand. "Sophie." He managed to rasp out the name, but his throat burned, as if he'd swallowed fire while he'd been asleep.

A smile flashed across her face, and she leaned closer. "When you say my name, it sounds like magic," she observed. "Why is that? Who are you?"

He tried to answer, but his voice wouldn't work anymore. The room seemed to darken. His vision blurred, and he lost sight of her. What the fuck? He blinked, but he still couldn't see anything, even though his eyes were open. Just blackness. "Sophie!" He rasped out her name, and bolted upright, terror ripping through him. He couldn't lose her again. "Sophie!"

"It's okay." Warm air rushed over him, and somehow, he knew it was her.

"Where are you?" He reached for her, but found nothing.

"Right here." Her voice was beside his ear, almost melodic in its rhythm "It's okay. It's the demon poison. It will take a while for you to regain full functionality. Your vision and hearing may go in and out for a while. You're in a safe place. Just lie down and let your body heal."

"No." Forget lying down. He had to get her to safety. See her. Touch her. He tried to stand, but he fell, crashing back down to the hard stone floor, his body too weak to hold him up. What the hell?

"God, you're stubborn." Her voice was firm, almost a little bossy, just as it had been so many times in the past when she'd gotten tired of him being too much of a pain in the ass. Jesus. It was really her.

He grinned at the same complaint she'd lobbed at him countless times over the years. "Yeah, I am. Always have been."

"Well, it's annoying. Lie down," she ordered.

"Annoying?" No one had told him he was annoying in centuries. God, he'd missed her.

"Stop grinning like an idiot and lie down."

He felt another push of energy at his chest, and this time, he surrendered to it and stretched out on his back. He closed his eyes, digging deep inside himself for healing energy. It surged through him, and he felt strength beginning to return almost immediately, slow but steady. He knew he'd be back to at least partial strength within a few minutes...which was good. He'd heard the hesitation in Sophie's voice when she'd said they were safe, and he knew that wasn't entirely true. He had to get healed fast. "Are we in the demon realm?"

"Yes. I shielded our location, so we should be okay for now."

His vision returned just as suddenly as it had left. Sophie was still leaning over him, but this time, her hands were moving across his face, almost touching him, but not quite. She stopped, apparently sensing that he could see again.

Her cheeks flushed red and she pulled her hands away. "Sorry, I just...I wanted to see what your face felt like."

"It's okay." He couldn't believe he was staring at her. It was surreal, almost too much to absorb. "You're alive. I can't believe it."

Her eyebrows knit. "How do you know me? Did you come here for me? Do you know me from before I came here?"

Her repeated questioning finally registered. She didn't remember him. He'd spent decades tormenting himself about her death, and she had no memory of who he was? "Yeah, I do." He started to sit up, and she jumped backward, her hand going to the handle of a dagger again. She moved away from him so quickly that he felt another brush of wind from her action.

Shit. She didn't trust him at all. A bleak darkness settled over him, but he shoved it aside. He had no time to take her response personally. He was here to rescue her, and that meant he had to gain her trust quickly. "My name's Vladimir Hawkings." He waited a heartbeat to see if that meant anything, but she was still staring at him expectantly. "Vlad," he tried.

She shook her head and held out her hands in a helpless gesture. "I don't remember."

He sighed. "We were friends. Best friends." He didn't mention they were married. She was so skittish, and he had a feeling that discovering she was bound to him might put her over the edge...either to shutting him out or killing him. Neither of which was high on his list of goals for the day, so, he didn't mention the husband-wife thing. But he couldn't keep himself from glancing at her left hand to see if she still wore his band. Her hand was hidden behind her thigh, out of his view, leaving him with no answers.

"We were friends? Really? Vladimir Hawkings," she said to herself, as if she were testing the name. She shook her head, her face furrowed in thought. "It doesn't mean anything to me."

She didn't remember. Grief and guilt flooded him, a sharp stab of isolation. How did the woman who'd consumed his every thought for the last two hundred years not remember him? To her, he was nothing. Nobody. A stranger not worthy of trust. Son of a bitch. He wasn't going to lie. That hurt like hell.

She cocked her head. "Why are you here?"

He sighed. "To rescue you."

Her eyebrows shot up. For a moment, she looked shocked, and then she burst out laughing. "Rescue me? I've been here for two hundred years. I think you're a little late. What have you been doing all this time? Napping?"

He was stunned by her laugh. It was exactly as he'd remembered. A genuine, heartfelt laugh that seemed to roll through her entire body and out into the air around her. "I've been saving kids," he snapped, his guilt making him cranky.

When her eyebrows went up, he swore. "Sorry." He took a deep breath. "Look, I feel like shit about it. I had no idea you were alive. When the demons took you, I felt..." Shit. What was he going to do, declare to her that he'd felt like his soul had been cleaved from his body, leaving behind nothing but an empty wasteland of isolation and hell? And that he'd thought that it meant she'd been severed from him by death, not just by a veil that separated the worlds? She wouldn't get it. Not now. Not with her thinking he was a stranger. "I thought you were dead," he said simply. "I didn't find out until yesterday that you were alive." He leaned forward, urgency coursing through him. "I swear on my soul that if I'd known you were alive, I would *never* have stopped trying to find you."

Her eyes widened, and she caught her breath. "Wow. Were you always this intense?"

"No. I used to laugh. Then you died, and I became a miserable, bitter, isolated bastard who hates the world and every person in it."

She stared at him. "I was that important to you?"

"Yes." He wanted to grab her, drag her into his arms, feel her body against his...but she wasn't his to touch anymore, regardless of whether she was wearing his ring. She clearly belonged to herself, not to him...as she should, after he'd abandoned her for two hundred years.

"Wow." Her cheeks were flushed, her eyes wary but vibrant as she studied him. "How do I not remember you then?

Did I feel that way about you?"

It was his turn to catch his breath. Did she? How had she really felt about him? What would she have done if he'd been the one to die? Would she have reclaimed her life and found a way to be happy? Probably. She was tougher than he was, in that way. He shrugged. "You used to sneak into my room at night and force me to take you to the river to search for fairies in the moonlight."

She smiled. "Fairies? I believed in fairies?"

"Yeah. You forced me to swear I believed in them too."

Her eyebrows went up then. "You don't seem like the type who could be forced into anything."

"I'm not. Except when it comes to you." Shit. He couldn't believe he was telling her all this. He felt like he was being stripped bare and raw, all his shields shattered, just because he wanted to help her, to connect to her, to give her back the past she'd lost...to give her back him. "I wouldn't have given up, Soph. If I'd known, I wouldn't have given up." He wanted to ask her for her forgiveness, but he didn't deserve it, not from her, and not from himself.

"I believe you," she said softly, searching his face. Her inspection was non-judgmental and genuine, as if a lifetime in the demon realm hadn't taken away the purity of her world view, her ability to see through the crap to find the scrap of beauty in a moment. That was why he'd gravitated toward her when they were kids: all he saw was darkness, and she'd changed that for him. She'd taught him to see light and sunshine...until he'd lost her.

And now, she was doing the same thing, looking at him as if he were a thing of wonder, not a stranger who'd abandoned her for two centuries.

"I feel the connection between us," she said quietly. "There's something there." She reached toward him again, her fingers drifting just above his forehead. "I've never wanted to touch a man before." Her blue gaze drifted to his. "But from the first moment I saw you, I wanted to feel your skin under my fingertips. I wanted to see how soft your hair was." Her gaze went to his jaw. "I want to run my fingers over your whiskers."

Jesus. Heat poured through him, the kind of dark, primal heat that could consume a man. Sophie had been his best friend, his partner in crime, his wife in name only. But the way she was looking at him made something inside him shift. Stunned, his gaze slid over her, across her lips, along her collarbone, over the swell of her breasts, down to the curve of her hips. Raw need arose hard and fast within him, shocking him. He realized he wanted her. He wanted to slide his hand through her hair, draw her to him, and taste her mouth for the first time ever.

She dragged her gaze back to his eyes. "Why do I respond like that to you? Why not anyone else? Why *you*?"

Why him? Her question jerked him back to the present, and he swore, trying to shut down his physical response to her. "We're connected," he said carefully. "Even though you don't remember me, your soul recognizes me."

She raised her eyebrows at his reply, but didn't deny his claim that her soul knew who he was, even if she didn't. "Connected how, exactly? More than friends?" she asked, astutely.

"Yeah." Slowly, he raised his left hand, showing his ring. It was still swirling with red, purple, and black, indicating that she was still in as much danger as before he'd arrived. Clearly, his mere presence wasn't enough to change the storm that was coming for her.

Sophie's eyes widened and a little gasp escaped from her throat.

Wordlessly, she held up her left hand, and he saw a matching band wrapped around her ring finger. Something lurched inside him at the sight of his ring on her hand, something deep, powerful, and primal. *She was still his.*

Her ring was equally turbulent, angry and dangerous. "What's our connection?" she asked, sitting back on her heels. Her dagger apparently forgotten, she tucked her hands over her heart, as if she were trying to protect herself from him. "Family? Brother and sister?"

"What? Your brother?" He sat up suddenly, forgetting that he was trying not to scare her. Was that really her response to him? Like a *brother*? This woman who had been a part of his very soul since he was a kid, thought he was like her *brother?* "Hell, no," he snapped. "We're married."

Chapter Eleven

"**M**ARRIED?" SOPHIE'S HEART lurched, and sudden fear seemed to paralyze her. For a moment, all she could think of was the bonding ceremony that demons performed with their lovers to trap them forever, to make them crave no one but their demon, to be unable to ever break away from the monster slowly killing her.

It was a marriage of sorts, and it trapped the women in hell...literally.

Instinctively, she recoiled, fisting her left hand against the burning from her ring. "No."

Vlad nodded at her ring, and held up his own. "Matching wedding bands."

"No." She jerked her hand back, her pulse hammering frantically. "That's impossible!" It had to be impossible. It couldn't be true. She knew too much about what happened to women who were bound to males. They died. Every single time. And this man had a claim on her? No, there was no way. It couldn't be. He was trying to trick her. Manipulate her. Something.

She scrambled away from him and stood up, pulling out one of the many knives she had strapped to her body. "Who are you?"

He leapt to his feet, then staggered slightly before catching his balance, not that she was going to feel bad for him. "We got married when we were sixteen. We did it in secret, to protect you."

"Protect me?" She couldn't keep the disbelief out of her voice. "Marriage was to *protect* me?" Bonding with a male was dangerous and brutal, not designed to protect the female. "From what?"

"Your parents. The man they betrothed you to." He grimaced. "And, apparently, demons, but I figured that one out a little late."

"My parents?" Her grip on the dagger faltered, and suddenly she couldn't breathe. "You knew my parents? What were they like? I have only flashes of memories of them, bits and pieces." Memories that always slipped out of her reach just when she was almost there, almost able to recover them. She didn't trust Vlad, but at the same time, the thought of learning about her past, her parents, and who she used to be was overwhelming. She wanted to cry, and at the same time, she wanted to leap over to him, grab him, and merge her mind with his so she could see all that he knew. "My mom? Was she nice? I think she was. I have memories of her reading to me...."

Her voice trailed off when she saw Vlad tense.

She paused. "What is it?"

He hesitated. "You don't remember?"

She shook her head once, fear tightening around her heart. "What don't I remember?" Suddenly, she knew. It was bad. Whatever it was that had happened before she'd arrived in the demon world was so bad that she'd blocked it. Her legs seemed to go numb, and she sank down on a nearby rock. "Tell me," she whispered, even as a part of her screamed that she didn't want to know.

Vlad walked over and crouched in front of her. His dark eyes were full of empathy, so kind that she wanted to fall to her knees in front of him and surrender to the raw strength of his being. "Your mom was a good person," he said quietly. "She loved you. She used to take you to the meadows around your palace and weave primroses in your hair."

Sophie touched her hair, just above her ear. "Primroses?" She whispered. "Were they purple?"

He nodded. "With yellow centers. You remember?"

She shook her head. "I remember flowers, but not my mom—" She cut herself off when she saw Vlad's grim expression. "What else? Tell me the rest."

"They were very...dedicated to their kingdom. They felt, as did my parents, that preserving the well-being of their kingdoms as a whole was their primary obligation." His voice hardened with bitterness, and he abruptly cut himself off. "We don't have time for this. Let's go." He turned around in the small cavern. "Which wall is adjacent to the earth realm?"

She pointed to the north wall. "What happened, Vlad? I want to know."

He walked across the room and pressed his hands against the rock. "Sometimes we forget things because we need to forget them. You forgot your parents for a reason."

"And you? What reason did I forget you?"

He braced his palms on the wall and bowed his head. "Because I was there when you died, and I didn't save you. I was the only one you trusted, and I failed you."

She stared at his muscular back, her heart turning over at the bitter self-hate in his voice. Despite her fear and distrust of him, she was beginning to believe he was who he claimed to be, if not her husband, at least a man from her past. This man, this strong, powerful, angry man was someone she'd depended on once. She didn't quite understand the concept. The only males she knew were demons, and she didn't trust them for anything, except pain, betrayal, and abuse. "And my parents? Why did I forget them?"

He didn't answer for the longest time.

"Vlad?"

Finally, he turned to face her. "Your parents and mine were threatened by demons. To ensure the safety of their kingdoms, they made a deal with the demons. They both agreed to trade their children to the demons in exchange for enough wealth to feed the kingdom for three generations."

A cold shock slammed into her, and suddenly she couldn't

breathe. "My parents *sent* me here?"

"Yes."

For a split second, a memory flashed through her mind. Of a man and a woman staring down at her, their faces impassive. She remembered screaming, reaching for them... "No." She turned away, trying to thrust aside the images.

She felt nauseous at all the information pouring into her. For her entire life in the demon kingdom, she'd held onto memories of a beautiful life she'd left behind, of people looking for her. She'd believed in the goodness she'd left behind, because she'd had to believe in something, and it was all a lie? "I don't—" She didn't what? She didn't even know what she'd been planning to say.

"I'm sorry, Sophie. I never would have let you go home after our wedding to get your things if I'd realized the threat was that imminent. We were going to leave in the morning..." Guilt flashed across his face, a soul-deep anguish that tore at her heart. "But it was too late."

The anguish in his voice tore at her, crumbling the steel walls she carefully maintained inside her. Betrayal ricocheted through her, pain unlike anything she'd ever experienced. Images started flashing through her mind. Of a woman with eyes like hers. Of fields of purple flowers. Of a boy with dark eyes like Vlad's, showing her how to shoot a bow and arrow. Of a bedroom with white flowing curtains drifting in the breeze. Of brilliant blue sky and puffy white clouds. Of nights that closed down on her, terrifying her. Of a boy sitting on the foot of her bed, promising to stay awake all night to protect her.

The images assaulted her with relentless speed, flitting through her mind before she could identify them, before she could hold onto them, before she could understand them. She stumbled back, holding her head, unable to breathe—

"Sophie." Vlad was suddenly beside her, his head bent beside hers so close that she could feel the warmth of his breath on her neck.

His breath sent shivers down her spine, and she froze, shocked by the sensation, by how her entire body seemed to go utterly still, reaching for his touch, for his warmth, for his strength. He raised his hand, as if to touch her, and she felt herself tingle, preparing to dissolve. "No!" She stopped him with a desperate cry. "Don't touch me."

She didn't want to dissolve. She didn't want to lose the feel of his breath on her skin. She didn't want to move away from his physical presence.

Vlad dropped his hand, but he didn't move away from her. "When you were eleven, one of the boys in the village tried to kiss you," he said softly. "You snuck in my window and cried for hours. When you fell asleep, I snuck out, found him, and..." He hesitated. "I made him promise not to ever bother you again. He didn't."

She couldn't prevent her tiny smile at the image he'd presented. "Did you beat him up?"

"It's entirely possible," he acknowledged. He still hadn't moved away, and his voice was soft, almost caressing. "I give you my blood oath that I will protect you from anything and anyone who tries to cause you harm, including your memories. I'm here for you, Soph. You owe me nothing, not even kindness, but know that no matter how bad things get, you don't have to fight alone anymore. Got it?"

Her throat tightened, and she opened her eyes, staring at his hands where they hung by his side. God, how she wanted to reach out and slide her hand into one of his strong ones, to feel that power emanating from him, to accept the help she so desperately needed. "I don't even know you," she whispered. "How come I want to trust you?"

"Because you do know me." He moved his hand over her heart, not touching her. Just hovering. She could feel the heat from his palm warming her, permeating through her chest. "Listen to your heart, Sophie. I know I broke your heart, but I'll do whatever it takes to help you trust me again, so you can remember."

Tears filled her eyes, and she blinked several times. The yearning to fall into his strength was so strong it almost hurt, so powerful that it made her heart ache with longing. When he'd said they were married, his words had reverberated through her with absolute rightness. She'd *known* he spoke the truth....and at the same time, she wanted it to be the truth. She'd wanted to be bound to this dangerous, muscular man who could bring down demons. She wanted him to be the one to teach her how to stay corporeal when touched by a male. She wanted *him* to belong to her.

And that terrified her beyond words. She'd seen what women did for the men who they were attracted to. Maria had been right when she'd said that not all the women would want to leave. Some of them liked an eternity of great sex and hot guys. They'd fallen for the demon who had chosen them, willing to die for him. The women weren't deterred by the fact that sex with their partners would eventually kill them, sooner rather than later if Maria didn't help them. They were lost to the males on every level of their being...exactly how Sophie had responded to Vlad.

It was terrifying, the power that a male could have over a woman, and there was no chance she was giving Vlad any kind of power over her. "I can't do this." She stepped back, putting distance between them, even though her heart seemed to shatter into a million fragments when she did so, as if she'd just severed a part of her own soul from her body.

"Do what?"

"Like you. Trust you. Respond to you." *Want you.* She held up her hands, trying to push away his influence. "Just...I just need space."

"Whatever you need," Vlad said, his fingers flexing restlessly. "But I'm not abandoning you again."

The movement of his finger caught her attention, and she suddenly remembered how he'd had his index finger pointed at Damon when he'd had the demon pinned against the wall by some invisible force. "Your magic is in your fingers."

He looked down at his hand. "Yeah."

She needed to neutralize him. "Make a fist."

He obediently did so, watching her face with astute observation. "I'm not going to hurt you. I would never use my magic against you, but I do need it to protect you."

"And I'm not naive enough to put any stock in promises like that." She dissolved into mist, streaming through the walls to retrieve two stones, blue ones with a trace of gold. When she found them, she fled back to the room, wrapped herself around his hands, and then brought the stone back to life.

By the time he realized what she was doing and jerked his hands away, it was too late. She'd encased his hands in stone. Very pretty blue stone, but stone, nonetheless.

Vlad gaped at her as she reformed. "Really?"

"Yes, really." She walked up to him, feeling much more confident. "I've been living with demons my entire life. I see what men do to women, and how they trap them. If you really think that by showing up here saying that you're my husband, you're going to get me to pull up a chair and a glass of wine and bask in your glory, then you're just wrong." She pointed at his hands. "I saw what you did to Damon, and I know I'm not as powerful as he is, so yeah, you get stones, or else I'll have to kill you. Which do you want?"

Something flickered in his eyes. Not the anger she was prepared for, but something softer. Guilt, maybe? "I'm sorry," he said. "It was my job to protect you, and I completely fucked up. I'm sorry as hell that you had to learn those lessons, and yeah, I get it."

She glared at him, unsettled by the sudden compassion that flowed through her. "Don't be nice," she snapped. "Nice makes me itchy—" She felt a push of energy from the stones that were guarding the door, and she whirled around. "Oh, God." She ran over to the stones she'd set up in the doorway and laid her hands over them. Instantly, she received messages from them, which they'd received from the other stones in the walls, in sort of a rustic game of telephone.

Her heart dropped, and she whirled around. "They're coming," she said. "We have to leave."

"Who's coming?"

"Demons. They're hunting me. Or Maria. Or any of us." She looked around, frantically, but Maria, Damon, and Vlad's friend were all still unconscious. "I can't carry them all. Oh, God."

Vlad sprinted over to Gabe and swung him over one shoulder. He slid his stone-encased hands beneath Damon's arms, and then, in some absurd show of strength, somehow managed to get him over the other shoulder as well.

Something pulsed inside her, an awareness of the sheer strength of this man, a shiver that went deep into her lower belly. If this man truly was her protector, could he keep her safe from Lucien? Did Vlad give her a chance to survive, a chance she wouldn't have without him?

The moment she thought it, desperate yearning coursed through her. She didn't want to be Lucien's concubine, and she didn't want to sacrifice herself for Maria. She would if she had to, but heaven help her, she didn't want to ever have Lucien's skin against hers. *Ever.* If there was another way, if Vlad could somehow be the factor that switched the balance of power to the women... God, it was worth everything to her.

She didn't trust him completely, but it was worth the risk. What was the worst that could happen? If she were wrong to trust him and he ended up being like Lucien, then what did she lose? It was trading one terrible fate for another, but at least with Vlad, there was a chance, no matter how slim, that he could be on her side. With Lucien, there was no possibility of a good outcome.

She was going with Vlad. "Okay."

Decision made, she raced over to Maria and hauled her to her feet. She managed to get Maria slung over her shoulder, staggering slightly under the weight of her friend. "There's one place that we could go," she said. "But it's deep underground. It's far, and we might not make it."

He glanced at the wall that she knew Damon pulled his women through from the earth realm. She assumed that's where he had come across as well. "Can we get through to the earth realm?" Vlad asked.

"No, there are barriers to prevent anything from going out." The stones guarding the doorway began to reverberate more emphatically. "We have to go!" She ran toward the door, waving her hand to take down the safeguards.

She saw Vlad take one last glance at the wall that led to the realm he was from. She felt his reluctance to leave his safety net, and disappointment surged through her. He'd come across to save her, but he didn't want to get too far from the earth realm he belonged to. She realized she'd already begun to count on him, that she'd already begun to trust that he would be there for her. Was he really going to stay behind?

It didn't matter. She'd made the decision to evade Lucien for now. She was taking Maria down below, with or without Vlad's help—

He suddenly caught up to her, and pulled Maria out of her arms. He cradled her friend against his chest, supporting her head with a gentleness that made Sophie's heart tighten. The man still had rocks wrapped around his hands, but that wasn't slowing him down, and he wasn't asking her to release his hands either.

That totally got him points.

He jerked his head at her. "You lead. I'm right behind you. Go."

She hesitated for a second. Was she really going to lead two men who were complete strangers into the only place in the demon hell that she could hide? The place she'd kept secret her whole life, waiting and waiting to use it, praying she'd never have to?

Her ring finger burned and she looked down at the band wrapped around her finger. It was even darker and more turbulent than before. She jerked her gaze to Vlad.

His face darkened. "I'm back, Sophie, and I'll do whatever it takes to ensure your safety."

His words settled deep in her heart, and they felt good. Once again, she was hit with an almost unstoppable urge to reach out and touch him. Her soul responded to him, and she was going to have to trust her instincts. "Let's go."

She broke into a run, racing through the halls, using the stones on the walls to guide her as she fled to the sanctuary that she'd always planned to use to escape from a male, not invite one in.

Chapter Twelve

THE STENCH WAS the first thing Vlad noticed as they emerged from a tunnel into a vast wasteland of lava, gravestones, and burned out vegetation. The upper crust of the rock had hardened into a blackened stone, but beneath it he could see melted rock glistening with fire as it moved slowly beneath it. "What is this place?"

"The Graveyard of the Damned. Step only where I step." She moved swiftly across the rocks, her boots landing with confidence as she leapt from rock to rock.

Vlad watched her closely, putting his feet where hers had been as soon as she'd moved on. They moved in silence, traversing the land quickly. He couldn't believe how agile she was, almost like a wild animal as she leapt across divides. In his mind, she'd been the defenseless teenager, but she'd become a bold and courageous woman who didn't need rescuing by him at all.

Pride pulsed through him, and he couldn't suppress his grin as he easily kept pace with her. She'd somehow managed to thrive down here, and now he understood why his ring had faded to gray all these years. She hadn't been in danger. She'd been surviving just fine.

Even as he had that thought, however, his ring burned. He couldn't see his hand through the rock that encased it (and he had to admit, that had been impressive as hell also), but it was a reminder that his ring had changed color to indicate she was in great, great danger.

His adrenaline jacked up, and he looked around, scanning for threats as they moved deeper into the Graveyard of the Damned. Whatever it was that Sophie had been evading for all these years was finally coming for her, and she needed him, whether she knew it or not.

Was she right that nothing could leave the demon realm? If so, he was there for eternity, which, quite frankly, didn't really bother him. It was as good a place to be as any, and at least as long as he was here, he could protect her—

"Watch below." She pointed toward her feet, and he glanced down. The rock was ebony black, flowing like a silent river. Embedded in the rock were faces, their hands pressed to the rock as if they were looking through a window, or trying to break free. All of their expressions were as empty of life and emotion as the rocks they were traversing. A haunted chill ran down his spine. "Who are they?"

"The souls of the people the demons have trapped here. They're all dead now."

He reached out with his mind, searching the cavern below for living matter, but he found none. She was right. They were dead, stripped of their eternity by the demons. He felt the sheer magnitude of the dearth of life force, a crushing emptiness that made his soul ring with hollowness.

He knew then that he couldn't survive down there. Living matter was not only his power, but his source of life. There wasn't enough for him to live off of down here indefinitely. It was empty of the brilliance of life, which was creepy as hell.

And they were still going deeper.

Sophie paused at a crevice in the rocks that appeared to be an opening to a small cave. "Put Damon in here."

Vlad raised his brows. "We're leaving him behind?"

She nodded. "He's a demon. They don't want him. I—" She hesitated, her gaze shifting toward Gabe's. "I don't want him to know where I'm taking you and the others."

Vlad understood then. "You don't trust him?"

She grimaced. "He's Maria's brother, but he's still a demon. What if he had to make a choice between me, and his sister? Or me, and his kingdom?" She shook her head. "Put him in there. He'll be safe until he recovers."

Vlad saw the pain in her eyes, and he knew how difficult it was for her to leave Damon behind. Guilt, and worry for his safety, but her fear of what he was ran even deeper. He swore under his breath, and ducked into the cave. It was narrow, but it stretched deep into the mountain. He jogged several hundred yards into the cave, then carefully set the demon down.

Damon didn't move as he rolled to the floor of the cave, and Vlad studied him. With his wings and horns retracted, he looked like a human male, strong and badass, but also human. A demon. Sleeping. Harmless, at the moment. He crouched down beside him. "Would you have betrayed Sophie?" he whispered.

There was no reply, and after a moment, Vlad stood up. He glanced around the cave, noting that it was barren. Instinctively, he reached out with his mind to scan for living matter, but there was none. Damon was alone, without threats.

Vlad knew he shouldn't trust the demon lying there. The dude had attacked him, and all. But as he shifted the position of Maria and Gabe on his shoulders and headed back toward the entrance, he couldn't summon up any hostility toward him. He'd defended his home from invaders, and Vlad respected that. Additionally, Vlad had seen the bond between Damon and his sister.

He'd once had that bond with his own sister, and he'd failed her completely. It made him feel emotions he'd shut down a long time ago, emotions that made his chest ache...emotions that made him feel alive again.

As he stepped out of the cave and saw Sophie waiting for him, those emotions became stronger. Sophie. She turned and smiled at him, a brief, tight smile that made his heart turn over.

He wasn't going to fail her again. No matter what it took.

Chapter Thirteen

A SHORT WHILE later, Sophie almost sagged with relief when she saw the white rock glistening above the vast wasteland. "That's the marker to the opening," she said. "Come on!" She broke into a run, her heart pounding as she leapt from rock to rock. The lava was cooling fast, and Rikker and the others would be out here soon. She was the only one who could read the stones well enough to traverse the graveyard safely when the lava was flowing, not that she'd ever let on about her talent.

Vlad was right behind her, keeping pace with an effortless ease that both made her nervous and relieved her. If he were going to help her, she needed him strong. If he were going to turn on her, she wanted him weak and pathetic. She hoped she'd made the right decision in trusting him.

She reached the white rock and knelt beside it. She placed her palms on either side of it, but just as she was about to move the rock, she hesitated.

Vlad crouched beside her, Maria still held protectively in his arms, with Gabe draped over his shoulder. "I know you don't trust me, Sophie. I get it. I blew it. I'd offer to put Maria down and walk away, but I can't do it. You don't owe me anything, but I will give my life before I'll let you face danger alone again, I swear it."

She bit her lip, desperately trying to make the right decision. She'd learned so well not to trust men of any sort. Only women. If she took him into the only safe place she knew in the demon realm, and he turned out to be a danger to her, there would be nowhere else to hide until she figured out a plan. "Vlad, I don't know you. We might have the same ring encircling our fingers, but that could be anything."

"I know." He swore under his breath. "Release my hands. I need to show you something."

"What? No. You might—"

"Do it, Soph. We don't have much time."

It was the way he'd said *Soph* that did it. The casual affection in his voice was too genuine to be fabricated. Even though she didn't remember him, there was something between them, something real, something that she wanted desperately to uncover.

Ignoring the trepidation rippling through her, she set her hands on the rocks encasing his hands. The stones heated up, and then dissolved into the finest mist, drifting off into the night. The only stone left behind was on his index fingers, trapping his magic within him.

He met her gaze, undecipherable emotions roiling in his eyes at the fact she'd left the trace of stone on the finger he used magic for. "I won't betray you," he said softly. "I swear it."

She swallowed. "What did you want to show me?"

He nodded, and then carefully set Maria and Gabe on the ground. He yanked his jacket off, and the metal spikes in the shoulder clanked as they landed on the hardened molten rock. When he grabbed the hem of his shirt, as if to yank it off, Maria shifted nervously. "Don't!" she said, holding up her hand. "I don't want to see—"

The shirt came off anyway, and he flung it aside.

For a moment, she was too shocked by the sight of his bare body to do more than stare. Maybe she did want to see after all. She was used to the demons running around shirtless, but they'd always been a threat, and any semblance of nakedness when it came to demons was only bad news. But with Vlad...it was different. His body wasn't the smooth perfection of an immortal being whose physical body could never be destroyed. Vlad's body was flawed and real: He was lean with corded muscle, and his skin rife with assorted scars, showing he was a man who could be hurt, instead of a demon who could just shift his skin whenever he wanted. Although he was strong and formidable, the scars changed everything. They made him breakable, and that took away all her fear of him.

Vlad was not a demon. She didn't know what he was, but he was different from all the monsters she'd lived with for so long. As she began to relax, her gaze instinctively slid off his shoulder to his muscular chest. The spattering of dark hair that tantalized down his belly toward a V at the waistband of his jeans was so deliciously human. He was male, pure, untamed male, and he was riveting.

Instinctively, she reached toward him, wanting to touch him, to feel his skin beneath her palm, but her hand dissolved just before her fingertips made contact.

Embarrassed and frustrated, she jerked her hand back, but Vlad didn't seem to notice. He was pointing to the front of his shoulder. "You see this?"

Dragging her gaze off his physical magnificence, she noticed a drawing inked across his right shoulder. It was an image of a castle with seven turrets, cast in the shadow of a mountain. Recognition rushed through her, and a lump formed in her throat. "Oh," she exclaimed. "I dream of that castle!"

"It's where you lived."

"My home? Where I grew up?" Disbelief and a tremendous sense of longing filled her. She wanted to touch the drawing and trace every line of the castle. This was her home? Her childhood? The secret to who she was? "Which was my room?"

He pointed to a small window in a turret. "This one."

"My room." She moved closer, staring intently, as if she could look inside the dark window and see the life she couldn't remember. She traced it with her eyes, her fingers drifting across it, just above his skin. The drawing on his shoulder stretched out of sight around to his back, and Sophie gestured for him to turn.

He obeyed and her heart seemed to freeze when she saw a teenage girl falling into a black abyss, her arms outstretched in entreaty, as if she were reaching for someone to save her. The girl was wearing a light blue gown with ruffles around the hem...just like the dress she had in her chambers, which she had worn for the first year she'd been in the demon realm. "That's my dress."

"I know."

She glanced at him, her heart pounding. She treasured that dress, because it was her only connection to the life she could barely remember. It almost felt like an assault to her most private memories to see it etched into his flesh. "How did you know what my dress looked like?"

"I was there."

As he spoke, her eyes shifted to the left side, and she noticed the image of a teenage boy etched on his skin. He was carrying a small bow and an arrow in his arms, and he was trying to shoot it as he ran. She could tell from the lines of his body that he was sprinting as hard as he could, but his feet were encased in what looked like quicksand, slowing him down. The look of anguish on his face was devastating, so vivid that she could feel his heartbreak in her own soul. His face was younger than it was now, less angular and softer, but there was no mistaking his dark eyes. It was Vlad, as a boy. It was the scene he'd described about the day that she'd been taken by the demons. For the first time, she felt his pain, and she understood the depths of the burden he carried.

She reached out, wanting to touch the boy's face, but her fingers dissolved before they reached his skin. Frustration tore through her, and she clenched her fist. Why couldn't she touch what she wanted? *Why?*

How would he have known all the details if he wasn't there? She couldn't imagine there was any other way. He was telling the truth. She suddenly noticed that the boy was bleeding from his chest. She looked closer, and saw a small dagger embedded in his heart. "You were stabbed?"

"No. Not literally."

He grabbed his shirt and dragged it back over his head,

cutting off her view of the tattoo. "The tattoo was my way of never forgetting my failure." His voice was steely hard, almost cold, but she could see the tautness of the muscles in his jaw as he dragged his jacket back on. "That tattoo is magic. The knife will not disappear until I've corrected my failure." He met her gaze. "I never thought I'd have the chance, but I do. I'm not failing you again."

She felt the truth of his words in her heart, and her throat tightened. "What if I don't want your help?"

"You're getting it anyway." He leaned forward, so close that she could feel the heat from his breath on her lips. "I swear on my sister's soul that I will never, *ever* hurt you. Do you understand?"

His sister. He had a sister? Who was dead? Sudden, almost unbearable sadness seemed to cascade through her. "Do I have a sister?"

He shook his head. "No, but you and my sister were close. Best friends. My parents threw her into the demon pit as well. She's dead. I know for sure, because I got her out, but she died in my arms." The pain in his eyes was so great, belying the lack of emotion in his voice.

Suddenly, he was no longer a stranger who had invaded her home and claimed to be her husband. He was a man who had suffered greatly, and still carried the pain. Demons didn't feel emotional pain, just lust and desire and hate. Maria felt emotions, but that was different, because she was a woman and half human. Vlad's pain was intense and almost overwhelming, and she wanted to hug him, chasing away his anguish.

Of course, she couldn't hug him, or even touch him, so she simply moved her hand so it was right next to his cheek, as if she could touch him in comfort. "You're different than they are," she said softly.

He nodded. "I'm a piece of shit bastard of the lowest kind. There aren't many like me around. I'm special that way."

To her surprise, she burst out laughing. "That wasn't what I meant. I meant you're actually a living, breathing human being in comparison to the demons." Her smile faded. "You feel.

They don't."

He stiffened. "I don't feel. I just have to make things right. It's my duty and my responsibility. That's all."

She smiled at his denial, uttered in the midst of the pain she'd just seen so stark in his eyes. She'd seen what men were like who didn't feel, and Vlad was not one of them.

He met her gaze. "I will not abandon you, Sophie. Ever." He went down on one knee, and went to lift her hand. It dissolved the moment he tried to touch it. His brow furrowed, but he didn't react. Instead, he braced his forearm on his knee and leaned forward. "I offer you my life," he said, his deep voice resonating through her like a hot wind. "It is yours to use as you wish. I hereby commit that I will sacrifice my life to preserve yours, should it ever become necessary." He bowed his head, and for the first time, she could see the prince he had once been. "It is my humble duty to serve you, Princess Sophie. Accept my offer."

Tears filled her eyes at his genuineness, and silently, she nodded, too overwhelmed to speak. For so many years, she'd been battling alone. To have Vlad by her side, backing her up, was almost too much to conceive of.

He nodded, but there was no triumph in his eyes. Just grim determination that probably should have terrified her, except that it didn't. She trusted him, and she believed in her own judgment. "Okay, you can come with me and be my servant and personal bodyguard, but if you try to harvest my soul, I'll destroy you. I'm handy that way."

It was his turn to grin. "Sounds like a plan." He swung Gabe over his shoulder, and then scooped up Maria. "Lead the way, Cap'n."

"Cap'n? I guess that will do." Captain? She liked that he'd made her boss. It made her smile, actually, and she was still grinning when she settled herself in front of the rock again. It was a heady feeling to have a man of Vlad's strength and talents deferring to her. She was so used to being around demons, who respected no one but themselves and certain female body parts. Maria had always been the badass, and all Sophie had been useful for was dissolving and hunting rocks.

She kind of liked the way Vlad had handed her the reins. "Okay, so I'm going to dissolve the rock, to reveal a narrow crevice." She studied him. "I hope you'll fit. You're kind of large."

"I can manipulate living matter." He shrugged. "I can adjust."

"Really?" Huh. Was he like she was? Able to dissolve and slide into any opening? Interest piqued, and she wondered if he would have any answers about her dissolution issues. "After you go through, I'll put the rock back and come through."

He shook his head. "Nope. I go last. I'm not leaving you behind."

Again, she wanted to smile at his stubbornness. There was something about having a man completely dedicated to her well-being that was just...well...awesome. "That won't work. I have to go last. I'm the only one who can close the door. Stop being difficult and—"

She heard a loud clang, and then the ground shook. She leapt to her feet, staring across the lava fields. In the far distance, she saw movement, and all amusement fled. "They're already hunting me," she said. "We have to go!"

She didn't wait for Vlad to agree. There was no more time for negotiation. She just dropped to her feet and prayed that Vlad would harness his protector instincts and do as she instructed. She dissolved into the rock and connected with it. As she'd done with rocks so many times, she bound herself to it, and the entire rock dissolved, as a part of her being connected with every fragment of rock.

She couldn't talk to Vlad from that form, but she felt his energy move past her. His shoulder brushed through the swirling mist of her body, and she felt the heat of his presence. Electricity leapt through her so powerfully that she almost lost her grip on her non-corporeal state. With Rikker and Lucien, the brief physical connections had never felt like that. Those moments had felt like she was embedding her soul in filthy slime, but Vlad's brush-by had been exhilarating and incredible. Was there more? Was this what it was supposed to feel like with a man?

The ground shook again, jerking her back to the present and the direness of the situation.

Vlad slipped beneath into the fissure that she'd opened, and she immediately shifted her position, separating herself quickly from the rock. This time, however, she placed herself below the rock in the crevice, and the massive guardian stone took shape above the crevice, blocking the entrance completely and sealing off the cavern from the outside. She was careful to mingle the bottom of the stone with the lava rocks, so that it was fused to the surface. No one would be able to move it, except for her.

Satisfied, she slid lower and assumed her corporeal form again in the cavern below.

She had just finished reforming when she heard a shout. She spun around to see a demon hound leap at Vlad, his teeth bared in fury. She realized instantly that a demon hound had started using it as his den since the last time she'd been there.

Vlad held up his hands to block the attack and the dog's teeth clanked into the stone that encased his index fingers.

The dog yelped and pulled back, then whirled around, its red eyes focusing on her as an easier target. Before she had time to move, it launched itself at her, teeth bared. She yelped and stumbled backward, but there were no stones to latch onto, just the ancient metal walls that had been there long before she had been.

"No!" Just as the dog's teeth reached her throat, Vlad threw himself against the dog's side, slamming him against the wall. The dog whirled on him, attacking viciously while Vlad fought him off. "Give me back my magic," he shouted at her. "Now!" His leather jacket was shredded, and blood was cascading down his hand as the dog twisted away from him and went after her again. "Sophie!" He dove at her, shoving her out of the way a split second before the dog reached her. They skidded across the stone floor, and wound up with her pinned beneath him.

He shoved his hands in front of her face. "Now!"

There was no other choice, and she knew it. She grabbed the remaining stone encasing his hand and dissolved it, freeing his magic. She had barely finished when he spun around and pointed his fingers at the dog. It stopped in midair and flew back against the wall, transported by an invisible force that she knew came from Vlad. It hit with a thud, and then landed on its feet. It went into a crouch, staring at Vlad as he imitated it, taking an aggressive posture.

Man and beast stared each other down, and then the demon hound turned and fled, disappearing through an almost invisible crack in the steel.

They both waited, the only sound in the cavern their heavy breathing as they watched the crack through which the hound had fled. There was no movement or sound.

Finally, she took a deep breath. "I don't think it's coming back."

Vlad didn't relax. "Will it report to the demons that we're here?"

She shook her head. "No. The demon hounds are wild creatures. They hunt what little life there is left down here. They'll even try to feed on demons." Wearily, she sank down, her legs suddenly giving out. "Thanks."

"No problem." Vlad glanced at his ring, and she saw him frown.

"What is it?"

He walked over to her and crouched in front of her. His nearness made her nervous, but at the same time, her body responded with a longing. She wanted to touch him so desperately, to feel his skin beneath her hand, to know what the curve of his muscles felt like beneath her palm. But she'd already tried to touch him, and she hadn't been able to. It was no different with him, despite their supposed bond with the ring.

He held up his hand, showing her the ring encircling his finger. "See how it's black and purple?"

She peered at it. It looked angry, almost like poison fermenting on his hand. "Mine looks like that, too. It just happened."

"Mine changed a couple days ago, too." He sighed and ran his hand through his hair and he sank down on the floor, leaning against the wall, putting distance between them. It was just a few feet, but it felt like he was too far. She wanted him close, so close that she could feel the heat of his body, even if she couldn't touch him.

She had no idea why she was responding to him on such a physical level. Was it just because something about her was shifting, something that had begun with Lucien and Rikker? Was Vlad just the man who happened to be near her at the right time? Or was it something more?

It was impossible to know, and it didn't matter. Either way, losing her ability to go incorporeal when a male tried to touch her was so very dangerous. No matter how much she craved the feel of Vlad's touch, she wasn't foolish enough to think that a moment of human connection would be worth the risk to her soul.

He didn't seem to notice her inner battle, as he pressed his hand to his wounded shoulder, stemming the flow of blood. "The magician who bound us by the rings tracked me down yesterday." His gaze was intense, scanning the cavern while constantly looking back at her. "He said that it had turned dark because you were in grave danger. I thought maybe it was the demon hound that was threatening you, but it's still black and purple." He met her gaze. "What's going on, Sophie? What's after you?"

She couldn't take her gaze off his injured arm. She could almost feel the pain in her own arm, mimicking his. "Are you okay?"

He glanced down at his arm and shrugged. "I'm fine. It's healing already. It's not like when the demon attacked me. I want to know about you."

She wanted to go to him and help him, which unnerved her. Instead, she got up and grabbed a pile of blankets from her stash on the wall and walked over to the unconscious pair. She put a folded one under Maria's head, and wrapped a blanket around her. "I'm fine." She was aware of Vlad watching her every move, which should have bothered her, but for some reason, it took some of the chill away from her bones. She put her hand by Maria's cheek, and frowned. "She's so cold. She drained herself too much saving you guys. She should be healing by now. It's been too much."

Tears suddenly filled her eyes, and she sank down beside her friend, pressing her hands to her eyes as the reality of their situation surged over her. She was hiding in a cavern with two dangerous men, and her best friend, who was dying, while Lucien, Rikker, and countless other demons were hunting her.

"Hey." Vlad crouched beside her, leaning in so his breath whispered against her ear. "I know you don't want to trust me, but you can. I came here to help you. That's all that matters. What can I do?"

She looked up at him, unable to stop the tears from streaming down her cheeks. "Can you get all of the women in this place across the border into the earth realm? Can you stop a demon king from claiming me? Can you stop the leader of the hunt from making me his concubine? Can you tell me why I'm losing my only defense system when I need it most? Can you heal Maria? Can you do any of those things? Because that's what I need."

He studied her for a long moment, his expression thoughtful as if he were actually considering all the ridiculous things she'd requested. "What does Maria need to heal?" he finally asked.

She blinked, surprised that he'd managed to discern the one that was most important to her in that moment. It was almost as if he were actually paying attention to her, and it felt good. Too good. Dammit. She couldn't afford to depend on him. She had to stay strong for herself. Feeling mutinous about her attraction to him, she glared at him. "Sex," she snapped. "She needs sex."

"Sex?" He blinked. "You want me to have sex with her? While she's unconscious?" He looked so horrified that she burst out laughing, a reaction that broke through the tension threatening to strangle her.

"No," she admitted with a smile. "I don't, actually." The thought of Vlad having sex with Maria was not a good thought. Maria was far too sensual and beautiful, and she did not want Vlad to notice that about her. And have sex with her? Once he had a lust demon, he'd never want anything else, and certainly not her.

Not that she was going to have sex with him. First, because she couldn't, and second, because that was just a foolish thing to do. She'd seen too many times exactly how addicting and disempowering great sex was for women, and there was no chance she'd relinquish that kind of power to a man.

But that still didn't mean she wanted Vlad to have sex with Maria. "No," she repeated, just in case he hadn't been paying attention. "I don't want you to have sex with her."

"Good, because you're the only one I—" He cut himself off, and the unspoken part of his sentence loomed big in the gap. He cleared his throat. "I'm not interested in having sex with her," he said instead, but not before she figured out what he was going to say.

This time, it was her turn to stare, and her stomach leapt. "You want to have sex with me?" she asked.

"If I say yes, you might kill me. If I say no, you might kill me." He rubbed his jaw, eyeing her so warily she almost started laughing again. "I think that it's in my best interest to pretend that the residual demon poison has killed my hearing again." He shrugged and pointed to his ear. "Sorry," he said loudly. "I can't hear you."

This time, her laughter filled the cavern. "You're such a liar."

"Me, never." He glanced back at Maria. "But what about her?"

Sophie glanced at Maria. Beside her, the other man was equally still, but the color seemed to be returning to his skin. Even in his unconscious state, he was well-built and muscular, almost a match for a half-lust demon princess.

"He's a jerk," Vlad offered in a conversational tone. "You don't want him."

She glanced over at Vlad, surprised by his comment, then grinned when she saw how cranky he was. Jealous? Of her looking at another man? Tucking a smile behind her hand, she stood up. "I think he would be enough for her. If we can arrange them so they're touching, she can start to feed off him while they both sleep."

Vlad raised his brows. "Seriously?"

"She's a lust demon. He won't mind. They never do."

His eyebrows shot up. "So, when they both wake up, they're going to be hot and heavy in a matter of seconds?'

"Hopefully. It's what she needs. It's been a while since she's taken a sexual partner. It has to be consensual, but as I said, men never turn her down." The moment she said the words, she felt her cheeks heat up. It was easy talking with Maria about sex, but it was completely different to have the conversation with Vlad.

His eyes darkened, and she felt the atmosphere become intensely sexually charged. There was no way to avoid the truth that she wasn't the only one responding physically to their connection. She cleared her throat. "So, the bed's in the adjoining chamber. Let's put them in there and seal it off." She managed a smile. "I don't really want to be in the room when they start having sex, you know?" Oh, God. Was she really having this conversation? But she had to. It wasn't like she could just avoid it, because when Maria woke up with Gabe beside her, things were going to happen.

Vlad grinned and stood up. "No, I think that might be a little awkward." He walked over and picked up Gabe. "Can you get her? I don't want to be the male holding her when her lust demon instincts kick in."

"Oh, yeah, good point." She quickly picked up Maria, staggering slightly under her weight, then led the way to the next room. There was a narrow bed up against the wall, with blankets piled neatly on it. She'd been furnishing the hideaway for years, slowly creating an oasis for herself and the others if they ever needed it.

But she'd never thought she'd really need it. It had been more of something to do, a way to feel like she was making progress toward *something,* instead of sitting around dissolving while the other women suffered. She set Maria on the mattress, and her friend slumped listlessly, her body completely limp.

Vlad set Gabe beside Maria. The Calydon groaned as his leg brushed against Maria's, and Sophie felt her cheeks heat up when she saw him roll toward Maria and drape his leg over hers, pulling her into the curve of his body as he wrapped his arm around her and tucked her against him. Maria was utterly still, and she looked tiny and vulnerable in the arms of the massive Calydon. Gabe was clearly still unconscious, but his instinct had been to tuck Maria into the shield of his body anyway. She stared at them, stunned by the way Gabe was trying to protect her. Maria had never had anyone but Sophie to protect her, and Sophie found herself hoping that Maria had also found someone to stand beside her and help her fight. *Please let her have found someone to help her.*

Sophie crouched beside Maria and smoothed her friend's hair back from her face. She was so used to Maria being the badass demon princess, but right now she looked small and frail, almost vulnerable, and it scared her. "Maria," she whispered. "Please don't die. We all need you."

Again, there was absolutely no response from Maria, and her skin was cold to the touch. Sophie bowed her head and rested her forehead against her friend's.

She felt something brush through her back, and she looked up to see Vlad crouching beside her, looking at his hand in confusion. She realized that he'd tried to touch her back, and she'd dissolved where he'd tried to touch her.

He noticed her looking at him, and put his hand down.

"I feel like I should get her a demon," she said softly. "I don't know anything about Gabe. I don't know if he'll be enough."

"Calydons are descended from demons," Vlad said. "He has demon heritage. They're sensual and need sex. I think it'll work."

She bit her lip, glancing again at the unconscious warrior who had, even in his sleep, pulled Maria protectively into his arms. A demon would be groping her, taking advantage of the fact that a lust princess was defenseless and available, but Gabe's hands weren't anywhere near her breasts. His forearm was locked across her belly, his leg was over her hip, and his face was against her hair, as if Maria was a precious soul he would protect with his life even while he was asleep.

No one had ever tried to protect Maria from anything, but Gabe was. It was sweet, and a part of her wanted to switch places with Maria, and see what it felt like to feel the warmth and strength of a protector.

"Her skin isn't as pale as it was," Vlad said, still crouched right beside her, so close that his shoulder was almost touching hers, but not quite.

She glanced at Maria, and noticed the faintest hue to her pale skin. Her heart leapt, and tears suddenly filled her eyes. "I think you're right."

"Then it's time to vacate, don't you think?"

Maria shifted slightly, and Gabe's arm tightened around her. He pressed his face deeper into her hair, and his leg wrapped more securely around her hip. She cleared her throat. "Yeah, I think it is."

Chapter Fourteen

TEN MINUTES LATER, Vlad was alone with Sophie.

He sat on a chair by the wall, watching Sophie move about the room, sorting through the assorted items that she'd apparently stored there over the years. She moved with the innate grace of royalty, but at the same time, there was a toughness to her stance that spoke of a survivor.

He was pissed at himself that she'd had to learn how to be a survivor, but at the same time, he liked it. He was riveted by her inner strength, as well as by the vulnerability she'd revealed when she'd been so worried about Maria.

He was leaning forward, his forearms braced on his knees, letting his body finish its healing as he watched her. Her hair was darker now, no longer the light blond of the teenage Sophie, and the way it tumbled in soft curls around her shoulders was entrancing. She was utterly female, but at the same time, she was prickly and distant, doing her best to keep him at bay. He got it. Yeah, he completely understood why she didn't trust him, but it was killing him not to be able to swoop in and fill the role he'd sworn to fill so long ago.

There were no sounds from the adjoining bed chamber, or from the lava rock above, and Vlad was able to focus entirely on the woman who had haunted him for so long. He could barely process the fact she was *alive*. He was desperate to touch her, to feel the warmth of her skin, to prove to himself that she wasn't simply a figment of his tortured imagination, but all efforts to do so had failed utterly. Was she even real? Or was all this really a dream. "Why can't I touch you?"

She froze, clutching a blanket to her chest as she stared at him. "What?"

"Why can't I touch you?" He stood up and walked over to her, his frustration softening as her eyes widened at his approach. She looked like a skittish fawn, afraid to be touched, but too curious to actually dart away. He tried to brush his fingers over the ends of her hair, but every strand dissolved a split second before he made contact. "What is this?"

Instead of answering, she cocked her head. "Have you ever touched me? When we were children? Could you touch me then?"

He nodded. "Yeah, I could. No problem."

"Really?" There was no mistaking the excitement in her eyes. "Since I've been here, no male demon has ever been able to touch me. Even if I don't see them coming, I still dissolve before they can touch me. Women aren't a problem. It's just the men."

He narrowed his eyes, thinking about her answer. He had to admit, he was damned glad to hear that no male had been able to touch her. No wonder she hadn't been in grave danger all these years. Some of the fear of what had happened to her eased its tight grip on his chest. "You don't do it on purpose?"

She shook her head.

"Can you do it on purpose?"

"Only if I'm hunting rocks. I can dissolve to connect with them, but I couldn't do it right now just for fun." She searched his face. "What do you know about me, Vlad? My parents? Is this from them?"

He rubbed his jaw. "Not that I know of."

"Can you dissolve?"

He shook his head. "My control of living matter isn't like that. I can move things around, but I can't change their shape. I connect with all their cells, and direct them that way."

Her face brightened. "That's what I do with rocks." She held out her hand. "Move me."

He almost laughed. "Move your hand? Just like that?"

"Yes." There was a deep yearning in her voice. "Even if you can't touch me, maybe you can connect with me on that level. Will you try?"

He was surprised by her request. "You're sure?"

"Yes." She wiggled her fingers. "You don't understand what it's like not to be touched," she said. "Please."

He nodded. "Relax your arm. Just let it hang by your side."

She let her arm drop. "Okay."

Vlad studied her for a long moment, and then he pointed his index finger at her. He focused on her hand, but he couldn't sense it. Frowning, he tried again, but he literally couldn't even sense that she existed, not when he was viewing her with his magic.

She frowned. "What's wrong?"

He shook his head, and he moved closer to her. She tilted her head back to look at him as he moved his fingers to surround her head. "What are you doing?"

"Trying something." He closed his eyes, directing his magic into her mind. He felt the hum of her energy instantly, swirling through him. Yet, when he directed his energy lower, toward her chest, he again felt nothing. He dropped his hands and stepped back, his mind whirring as he tried to process it.

"Tell me."

He met her gaze. "Your body isn't made of living matter," he said. "Your mind is alive, but your body...it's not alive."

Her face paled. "What? Of course it is." She smacked her palm against the wall and a loud thud sounded in the room. "See? And I can pick up things and touch them. Of course I exist."

He shook his head. "A rock isn't living matter, but it exists. I can't move a rock, and I can't connect with it."

She stared at him. "But you have to be wrong. That's not possible. I mean, Lucien touched me tonight, and I felt Rikker's energy. I even felt yours!"

"Lucien?" Foreboding crept down Vlad's spine. "Who's Lucien?"

"The demon king. He wants to have sex with me, and he almost did it tonight." She whirled away from Vlad, apparently oblivious to the sudden fury that raced through him. "I touched him tonight. I didn't mean to, but I touched him." She spun back toward him. "How could he touch me, but not you? I don't understand." She hugged her arms across her body, and leaned against the wall, sliding down until she was sitting as she stared up at him. "Don't you get it, Vlad? Rikker and Lucien know that they can break through my protections. They're not going to give up. I need to understand what is going on, and I need to know now. I have to learn to control it, or they're going to take it away from me."

Vlad ran his hand through his hair, trying to focus. He was being assaulted with emotions, the primary one being a sudden, debilitating fear of the fact that he couldn't sense any living matter in her body. Was she really dead? Living in some sort of physical body that wasn't hers? Her mind and soul trapped in a vessel of the dead? If so, it was his fault. His damned fault. And the fact that two demons wanted to rape her? *Jesus.*

Swearing, he knelt in front of her, his mind spinning as he tried to think of what was going on. "Tell me what happened with Lucien. When you touched him." He didn't want to hear about it, but at the same time, he needed every detail. This was why the old man had sent him. She was in grave danger, and he was the one who had to help her.

She rested her chin on her knees as she stared at him, her eyes wide and vulnerable. "He had jewels," she said softly. "I respond to jewels."

He nodded. "You always did."

"Did I?" She looked like she wanted to ask more questions, then sighed, clearly deciding to focus on the bigger issue. "Lucien had some tonight. I was overwhelmed by the sensation, and when I reached for them, my hand stayed corporeal and I wound up touching Lucien's shoulder." She shivered visibly, and Vlad wanted to pull her into his arms to take away the memory. "It was like touching death and evil," she said. "I know he's gathering more jewels, and he's going to use them on me next time." She looked at Vlad. "I'm really scared it's going to work," she whispered. "I've never been scared my whole life, not like I am now."

Vlad ground his jaw, needing to reach for her, to touch her, but he didn't move. "So, you're starting to stay corporeal for him." He worked his jaw, struggling to keep his voice calm. "Are you attracted to him? Could that be it?"

"Him?" She looked shocked enough that some of the tightness in his chest eased. "God, no. He's a nightmare. The only male I've ever been attracted to is you, but you're not the one I can touch!"

Heat flared hot and fast in him at her confession. "You want to touch me?"

Her cheeks turned red, but she nodded. "So much," she said softly. "It doesn't make sense, but I can't help it."

"Of course it makes sense. We're connected."

"Married."

He nodded.

She looked down at her hand and traced the ring still out-lined on her hand. His ring. "Marriage that young isn't real. I'm not your wife."

He decided not to argue that point, realizing that the depth of his need to protect her would scare her, not entice her. Instead, he simply said, "We've known each other since the beginning of our lives," he said. "That connects us, regardless of the ring." He pointed at his tattoo, which was now hidden. "I'm your reference to your old life. To the time when you felt safe." Which was, of course, a complete lie. They'd never been safe. Not him, not his sister, and not Sophie. He still didn't understand what had happened with his parents that day. He'd walked out with his sister's body in his arms, and by the time he'd gone back, years later, both kingdoms had long been abandoned. "Deep inside, you know that. You feel that connection. Your soul recognizes mine."

She bit her lower lip, but said nothing.

Swearing, he tried again, knowing that he would never be able to ensure her safety until she trusted him. "What does your gut say, Sophie? Not your mind. Your heart."

She looked up at him, her eyes steady and calm. "I brought you into the only safe place I have in this entire realm."

Her words were simple, but they said it all. Relief settled in him, and he nodded, understanding the significance of the trust she'd offered. Slowly, he eased himself all the way down in front of her, sitting cross-legged before her. "I felt you," he said. "I felt your spirit several times when I brushed past you."

She said nothing, but he saw acknowledgement in her eyes. She'd felt it too. He nodded, slowly working his way through the possibilities. "When you were looking at the jewels with Lucien, were you afraid?"

"Of course! I was with him. I was terrified—"

"No." He interrupted her. "In that moment you touched him, were you afraid, or were you so connected with the jewels that you forgot his existence?"

"I—" She hesitated, then inclined her head. "I forgot about him. I was only focused on the stones."

"And Rikker?"

"I was holding a stone again. He grabbed it from me, and I was trying to protect it from him." Her words were slow, thoughtful. "And the other time Lucien touched me, I was terrified he was going to hurt Maria. I wasn't afraid of him myself. I was trying to protect her."

"So, perhaps, despite what you said, you've been afraid all this time, and your instincts have protected you."

She cocked her head. "I haven't felt afraid."

"No, but maybe you have been." He leaned forward. "Do you want to try?"

She stared at him. "Try what?"

"See if we can do it."

"Touch?"

He nodded.

For a long moment, she simply stared at him, then she nodded once. "Okay."

Anticipation rushed through him. "Hold out your hand."

She did.

Chapter Fifteen

SOPHIE'S HEART WAS racing as she held her hand out to Vlad. She was terrified it wouldn't work, and terrified it would. She didn't want to lose her defenses, but the truth was, she was losing them anyway. Maybe Vlad could help her understand them and learn to control them.

And she wasn't going to lie. After seeing the way Gabe had cradled Maria in his arms so protectively, she wanted to experience that, too. Just for a minute, or even a second, she wanted to know what it felt like for a man to touch her, a man she didn't fear.

Vlad bent forward, his dark eyebrows furrowed in concentration as he set his hands on either side of hers, as if he were trying to press the air into her flesh. "Imagine what it would feel like to have my skin against yours," he said, his deep voice rumbling through her like a caress.

She swallowed nervously. "Okay."

He looked up at her. "No fear, sweetheart," he said. "This isn't about fear. It's just you and me. I already swore on my sister's soul that I would give my life for you. That means I would die before I would allow harm to befall you, including any that I might cause. Do you understand?"

She nodded once. She'd heard his words, and she believed he meant it, but to actually, completely, put her trust in a man who was essentially a complete stranger was a different matter.

Something flickered in his eyes. Guilt? Pain? Resignation? It was too quick to tell, but the mere fact that she'd glimpsed emotion in his dark eyes was reassuring. A man who could hurt was a man who was real. "Okay," he said. "Close your eyes."

She hesitated for a split second, searching his face for any sign of deception, but she saw none. Just the strong, angular face that had compelled her from the first moment she'd seen him. Slowly, she let her eyes drift shut, but her heart was thundering through her as she strained to sense him.

"I'm going to move my hands along your arm," he said. "Imagine that they're on your skin. What does it feel like to have my skin against yours?"

Scrunching her eyes shut, Sophie opened her mind as widely as she could, seeking his presence with all her senses. He smelled faintly of sweat and earth, and something deeper, more intoxicating. She inhaled deeply, bringing his scent into her lungs. She let his voice roll through her, soothing her tensions and relaxing her muscles. She pictured the strength in his shoulders, the aura of lethal danger that seemed to bleed off him at every moment. She imagined his hands, strong and callused, gliding over her skin. "Warm," she whispered, almost able to imagine what it would feel like. "Your hands are warm."

"What else? I'm by your shoulders now, gliding my fingers above your collarbone."

She imagined his fingers drifting across the curve of her collarbone, and her belly tightened. "It feels amazing," she whispered. "No one has ever touched me like that."

"Let me kiss you," he murmured, so close she felt his breath against her cheek.

"Okay," she whispered. She didn't open her eyes, every sense attuned to Vlad, waiting for where he would be next.

She felt a pulse of warm air across her mouth. His breath? His lips? "More," she whispered. "Again?"

"I dedicate my life to you," he said, and this time, she was certain she felt his breath against her mouth. Her mouth tingled from the touch, and a deep yearning began to build inside her.

"My soul is yours," Vlad said. "It always has been, since the day we were bound. Can you feel that?"

She nodded once, breathless as she felt something brush against her ring finger. She jumped, startled by the touch, but before she could panic, Vlad's low voice was whispering in her ear again. "It's okay," he said. "It's just me."

"Okay." She scrunched her eyes shut, trying to catch her breath. "What are you doing now?" She felt something brush against the corner of her mouth as she spoke, and her heart jumped.

"The left side," he whispered. She felt something against the other corner. "The right side," he said.

"I can feel that." She couldn't keep the excitement out of her voice. "I can feel you."

"When I kiss you," Vlad said, his mouth next to her ear again, "I feel the pulse of your energy. You're alive, Sophie, just buried in fear so deep that it has shut you down. But you're not there. You're *here*. With me. Right now."

The yearning inside her increased, and she was almost desperate to really feel his mouth against hers. "Kiss me for real, Vlad. Please."

There was a pause of a heartbeat, and for a moment, she thought he was going to refuse, or tell her it was impossible. "I'll think of jewels," she promised. She opened her eyes, startled to see his face inches from hers, his eyes turbulent and intense as he studied her. "It might work."

He shook his head. "When I kiss you, I want you to be thinking about *me*. My touch. My lips. My body. Nothing else."

She swallowed. "What if it doesn't work?"

"Then we try again." He leaned forward, as if to press a kiss to her eyelid, and she instinctively closed her eyes.

"Perfect," he said softly. "I want you to think about me. Nothing else. Just me."

She took a deep breath, once again bringing him into her

lungs. His energy seemed to swirl through her like a warm seduction and a protective shield. Her fear slid away, and all that was left was a need for him, for his touch, for Vlad to free her from the isolation that had bound her for so long. "I want this," she whispered. "I want it to be you." She'd never wanted a man to touch her before, but with Vlad, the need was so strong she felt as if it would tear her apart if she didn't.

"Breathe," he whispered. "Just breathe."

She took a deep breath, and then suddenly, shockingly, she felt his lips against hers. She froze, afraid to move, afraid to break the spell, but her mind was whirling. His mouth was hot and his lips were decadently soft. Desire flooded her, a raging inferno of need so great she wanted to cry out, but she was too terrified to move. Not terrified of him. Terrified of losing the ability to feel him.

His kiss deepened, becoming more demanding, asking for more. Tentatively, unsure what to do, she parted her lips. The moment she did so, he took over the kiss, a sensual assault that made every cell in her body come to life. His tongue slipped between her teeth, a hot, wet caress of pure seduction that overwhelmed all her senses. Instinctively, she reached for him, and she was shocked when she felt her arms wrap around his neck. She could feel the heat of his skin against hers, and the strength of his body.

With a low groan, he palmed her hips and pulled her onto his lap. Her breasts pressed against his chest, sending waves of desire cascading through her. Her nipples were so taut they almost hurt, and her nerve endings were on fire, exploding everywhere he touched her. In one swift move, he grabbed her legs and locked them around his hips, dragging her more tightly against him.

She felt his erection pressing against the front of her jeans, and she shifted restlessly. She knew plenty about sex and had seen far too much in her time in the demon realm, but never had she expected that a kiss, a touch, and an embrace would feel so intense.

Vlad cradled the back of her head, angling his head to kiss her more deeply. She didn't hesitate now, following his lead, their tongues dancing like two lovers in a moonlight rendezvous. He slid his hands across her ribs, every move eliciting the most intense sensations from her. By the time he cupped her breast, she could barely think. All she could do was hang onto him, drinking every sensation into her soul, knowing that at any moment, she could lose it all.

But it didn't end.

She didn't fade.

And when he tugged down the collar of her shirt to press a kiss to the swell of her breast, she felt her whole body clench in response. "Vlad—" She gripped his shoulders, twisting in his arms, unable to stay still as he kissed his way across her breast.

Then his mouth clamped down on her nipple. She yelped as fireworks seemed to explode through her mind, and her body convulsed violently in his arms. The orgasm took her hard and fast, and she clung to him as he coaxed it out of her, his lips and tongue working magic on her nipple, drawing it out until she collapsed against him, utterly drained.

Vlad laughed softly, his arms tight around her as he kissed her temple. "Good?"

"Wow." She rested her head on his shoulder, sagging against his strong frame. She could still feel his erection pressing against the seam of her jeans, and she was viscerally aware of her bare breast against his leather jacket. Despite all the clothes they had on, the heat from his body was intense, penetrating all the way to the core of her being. "How am I sitting here like this? On your lap? In your arms?" She didn't want to move. Ever. After a lifetime of being physically isolated, the sensation of his body wrapped around her was incredible. She felt like the part of her soul that had been empty and crumbling, was suddenly beginning to heal, no longer torn apart by the raw isolation of being physically alone.

"Because it's me." There was no arrogance in his voice, just a statement of fact. "You've been waiting for me all this time." He kissed her hair again. "I'm so sorry I took so long," he said softly.

She closed her eyes, suddenly tired, so tired. She felt as if she were falling off a cliff into a place where she didn't have to fight or be on guard, as if she could truly relax for the first time in her life. She never slept hard, always waking up every few minutes to see if a demon was lurking, or a woman was in trouble. But in Vlad's arms, she felt safe, safe enough to finally let go. "It's okay," she mumbled. "I had things to do. I didn't need a man around to interfere. I had to save the women and Maria. Girl stuff."

He chuckled, his arms tightening around her like a protective shield. "Want some help with that?"

"Maybe." Her muscles were growing heavy, and she was too tired to think. "Vlad?"

"Yeah?"

"Will you watch over me while I sleep? Promise me you'll stay, and wake me up if anything happens?" She could barely mumble the words she was so tired, but she felt his nod.

"Of course. I won't let you down again."

"I don't need your help," she mumbled as she felt Vlad shift their positions, stretching out on the floor beside her so they were horizontal. She sighed as he pulled her against his side, wrapping her up against him just as she'd seen Gabe do with Maria. "Just a nap. That's all I need you for."

"Ask me for anything, sweetheart. I'm here for you." She felt him kiss her again, and she smiled to herself.

She'd never wanted to be kissed. She'd never wanted to be held. But now that she had been, she knew she would crave it forever. Which was bad. She didn't need this in her life. She had a mission that was about women, not seduction, orgasms, sex, and self-proclaimed husbands sneaking over from the earth realm.

She didn't have time to sleep. She had to fight. But she was too tired. She was tired all the way to the depths of her soul, and she knew she needed this moment in Vlad's arms if she had any chance of finding the strength to win a battle she had no chance of winning.

Maria was still asleep. When she awoke, they would make plans. Right now, though, right now, was her moment. As she fell asleep, Vlad's body wrapped around hers, her last thought was that everything had changed now. Would she be able to go incorporeal with demons now, or was all that gone? The thought jerked her back to consciousness, and she gripped Vlad's arm in sudden fear. "Vlad?"

"Yeah." His voice was wide awake and sharp, and she realized he'd been on full alert the entire time, ready for danger at any moment.

"What if I can't go incorporeal with demons now? What if I have no defense?"

He was silent for a moment, then his arms tightened around her. "We'll deal with it. You aren't alone anymore, Sophie. Never forget it."

"But—"

"You need to rest. Take advantage. When things start happening, there won't be another chance. I'll stand guard."

She bit her lip, but she knew he was right. "Promise?"

"Swear."

She nodded, relaxing back into his arms. This time, she let herself fall asleep, and she dreamed of Vlad, of kisses, and of being pinned to the bed by a deadly demon king.

Chapter Sixteen

VLAD WAS PRETTY much in awe of the feeling of Sophie in his arms. He couldn't stop running his hands down her back and through her hair. For so long, he'd thought she was dead, and now he was actually holding her. She smelled good, like the sunshine that she probably hadn't seen since the day she was taken by the demons.

The moment that he'd felt her lips against his, his world had stopped. He'd been with women over the years, but he hadn't cared. It had been mindless sex in an attempt to drag himself from his self-imposed hell into the land of the living long enough to breathe. It had never worked, and he'd given up long ago. But the moment he'd seen Sophie, he'd wanted her. Not being able to touch her had been torment, but when she'd offered herself up to him, trusting him enough to ask him to try to touch her...hell...he felt like he'd just been offered a gift that he didn't deserve in any lifetime.

It had been unbelievably sensual and erotic to slide his hands along her arms and shoulders, not touching, but trying to drink in the sensation as if they were. And then, when he'd bent to kiss her, and he'd actually felt her lips beneath his...hell. That had been a moment he'd never forget. Pure magic. The amount of trust she'd poured into that kiss had floored him, because he knew the only things that had been keeping her corporeal had been her intense desire for him to touch her, and her utter absence of fear.

She shifted in his arms, suddenly restless. He heard her mention Lucien, as if she were fighting him off, and he swore, all his good feelings dissolving. He tightened his arms around her. "I'm here, Sophie. You're safe."

Her restlessness died down momentarily, but the impact on him hadn't. She was sound asleep, dreaming of a demon who wanted to claim her, and yet she was still corporeal in his arms. Was she corporeal because her trust of him was so absolute, or was it because he'd robbed her of her one defense? Instead of trying to get her to own her body so that they both could fulfill their desires to touch, maybe he'd done the opposite, dragging her out of the self-defense mode that had kept her safe for so long.

Swearing under his breath, he rolled onto his side, scanning the room with ever increasing vigilance. Instead of protecting her, he might have made her more vulnerable. She could be in even more danger now, thanks to him. So, what was he going to do about it? And what would she even *let* him do?

GABE AWOKE FROM his healing sleep in an instant, going from total submersion to complete readiness in a split second. The first thing he noticed was that there was a woman in his arms, and the second thing he noticed was that he had no idea where the hell he was.

His eyes snapped open, and he scanned the room, assessing every last detail with rapid speed. They were deep underground, and the walls were volcanic rock laced with magic and metal. Where there had once been a door was now solid rock, and there were only a few pieces of furniture scattered about the room.

He sat up, too fast, and the room began to spin violently. Swearing, he gripped the mattress while he fought against the vertigo. Memories came flashing back of the demon attack after Vlad had brought him into the demon realm. He recalled instantly the woman who had rushed into the room, warning him off her brother.

Brother?

He looked down at the woman still unconscious beside him, noting her lacy bodice, black pants and badass boots. Same woman. Her brother was a *demon*? The room kept spinning, and he stretched out beside her, fighting against the onslaught of dizziness. He did a quick scan through his body and found remnants of the poison that the demon had thrust into him. It was mostly gone, wiped away by a healing energy...a female energy...*hers.*

His attention snapped to the woman beside him once again. She had saved him? And she done so by invading his body with her energy? He swore under his breath, summoning the focus to prop himself up on his elbow so he could inspect her more closely. His gaze swept over her high cheekbones, the curve of her mouth, and her breasts that were pushing up out of her bodice. Her hips had the soft angles of a woman, and for a split second, he had a sudden urge to run his hand over her hip, to feel the curves beneath his palm. His hand actually started to move, but he jerked it back by his side, shocked by how strong the temptation to touch her was.

He was carefully and intentionally immune to women, and he had been for centuries. Celibacy had always been a part of his life, because even when he was a kid, he'd known that he wanted to be part of the Order of the Blade.

As a Calydon, he was vulnerable to women. Every Calydon was destined to meet his *sheva*, which was his soulmate. The attraction was instant and unstoppable, forcing both parties to complete the bonding stages. Once complete, they were fated to destroy each other and everything that mattered to them. The Calydon would go rogue, turning into an insane monster that destroyed everyone and everything, stoppable only by the hand of his *sheva*...or by the Order of the Blade. Even Order members had gone rogue over the years, and there was no way in hell he was going to risk his duty by deciding to fuck the wrong woman.

Yeah, sure, some of the Order members had recently met their *shevas* and had managed to hold off the fate of hell for now, but they had still lost their focus. No man could give a hundred percent to his mission if his time was split with a woman. It simply wasn't possible.

With the Order crumbling since Dante's death, Gabe knew he was the last chance the Order had to survive. He had to find Dante and bring him back, because no one else was doing it.

Which meant he had no time for women. He didn't even notice them as women, and he never wanted them. It had never been an issue...until now.

He could still feel her presence inside him, like a silken seduction that had caressed every cell in his body while he'd been unconscious. It was a feminine energy, soft, seductive, and tempting, utterly unlike anything he had ever experienced in his life.

Slowly, reluctantly, he leaned forward and inhaled. She smelled like untouched beauty, dark and sensual, with a hint of something lighter and more feminine, like some sort of flower. It was intriguing as hell, and he wanted more of it.

Her hair was dark and thick where it tumbled over her shoulders and across his upper arm. He moved his fingers slightly, rubbing the strands. Soft. Like silk. He hadn't even realized that anything that soft existed, not that he'd ever thought about it. He was always working, always focused on the mission of the Order, always alert for threats. Yeah, he'd seen his team members fall for women, but he'd never noticed or cared about it, other than to assess whether the situation adversely affected the ability of the Order to discharge their duties. He'd never even been curious.

But now, with this woman lying so still in his arms, he was riveted by her, and he wanted to know why. Was she his *sheva*? The thought made his blood run cold, but he didn't shy away from the possibility. He had to know what he was facing, why she had managed to get him to notice her.

He studied her again, systematically going over her, trying to figure out why he was reacting to her. A dozen weapons were strapped to her body, and those were just the ones he could see. A warrior, then. He recalled how she'd strode right into the middle of battle, utterly without fear. Not just a warrior. A brave, fearless one who would risk anything to save her brother.

He nodded, respect for her flooding him. He appreciated a warrior who was willing to risk her life to save those who mattered to her...but then why had she saved him? His goal had been to kill her brother, and he'd been well on his way to accomplishing that. So...why had she saved him?

Frowning, he brushed his finger over her cheek, as if her skin could tell him what he wanted to know. She was cool to the touch, a fact which deepened his frown. Her skin was pale, almost ashen, and her breathing was much too shallow. She wasn't well, he realized, and that thought didn't sit well with him, not after she had saved him. He moved his hand to her chest, letting his palm hover over her heart while he sent his energy into her, assessing her injuries.

No broken bones or injuries that he could find. Just a fading spirit, and a body that was full of darkness and taint. The darkness that had been in him. Swearing, he closed his eyes, reaching more deeply inside her, retracing the connections that she'd built between them when she'd healed him. He could feel his own presence inside her, and he realized that when she'd healed him, she brought his energy into her own body, along with the poison that had been killing him. He realized that she'd healed him by taking the poison into her own body, and now it was trying to kill her.

Shit.

Swearing, he looked up again at the walls surrounding him. He reached out with his preternatural senses, searching for any vulnerability in the walls that would allow him to escape the tiny cavern, but he found nothing. It was rock in all directions, thick, heavy rock laced with metal. There was the faint scent of sulfur in the air, and he knew that they were still in the demon world...near Dante.

Anticipation rushed through him. *He'd made it into the demon realm.* But where was he? And where was Vlad?

"Vlad!" He shouted the name, but his voice simply bounced off the walls, rebounding back at him.

There was no reply.

He looked down at the woman in his arms. She was of the demon realm, and was of demons. She would know where they were, how they got here, and how to get out. She was his only chance. He knew better than to allow his attraction to her to go any further, but he wasn't going to risk Dante's future, not when he was so close to saving his leader. Gabe's job was not to save himself. His loyalty was to the Order, and if saving the Order meant getting involved with a woman, then he would do what he must.

He let out his breath, but he didn't move. He had no idea what to do with her. If she were a Calydon, he'd simply merge with her and heal her. But she was a woman. A demon, possibly. He was so used to keeping his distance from females that he wasn't even sure where to start. He literally had no experience with women to draw upon. If she were his *sheva*, he would be able to heal her the same way he'd heal a Calydon, by merging his energy with her, but he didn't want to even try that.

It was too intimate, and he wasn't going there. So he had no damned idea what to do.

What he did know was that she looked like hell, and she was dying because she'd taken the poison out of him. Since she wasn't a Calydon, he couldn't heal her with his energy. So, what could he do?

Frowning, he put his hand on her hip. She was on her side, with her back toward him, so it seemed like the most logical place to touch, but it felt awfully damned invasive to touch her like that. The leather of her pants was smooth and sleek beneath his palm, an assault to his senses, but it was blocking his ability to sense her. With a groan of resignation, he slipped his hand beneath the waistband of her pants and spread his hand across her bare hip, so he had skin to skin contact with her.

Her skin was incredibly soft, but it was cold. Too cold. There wasn't enough life left in it. Swearing, he closed his eyes, summoning all his healing energy to his hand. His hand began to heat up, and he offered it to her, but she didn't let him in. For a split second, relief rushed through him. If she were his *sheva*, he was pretty sure she wouldn't have been able to reject his healing energy. Then, he realized that meant he wasn't helping her, so his relief quickly faded into frustration.

Swearing, he moved his hand lower, trying to find a place where her barriers were less strong, and then he tried again...and again, she didn't let him in.

Shit.

He withdrew his hand, irritated by the fact that his cock was starting to get hard. He needed to focus. Getting a hard-on was a ridiculous lack of discipline that hadn't happened to him in centuries.

He studied her for another moment, trying to decide the best place to touch her. The skin on her face was too soft. Her hip...too dangerous. Her arm or leg? Not connected closely enough to her vital organs. That left her torso. He could try her heart, but with her breast spilling out of the bodice, he'd be getting a handful of flesh that he didn't want to risk.

Her stomach then. The belly was a powerful source of energy for the soul and the physical being. With another groan of resistance, he tugged her bodice up and shoved her high-waisted pants lower on her belly. Her stomach was flat and muscled, but there was a softness that was pure woman.

Jesus.

Gritting his teeth, he flattened his palm over her stomach. Her body was soft and womanly beneath his touch, not the hard steel of his own flesh. She was strong and muscular, but her body was so different than his. Swearing under his breath, he closed his eyes, sending his energy into her belly through his hand. His palm burned with heat, but again, she didn't accept his help.

He tried three more times, and got nothing, except a bigger hard-on.

Swearing, he extricated himself from her and got off the bed. It took a moment to get his balance, but he walked across the room and sat down on the floor, draping his hands over his knees while he took some space from her. "What do I do with you?" he asked her. His voice was low, bouncing off the walls, echoing his question back at him.

He had to get out of the room. He had to find Dante. And he needed her help to do it.

Her breath stuttered in her chest, and he studied her. Did she look even paler than she had before? Was her breathing shallower? Shit! He jumped up and walked back over to her. He crouched in front of her and touched her cheek. Her skin was definitely colder now. Son of a bitch. What was going on?

Her eyelids suddenly fluttered, and then opened. He found himself instantly staring into the most vibrant blue eyes he'd ever seen in his life. They were icy blue, like a glacier that was ruthlessly tearing apart everything in its way. But, at the same time, there was such pain and fear in her eyes, vulnerability that violated everything that a warrior should be. "I can't die," she whispered. "They need me."

Her voice was soft, so soft he could barely hear it, but it was laced with fierce determination. She was vulnerable and powerful, both at the same time, a combination he wasn't accustomed to. Male warriors were only hard. Never vulnerable. But this woman was both, which intrigued him. He leaned forward, his hand still on her cheeks. "What can I do?"

Her gaze was steady and unyielding, but her breath was becoming shallower and more labored. "Kiss me."

Chapter Seventeen

GABE BLINKED AND instinctively dropped his hand from her cheek. "Kiss you?"

The moment he released her, fear ran starkly across her face, and she cried out in protest. "Don't let go!"

He immediately placed his hand against her forehead, and this time, he saw her body shudder in response. "My touching helps you," he said. "Why?"

Her gaze met his, and he saw a hint of something in there. Embarrassment? Vulnerability? "I'm a lust demon," she whispered. "I get my energy from sex. I need you."

"Oh...shit." His cock got harder instantly, and he jerked backward, away from her. "I don't do that."

"Don't let go of me!" She snapped the command at him.

For a long moment, he didn't move, every instinct screaming at him to back off and not get involved. But when her eyelids fluttered shut and her body went limp, fury tore through him. "No." He crouched in front of her again and framed her face with both hands. "I need you."

For a moment, she didn't respond, but then her eyes opened again. "Mutual need, apparently. Take me, I'm yours."

Again, with the surge of blood to his cock, like he was some animal who couldn't control himself. "My leader is trapped in the demon realm. I need your help to find him."

She studied him. "You'll give me sex only if I assist you?"

He grimaced at the way she'd phrased it. "I don't have sex. How else can I save you?"

Her eyes grew thoughtful. "Never? You've never had sex?" Her gaze slid over his body, and then back to his face. "How is that possible?"

"It's undisciplined," he snapped. "It's dangerous. I can't risk it. How else can I save you?"

She shook her head, and her eyes fluttered shut again. "Lust demon," she murmured. "Only sex." She took a shuddering breath, and then went still.

Shit. He didn't do sex, and now he was supposed to make out with an unconscious woman? What the *hell*? If there was any way, *any other way*, he would do it, but there was nothing else. He had no other choice if he wanted to save his leader. Whatever it took to engage his mission. He'd made an oath, and there was *no other path.*

With a deep inhale, he calmed his mind, shutting down his physical response to her. He steeled himself against her femininity, and then he lowered his head and pressed a kiss to her mouth.

The moment his mouth touched hers, he froze in absolute shock. Her lips were softer than he could even conceive of, like the air itself had come together to form her lips. He'd never experienced anything like it, and his entire body came alive. Energy rushed through him in a violent frenzy, and lust slammed into his gut violently.

He gritted his teeth against the warring urges to drag the woman into his arms and unleash himself onto her, and the equally strong instinct to hurl her aside and bolt for safety before anything further could happen.

He did neither. He simply kept his mouth against hers, hoping that the closed-mouth kiss would be enough. Even aside from the fact that he wasn't going to have sex, there was no way in hell he was going to take advantage of an unconscious woman, no matter what she'd said during her brief moment of lucidity—

Her lips suddenly parted beneath his.

Desire rushed through him, and before he could stop himself, he kissed her again, running the tip of his tongue over her lips. The moment he did, she responded. She began to kiss him back, her decadent mouth moving under his in a rush of sensual temptation that was beyond anything he'd ever experienced.

Swearing, he gripped the edge of the bed, refusing to touch her, even as the kiss deepened. She slipped her tongue between his teeth, and he groaned when he felt it slide across his in a sensual caress. Sweat broke out on his forehead with the effort of restraining himself, but he kept to the script, deepening the kiss while never moving his hands to her body.

Then she moved *hers*, sliding her arms around his neck and pulling him closer. He lost his balance and went to his knees, falling against the side of the bed as she took over the kiss. Her mouth was hot and sensual, a temptation of the most sinful kind. His cock was hard as a rock, straining against his jeans, and his entire body was screaming for more.

She deepened the kiss, a sensual assault against his defenses, stirring up desire in him that he'd never experienced before. Was this what his teammates had felt when they'd met their soulmates? Was this what all men felt when they fell under the spell of a woman? For the first time, he comprehended the power of a woman over a man. He'd always kept himself so far removed that no woman could access him, and yet with one kiss, he was consumed with thoughts about what he wanted to do to her, of what her breasts would taste like, of how he wanted to part her legs and—

Shit!

He jerked back, breaking the kiss, but she didn't release him. Her grip was surprisingly strong, and he didn't want to hurt her by exerting the effort it would take to break her hold. "I don't do this," he said.

Her eyes were brighter now, and sharper. "What's your name?" she asked.

"Gabe."

"Mine is Maria. No man has ever been able to say no to me," she said, her fingers softening against the back of his neck. He realized she was playing with his hair, a tender gesture that felt incredible. "It feels good to know you can keep your mind when I kiss you. No one ever can." There was a wistfulness in her voice that softened his resistance.

He leaned forward, and traced his finger over her cheek. "No woman has ever gotten past my shields," he said. "I haven't had an erection in hundreds of years. You're very powerful."

She smiled, her fingers still tracing circles on his neck. "I need to get stronger," she said. "I've waited too long to replenish my energy, and now I'm paying for it."

"Why did you wait?"

She shrugged. "I hate having sex with the demons in this place. It's like selling my body to the highest bidder every time I need to be restored. They use me as much as I use them, and I have no choice. I have to do it."

He understood what she was saying. Like him, she had a duty to others, and she did whatever it took to fulfill it, even if it meant handing her body out to whoever would take it. He might not have spent any time between the sheets with women, but he'd been around enough to understand that a woman's right to say who touched her was sacred and critical for the sanctity of her soul. Protectiveness surged through him, and he cupped her face. He didn't even know her, but her plight affected him. He didn't like what she had to do. "I'm sorry you have to do that."

She met his gaze, and he saw that now-familiar fog beginning to overtake her eyes again as the momentary high of the kiss began to fade. "It's okay," she said. "I don't waste time worrying about it, but the fact I can have a sane conversation with you after I've started kissing you made me think about it." Her words began to slur, and he realized the effect of the kiss was already wearing off. "I need to heal," she whispered. "I need your help. At least give me enough to help me survive until I can find a demon. You don't have to have sex. Just enough to keep me going." A faint smile curved her lips. "It would be a miracle to be with a man who could manage not to have sex with me. Just once. It might be nice to experience, before I go back to doing what I do."

He ground his jaw at the idea of her handing her body over to some demon who would fuck her like an animal, anger pulsing through him at the mere idea. "That is going to have to change," he said as he bent his head to kiss her again. "No more of that shit."

Then he kissed her again, and this time, he knew it wasn't going to stay chaste.

Her mouth was warm and ready for his when he kissed her. This time, he took over the kiss, no longer allowing her to control him. He kissed her hard, he kissed her deep, he kissed her with the passion she stirred up in him. He held rigidly onto his control, however, refusing to become the mindless sex fiend that she'd had to deal with her whole life. He had no idea what the proper methods were for kissing, but he didn't give a shit. He was a Calydon warrior, for hell's sake, born and bred to be consumed by his lust so that it would drive him into the arms of his soulmate. He might not have been trained in sex, but every nuance of seduction and sex was imprinted on his being, and he knew exactly what he wanted to do to her.

He was going to kiss her like she was worth something, not like she was some piece of ass to be ridden until there was nothing left. He pressed a kiss to the side of her mouth, then trailed his lips along her jaw, and then down the side of her neck. Yeah, she might be a lust demon who'd been with men too many times to count, but she hadn't seen anything yet.

Her arms tightened around his neck, and she gasped as he lightly bit the side of her neck. A heady sense of power surged over him at her response, and he bit again, this time harder. Then he worked his way up her neck. He trailed his tongue along her earlobe, need surging through him as he tasted her skin. "You taste incredible," he whispered as he worked his way back to her mouth. "Like fresh honey and peaches."

"No one has ever said that," she whispered. "Thank you—"

He cut her off with another kiss, deeper now, sensual and passionate, unleashing a thousand-year-old untapped instinct into the kiss. She leaned into him, almost falling off the bed, and he grabbed her, his hands flanking her hips. Her curves filled his hands perfectly, and he tightened his fingers on her, using his body to push her back onto the bed. He followed her onto the bed, never breaking the kiss, never taking his hands off her hips. The kiss was wild and out of control, and he loved every second of tasting her.

He settled beside her on the bed, his cock hard as he draped his leg over her hip, trapping her against him. She was strong, but he was stronger, and for some reason, he wanted her to know it, not to show he was the aggressor, but so she would know that he was a shield that was available for her use.

Her slim fingers wrapped around his wrist, pulling his hand off her hip. He knew what she wanted instantly, but he let her move his hand and place it on her breast. If every demon she kissed turned into a lust-crazed sex-fiend, he doubted that she'd ever had to put a man's hand on her body, or that she'd even had the chance to control the pace.

So, he didn't move his hand until she put hers on top of his and squeezed lightly, as if she thought he were some innocent who had no idea what to do with a woman's body. He grinned, and instead of squeezing her breast through the wire bodice, he grabbed the edge of her top and dragged it down to expose her breast.

Hell. His cock quivered at the swell of flesh as it tumbled free. Her nipple was hard and dark, a salacious bud of temptation. He cupped the underside of her breast, drinking in the feel of the soft mound in his hand. It felt unlike anything he'd ever touched, and it felt right.

Maria shifted against him, and he glanced at her face. Her blue eyes were riveted to his face, and she smiled when she saw him look at her. "No one has ever slowed down enough to notice my body. The look on your face when you saw my breast made me feel like the most beautiful woman ever. Thank you for that. Thank you for making this different than it ever has been."

Emotions shifted inside him, feelings that he'd never allowed to surface before. Emotions that were soft, and, at the same time, cloaked in a furious, possessive rage at all the men who had used her body with so little appreciation for what they had been gifted with. "You must be the most beautiful woman ever. You're the first one I've ever responded to." He thumbed her nipple as he took her mouth in a deep kiss of tongue, seduction, and possession.

She shifted against him, a low groan escaping her mouth as he continued to play with her nipple, rolling it beneath his palm and pinching it lightly. "That never feels this good," she whispered into the kiss. "Why does it feel so amazing with you?"

"Because I'm incredibly good at everything I do." He palmed her breast and bent his head, taking the taut bud into his mouth. Her skin tasted like heaven, something far purer than he deserved to experience. He traced circles with his tongue, vividly attuned to every breath Maria took, to every flinch of her body, memorizing what she responded to, and what she loved. Within a minute, she was twisting on the bed, held in place only by his leg locked over her hip. His balls were hurting like hell, and he knew that he needed release, the kind of release he'd never granted himself.

But he ignored it. Instead, he focused on Maria. How far did he need to go with her? Was it enough? He had to knock it off soon, because it was getting more and more difficult to suppress his own needs, needs that he'd never had to fight off before. He pulled back from her breast and kissed her mouth. "Enough?" he whispered.

"No."

Shit. "What do you need?"

"I need physical release. An orgasm." She pulled back. "Do you know what that is?"

"Do I—?" Jesus. She really thought he was that pathetic? "Hell, yeah, I know what that is."

She raised her brows.

He groaned under his breath, aware of how hard his cock already was. He couldn't afford to get more entangled with her, but what choice did he have? "Okay."

This time, when he bent to kiss her, he knew he was in danger...from her, from himself, from the instincts that he'd managed to control his entire life.

His control was about to snap, and he had to let it happen.

Chapter Eighteen

GABE DIDN'T GIVE himself a chance to think about what he was about to do, or how dangerous it would be if she turned out to be his *sheva,* or how it could awaken instincts that he'd suppressed for so long. He simply moved over her and kissed her hard. Desire poured through him, as he reached for her pants, hooked his fingers over her waistband, and pulled them down over her hips.

Her skin was like satin, tempting him as he dragged her pants over her feet. She propped herself up on her elbows, her gaze hooded and sultry as she watched him. There was so much yearning in her eyes that he felt something deep inside him lurch. Something more than lust or need. He took a deep breath, meeting her gaze as he locked his arms around her thighs. "You're sure?"

She nodded. "Yes," she whispered, her voice raw with need.

He swore under his breath, feeling guilty that she'd been forced to accept him, that she was trapped by her body's need for sex. He was a stranger, and yet she had to give him her body to save herself. He admired her courage, but couldn't deny the vulnerability in her eyes. Determination flooded him, a sudden protectiveness, and he knew he was going to do everything in his power to make it good for her, to honor her and

to touch her, how to kiss her, how to
satisfaction pulsed through him each t
realized that he loved making her re
whisper that slipped from her lips witl
and he loved feeling her legs tense arc

He unwound his right arm from h
fingers inside her. Her body welcom
entire body shudder as her muscles t
gers. He kept up his assault with his r
ing her onward, giving her no time
breath. She bucked against him, and l
bed with his forearm, locking her dov
gers were tight in his hair, and he felt
ter and tighter.

"Now," he whispered. "*Now.*" He
and moved his fingers inside her, ha
lute precision.

"Gabe!" She gasped his name,
against him. The orgasm ripped throu;
siderable portion of his strength to h
lose his spot. The orgasm held her i
like an eternity. He could feel himsel
plunge inside her, and to complete wh

But he didn't move. He just kept
her as the tremors wracked her bod
body was rigid, and her skin was dam
eral minutes before the tension eased,
mattress, still gasping for breath. Her
head on the pillow, making her breas
She was sexy as hell, and he was all to

"Wow," she gasped. "That was amazing."

He grinned, kissed her belly button, and then eased up beside her. He propped himself up on his elbow, resting his head on his hand, grinning as he watched the play of expressions across her face. Her skin was flushed and rosy now, darker, a caramel brown that made her eyes even more brilliantly blue than they were before. Beads of sweat dogged her forehead and her upper lip. Her lips were fuller than before, and darker...and he wanted to kiss them again.

He let out his breath, examining his urge to kiss her, assessing it. He knew he couldn't shove it away into a black abyss right now, not when he could still taste her on his lips, and smell the scent of sex in the air. So, instead, he faced it, knowing that the more he understood about his reaction to her, the better he would be able to control it. "I'm good, huh?"

She smiled, her gaze moving over his face assessingly. "That was your first time?"

"Yeah."

"Want to try it again?"

He grinned. "Yeah, actually, I do."

Hope lit her eyes. "Really?"

"Yeah, but I'm not going to."

"Oh." Some of the hope faded, but she didn't look overly disappointed. "No one ever turns me down. It's nice." She touched his face. "No one has ever done that to me before."

He cocked his brow. "Done what? Oral sex?" At her nod, he grinned. Yeah, she was a lust demon who'd been with a lot of men, but he was also her first. He liked that idea. He liked it a lot.

Maria sighed. "It's always just about sex, as fast and as hard as we can make it."

His amusement vanished. "Is it." It wasn't a question. It was a thinly veiled attempt not to descend into some possessive, testosterone-induced male rage.

"Yes. It's functional, not for pleasure." She raised her hand and brushed her fingers over his hair, in a touch so gentle he wanted to close his eyes and simply absorb it. "That was pure, sinful pleasure, Gabe. Amazing. Thank you."

He inclined his head, still focusing on her fingers in his hair. "How do you feel?"

She smiled. "So much better."

"Totally recovered?"

Her smile faded, and she shook her head. "I'll still need to have sex soon, but this gave me time." She began tucking her breasts back into her bodice, and Gabe couldn't help but feel cranky about it. He liked having her breasts where he could see them.

Shit. This wasn't good. He rolled off the mattress and walked away from the bed. He placed his hands on the walls, sending his energy into the rock, trying to focus on Dante, and not the fact that he couldn't stop thinking about the woman behind him. "So, how do we get out of here? Where are we? And where would Dante be?"

"So many questions. You're awfully demanding, aren't you?"

"I have a mission." He heard the sound of her sliding her leather pants over her legs, and he ground his jaw. He knew exactly how soft that leather was, and how it clung to her body as if it were part of her skin. He knew the way it curved over her hip in a sinfully decadent way that would make any guy forget about anything but seeing what was hidden beneath the fabric. He bent his head, resting his forehead against the rock, using the cold surface to distract him. "My leader, Dante Sinclair, was murdered recently. His spirit is still circulating, so I need to get his body back to the earth realm to reunite them." As he spoke the words, the enormity of what he was planning struck him. He didn't even know if it was possible to do what he was planning. "He's a Calydon, which means he's descended from demon blood. I think that his body may have returned to the demon realm when he died. All Calydon bodies disappear when they die, and I'm guessing they come here."

She was quiet for a moment, and he could hear the rustle as she finished getting dressed. Shit. He wanted to turn around and rip those clothes off her, to see how far she could take him. Swearing, he pressed his forehead harder against the wall, and braced his palms on the rock. "Is that possible to

160

do?" he asked. "Retrieve him and bring him back to life?"

Her hand touched his back, and he jumped a mile. He whirled around, grabbed her around the waist, and pinned her to the wall with his body in one swift move that was pure instinct, completed before he even had time to think about it.

Maria's eyes widened as she stared at him, her breasts pressed against his chest. "I didn't mean to startle you," she said softly.

"I want you."

A small smile curved her mouth. "It's okay, Gabe. Every man wants me. It's not your fault."

"It's my fault. I have better discipline than this." He bent his head slightly, so that he could inhale the scent of her hair. "God, you smell good. I shouldn't even realize that, but instead, I can't stop thinking about it." He tangled his fingers in her hair and tugged on it as he lifted his head so he could see into her eyes. "Why do you affect me like this?"

She shrugged. "Lust demon."

"Is it? Because I've been around other women with supernatural sex appeal, and I was never remotely affected. A lust demon isn't the only sensual female around, you know."

She raised her eyebrows. "I'm very powerful."

"So am I." He pressed closer with his body, needing to feel her against him. "No woman has *ever* penetrated my shields. *Ever.*" He trailed his mouth over the curve of her neck, intense satisfaction pulsing through him when he heard her sharp intake of breath. "Do you know what a *sheva* is?"

She leaned her head back against the wall and closed her eyes, as if she were having to concentrate to hold herself aloof from the heat building between them. "A Calydon's soulmate, who is bound to destroy him and then kill herself because she is so bereft at losing him? Yes, I know what that is, but that's not me."

"How can you be so sure?" He kissed her collarbone. Even her skin tasted fresh and pure, nothing like a demon who had lived several lifetimes in the darkness of their cursed realm.

"Because I'm not an ordinary female. I'm part-demon, which means I'm a monster to which none of the regular rules apply." She slid her fingers through his hair. "My instinct is to suck every last bit of sexual energy out of you until nothing remains but a shriveled shell and a broken soul. That's why you're reacting to me." She tugged him closer, until his mouth was just above the swell of her breasts. "I haven't done that to anyone in a long time. I can always stop myself. But with you, it's different. I want more of you." Her voice was so sultry and decadent that Gabe felt his entire body surge in response. "I don't know if it would ever be enough with you."

He pressed his pelvis against her belly, grabbed her hands, and pinned them to the wall on either side of her head, searching her face. "You can't have me," he said.

"Of course I can." She looked saddened by the words. "This thing between us is supernatural sex. Nothing more. It's never anything more."

"It's going to be more this time." Gabe refused to look at her mouth, staring instead into those riveting blue eyes. "This time, you're going to be partners with a man. You're going to help me find my leader's body, and you're going to help me get it out of the demon world. We have a deal, princess, and I won't let you out of it."

Maria searched his face. "You really believe you can spend time with me and not have sex with me, don't you?"

"Yeah." He had to admit, however, that she'd made him fully grasp the power of a female for the first time in his life. "It's not a choice. I've given an oath to the Order of the Blade, and I will see that oath through at any cost."

She met his gaze, a small smile curving the corner of her mouth. "You sound like me, except I'm willing to have sex with anyone so I can save the women who are trapped here. I admire that about you."

He inclined his head. "I admire you as well."

For a moment, they simply stared at each other, and Gabe was acutely aware of her breasts pressed against his chest. He wasn't going to jerk off his pants and sheathe himself inside her, but he had to acknowledge that he damn well liked having her body crushed up against his.

She smiled, and set her hands on his shoulders. "I'm not

used to having time to enjoy a man. I forgot what it feels like to simply touch one." She slid her hands down his arms, watching the progress of her hand with a look of almost-innocent fascination. A small giggle escaped her lips. "It's an incredible luxury, the sense of leisure you give me." She glanced at him. "Thank you."

He shrugged. "It's my steel will and iron discipline. Comes in handy around lust demons."

She nodded, and dropped her hand, her face becoming serious. "I understand about your leader, but I also have a situation to deal with. Before we find Dante, I have to check on my friend Sophie—"

"Sophie?" Gabe frowned at the name. "That's the name of the woman that Vlad came to find. She's really here? And alive?"

"For a brief while longer, yes." Maria frowned back at him. "Why would your friend want to find her?"

"They're married, I guess." Gabe shrugged. "I didn't pay much attention. I'm only here about my leader."

"Married?" Maria looked shocked. "But she was a teenager when she came here. *Married?*" She twisted around in Gabe's arms and pounded her fist on the solid rock that was functioning as the wall to their prison. "Sophie! You're *married*? We need to talk!"

Suspicion settled on Gabe as he watched Maria hit the wall. "She's on the other side of the wall?"

"Of course she is. How else would we get locked in by a solid wall of rock? It's not like anyone else can manipulate stone like she can. *Sophie!*"

When the stone wall began to dissolve to form a door, anger began to swirl through Gabe. There'd been a way out the entire time? Sophie had *locked him in* with Maria, to use him as food so she could have sex with him? He'd broken his life-long celibacy to help Maria when there'd been a way out *the entire time?* He was no fool. He knew he was at risk now from Maria, and, more importantly, from his *sheva*. All it would take would be one glance at the wrong woman, and he'd be more interested in nailing her than doing his duty. He'd risked so much to bring Maria back to life, because he'd thought it was his only option, and the whole time, he'd simply been set up as *food*?

Fury settled deep in him as the doorway completely opened, revealing a blond woman standing in the opening. Behind her stood Vlad. Son of a bitch. The other man had been in on it as well?

That same hated feeling of impotence began to settle on him, the same one he'd felt since the day Dante had died and Gabe had realized that none of the remaining warriors were strong enough to replace him. The Order had begun to fragment that day, and it was continuing to shatter.

Rogue Calydons were becoming more rampant, Dante's own son was becoming increasingly dangerous, and there would soon be no Order left to defeat them. Gabe was their last chance, and he had been tricked into almost dropping his pants for a *woman*.

Vlad met his gaze over the women's heads, both men ignoring the chatter of the women. Vlad raised one eyebrow in question, clearly asking what he'd done to bring Maria back to life. Gabe shook his head once, indicating that they hadn't had sex. Vlad's other eyebrow went up and he made a drooping motion with his index finger, suggesting that flaccidity had been the enemy. Gabe snorted, chuckling under his breath. "No chance," he shot back.

"If you say so," Vlad said, injecting just enough of a patronizing tone into his voice to make Gabe laugh.

"Shut up." The ribbing by Vlad took the edge off Gabe's anger. It reminded him of what the Order had been like back when they'd been intact, when Thano had been around to give them all grief, before he'd gone off with some broken-off branch of the Order that none of them had ever heard of. He missed the team atmosphere, and Vlad reminded him of it.

He moved past the women and walked up to Vlad. "You found her."

"Yeah." Vlad's gaze flicked past him. "She won't leave, though. She wants to stay and help the other women."

"So, you going to stay?"

Vlad raised his brows, then shrugged. "I hadn't thought of staying, but yeah, if she stays, I stay."

"Then you want to help me?"

Vlad glanced at Gabe. "Find your leader?"

"Yep." He watched Maria and Sophie hugging, studying the visible affection between the women. "Maria's my guide in the demon realm, but I have a feeling that it's not going to be a friendly trip. I could use backup." He could tell that the bond between the women was genuine, and that eased some of his anger about being locked up. He respected Sophie's decision to do whatever it took to save her friend. That was the stuff that made a solid team.

"Sophie's being hunted by the demon king because he wants to have sex with her until she dies, as well as by the leader of the hunt, who wants the same thing. Not to mention, the thousands of demons she's sexually frustrated over the years. I'm going to be a little busy cutting off their horny little heads until I find a way to kill the fuckers."

Gabe glanced at Vlad, and then started chuckling.

"You think that's funny? Because I don't."

"It's just not something I'd ever thought I'd hear in my life." Gabe ran his hand through his hair, studying the blond woman. Sophie didn't have the raw, untamed passion of Maria, but she was relatively attractive. He could see the appeal. "If you have all those demons lusting after your woman, you're going to need some help, too."

Vlad looked back at him. "You want to team up?"

Gabe shrugged. "I saw you fighting earlier. You're good. I'm better, but you're close enough to be an asset."

Vlad studied the women, who were sitting on a small couch, hunched over in whispered conversation no doubt meant to exclude the men. "So, we go deep into the demon realm, grab Dante's body, and then together we all fight our way out and we get the women out of here?"

"I thought you said she wouldn't leave."

"It's not safe for her here anymore. She'll have no choice." Vlad ran his hand through his hair, and Gabe noticed that the band on his ring finger was black and purple, swirling like a turbulent poison around his finger. "I agree. It's a deal."

Gabe held out his hand, and the two warriors shook on it. It was good. It was right. With Vlad and Maria on his team, he could make this happen—

He suddenly noticed Maria and Sophie had gone silent, and he saw Vlad tense at the same moment. Both men whirled toward where the women had been sitting, and they were gone. A sound creaked from above, and Gabe looked up just as Maria's stilettoed heel disappeared through a hole in the ceiling. "Hey!" He leapt up just as Vlad pointed toward the ceiling, power bursting from his hand as they lunged for the women—

The rock reformed the instant before they got there, and Gabe's fist slammed into the rock. Vlad's magic bounced off the ceiling and hit Gabe, throwing him down onto the stone floor. "Hey!"

"Sorry." Vlad leapt over Gabe and put his hands on the rock. "Shit. They locked us in. I can't believe it."

Gabe rolled over, trying to catch his breath from the hit Vlad had inflicted upon him. "You aimed at Maria with that shit? You could have hurt her."

"She was locking us in!"

"She's still a woman!" Gabe coughed and made it to his hands and knees. "If you ever fuck with her again like that, I'll kill you."

"For a man who just turned down a lust demon, you're awfully possessive of her." Vlad leapt over to him and sprinted toward the opposite wall. As soon as he reached it, he stopped and began running his hands across it, as if he were looking for something.

"She's had a tough life. I respect that. I kind of admire her ruthlessness in tricking me into sex so she could survive, although, I am, of course, morally opposed to that deception." Gabe made it to his feet. Shit. He was still weak from the demon poison. A hit like that shouldn't have taken him down. Why the hell was he having so much trouble recovering? "We need to go get them."

"Yep." Vlad slapped the wall. "Get over here, Gabe."

Gabe managed to walk across the floor without stumbling. "What do you have?"

"A crack. Can you open it?"

Gabe crouched down and ran his hand over what appeared to be a solid wall. It took three passes before he finally saw the hairline crack Vlad was talking about. "That? You think we can get out through that? I don't know about you, but I eat my Wheaties for breakfast, and I'm not that skinny."

"A demon hound got through. It goes somewhere. Open it."

"A demon hound? Shit, you guys were busy while I was being used for my body." Gabe reached out with his preternatural senses, sending his energy through the hairline fracture. He felt the air move on the other side, and realized Vlad was correct. "You get anywhere with Sophie? Reunion sex? I've heard it's good."

Vlad crouched beside him, studying the crack. "You ever get personal about my wife again, and I'll kill you."

Gabe considered that, and then he shrugged. "Can't make any promises. I probably will get personal about her again."

"Yeah, well, I'll probably use my power against Maria again, if I have to."

The two men looked at each other.

"I'm a better warrior," Gabe said. "I'll win."

"I'm better. I'll win. I'm highly motivated because I actually like the woman I'm defending."

"Who said I didn't like Maria? You do realize it's possible to respect a woman and not want to have sex with her, don't you?" He held out his arms. The weapons branded on his forearm began to hum with energy as he prepared to call them out. "Besides, saving Maria isn't simply about saving her. It's about using her to find my leader." The weapons exploded into their solid state with a crack and a flash of black light, appearing in his palms, ready for striking. "My dedication to my team is a hell of a lot stronger than your need to help a woman."

"Said by a guy who has never betrayed the woman he was born to protect." Vlad stepped back. "There's no higher purpose in life, my friend."

"Sure there is. It's called duty." Gabe gripped his weapon, and then swung hard, slamming it into the hairline crack in the wall. His blade sunk deep into the crevice, and he felt the rock strain against the assault upon its vulnerability.

"The wall's still up," Vlad pointed out.

"Shut up." Gabe slammed his second weapon into the crevice and then swung his weight into the handle, using it as a lever. The rock strained under the assault, groaning as it fought not to break. The room began to spin as Gabe braced himself, using his entire body weight to wedge the rock apart. Shit. What the hell was wrong with him?

Without a word, Vlad moved up beside him and added his own weight to the weapon. Together, the two warriors thrust all their combined strength into the blade, gaining a fraction of an inch, and then another and then a huge chunk of rock exploded out of the wall. It slammed into the couch, leaving a gaping hole in the wall that led to a narrow, pitch-black tunnel that stank of rot, corpses and the same poison that had nearly brought them both down.

The two warriors stood side by side, peering into the blackness. "You got night vision?" Vlad asked.

"Yeah, but not enough to penetrate that. There's nothing in there but an abyss of darkness."

Vlad raised his brows. "We could always wait here for the ladies to return. Maybe they went out for takeout."

"Maybe. Their couch has a rock on it now, though. Nowhere to sit while we wait."

"Well, then, we might as well go." Vlad raised Gabe's sword. "To marital loyalty.'"

Gabe tapped his blade against Vlad's. "To duty. And give me my damned weapon." He jerked his sword from Vlad's hand, and then the two of them headed into what could be a really big mistake, or a great chance to show two badass women that it had been a mistake to underestimate them.

Chapter Nineteen

F OR THE FIRST time in her life, Maria felt what she was pretty sure was guilt. She glanced at Sophie as they raced across the rocks. "I kind of feel like we shouldn't have left them. Gabe did help me recover. I promised I'd help him find his leader."

Sophie didn't slow down. "We'll go back and help them. But I can't be defenseless. I need weapons." She led the way down a twisted, curving trail that was carved into the side of a deep canyon.

"Why didn't you put these stones in your cave with you?"

"Because they're jewels. If we went across the top of the cave while on a hunt, I wouldn't have been able to hide the fact I sensed them. Rikker would have known they were below, and he might have found out what was down there." She was running hard, sweat beading on her brow.

Maria realized that Sophie was scared, and her heart sank. "You really think Lucien can make you stay corporeal?"

Her friend looked back at her, and Maria's heart skipped a beat when she saw the tears in Sophie's eyes. "What happened?"

"Vlad gave me an orgasm—"

"What?" Maria jerked Sophie to a stop. "You had an *orgasm*? Why didn't you tell me? How was it? Good?"

"Amazing, of course." Sophie waved her hand with exasperation. "Don't you understand what that means? I didn't go incorporeal with him. I stayed in my body the whole time. I even *slept* in his arms afterwards."

"You did?" Maria was shocked. "You trusted him enough to *sleep* with him?" She'd never slept with a man in her life. Waking up in Gabe's arms should have been terrifying, but she'd been too far gone to care about anything other than self-preservation. She'd never have put herself in that situation intentionally, but Sophie had chosen to do it to save her life. She trusted Sophie's judgment, but she'd still felt the need to put some space between her and Gabe.

Her reaction to him unsettled her. She was riveted by the fact he didn't lose his mind when he kissed her. She was astounded at what it felt like to have an actual conversation with a man while she was half-naked. As strong as she was, she wasn't stronger than Gabe. The idea should have terrified her, but instead, she'd been fascinated by it, which made her even more alarmed. As a man, Gabe was an enemy. As a Calydon, one of the immortal warriors descended from demon blood, he was exactly the kind of creature who had stolen so much from her and all those who mattered to her.

And the *sheva* thing? She'd totally fabricated her claim that she couldn't be a Calydon's soulmate. She had no idea whether she could or not, but the idea of being victimized by an irresistible need to be with a particular man was devastating to all she'd struggled to attain her whole life.

Which was why she'd left.

Okay, so forget the guilt. It had been the right choice to leave him. Sometimes, breaking a promise was the only valid option available. "Okay, so what now?"

"I hid them down here." Sophie turned away and started running down the trail again. "Rikker almost never goes down here with his team, so we should be safe."

Maria tripped on the narrow trail, losing her balance and catapulting forward, toward the edge of the precipice.

"Maria!" Sophie shouted as Maria twisted to the right, throwing herself against the side of the mountain. She hit the rock hard, and landed on a craggy outcropping that tore the palms of her hands and her knees. Grimacing at the shot of pain, she leapt to her feet. "I'm okay."

She caught up to Sophie, then braced her hand on the wall, trying to catch her breath.

Sophie's forehead furrowed. "You didn't have sex with him, did you? You're still weak."

"He wouldn't have sex with me."

Sophie's eyes widened. "*What?* How is that possible? What happened?"

Maria shook her head. "We don't have time for that. We need to get your jewels, and then we need to figure out what to do." Even as she said it, her mind whirled with possibilities. She looked at Sophie, and knew she was thinking the same thing. "We have to kill Lucien, don't we?"

"It's time." Sophie's face was stoic, but Maria knew how much it was breaking her to say it. Sophie was a gentle soul, one who had never caused any harm in her life. She was the one who had organized the healing chain for Maria to help the other women. She had always talked Maria out of fighting him, unwilling to risk the dangers that would befall them if they engaged the demons.

They were deep in the demon realm with no way out, and they both knew it. If they took out Lucien, other demons would take his place. It would never end, and they would become outcasts, always on the run. But Maria didn't care. Sophie was her best friend, and if she'd lost the ability to stay safe, the only option was to take whatever action would keep her safe.

"Then you have to leave the demon realm." The words felt like they tore Maria's heart in half, but she knew there was no other option. It was no longer safe for Sophie to be there. She had to get her out, no matter how much it would break her heart to separate from her best friend.

"What? No." Sophie took Maria's arm and supported her as they resumed their descent. "You need me. Besides, it's impossible."

"You're not demon," she said gently. "No demon has had sex with you, so you have no demon taint in you at all. The shields won't stop you."

Sophie frowned at her. "I tried to go across when I first got here, remember? I can't go. It's not like it's simply a wall of rock that I can dissolve. It's a metaphysical layer between two realms."

"You need someone on the other side to take you across," Maria said quietly. "That's how Vlad and Gabe came in. That's how they'll get out, and you need to go with them."

Sophie stopped in place, staring at her. "You mean that. You want to send me out of here."

"It's your one chance," Maria said, trying to blink back tears. She couldn't imagine surviving the demon realm without Sophie. Yes, she was half-demon, and therefore predisposed to a certain amount of ruthlessness, but the other half of her could break just as much as anyone else. Sophie's mission to help save the other women gave Maria's life meaning, and it gave her a reason to continue to offer her body to the demon bastards who would use her until her body lay in broken smithereens, if she didn't always stop them with a blade to the throat when she'd had enough. "I'll keep healing the women."

Sophie met her gaze. "But who will take care of you when you push yourself too far?"

She shrugged. "My brother—"

"Is not as great a guy as you want to believe." Sophie shook her head. "He's a demon, Maria. There are limits to how much he can offer you—"

A rock rattled above their heads, and both women froze and looked up, searching the cliffs above their heads for movement. Maria's heart started to pound, and she realized that she'd made a grave mistake in letting Gabe not have sex with her. She couldn't be running around out here at half-strength. She was Sophie's only protection, and lust-crazed demons were almost unstoppable.

She searched the rocky shadows above their heads, but she didn't see any movement. She touched Sophie's arm in silent question, and her friend shook her head and gestured ahead. Maria nodded, and the women silently resumed their descent. This time, there was no chatter, just the whisper of their feet over the rocks as they hurried below.

They reached the bottom of the trail, but Sophie kept close to the bottom of the precipice, sliding through the shadows as she led Maria deeper into what she knew was the perimeter of the demon burial ground that housed the most powerful demon essences. Very few demons could be killed, and all it really meant was that their spirits had been trapped here, bound to the bowels of the realm for all eternity.

She could almost feel the ground pulsating with power as she followed Sophie, and the bottom of her shoes felt like they were burning through her feet. "How can you survive down here?" she whispered to Sophie. "You have no protection from the demons."

Sophie looked over her shoulder at her. "I don't feel anything," she whispered back. "What are you talking about?"

Maria was startled by Sophie's reply. "You can't feel the demon energy?"

Sophie shook her head, but she glanced around, suddenly wary. "Are they close?"

"They're trapped." Shit. Maria pulled out two of her swords and gripped them loosely as she moved closer to Sophie. She'd never been down here before, but it was dangerous and ugly. "Let's hurry."

Sophie nodded. "In here." She ducked into a crevice in the wall.

Maria hesitated at the opening to the crack, glancing upwards. The crack went up to the top of the precipice, and it was less than a foot wide. They would be utterly trapped if something came after them while they were in there. "What's in there?"

"It's a pathway about three hundred yards long. My stuff is in a cave at the other end." Sophie looked back at her, her palms on the rock wall as she inched her way through.

Maria swore under her breath, debating about whether she could protect Sophie more by waiting by the entrance, or by going with her. She knew Sophie might still be able to dissolve if they were threatened, but Maria couldn't. She would have no room to fight. Sweat broke out over her palms as she watched Sophie inch further along. "What if you can't dissolve?"

Sophie looked back at her. "These jewels are my only chance, Maria. I had to hide them here, because the crevice is too narrow for most demons to fit through."

"Most, not all." Maria looked up at the top of the cliff, and then surveyed their surroundings. She saw no movement, nothing to suggest they were being hunted, but she still didn't like it. Demons could move like magic, and she knew they could be anywhere...including waiting at the end of the crevasse for Sophie. What if Rikker knew she'd been hiding jewels there?

Swearing under her breath, and hoping she was making the right choice, Maria sheathed her swords, turned sideways, and then slithered into the crevasse behind her friend.

VLAD HAD BEEN in some pretty rank places during the last few decades of self-abuse and self-hate, but this was a new low for him.

The tunnel was rancid with the stench of rot and death. The ground was damp and spongy beneath his feet, and he had a bad feeling it was the blood of the unfortunate that had softened the earth. The walls were dripping with something that made his fingers burn when he touched it once to test it.

He led the way, continuously scanning the tunnel ahead for living matter, though he wasn't sure whether some of the beasts in the demon realm would show up on his radar. Even Sophie hadn't. The thought made guilt stab through his gut, and he shook it off.

He didn't have time for guilt. He'd touched her. He'd talked to her. He'd given her an orgasm. Whether she was incorporeal or not, her soul was clearly alive, and he wasn't leaving without her.

But he was also grimly aware that she didn't share the

same goal.

Gabe touched his back, and Vlad stopped. "What?"

"We need to blood bond." Gabe's voice echoed out of the darkness.

Vlad turned around, but he couldn't discern Gabe in the dim light. "What?"

"Blood bond. Calydons do it when necessary to communicate over great distances. If we do it, we can talk mind-to-mind. I have a feeling we're heading into serious shit, and we need all our resources."

Vlad scowled. "I'm not Calydon."

Gabe laughed softly. "I'm sure you've got some somewhere in your heritage. Most males with any kind of power do."

"Fuck that." Vlad turned and started to walk again. "My only loyalty is to Sophie. I'm not hooking up with some Order of the Blade groupie who thinks his duty is all that matters—" He suddenly found himself shoved up against the side of the tunnel. Acid coating the walls burned into his back, but Gabe didn't let go.

"Don't denigrate the Order of the Blade."

"The skin is disintegrating off my back right now. Let me go." Vlad fisted his hands, resisting the urge to hurl the other warrior backwards with the flick of his finger. He had no idea what was around him, and if they were attacked by something that wasn't living matter, Gabe's weapons were going to come in handy.

Swearing, Gabe pulled him off the wall. "I need your help," he said.

Vlad heard the edge in Gabe's voice. "I am not a team player," he said softly. "It's not my thing." He'd heard enough about the Order of the Blade to know that they were a major boys' club. The members always had each other's back, and usually worked in pairs, if not in larger groups.

"It goes both ways," Gabe said. "You help me with Dante, and I've got your back with Sophie. If the demon king goes after her, it wouldn't be bad to have backup. What if you die, Vlad? What if you fail again? You want to leave her behind unprotected again, or do you want to die knowing that I've got your back, and hers? Because that's how it works."

Vlad ground his jaw. "I don't trust people," he said. "They fuck you over the minute you count on them." For hell's sake, he'd watched his own parents throw him and his sister to the demons, and he'd watched Sophie's parents do the same. "My parents sacrificed me for some delusional duty to their kingdom. Duty is crap. It makes people betray those who really matter. I don't want to be part of the Order, and the last thing I'm going to do is trust Sophie's safety to anyone."

"And if you die? Aren't I better than no one?"

Vlad swore under his breath. "Your duty is to Dante," he snapped. "I'm not an idiot. You want to team up with me so I'll help you. If you have to choose between Sophie and Dante, you're going to leave her high and dry."

"Yeah, I would, but I'll do whatever it takes to make sure I don't have to make that choice. I believe in honor." His voice grew harder. "If I promise to stand by Sophie for you, then I will honor that. The only thing that could come before that would be my oath to the Order. Other than that, I will do everything possible to get her to safety. Honor is all we have, my friend."

Vlad ran his hand through his hair. "I don't have honor."

"Yeah, you do actually."

Vlad was silent. He wasn't honorable. He knew that. He was a piece of shit who had let his sister die and his wife be dragged into hell, and then sat on his ass for a couple centuries while Sophie suffered. He didn't trust the Order because they valued the greater good over individuals, but at the same time, he knew that their loyalty was to protect the innocent, and he respected that. He also knew he could never play in that ballpark.

Gabe's hand settled on his shoulder. "The Order is falling apart. Without us, the rogues take over, and the demons won't be far behind. The demons are your enemy, Vlad. We're on the same team now. We're never going to make it out of here without teaming up. You know that. I know that. We need both of us, and we need every advantage we can get."

Vlad ran his hand through his hair, swearing under his breath. He'd done everything wrong in his life. He'd failed everyone who mattered to him. He just wanted to get one thing right, and get Sophie to safety. That was his only path to redemption. Could he really turn down Gabe's offer for help? He already knew damn well that he'd failed to save his sister, and he'd failed to save Sophie once before, even though he'd been present. He'd had to stand there and watch them die. "I don't do the team thing."

"I know. You broadcast anti-social isolated loner like it's tattooed on your forehead. That's okay. I'm a team guy. I'll smack you around until you figure it out." His voice lowered. "My team has gone to hell, Vlad. I've got no one to back me up except you. I know when someone can be counted on, and you're it, whether you want to own up to it or not."

Shit. He wished he was that guy, but he knew he wasn't. But he also knew Gabe was right. They were in this together, and two women's lives were at stake. "If I do a blood bond with you, is that going to turn me into a Calydon? Or is it going to trick me into being an Order of the Blade groupie?"

Gabe laughed. "No chance of either. Just the ability to communicate telepathically and keep track of where we are. It'll help us communicate in battle and become a more effective force."

"More badass? I like that." Vlad made his decision. "I'm in. What do we do?" It was too dark to see Gabe at all, which was probably good. It was weird as hell to be bonding with another male, or anyone, and the darkness made it easier to separate himself from it.

"Cut your palm, and I cut mine. We grasp hands, and I'll chant the words. Once you figure them out, do it with me. When the blood bond is complete, you'll know because you'll hear my voice in your head."

Vlad grimaced. "I don't want your damned voice in my head." What the hell?

"You will when we're fighting down an entire kingdom of demons standing between you and your woman."

"Good point. Got a knife?"

"Hook sword work?" There was a crack and a flash of black light that lit up the tunnel for a split second. Vlad caught a glimpse of Gabe's grim face, and resolution flooded him. There was pure focus on Gabe's face, the visage of a warrior bent on doing his duty. Vlad knew then that the alignment would only strengthen them both, and he knew damn well that the honor of the Order of the Blade was legendary. He could trust Gabe.

Shit. It had been a long time since he'd trusted anyone.

Gabe set a sword in Vlad's hand. The metal was cold to the touch, and Vlad didn't flinch as he opened his palm and dragged the blade across his flesh, opening a fissure in his hand. He held out his hand, and, despite the darkness, he found Gabe's hand with unerring precision. The two warriors clasped hands in the darkness, and Vlad's palm began to burn as Gabe's demon-tainted blood mixed with his.

Gabe's voice filled the tunnel with a chant that felt ancient with its power and strength. "Warrior to warrior. Bonded by blood. Connected across all distances. Sworn to defend and fight side by side, at all costs. So be it."

The words settled inside Vlad, as if they were born to be a part of him. He spoke the words with Gabe the second time through, already knowing every syllable and intonation. "Warrior to warrior. Bonded by blood. Connected across all distances. Sworn to defend and fight side-by-side, at all costs. So be it."

Power surged through him, a raw, untamed force that came from deep within him and charged across their joined palms. His muscles flexed involuntarily, and he felt the flesh on his forearms burn.

The chant burned in Vlad's mind, and he spoke the words silently, his unspoken voice melding with Gabe's as the warrior's voice reverberated in his mind. *Warrior to warrior. Bonded by blood. Connected across all distances. Sworn to defend and fight side-by-side, at all costs. So be it.*

Pain shot through his hand, but he didn't pull away, gritting his teeth against the raging burn that raked through his body, as if it were burning off all the shit that no longer served it. Gabe's grip tightened as well, as if he were experiencing the same thing.

Finally, the pain stopped, but there was still power humming through Vlad's ears, like the roar of an ancient tidal wave that had spanned centuries of time to hunt him down.

The two warriors released their grip, and Vlad dropped his hand to his side. *That was weird.* He tested the mental communication, having no damn clue how it worked.

To his surprise, Gabe answered, in his own head.

Yeah. That was different from how it works with Calydons. Gabe's voice had an edge to it. *What was all that burning? You get that?*

That's not supposed to happen?

Who knows what's supposed to happen? It's against the law of nature to blood bond with a non-Calydon. Gabe sounded surprised. *I didn't actually think this was going to work. This is good, man, it's really good.*

Vlad felt like his senses had magnified a thousand-fold. He could hear the thud of Gabe's heart, the distant sound of toenails scrabbling on rock, as if there were hell hounds a hundred miles away that he could hear. He could feel the weight of the demon taint in the tunnel, mixed with the remnants of what had once been living creatures. It was as if the entire world had descended into technicolor, and he tried to quickly attune his senses and manage the sudden influx of sensory overload. *You broke rules to do that?*

Yeah. Gabe walked past him and began leading the way down the tunnel. *Got a problem with that?*

Hell no. I hate rules. Vlad fell in behind Gabe, using his heightened senses to reach behind him and assess whether they were being followed. He was accustomed to being able to search only for living matter, but now he could pick up so much more. *I thought you were too uptight to do things like break the rules.*

I'm focused on my duty. I'll do whatever it takes to make that happen, including breaking the rules that underscore the very fabric of my race.

Vlad grinned. *Damn, man. I might actually end up liking*

you after all.

He felt a ripple of humor from Gabe. *You trust only people who break rules for their own agenda?*

Yeah, pretty much.

Gabe laughed then. *I knew I chose well. Let's go find some women, my leader's inert body, and get the hell out of here.*

Deal. Sophie first.

Dante first.

Vlad narrowed his eyes, and sent a pulse of psychic energy at Gabe's brain, channeling it the same way he channeled his magic when he was trying to manipulate living matter. The energy gathered itself and torpedoed right into Gabe's mind, hitting harder than Vlad had intended, much to his delight.

The other warrior grunted in pain. *You're a pain in the ass.*

So are you. He did it again, more lightly this time, and then grinned when Gabe tried to do the same, but failed. *Psychic attacks are my thing,* he said cheerfully. *It's like how I can manipulate living matter. This is fun.* He did it one more time just to practice his new skill, grinning when he felt Gabe flinch. *Sophie first, or I harass you so relentlessly that you'll eventually be reduced to curling up in the fetal position and screaming for mercy.*

Fuck that. You do that again, and I'll cut off your head.

Vlad grinned. *Relax. You're too handy with a sword to be of any use if you're in the fetal position. I'm just practicing for when we have our encounter with the demon army.*

Gabe was silent for a moment, then Vlad sensed him nod. *Keep it up. I'll practice my shielding.*

Vlad was surprised by the remark. *Really?*

We're at war, my friend, and we can't afford to lose. We need to be ready. Who knows what the hell the demons are capable of. All I know is I doubt they're going to sit back and do their nails while we steal from them.

The grimness of Gabe's words hung thickly in the pitch-black tunnel, sobering Vlad. They had a long way to go to get Sophie to safety, and he was damned glad to have Gabe at his back.

Chapter Twenty

SOPHIE FELT A renewed sense of urgency when she saw how Maria was struggling to get through the narrow crack in the rocks. She realized she shouldn't have been so quick to ditch the men. She was so used to being on her own, she hadn't stopped to think about how reliant Maria was on them, or how much she'd be impacted by the fact she hadn't actually had sex with Gabe.

Soon, Maria would be forced to accept the first male who crossed their path, and that could have disastrous consequences. What if it was Rikker? Or Lucien? A shiver crept down her back and she renewed her efforts to get through. "You okay, Maria?"

"Peachy, but after this is over, let's have a little chat about appropriate hiding places for weapons. They do you no good if you can't get to them, you know?"

"I know. Almost there." Sophie reached the end of the crack and slipped out into the small clearing that she knew so well. There was a tall rock ahead, blocking a cave. She had just started to move toward it, when she felt something watching her.

She spun around, searching the shadows, but she saw nothing. Her heart started to hammer. "Stay in the crack, Maria. I'll be right there."

She hurried across the clearing, the hair on the back of her neck standing up as she ran. She braced her palms on the two-foot wide black rock, and asked it to dissolve. For a moment, nothing happened, and fear reached through her. What if she couldn't even manipulate rocks anymore? But then it dissolved, revealing the small opening. She quickly squirmed through the opening, her heart pounding.

Relief rushed through her when she reached the inside of the cavern and saw the rows and rows of jewels that she'd stashed there, specifically chosen because of the burst of power she'd felt when she touched them. She raced across the rocky floor, quickly gathering as many small ones as she could find, slipping them into her pockets. She found the portable cache she'd already assembled, and slipped it over her shoulders, strapping it around her waist. There were dozens of small pockets, each of them hosting a small, uncut jewel.

As she packed on the rocks, she felt energy surging through her, a sense of power. She'd never had so many jewels on her, and there was no mistaking the surge of power. Hope leapt through her. Was it possible that she could become an offensive force with the stones? See? She'd been right to leave Vlad and Gabe behind. It wasn't as if they needed any men to help them.

But even as she headed toward the opening of the cave, she couldn't stop the surge of regret that she'd left Vlad behind. There was something about him that was so compelling. Was it simply that they were really married, like he'd claimed? She wasn't sure, but she couldn't stop wishing that she'd met him in a different time and place, and that she was the kind of woman who had time to pursue a man who caught her interest.

But that wasn't her life. Her life was about helping other women, at whatever cost. Vlad was just a distraction. She had always justified her kidnapping to the demon realm by the belief that she was needed here, that she was meant to be here to help the women. Vlad was a distraction from that, and she couldn't afford them.

Resolutely, she took a deep breath as she stepped outside, determined to focus on what she was meant to achieve—

Then she stopped, her blood freezing in her veins.

Rikker was standing in the clearing, holding Maria against his chest with a knife to her throat. Her friend was pale, the kind of pale that came from an energy depletion that could not be restored without sex. Surrounded by Rikker were the rest of his team. Eleven demons all armed with knives, all of them gazing at her like she was dinner that had been served up to them for their pleasure.

Fear tore through her, but she lifted her chin, sliding her hand into the front pocket of her jeans for a ruby. She hadn't even gotten her fingers far enough in to touch it when Rikker snapped at her.

"Freeze or she dies."

Sophie froze, her gaze snapping to Maria's face. Her friend's eyes were haunted, and she knew that Maria didn't have the strength to fight. Rikker's knife was so tight against Maria's throat that a trickle of blood was easing down her pale throat.

Unlike demons, who were largely immortal, Maria was only half demon. She was difficult to kill, but not impossible. Decapitation would do it.

Her heart thundering, Sophie tried frantically to think of what to do. She looked above Rikker's head and saw a large rock outcropping. If she could dissolve it and make it fall—

"If you dissolve, she dies. Instantly."

Sophie's gaze shot back to Rikker, her heart sinking at the look of smug satisfaction on his face. "There's no out, Sophie. Come to me."

Desperation hammering through her, Sophie began to inch toward Rikker, her mind whirling with options. She had to get her hands on her jewels. But once she did, then what? She'd never used them as weapons. How would they work? She'd always thought she'd have time to figure it out, but the time was now.

She reached Rikker, stopping just in front of him. "Let her go."

Without a word, Rikker shoved Maria at the demon next to him. That demon yanked her against his chest and lodged his knife against her neck, taking up the same position that Rikker had had her in. Sophie caught the scent of lust from him, and hope sprang to her heart. If the demon was unable to resist Maria's allure and had sex with her, Maria would recover...

But as she looked at the demon's twisted face, and the pure, merciless hate in his eyes, her heart sank. Was that really what their life was like? That the best option was for Maria to give herself to an odious creature? Was this really what they both considered satisfactory?

"Sophie. Look at me."

She jerked her gaze back to Rikker, her fingers burning with the need to grab her jewels.

Unlike most demons, Rikker was handsome, with sculpted cheekbones and short dark hair. His horns were invisible now, hidden at his command to look more human. He often did that around her, as if he were trying to make her forget what he was. "If you dissolve," he said softly. "My demon will cut her."

Sophie glanced at Maria, whose eyes were closed now. She saw bruises on her friend's shoulders, and she realized suddenly that Maria had tried to fight all of them while she'd been in the cave, draining herself of her last reserves. "Don't let him touch you," Maria whispered. "I don't care if I die. You matter more."

Rikker's eyes darkened. "She will suffer," he snapped. "You know she will." Then, without another word, he reached up and grabbed Sophie around the back of the neck.

Sophie yelped in fear, but she didn't dissolve. Not one bit.

Surprise flickered across Rikker's face, then he tightened his grip on the back of her neck. "What the hell?"

The other demons shifted, and she smelled the sudden influx of lust.

Fear hammered in Sophie's chest, but she met Rikker's gaze. She couldn't believe she wasn't dissolving. She didn't have time to fear it. The time was up. Her body was about to belong to a demon if she didn't do something.

He grinned, his thin lips stretching across his glistening white teeth. "Fuck Lucien," he said with a low growl, then he yanked her against him and slammed his mouth down on hers.

The moment his mouth touched hers, Sophie shoved her hand into her pocket, grabbed a ruby, and then slammed it against his chest. It dissolved through his skin, and he shouted, jerking back. But as she released the stone, it reformed inside him, right in the middle of his heart.

Rikker staggered, clutching his heart, trying to dig it out of his body, but she knew it was in too far. She'd melted it to all his cells. It wouldn't kill him, but it would take him time to recover. She stumbled back, horrified by what she'd done, but before she could even register it, she was surrounded by the howl of predators. She whirled around as Rikker's demons broke rank and attacked, nothing holding them back from what they'd craved for so long—

The nearest one grabbed her, and she felt his claws sink into her breast. "Get away from me!" she shouted as she shoved an emerald into his chest. She hadn't even merged it with his body when another demon grabbed her shoulder, yanking her backward. She landed on the ground, then dove to the side when he went for her.

They came at her from all sides, and she started throwing the jewels, hurling them as fast as she could, knowing that she was going to lose. She didn't even know where Maria was, or whether she was surviving. A demon grabbed her and hurled her against a rock. She gasped, groaning as her head hit. She rolled onto her side, trying to pull herself to her feet when she saw the band on her ring finger. It was black and purple now, burning her hand. *Vlad.* "Vlad!" She screamed his name, desperation tearing it from her. "*Vlad!*"

As the demon grabbed her arms and locked them behind her back, she knew it was too late.

VLAD WHIRLED AROUND when he heard Sophie shout his name. "Did you hear that?"

Gabe stopped in front of him, both men going still. "Yeah, I did. Where's it coming from?"

She screamed his name again, and Vlad felt the ring burning on his finger. He reached out with his senses, but couldn't pick up any life force. Swearing, he went deeper, calling upon his new skills. He opened his mind to Sophie, to the essence of her soul.

Instantly, he found her. "This way!" He broke into a sprint, racing down the tunnel. It was still too dark to see where he was going, but he kept hurtling energy outward, letting it rebound off the walls like a radar.

Pain shot through him, and he knew it was her pain. Jesus. His ring was burning so badly he felt like acid was being poured over his flesh. "Sophie!" He bellowed her name, sprinting through the tunnels, turning unerringly at each fork, his need for her growing stronger and stronger.

And then, he was there. Up ahead he sensed a weakness in the rock, a hairline crack like the one that he'd gotten through before. "Gabe!"

"On it." Gabe tore past him, connecting with Vlad's mind to see where the crack was. He attacked ruthlessly, his weapons tearing through the rock with pinpoint accuracy. The rock exploded, and both men leapt through, emerging into the midst of a full-on battle.

There were demons everywhere, and the stench of sulfur was almost overwhelming. Maria was on the ground, inert, being dragged toward a crevice by two demons. *Over there!* He pointed out the location to Gabe, who bolted after Maria instantly.

But where was Sophie? Vlad spun around, searching the melee, until he saw a cluster of demons on the far side of the pit, bent over something. Rage tore through him, and he pointed both hands toward them. He unleashed more energy than he'd ever accessed before, ripping the demons aside and hurtling them against the walls of the crevasse. Sophie immediately rolled onto her knees, trying to stand. Her shirt was torn, revealing a massive bruise on her shoulder, and she stumbled

Swearing, Vlad raced across the clearing toward her, catching her just as she fell again. He'd barely gotten his arms around her when the demons attacked again. With a roar of fury, he swept them aside. He kept his attention on them this time, pinning them to the rocks around them, holding them there as they fought to break the grip of his energy. Some of them were motionless, victims of Sophie, he suspected, but the others were raging and furious, howling like predators in a feeding frenzy.

They were fighting against his hold, incredibly strong. He knew that without the blood bond with Gabe, he wouldn't be able to hold them at all, but even with his added strength, he wouldn't be able to hold them for long. "Gabe?"

Gabe picked up Maria, cradling her inert body in his arms. *She's ice cold. She needs help.*

Vlad kept his focus on the screaming demons, still holding Sophie, who was on her feet now, leaning against him as she dug into the leather straps crisscrossing her body. *I'm not going to have sex with Maria. That's your job. Take her somewhere safe to heal her. We'll buy you time, and then catch up.*

Got it. Gabe swung Maria over his shoulder, raced over to the wall of the precipice, and began to climb straight up, moving swiftly as his fingers and toes found handholds that didn't exist. Within minutes, he was gone, but Vlad could feel his presence moving swiftly to the south. Son of a bitch. He knew exactly where they were. That was weird as hell. *Let me know if you need help.*

Will do. Now get the hell out of there. More are coming. I

can see them on the horizon.

Shit. Vlad thrust another burst of energy at the demons pinned to the walls. "Sophie, we gotta go. Fast. More are coming."

She looked over at him. "Lucien," she whispered. "Oh, God." She looked frantically around. "There's nowhere to hide."

"We go back through the tunnel. Can you seal it?"

She looked over at the rock, and nodded. "Yes."

"Then let's do it." He grabbed her arm, still focusing his energy on the demons he'd pinned to the wall as they turned and sprinted toward the opening. Sophie paused on the threshold. "Wait."

She pulled her hand out of her pocket, her fingers clenched around a small, rough rock. She narrowed her eyes, then hurled it at one of the nearest demons. It hit him in the throat, then seemed to disappear. The demon immediately started gagging.

"Did you just merge the rock with his cells?"

"Yes. It won't hold for long, but it will give us a few minutes." She threw another, and another, until every demon he'd pinned up was gasping in agony. There was only one left, a massive demon at the far end of the clearing. His hand was on his chest as if she'd already attacked once, but he was watching Sophie with brutal intensity.

"Rikker." He didn't need to ask. Vlad knew ownership when he saw it, and that demon had claimed Sophie for his own. Shit. He was a formidable opponent. "Hit him again."

Sophie threw two more rocks at him, but this time, they both bounced off him. She paled. "He's figured out how to block them."

"Then it's time to go." Vlad stepped back into the tunnel, pulling Sophie with him. "Seal it up."

She immediately placed her palms on the rock that Gabe had blown out. She dissolved it quickly, and rebuilt the wall, turning the rock from floating particles into solid form almost instantly. The moment she sealed them off, Vlad lost contact with the demons, severing his grip on their minds. "Let's go."

He grabbed her hand and started to run, using his radar-like skill to guide them.

Deeper and deeper they went underground, running as fast as they could through the rank, dark tunnel. Sophie never complained, but after she tripped twice, he picked her up. She didn't even argue. She just wrapped herself around him, and held tight, allowing him the freedom to run even faster. As he ran, he pinged his radar in all directions, rapidly amassing a map of the tunnel system. It was entirely uninhabited, but he found several entrances.

"Go deeper," Sophie told him. "The demons don't like to go into the graveyard. We'll have time to regroup there." Her voice was taut with pain, and he remembered the bruise on her shoulder.

"You got it." He chose the path he wanted, and hauled ass, his quads burning as he ran. He kept one arm locked around Sophie's back, holding her against him as he traversed the rocky ground. He kept searching ahead, and finally found what he wanted. An untraveled section of the trails that held no trace of past inhabitants, a place that no one had found in many, many years.

He made several turns, then slowed as a sudden roaring filled the tunnel. Sophie twisted around in his arms, peering into the darkness as he rounded the corner to reveal a massive waterfall cascading down the side of the tunnel. It appeared to be rolling down solid rock, but behind the roaring falls, he knew there was an opening in the rocks that led to another cavern.

"You trust me?" he shouted to Sophie over the roar of the water.

"Yes!" she yelled back.

"Then hang on!" He raced forward into the water, plunging deep beneath the water. Sophie gripped him tightly as he swam, hauling ass through the water to the crack he'd sensed deep beneath the surface. He reached the edge, found several rocks protruding, guarding the opening. He immediately swam through, keeping Sophie tight against his chest.

His lungs burning, he kicked them to the surface, their

heads burst out of the water just as his lungs felt like they were going to explode. Sophie gasped, gripping tightly to him as they cleared the water.

The cave was dark, but not impenetrable darkness. Littered across the ground were a number of glowing yellow stones that cast a filtered light across the smooth walls of the cave. Vlad kicked over to the edge of the water, and hoisted Sophie onto the ledge. She dragged herself onto it and rolled onto her side, her lungs heaving as he hauled himself up beside her.

He stayed on his hands and knees for a moment, casting his senses about to double check they were indeed alone, but the place was pristine. No living matter had been there. Ever. They were safe, for the moment.

He turned his head toward Sophie. "You okay?"

She had her arm over her face, and appeared to be having difficulty breathing. "I think I have a problem," she said, her voice strained.

Tension ripped through him, and he crawled over the stones to her. "What's wrong?"

She pulled her arm down to look at him. Her face was pale, and there were dark circles beneath her eyes. "One of the demons clawed me," she said. "I think it poisoned me." She pointed to her shoulder. "It hurts," she whispered. "It really hurts, Vlad."

Swearing under his breath, Vlad grabbed her torn shirt and pulled it down over her shoulder. The bruise he'd noticed before was twice as big as it had been, and the skin was mottled with black and blue bruises, much like what his ring looked like. "Roll over," he said softly.

He helped her roll onto her side, and then he pulled the torn fabric aside. He swore when he saw the torn, ragged skin, already decaying. "Shit."

She rested her head on the ground, not moving. "It's bad, isn't it?"

"Yeah. How do you heal from demon poison?"

"Maria's the only one who has the skill. She can do it."

Gabe. Where the hell are you?

I don't know. Maria's directing me. We're still on the run. We need to get to a safe place. She's in trouble, mate. I don't like it.

Sophie's been poisoned. She needs Maria's help.

There was a moment of silence while Gabe apparently conferred with Maria. *She said you need to purge her blood of the poison and take it into you.*

How the hell do I do that?

There was another moment of silence, which grew too long. Swearing, Vlad crouched beside Sophie. "You still with me?"

She nodded, rolling onto her back to face him. Her eyes were still bright as she looked at him. "Thanks for coming after us."

He shrugged. "Always."

Gabe finally reconnected. *Here's the plan. I'm going to blood bond with Maria. Shit. Did I just say that? Jesus. But yeah, I'm going to do that, then I'm going to hold a bridge between the two of you. She'll help you heal Sophie. She thinks that because of your bond with Sophie, you will be able to heal her, but you gotta get her to trust you. We'll touch base when we get to a safe place. Keep her alive. But you gotta promise me something.*

You name it.

If this blood bond with Maria goes wrong, and I lose my shit, you have to get Dante out of here. He has to be reclaimed from the demon realm. Give me your oath that you'll do it.

Vlad looked down at Sophie, who was still struggling to breathe. *Yeah, whatever it takes.*

He felt Gabe's intense relief. *Stay tuned. I'll be in contact as soon as I can. Maria says she'll cut out your throat and your intestines if you let Sophie die before she can help her. I believe her, so you'd better do it. Man, these women are a pain in the ass— Ow. She just hit me. What the hell? How did she hear that?* Gabe cut the communication as his attention shifted to Maria, leaving Vlad to deal with Sophie.

"Sophie." He leaned over her.

"What?"

He explained the plan, and she nodded. "Okay," she said. "You think that will work?"

"It has to." He realized she was starting to tremble. "You're cold."

She nodded. "Just a little. I'm okay."

"No, you're not." He stretched out beside her and wrapped his arms around her, pulling her into the curve of his body. "You have to preserve your strength. I don't know how long they'll take."

Without hesitation, she burrowed against him, tucking herself into the shield of his body. "Thanks for your help to-day," she said softly. "I thought I could manage it alone. I'm not used to needing anyone's help, especially not a man's."

Guilt bit at him. "Yeah, my fault, but you're damned im-pressive." He wanted to kiss her hair, but he didn't dare. How could he cross boundaries with her physically like that? "I'm guessing that you don't go incorporeal with the demons any-more." Shit, that truth hurt. "That's my fault. I can't even tell you how sorry I am that I stripped that from you."

She lifted her head to look at him. "It's not your fault. It was starting to happen anyway."

"You don't know what might have happened. I taught you to trust me." He grabbed her hand and held it up for them both to see it caught in his grasp. "I taught you to do this, and now you can't undo it. I'm sorry, more than I can ever express."

She sighed and snuggled more deeply against him, her body still trembling. "I think," she said softly, "that you were right. The reason I have always turned incorporeal is because I was afraid. I lived my whole life in fear, and when I was with you earlier. I wasn't afraid." She pressed her face to his throat, and he could feel the warmth of her breath against his skin. "When the demons found us, my first instinct was to fight. I felt, for the first time in my life, like I could defend myself. You taught me how to not be afraid, and that's why I didn't dissolve, because I didn't feel like a victim anymore."

He pulled back to look at her face. "Really?"

She grinned at him, and he saw sparkle in her eyes that hadn't been there before. "My whole life, it's Maria who has been the strong one. She's the fighter, and she's the healer. My only job was to direct women to her and to make sure she didn't drain herself. But today, in that battle, I felt strong. I felt like I didn't want to run away." Her smile widened. "It felt good to not be afraid, Vlad, and I owe you for that."

He grinned at her. "Being afraid sucks."

She nodded. "I know. I didn't even realize I was, until I felt the difference today." She grinned and settled more deeply against him. "Of course, apparently, I need to do a little work on becoming as badass as I thought I was. We were in trouble, Vlad. If you hadn't come..." She shuddered against him. "It was bad. I think being afraid was the safer choice."

He pulled her more tightly into his arms, trying to infuse his warmth into her. "Nah. I had your back. Standing up for yourself is always better." He held up his hand, and she put hers in his, lacing their fingers together. "But can I ask you a favor?"

She closed her eyes, her body becoming heavier. "Sure."

"Don't ever take off on me again like that. I was scared shitless when I realized you were in trouble and I couldn't get to you."

She was silent for a minute. "I don't think I can promise that, Vlad. I mean, I'm sorry I left but at the same time, my duty is to those women. If they conflict..." She shrugged. "I have to do what I do."

He gritted his teeth, frustrated by her response, by her refusal to understand that he was on her side. Yeah, he got it, she'd been going solo her whole life, but at the same time, he'd been born to protect her, and he needed to make it right. He could tell her again that he wouldn't let her down, but he knew it wouldn't matter.

He had to prove it.

But how?

"Vlad?" Her voice was a low murmur, so quiet he had to bend to hear her.

"Yeah?"

"If I die, will you save the women and Maria for me?"

He tightened his grip on her as his blood went cold. "You

won't die," he said vehemently. "I swear it."

Her eyes fluttered open, and he saw they were bloodshot "I've been infected with demon poison, straight into my blood stream," she said. "I'm not as immortal as you are. I don't have much time." Her finger drifted to his cheek. "But thank you for showing me what it's like to be touched. I'll never forget it."

Then her eyes closed and her head slumped against his shoulder.

He swore vehemently, and reached out to Gabe. *She's dying, Gabe. What the hell's keeping you? She needs help right now.*

Chapter Twenty-One

GABE WOULD HAVE staked his life on the belief that he'd never care enough about a female to take it personally if she died, but he would have been dead wrong. Dead *fucking* wrong. Maria was dying, and his entire soul howled in fury at that possibility. She was too courageous and too vulnerable to die this way.

Urgency pounded through him as he raced along the rocky ledge, following Maria's whispered instructions. Below him was the desolate carnage of the Graveyard of the Damned, and to his left was the distant sight of the demon kingdom. A tall, black castle rose high above the scorched earth, and hundreds of small villas were nestled in the crevices of the rocks. It was stark and barren, with no vegetation, no warmth, and nothing but black, burned out rocks.

He'd never been a scenic guy, but the sight of the demon kingdom made him hope to all hell that he was going to make it back to the earth realm. "We need to find a spot fast," he said, Vlad's urgency galvanizing him. "Sophie's in trouble."

"To your right," Maria whispered, slumping weakly against his chest. "There's an opening to a cave. It's the best we can do right now."

Gabe immediately scanned the rocky mountain on his right, using his preternatural senses to search for the opening. He found it halfway up the side of the mountain, hidden between two giant rocks. He leapt effortlessly up the rocky shale, keeping Maria tight against his chest as he ran.

Before sliding into the cavern, he took one last scan of their surroundings. Nothing had tracked them. They were safe for the moment. He ducked inside, his shoulders barely squeezing through the narrow opening. Inside was dark and damp, and he saw a few blankets folded neatly in the corner. The cave smelled like Maria, and it was clear that this was a place she often went.

Anger pulsed through him. "Is this where you take your men?"

"No. It's where I hide when I can't take it anymore. Sometimes, I just need a break. Even Sophie doesn't know about this place." Her breath was rasping now, as if every breath was a strain.

As she spoke, he realized that there were no other scents in the cave. He'd been so caveman about the idea of her with other men that he hadn't even bothered to notice that hers was the only energy present. Satisfaction pulsed through him at her answer. This was her private sanctuary, and yet she'd let him in. "I won't betray you," he said as he strode across the cave and grabbed a couple of the blankets. They were thin and ho-ley, and his gut tightened at the thought that sleeping on rock with a couple threadbare blankets was her oasis. He thought of Dante's luxurious mansion, and what it would be like to take her there, to give her the luxury she'd never had.

He immediately scowled as he spread out the blankets with one hand, his other arm keeping her locked against his chest. Since when did he give a shit about luxury, or taking care of a woman?

He didn't.

This wasn't about her. It was about his mission, and he had to remember that.

He knelt on the blanket and eased her to the hard ground. She kept her arms tight around his neck. "Don't let go of me," she gasped.

"I've got you." He stretched out beside her, dragged her in-to the shield of his body, and then kissed her, without any of the hesitation of before. He knew what he had to do, and in truth, it felt right.

She melted into him just as before, and his entire body seemed to vibrate in response. Her lips were cold and her kiss was weak, and he swore under his breath. *Come on, Maria. You can do this.*

He felt a rush of surprise from her. *I heard that in my head.*

For a split second, he froze. The only way she could have heard his thoughts was if she was his soulmate. His *sheva*. His fate. Fuck. But even as he recoiled, a part of him wasn't surprised. It was the only explanation for his response to her. He'd accepted it already, and this was merely confirmation. Better to know what he was facing than to deny it. His teammates had found a way not to succumb to the *sheva* destiny, so he'd have to find a way as well. It was too damn bad he hadn't paid much attention to it at the time.

Yeah, he had the runes on his arms to protect him from his *sheva,* but clearly, there were limits to what they could shield. How vulnerable was he? He didn't know.

Gabe? Her voice was weaker now, and her skin even colder.

Swearing, he rolled on top of her, keeping his weight from crushing her as he slid his fingers through her hair and kissed her the way he'd wanted to since the first moment he'd seen her stride into the cave in defense of her brother. Lust poured through him, and he embraced it. The kiss turned carnal within seconds, and she locked her arms around his neck, kissing him back just as fiercely. His body was hot and hard, primed for the woman beneath him. Every instinct inside him was screaming at him to claim her, to make her his, to leave his imprint on her body and her soul.

Her tongue met his with equal fire, and he deepened the kiss, consuming her with the fires raging within him, the fires he'd kept crushed mercilessly for so long. Everything about kissing her felt right and natural, as if he'd been born to do it, and he knew he was.

He grabbed her bodice and tore it down the front, freeing

her breasts in one move. She gasped, shifting beneath him as he cupped her breast, never letting up on his relentless assault on her mouth. She tasted incredible, like the nectar he'd been craving his entire life.

"I need to feel your skin against mine," she whispered between his kisses. "Please."

He broke the kiss just long enough to rip off his shirt, and then he was back on top of her, his senses reeling at the sensation of skin against skin. Her breasts were perfection, fitting his palm as if they were made for him, her nipples taut and pert between his thumb and forefinger.

He knew he had to go all the way this time. There was no holding back. He could not allow her to die, and the fate of Sophie and Dante were also inextricably tied up in his ability to save Maria. He'd made too many promises and taken too many oaths for there to be any choices left except to do what he had to do.

So, he didn't fight it. He just opened himself to the moment, pouring thousand-year old instincts into every kiss, every touch, every caress. He knew she'd been used and abused, and he wanted to show her something else. Regardless of what else happened, she was his mate, the woman destined for him, and he would never allow her to feel anything but treasured.

That was his job. That was her right.

So, even though his cock was rock hard and straining against his jeans, he ignored it. Instead, he swept his palm across her ribs and belly in a seductive caress meant to tantalize her.

Maria's belly quivered in response, and her fingers dug into his shoulders. *I can't believe how good that feels to be touched like this. It's...it makes me feel alive, like this moment is real, instead of some frenzied blur of feeding that sex always is.*

It is real. He bent his head and took her breast into his mouth, swirling his tongue over the hard nipple. *You do matter. You're not feeding on me. I'm strengthening you. There's a fundamental difference.*

God, that sounds good. She made a small noise of desire in her throat, her head going back as she arched into his kiss. *More, Gabe. Please. Make love to me.* She laughed as she said it, her laughter echoing through his mind. *I can't believe I just said that. I've never had to ask before. It feels good to have to ask.*

I'll never take you without your permission. Gabe shifted his position just enough to get his pants and boots off. He tried to undo the zipper on her pants, but the leather was too slick and his fingers not delicate enough. *Sorry, sweetheart.*

She giggled again, sounding more like a woman than the embittered, hardened warrior he'd first met. *It's okay. I have more clothes here.*

Sweet. He gripped the leather and ripped it, quickly sliding it over her legs and off her body, along with the sexiest bit of black lace he'd ever seen in his life. *I really want to leave that on you, but we're kind of in a rush. Next time.*

Because there would be a next time. He knew it in his gut. This time was about his mission, but next time, it was going to be because he wanted it. Not it. *Her.*

Trust me, this is leisurely compared to what I'm used to. She clasped his jaw, and he looked at her. Her eyes were burning with emotion. *You don't understand what it's like that you're still in your own mind right now. All the men who'd ever served me have been insane with lust by now. I don't exist for them. It's just a body for them to fuck.*

Anger rolled through him at the words. *I know it's you. I see the blue of your eyes, the curve of your mouth, the mole on your collarbone.* He ran his fingers through her hair, searching her face. *I feel the softness of your hair over my skin.* Her face softened, and he grinned. He knew they were in a rush, but at the same time, he needed to do this for her, to let her know that she mattered. *I know that I'm with a woman who is loyal, honorable, tough, and vulnerable, all at the same time.*

He cupped her face. *I see you, Maria.* She smiled, and something inside him softened. He wanted to say more, but he didn't know what it was he wanted to say, and he knew he had no time anyway. So, instead, he slipped his fingers behind the back of her neck and kissed her again, taking possession of her mouth as he moved over her. Maria's arms locked around his neck, and she pulled him closer, kissing him back as frantically as he was kissing her. *Now, Gabe. Make love to me now.*

He slipped his thigh between hers, moving her legs apart as he settled between them. Desire and lust roared through him as he kissed her, his cock rock hard with a lifetime of suppressed lust surging through him.

Maria locked her legs around his hips, her arms tight around his neck as she kissed him. He paused, his cock poised at her entrance. It was his last chance to say no, to reclaim the iron-willed control that had served him so well. If he made love to her now, he knew that his soul would never entirely belong to himself and the Order again, no matter how hard he tried. If he made love to her, a part of his soul would always belong to her.

He understood suddenly, why his team members had bonded with their women. In this moment, with Maria in his arms, she was his entire focus. Tension gripped him, a need to refocus on the Order, but he couldn't make himself do it. Right now, in this moment, with her on the edge of death, *she* was what mattered. He had to continue. *He had to.*

She broke the kiss suddenly, pulling back to look at him. "You don't have to do this," she said. "I know the cost. We can find another way."

It was that offer, that pure, genuine willingness to sacrifice on his behalf that erased the last bit of his hesitation. The woman in his arms was a warrior, a selfless, courageous warrior who lived her life for others. There was no other woman worthy of him, and no other man worthy of her. He'd always lived with honor, and he knew damn well he was one of the good guys. He would honor her the way she deserved, and he knew that she would do the same for him, and for all those who were counting on her. "I want to," he said simply, and then he drove into her, sheathing himself inside the woman who was meant for him.

Chapter Twenty-Two

THE MOMENT SHE felt Gabe inside her, Maria knew that everything had changed for her. She'd never be able to live the life she'd led for so long. Her whole body seemed to cry out for him, and she had to bite back tears as he held her in his arms and kissed her, sensual, beautiful kisses that ignited not just her body, but her soul.

His lovemaking was fierce, his hips driving into her with enough passion and force to tear apart the veil of death trying to take her. She could feel power surging into her, cleansing the poison from her body and igniting a fire within her. He was giving her everything she needed, but at the same time, it was completely different than anything she'd ever experienced before.

The way his lips caressed hers, the way his hand was on her hip, supporting her, holding her, the way he'd let her into his mind, allowing her to feel his need for her, it made her feel like a woman. For the first time, she understood why some of the women wanted to stay with their demon lovers. In Gabe's arms, she felt safe and protected, even treasured, for the first time in her life.

"Hey," he whispered against her mouth, breaking the kiss while his hips stilled, leaving himself sheathed deep inside her, but no longer moving.

No man had ever stopped in the middle. *Ever.*

"Maria." He caught her chin, lifting her face.

She opened her eyes to look at him, her heart constricting when she saw the tenderness in his eyes.

"You're crying." He rubbed his thumb over her cheeks, wiping away the tears she hadn't realized had escaped. "What's wrong? Am I hurting you? Do you want me to stop?" He started to pull out, and she panicked.

"No, don't."

He stopped, sliding back deeper inside her, moving gently, not hammering at her. "What's going on?" His voice was soft, more tender than she would ever have expected from a hardened, committed warrior like him.

She shook her head. "It's okay. Let's keep going."

He laughed softly, and kissed her forehead. "Let's keep going? Really? You're my soulmate, sweetheart. You've been misused by men your whole life. There's no chance in hell that we're going any further while you've got tears on your cheeks." He searched her face. "I know this isn't your choice, and I'm sorry that you have to do this, but I want to make it right for you. What can I do?"

His question was so genuine that she couldn't stop the fresh surge of tears. "No," she managed, lacing her hands behind his neck. "It's not that. It's...it's just that you make this beautiful. It's never been beautiful before. I didn't realize how awful it was, until this moment, until you made me feel like I mattered, like you saw me as a woman, like you were here, only because it was me."

His face softened. "It *is* only about you, sweetheart. I'm not going to lie about how much I want you. I find you sexy as all hell, but that would never be enough to control me. Being with you is my choice."

"I know." She framed his face with her palms. "I realize that the only reason you're doing this is to save Dante, but—"

"No." He cut her off, his face darkening. "Don't ever think that. Don't ever think that I'm using you for your body."

She searched his face, trying to understand. "But—"

"Listen to me, sweetheart." He kissed the palm of her hand

and then pressed it to his face again. "I've been around for over a thousand years. I have gone to hell and back for my mission, and I have *never* made the choice of bringing a woman into my plans. I'm an amazing warrior, and I don't make bad choices." His voice grew deeper. "If having you alive was my only goal, I would have dragged one of those demons with us and set him up as your sex slave until you were better. I would have sat in the doorway of this cavern with my weapons, guarding the entrance while you fucked him, right?"

She stared at him. "That would have worked."

"Yeah, it would've, but I never even considered it." He shook his head. "Someone has to have sex with you, and there's no way I want it to be anyone but me. Ever. End of story."

Ever. The word hit hard and deep, making her want to cry again. The thought of never, *ever* having to prostitute herself to a scumbag again was almost overwhelming, a concept she could barely even grasp. It was a fantasy she'd never even entertained, and the mere thought of it as a possibility was overwhelming. She couldn't hope for that, or she would never be able to do what she had to do. She pushed at his shoulder, trying to get him off her, but he was immovable. "Why? Why are you saying this to me? Is it some kind of Calydon he-man thing? I don't want to be owned, and I'm not a trophy—"

"No. You're not." He withdrew slightly and then slid deeper inside her, a small movement that made desire rush through her again. "Here's the deal, sweetheart. You're my soulmate, and when we finish making love, there's going to be a mark on your arm that matches the brand on my arm. It marks you as mine, but—" He kissed away her protest, breaking the kiss only when she stopped trying to talk. "Listen to me. I don't want or need some concubine to make love to and come home to. I will never walk away from my duty, and I need a woman who's my partner, one who makes me stronger, one who I make stronger. I admire you because you're a warrior, you have honor, and you and I will make the best damn team the earth has ever seen."

She stared at him through her tears. "You want a partner?"

"An equal. I'm a team guy, Maria. I don't like to go solo. Hell, I even blood bonded Vlad on this mission. That's how desperate I am, though, I have to admit, he's pretty impressive. But that's the thing. I need you as my backup, and I'll be yours." He started moving inside her again, a slow, tantalizing sensation that began to coil through her. "But I'll be honest, being inside you makes me feel like the world has shifted on its axis. I need you as my partner, but I want to be your lover, the man who makes you feel like the most treasured woman on the entire planet." He swore under his breath. "I can't believe I'm saying this to a woman, but it is what it is. There's no point in fighting it, so we need to work it to our benefit."

She bit her lip, trying to hold her emotions in. "I don't even know you. You're a stranger—"

"Am I?" He opened his mind to her, and she was suddenly bombarded with a thousand years of emotions, battles, sacrifices, and losses. Everything he'd experienced, everything he'd failed at, every victory he'd bled for, all laid out for her to experience. She saw his courage, his honor, his bravery, his single-minded focus toward his job, his absolute refusal to accommodate any female in his life, and his absolute unrelenting commitment to his mission, the Order and Dante. He was a true warrior, a man of honor and faith, a man who lived by the same code that she'd tried so hard to adhere to, even in her world of lust, debauchery, and mercilessness, where she tried so hard to stay above the darkness.

He met her gaze, and then she felt something else. His soul, reaching for her, enfolding her in his strength and kindness, like a shield of compassion that would never, ever fail. She felt like he was holding her very soul in his hands, cradling it against his chest as if she were the most precious being in the world.

This time, there was no stopping the tears. "I can't be your teammate," she said. "I have to save these women—"

"We do it together." He kissed her then, a deep, relentless, passionate kiss that stripped her of all that remained of her protections. She didn't want to believe in him. She didn't want to count on him. She knew his devotion to the Order and to

Dante, and she knew that despite his words, her own mission, her women, would have to come second. As long as he could fit it all in, he would stay true to his word, but if he had to choose, she knew what he would choose.

She would be second on his list, a high second, a treasured second, but second nonetheless.

Trust me, Maria. I could never hurt you. His voice drifted through her mind like a soft caress. *I'm a really good warrior. I can do it all. We will do it all. The impossible choice will never have to be made.*

She gasped as he continued to move inside her. *And what if we have to face it? What then?*

He was silent for a moment, and his hips stilled. He looked down at her, and she saw the anguish on his face, the truth he didn't want to face. "I can't fail my team," he said softly.

She nodded, understanding. "I can't fail my women."

They stared at each other for a long moment. The torment on his face touched her heart, and she felt the depth of his struggle to accept that he might have to make a choice. She knew how much his Order of the Blade meant to him, and the mere fact that he could even consider the possibility of putting her first was enough. She mattered, and she understood the place she occupied, because he could never be higher on her list either. "As long as we're honest," she said softly. "Just never lie to me. Never make promises you can't keep. As long as you do that, I can trust you." Her fingers tightened behind his head. "I need to trust you," she whispered, realizing she did. He made her realize how empty she'd had to make her heart in order to survive the life she was bound to. Being able to count on a man was a luxury that she'd never thought she'd have.

He nodded. "I'll never lie to you," he said, his voice raw with honesty. "And you?"

"I promise."

"And you know what else I promise?" He began to move inside her again, and this time, she didn't resist. She just opened herself to him, and all he had to offer.

"What else do you promise?"

He kissed her, deeply, passionately, and tenderly. *I promise you'll never have to be with anyone except me again. No more demons. Just me.* There was a slight hesitation. *Please tell me that's okay with you.*

She almost laughed at the strain in his voice. *Yes, Gabe, that is more than okay with me if you make it so I don't have to endure sex with anyone else.*

Endure? Is that how you see this? He moved deeper, and faster, making desire rush through her.

With you, never. It's...magic. There was no other word to describe what it felt like to be with him. He might be the one who'd never had sex before, but she was the one who felt like he was showing her a world she'd never known before.

Magic. I like that. He caught her mouth in a kiss that seemed to knock *her* world off *its* axis. The kiss wasn't about sex. It reached inside her and touched her as a woman. It awakened the human part of her, the side of her that felt fear, hope, sadness, and joy, the part of her that she worked so hard not to acknowledge, because feeling emotions made it impossible to endure the life she had. She didn't want to feel, but at the same time, responding emotionally to Gabe made the world seem brighter and more vibrant. It made her feel treasured, and powerful, as if she'd just begun to tap into a second source of power that she'd never acknowledged.

Was it really possible that aligning herself with Gabe and caring about him could make her stronger? She'd worked so hard to be solo, trusting only Sophie, but now, everything was different.

You're thinking too much, sweetheart. Gabe cupped her breast as he moved his hips, driving deeper inside her. *I'm not doing my job if you can be over-analyzing while I'm making love to you.*

She smiled, gasping at the surge of desire he evoked inside her. *I always do that. Staying distant from my body is the only way to survive sex.*

It's not like that anymore. I want you to be here with me. He kissed her again, more deeply, pouring heat into her. His tongue swept across hers, a magical seduction that sent waves of desire rushing through her.

She fought against the tidal wave of need, struggling to stay in control, but with each kiss, and each delicious move of his hips, the need for him escalated, and her ability to hold it off faltered. She realized she didn't want to stay in control anymore. She wanted to lose herself to Gabe and his lovemaking. Surrender sounded like a gift she'd never had before.

That's my girl. He nibbled her earlobe, a ridiculous gesture that made chills explode through her body. She let out a small cry, gripping his shoulders, unable to contain herself.

She felt his smile. *You like that, do you?* He kissed her ear, sliding his teeth over the edge of it, still gliding in and out of her with increasing force.

It feels amazing. She twisted beneath him, her body begging for more. *I don't understand. How can it feel so good?* She let out another yelp as he thumbed her nipple. Her senses were fragmenting as he came at her from so many angles. Another nip on her earlobe, her nipple, his cock deep, and his need pouring into her, a sensual, heated need that evoked an answering need from her.

Suddenly, it was no longer about enduring. She wanted more of him. She wanted everything he could give her. With a low cry of need, she wrapped her arms around his neck, dragging his face to hers. His kiss was exotic and intense, a primal claiming that escalated the tension building within her. He wasn't holding back now, pouring all his strength and need into the lovemaking. She was a lust demon, and she should be the one with the greater need, but his was devouring her, claiming her, branding her with each kiss and each thrust.

She loved the way he loomed over her, the strength of his body as he made love to her, controlling the pace and the depth, until he was so deep inside her that she wanted to scream his name and hold onto him forever.

Tell me you're mine. Say it. I need to hear it. He drove deeper and faster, harder, dragging her into his frenzy.

She could barely breathe now, her entire body screaming for his. *You're mine*, she gasped.

He laughed, and kissed her again, his fingers pinching her nipple. *Okay, I concede. Partners. I'm yours. You're mine. Equal authority.* He reached between them and ran his fingers across the swollen nub between her legs.

She gasped and bucked, but he followed her, ruthlessly making her his, unleashing a spiral of heat and desire beyond anything she knew she was capable of.

Say it, he demanded. *Say you're mine. Say we're partners, in it to the end.*

But my women come first. And your mission comes first. She'd been lied to so many times, she wouldn't do it again, even though she could barely think over the desire rushing through her.

His irritation rushed over her, quickly followed by a surge of admiration. *Shit. You're exactly what I need to keep me in line. Partners, coming in second, but a strong, unassailable second. Deal?*

She grinned, arching back as he upped his assault on her body. *Deal.*

That's my girl. He caught her mouth in a searing, ruthless kiss that was pure male, pure claiming, pure ownership, that exploded through her, sucking the last vestiges of control from her grasp. The orgasm swept through her, yanking her out of her world and thrusting her into his arms. She gasped, clinging to him desperately as her body shook from the sheer force of the orgasm.

Maria. Gabe's stunned gasp filled her with more power, more emotion, more need. Then he bucked against her, his muscles going rigid as the orgasm claimed him. He swore aloud, driving into her harder and harder, sending them both hurtling out of control, until there was nothing left but the sheer force of the orgasm, searing every cell in their bodies, and laying raw, stark claim to their battered souls.

She screamed his name, her fingernails digging into his back as the orgasm thrust her mercilessly over the edge. He pounded into her, somehow protecting her from the sheer weight of his body, shouting her name over and over again, as if his entire world had become only her.

With one last roar of possession that made her scream again, the orgasm finally released her. She free-fell out of its grasp, tumbling into Gabe's powerful arms as he collapsed, half on top of her, half beside her, the bulk of his weight against her side instead of crushing the breath from her lungs.

His arm was wrapped around her waist, his leg locked around hers, his face buried in her hair as he fought for breath. His lungs were heaving, and so were hers. Perspiration cascading between her breasts, her body aching from the force of their lovemaking. "Holy crap," he muttered. "Is it always like that?"

"It's *never* like that." She could still barely breathe, her lungs gasping for oxygen. Her skin felt as if it were on fire, with every nerve ending screaming for more.

"I get it now." He lifted his head, his dark eyes searching out hers. "I understand why the guys get obsessed with their women. I thought they were weak, but that's not it. I'm strong as hell, in every way. It's just that you're more."

Warmth filled her at the stark wonder in his voice, and she couldn't help but smile. "You're the first man to be conscious after lovemaking," she said. "I like it."

His eyes darkened. "I gotta be honest with you. I'm thrilled as shit that I'm ten times the man that any other guy has been, but it triggers something dark inside me whenever you mention being with anyone else. I have demon heritage, and I'm destined to go rogue. I think that's crap, and we're not going there, but *hell*, you have to stop putting images in my head of other men seeing you naked. If you keep doing that, the fact I'm awesome isn't going to mean shit."

She almost laughed at his combination of ridiculous arrogance and total vulnerability. She loved his confidence, but it was also incredibly appealing that he knew his limits. "Okay, it's a deal."

He nodded, but there was still a dangerous glint in his eyes that made her belly tighten. She had to admit, the fact that he could go rogue because she'd been with other men was sort of intoxicating. She was used to dangerous, deadly males, and if he were anything less, she knew that he wouldn't be enough.

The fact he was possessive of her? She liked it. It made her feel like she mattered, and not just because of the sex. The man was sane, for heaven's sake, and they'd just had a love-making session that would be imprinted upon her soul forever. He might be a sensual god, but the man had a brain beyond sex, and she liked that. A lot.

"How's your forearm?"

The moment he asked the question, she felt a strange burning on her skin. She looked down, and her stomach tightened when she saw silver lines appearing on her arm, as if someone were using an invisible marker to draw. She grabbed his arm and held it beside hers. "They match your handle."

He rolled onto his side, his head leaning against hers as he watched. He whistled softly, running his fingers over the marks on her arms. "There's nothing that can prepare a guy for how damn awesome it is to watch his brand appear on his woman's arm. I feel like a megalomaniac cavemen watching that shit. Makes me want to beat my chest, throw you over my shoulder, and parade you in front of my team."

She laughed. "A megalomaniac? Really?"

"Hey, I'm not just a dumb, badass, hot warrior you know. I even know what a dictionary is." He pressed his palm to her arm. "You okay?"

She nodded, surprised that it was the truth. She trusted Gabe. He was an honorable warrior, and she needed him by her side. Having them bound by the *sheva* bond simply ensured his willingness to help her. She had to admit, it felt amazing to have a man on her side, instead of being the enemy. "But my women come first. I need your help with them."

"You got it." He pressed a kiss to her arm. "Ready for the blood bond? We need to help Sophie."

"Oh, God. *Sophie.*" Guilt tore through her. She'd been admiring the brand and languishing in the glow of amazing sex while Sophie had been dying. What was wrong with her? One hot guy liked her and she forgot what mattered? She sat up instantly, dislodging him from her shoulder.

He raised an eyebrow, but made no protest as he sat up as well. "This is going to create a very strong connection between us. I'll be able to track you down no matter where you are, and no matter how hard you to try to hide."

She looked up at him, and her gut tightened. What if he turned out like Lucien, and there was nowhere to hide from him? "Are you trying to scare me?"

"Just want you to know."

Sophie needed her. It was too late to back out now. "Okay, I know." She held out her palm, not wanting to think anymore. She was so far outside her comfort zone, plummeting down a slippery slope. She had no choice but to continue forward. The people she loved were in too much danger, and she couldn't save them alone. "Do it."

For a split second, she thought she saw fear flash across his face, but it was gone almost instantly. Instead, he called out his hook sword with a crack and flash of black light. The weapon appeared in his hand, a dangerous, lethal instrument of death.

Without hesitation, he dragged it across his chest, slicing a deep wound across his body. Then he looked at her, and fear wrapped around her. Her hands started to shake, but she held out her palm to him, lifting her chin. *For Sophie.*

She clenched her jaw in anticipation of the pain as he took her hand in his. God, could she really do this?

Chapter Twenty-Three

SOPHIE HADN'T EVER thought of dying. She'd never really worried about it. Life had been too busy trying to save others to worry about herself. But she knew she was dying now, and it scared her. It wasn't the right time to die. People needed her. "Vlad," she whispered, her voice raw.

"I'm here, sweetheart." He caught her hand in his, and pressed a kiss to her fingers. "Stay with me. Gabe said Maria's better now. They're going to do the blood bond, and then she's going to heal you."

"I'm not going to make it." Pain shot through her stomach, and she doubled over, curled into a ball in Vlad's arms. Her skin felt like it was on fire, and her organs felt as if acid was eating away at them. "Dammit, Vlad. I'm not ready to die."

His grip tightened on her. "Don't give up. It's just a couple minutes."

She couldn't keep her eyes open, sagging against him. "Make me a promise," she whispered, her voice hurting her throat.

"Dammit. You're not going to die—"

"Get all the women out. Make sure Maria gets out, too. The demons are killing them." Another wave of pain hit her. "Promise me."

"No, I'm not promising. You're going to have to take care

of it yourself." His voice was hard and unyielding.

She pried her eyes open. "What? What happened to all your declarations of support?"

"Your problem isn't mine. My job is to rescue you. If you die, I'm out of here."

Betrayal bit deep when she realized he meant it. "You bastard," she hissed, trying to crawl away from him. Dammit, where was Maria? *Maria!* She screamed her name, but of course, there was no response. She didn't have that connection with her.

After all these years, she should have been smart enough not to trust a man.

Damn him.

She was going to have to stay alive long enough to save the women herself, and when she finished with that, she was going to get that damn band off her ring finger and burn it.

GABE WAS IMPRESSED as hell when Maria stoically held out her palm, so he could cut it. "God, woman, you're hot as hell."

She raised her brows. "You're just saying that because your brand has defaced my flawless skin."

"No. It's because you're you."

Vlad's voice hammered into his mind. *What the hell are you doing? Sophie's dying! We need help!*

Maria's eyes widened, apparently able to hear Vlad through their *sheva* connection. "We have to hurry." She slammed her hand down on the edge of the blade, her face contorting in pain as the razor-sharp edge cut through her hand.

Gabe sheathed the blade and grabbed her palm, pressing his mouth to her wound. The moment the coppery taste hit his tongue, raw, untamed lust exploded through him. The need was so intense he almost doubled over. *Sweet Jesus, Maria.*

She didn't hesitate, climbing onto his lap to press her

mouth to the wound on his chest. The moment she took his blood into her body, he felt his entire soul explode with need for her. He grabbed her around the waist, dragged her against him, and captured her mouth with his. The moment he kissed her, he tasted the coppery blood mixing and blending, lighting a fire within him so intense he felt like he was going to explode out of his skin. *Maria.*

Her arms were tight around his neck, and she was kissing him just as fiercely, pouring such need into the kiss that he knew he'd never be the same. Words began to hammer in his mind, words he didn't know, words that were screaming to be acknowledged. He didn't mean to say it, didn't even know where the words came from, but suddenly, they were in his mind, pouring into her with every last bit of his strength. *Mine to you. Yours to me. Bonded by blood, by spirit and by soul, we are one. No distance too far, no enemy too powerful, no sacrifice too great. I will always find you. I will always protect you. No matter what the cost. I am yours as you are mine.* The words reverberated through him with such rightness, he knew it was the truth. He'd give his soul to protect her, no matter what the cost.

His words were still echoing between them, when he felt her reach out to him, offering her vow to him. *Mine to you. Yours to me. Bonded by blood, by spirit and by soul, we are one. No distance too far, no enemy too powerful, no sacrifice too great. I will always find you. I will always keep you safe. No matter what the cost. I am yours as you are mine.*

Yes. His entire being trembled with the magnitude of their bond, and he pulled her up on his lap, sheathing himself inside her in a single swift move. She gasped, welcoming him into her body as she clung to him, still kissing him fiercely.

The orgasm took them both almost instantly, whipping their lovemaking into a frenzy beyond comprehension. His body bucked beneath hers violently, beyond his control as she held onto him, her hips moving as she tried to drag him more deeply inside her. In that moment, Gabe knew they had become a single unit, more powerful, more dangerous, and more vulnerable than either of them could ever be on their own.

This was his woman, his life, his world, and he wanted every last bit of it.

Don't. Maria's breathless protest whipped through his mind. *We can't lose our vision of what's important. I can't be your everything. Don't let that happen. Please.*

It's too late, sweetheart. We're going to have to find a way to work with it. The orgasm hit with a final blow, and he gasped, holding her more tightly as it stripped from them any last sense of who they had once been, before they had become one.

The instant the orgasm released them, they collapsed as a unit, utterly spent. Gabe put his hand on Maria's arm, feeling the heat from the brand as it marked her, even as he reached out to her with his mind. He felt her resistance, and knew she was rebelling against the closeness of their bond. They didn't have time to fight it. *Open your mind to me, sweetheart. You can't hold back if you're going to help Sophie.*

Okay. Her shield dropped instantly, opening herself to him so completely that he felt every emotion she harbored. Fear for her friend, fear of him, self-loathing, pride, courage...the full array of what made her who she was. He caught glimpses of her memories, of times of such torment that he wanted to rip the memories from her mind so she never had to relive them again.

Except they didn't have time for that. They had time for nothing, except Sophie. *Perfect.* He held the bridge with her, and then reached out for Vlad, trying to open the connection between them. *Vlad. You ready?*

There was no reply.

VLAD CRADLED SOPHIE to his chest, his back up against the side of the cavern. He could hear each step of the demons as they crept along the stone beside the water. They were less than ten yards away, separated only by the thick waterfall.

How the hell had they tracked them already?

Sophie was utterly still against him, her heart so slow it was barely beating. Sweat was trickling down his spine, driven by the urgency to connect with Gabe and save her, but the demons were so close.

They would hear everything.

He reached out with psychic energy, testing the air. Eleven demons. Shit. He couldn't fight them all, not with Sophie in his arms. He could feel their lust and their eagerness, and he knew that they'd picked up Sophie's scent. They knew she was nearby. Shit.

He could feel Gabe trying to bridge a mental connection with him, but he kept his teammate shut out, needing full focus on the situation. He heard a small trickle of water, and he knew one of the demons had slipped a foot into the water. *Shit.* All that was between him and the demons was a thin wall of rock and a deep pond.

He took a deep breath and closed his eyes, shifting Sophie in his arms enough to free his right hand. He pointed his index finger toward the nearest demon, using his senses combined with his new, heightened ones, thanks to the Calydon blood bond, to pinpoint its location. He targeted every one of its cells, and then, on a whim, he tried to touch its mind, combining his powers with the psychic energy that Gabe had given him. He immediately became aware of every pulse of energy in the demon's mind...and the demon became aware of him.

Before the demon could react, Vlad flicked his finger, pushing a subtle wave of energy at the demon. It took a step back, and he felt its focus on him blur. He immediately pushed harder, sending his energy out toward the other demons.

He caught them unaware, thrusting them into a state of confusion. He could hear them milling around, trying to refocus, and he kept up the assault, directing their bodies and minds away from the pool. Not wanting to awaken their battle instincts, he kept his assault subtle, trying to urge them away instead of forcing them.

Sophie convulsed in his arms, and he pulled her more tightly, trying to infuse his body heat into her while he pushed the demons away. "Hang on, Sophie." The wait was interminable as he worked the demons, redirecting them. He drew on limitless patience and the focus of battle to drive them away, somehow maintaining his focus despite the rising danger to Sophie.

Finally, they were around the corner. It wasn't as far as he wanted, but he knew he had no time.

He broke his connection with the demons, and opened his mind to Gabe. The Calydon's energy surged over him, bridging a connection with Maria. Her feminine strength was such a contrast to Gabe's, powerful and lethal, but definitely warmer. *Tell me what to do,* he said.

Maria's energy swept through him. *Look at her so I can see.*

He immediately looked down, and his gut clenched. Her skin was almost black, her head lolling back lifelessly, her eyes closed. "Come on, Sophie, we can do this." He sank to his knees as Maria's grief tore through him. *Maria,* he said sharply. *Tell me what to do.*

He felt her pull herself together. *Cut your palm, and then hers. Then hold her hand so your blood mixes.*

He immediately did it, and Sophie didn't even flinch when he cut her hand. He did as instructed. *Now what?*

I don't know if this will work. You have Gabe's blood, but not mine.

Gabe's voice cut in. *Our blood is mingled now. It's the same as if Vlad has your blood. It'll work.*

Tell me what to do, Vlad ordered.

We're going to go into her body and find the tainted cells. We're going to break them up, and then draw them into your body. Then, hopefully, I'll be able to take them out of yours, through your blood bond with Gabe. Let's go.

She took control of their connection, and Vlad suddenly became deeply aware of the way his blood was mingled with Sophie's. Following Maria's lead, he focused his psychic energy on their merged blood cells, and then began following the path of her blood into her body, using each cell as a stepping stone. His mind began to merge with Sophie's energy, and he became aware of a vicious, lethal taint rushing through her, as if a million microdots of death were cascading through her body, killing every cell it touched. Maria guided him forward, and his energy merged with one of the dots, drawing it into his own energy source. He was much stronger than Sophie's depleted body, and it willingly released her and flowed into him, binding to his energy.

He found another, and another, and soon the poison was all flowing toward him, as if the droplets had communicated with each other and decided to prey on the stronger host. He gasped as the poison surged into him, attacking him with such force he could barely hold his focus, attacking him on both a psychic level and through their mixed blood, traveling through his open wound and into his bloodstream.

He swore, nearly doubling over at the pain, but he held his connection, refusing to break it until Sophie was clear.

Vlad. Maria's voice broke through his focus. *You need to let go of Sophie. The poison is too strong for you to handle. It's hitting you harder than it hit her. You're weak from the poison that was in your system earlier. You need to stop.*

Sophie was still limp in his arms, and he could sense the amount of poison still in her body. *No. She's still carrying a lot. I need to clear it.*

You got enough to hold her until I can get there. Break off your connection!

No.

Maria pulled back from Sophie, but Vlad's grip on her was too strong. He didn't need Maria to bridge his connection with Sophie anymore. He understood what Maria had been doing, and he was able to use his own energy to continue it. *Dammit, Vlad! She needs you alive! If you die, she has no one to protect her until I get there!*

If she dies, it doesn't matter if I'm here or not. I'm not walking away. This was it. His moment. Why he'd come. He knew he was the only one who could save her. This was his job.

Can you pull the poison out of Vlad? That was Gabe's voice, consulting Maria.

I'll try, but it's hitting him really hard.

Vlad felt Maria's energy swirl through him, a powerful invasion that swept through him with ruthless force. His instinct was to block her, but he forced himself not to fight her, keeping his focus on Sophie. His psyche was being assaulted in all directions, but he didn't release his focus. He just kept pouring his energy into Sophie, cleansing her body as he went systematically through each part of her body. Her heart. Her lungs. Her mind.

The moment she sucked in her first breath, a shuddering, painful inhale, triumph cascaded through him. "That's my girl."

She stirred in his arms. "Vlad?" Her voice was weak, and it sounded distant, as if the wind was carrying it on the breeze. His body was getting weaker, the poison breaking down his muscles with surreal speed.

He lowered them both to the floor of the cave, no longer able to support her.

"What are you doing?" Her voice sounded even more distant.

He tried to answer, but it seemed to take too much energy to speak. His tongue felt too thick and heavy to move, but he kept his focus on her, drawing out the rest of the poison.

Vlad. Get out of her. Maria's voice was bossy and commanding in his head, even as her energy continued to pound him ruthlessly.

Not yet. Almost there. Almost done. He found the last little bit of poison tucked in behind Sophie's heart, and he dragged it out of her, taking it into his own body. *Done.*

He broke the connection with Sophie, and collapsed beside her on the hard stone, gasping for breath as his lungs began to shut down. He'd pushed it too far. He knew he had. Maria wasn't going to be able to save him.

And he was okay with that.

Sophie was going to survive, and that was what mattered—

But just as he thought it, just as he was letting himself go, he felt another push of demon energy.

They were back.

Swearing, he shoved himself back to his hands and knees. "Sophie," he whispered.

Her eyes flickered open. "Vlad?" Her voice was slurred, and he put his hand over her mouth.

"The demons are here," he whispered into her ear, struggling to stay conscious. He would not leave her. *He would not leave her.* He could feel Maria inside him, still battling the poisons, but he didn't care. He just had to make sure Sophie was safe first.

Her eyes widened, and she turned her head, looking toward the waterfall. She then looked around, searching their cavern.

"What are you looking for?" The room was spinning, and he swayed. He reached out with his psychic energy toward the demons, and this time, he felt their readiness for his attack. Their mental shields were up, and he felt their energy swarm his, trying to track where he was. Swearing, he broke mental contact, keeping his energy focused on their physical being. He pushed at them, holding them back from the edge of the water as they neared it.

He closed his eyes, willing all his energy into the energy shield he was creating. "Find a way out," he said. "Now."

Sophie moved behind him, falling against his side as she tried to sit up. He knew she was as weak as he was, but at least she was on the right side of the poison. "There's a crevice. Come on." She tugged on his arm, but he didn't move.

"I'll hold them off. You go."

"What? No." She pulled harder, but he couldn't muster the energy to rise. "Come on, Vlad."

The poison was encroaching on his heart. He could feel Maria battling with it, but it was too late, too little. "You go."

"Really?" Her voice was next to his ear. "Listen, Vlad, I know that you said you wouldn't help the women because you knew I wouldn't try to stay alive if I was certain you would take care of them. You were right, and you saved my life."

She took a shuddering breath. "Thank God you can be such a convincing ass sometimes."

He managed a half smile. "Smart woman."

She tightened her grip on him. "Here's the thing, Vlad, the demons outside aren't the only ones after me. If I get away from them, Lucien and Rikker are still hunting me. The threat doesn't end until every demon in this kingdom is dead, or I'm in the earth realm. You do realize that, don't you? If you die, I'm on my own."

Vlad swore at her words, realizing that she was right. He could still feel the burning of his ring finger, indicating that she was still in danger. Son of a bitch. *Maria, you better make this work.* With a muffled groan, he rolled onto his side, still keeping the demons pinned back from the pool.

His vision swam in and out of focus, as he let Sophie half-pull him across the floor of the cavern. There was a slim crack in the wall, and as he watched, she placed her hands on it. The rock seemed to disappear, along with her, revealing a narrow tunnel that ran alongside the cavern they'd been hiding in. He didn't hesitate. He knew the drill by now. He just dragged himself through it on his elbows, every muscle in his body screaming in agony. He had just gotten his feet through it when the rock wall reformed, with Sophie standing on his side of the wall, her palms pressed to the rock.

The minute the rock was sealed, he lost contact with the demons. How long until they found their hideaway? How long until they broke through the wall? The moment the wall formed, Sophie stepped over him, and pressed her hands to the rock on the opposite side of the tunnel. Again, the stone disappeared, creating another opening. This one was small, just a cavern, no tunnel. It was a dead end, and a trap, a hole that she'd created for them.

"Come on," she whispered.

He heard the demons on the other side of the wall now. They were already in the cavern that he and Sophie had just vacated, trying to figure out where they'd gone.

In their weakened state, he and Sophie had no chance of

outrunning them. Their only hope was to outsmart them. Gritting his teeth against the pain, he dragged himself through the opening, and collapsed on the floor of the tiny cavern. Sophie took her hands off the wall, then turned toward him. "Call me back." Before he could answer, she turned away and then sprinted down the tunnel.

Hell. What was she doing? Trying to create a false trail?

The demons were pounding on the stone now, clearly trying to break through. She wouldn't make it back in time. Call her back? Suddenly, he realized what she'd meant. She wanted him to use his magic to drag her back at warp speed before the demons broke through, after she'd set a trail for them to follow.

Sweat trickled down his back as Vlad rolled onto his side. The rock wall on the other side of the tunnel shuddered, and tiny fragments fell as the demons started to hammer on it. He closed his eyes, pointing his index finger in the direction Sophie had gone. He reached out with his mind, searching for her. His focus faltered, and he swore. He didn't have the strength to reach that far. *Gabe. Give me some of your strength. Can you do that?*

Yeah, I think so. Gabe's energy surged through him, the demon-laced strength of a Calydon warrior. Vlad bolted upright just as a tip of a blade broke through the wall. His psychic energy surged outward, and he found Sophie instantly, already a mile away, running at lightning speed. Unlike the last time, when he'd been unable to find living cells in her body, this time, she was vibrant with life and in solid form. He locked onto her, and then flicked his finger, jerking her back off her feet.

The tip of another blade broke through, creating a second hole. Vlad kept his focus, using more of Gabe's strength as he called Sophie back to him, moving her faster than he'd ever moved anything in his life.

Another crash on the wall, and then Sophie careened around the corner. He held up his arms and caught her as she slammed into him. She spun around and slammed her hands down on the rock, disappearing into mist, and then, just as fast, the rock wall took shape again, cutting them off from the demons.

She collapsed against him, both of them going utterly still as they heard the demons break through. They were so close that Vlad could hear the murmur of their voices, and the scrape of their axes on the stone. He and Sophie were both utterly drained. They'd no chance to defend themselves if the demons found them.

They were milling around in the tunnel, no doubt trying to figure out which way to go. Vlad tightened his grip on Sophie, his mind going frantically as he tried to figure out an option if the demons broke through. *Gabe.*

Yeah.

If they come after us, you need to help me hold them off until Sophie can get away.

I don't have much left. I'm feeding life force to Maria while she drags that shit out of you.

Without Gabe's infusion of strength, they had no chance to fight the demons. Vlad swore under his breath, staring at the rock wall. Sophie stayed still in his arms, both of them waiting...waiting...waiting...

Then, suddenly, mercifully, the voices of the demons began to fade, as they headed down the tunnel, following the trail Sophie had left for them.

Sophie collapsed against him with a small groan. "We should move further. I can make a couple more holes."

"Do it."

Somehow, they both managed to drag themselves through three more holes she made in the solid rock, until finally, exhausted, they both collapsed. They could go no further. It would have to be enough, even if the demons backtracked. She'd refilled each of their caverns with the rock from the new one, so there was more than ten feet of solid rock between them and the tunnel.

It had to be enough.

I'm pulling Maria off you. Gabe's voice brushed over his mind. *She says you'll live, but she's in trouble now. How come I'm the only one who can strip poison without getting af-*

224

fected? Clearly, I'm a god. Let's touch base in a few. You good?

Vlad closed his eyes as he pulled Sophie against him. She sagged against his chest, her exhaustion beating at him. *Yeah, we're okay. For now.*

Chapter Twenty-Four

MARIA LAY ON her side, tucked up against Gabe's naked body, too exhausted to move. The healing of both Sophie and Vlad had nearly killed her, and the lovemaking needed to save her had been more intense than anything she'd ever experienced. Through it all, Gabe had stayed sane and focused, concentrating on taking care of her.

This incredible warrior who was so dedicated to his mission and so skilled at what he did had enabled her to reach beyond her capacity in her healing, and he'd made it safe for her to rebuild herself.

She had never had the luxury of resting in a man's arms, of being cradled against his chest, of being able to sleep and relax and feel safe, but Gabe gave it to her.

"How are you doing?" His voice was quiet, but it was sharp and alert. She knew that despite the exhaustion he must be facing from the numerous orgasms they'd both had, he was on guard, watching out for her so she could heal.

Her back was up against his chest, tucked tightly against him. His thigh was over her hip, and his arms were wrapped tightly around her, his forearm resting across her breasts. She felt cherished and protected, like a woman, not like a lust-driven lunatic willing to sell herself to any male who could feed her. "Sex is different with you," she said softly, running her hand over the soft hair on his forearm. The hook sword branded on his forearm was intricate artistry, so lethal, but so beautiful as well.

"Good." He pressed a kiss to her hair, making her smile.

It hadn't been a kiss of sex. It had been a kiss of intimacy, something she'd never experienced before. She moved her arm so she could see the markings on her skin, smiling at the sight of his brand forming on her arm. She couldn't believe she wasn't freaking out at the idea of being linked to him, but it felt good. Maybe it was because being connected with Gabe actually gave her freedom and self-respect that she'd never had before. "What's the deal with the *sheva* bond?"

"Five stages. Sex, which we did. The blood bond, again completed. The other three are transference, when you are able to call my weapon—"

"Really?" She sat up, excitement pulsing through her. "I can call your weapon?"

He raised his brows, amusement flickering across his face at her excitement. "When you need it, yeah. It won't come so you can admire it."

She grinned. "I like that." She held out her hand, flexing it. "Imagine what I could do with a Calydon weapon? I bet that could take down any demon."

He grinned. "You're so bloodthirsty. That's sexy as hell, you know."

She beamed at him. "I love that you think it's hot that I'm not a girly girl. I'll always be a protector, you know."

He nodded. "I like it."

Her smile widened. "What are the other stages?"

"Trust, where we give one another the power to kill each other, or entrust the other one with our greatest secret."

"Trust?" She wrinkled her nose at the thought of having that kind of faith in anyone. Sophie, yes, but a man? "Sorry, but with the exception of Sophie, I don't really trust anyone, especially men. So, I don't think we need to worry that I'm going to be pouring out my innermost secrets to you." She almost felt a little sad. The idea of being fully connected with Gabe appealed to her on some level. Maybe it was because she'd been on the outside, struggling to survive her whole life.

She'd never felt safe or balanced, but Gabe made her feel like she could be. He gave her a place to breathe, to respect herself, to be herself, whether that was courageous, a warrior, or too exhausted to even move.

She'd collapsed, and he'd carried her for miles to get her to safety, then he'd made love to her until she was better, and then helped her save her friends. With Gabe, she had someone to share the burden, and it felt good. It wasn't that she *trusted* him, but...he'd given her faith in humanity that she'd never had before.

He made the world seem a little more three dimensional than it had been before, and she liked it.

Gabe didn't seem concerned about her lack of trust. He shrugged. "We'll just take it as it goes. Do what needs to be done. I'm not worried."

She smiled, running her fingers over the corded muscles in his forearm. After all her time with demons who tried to control everyone in their path, it was incredible and unexpected to meet a man who wasn't the least bit concerned with trying to manipulate her behavior. "What's the last stage?"

"Death stage, when we kill to save each other, or offer our own lives to save the other."

"Death?" She thought about that. "Trust may not be likely, but that stage probably is. I'd have no problem killing to save you..." She grimaced, realizing how that might have sounded. "I mean, I'd kill to save anyone from a demon. It's not like you're special or anything." She then grimaced again. "I mean, not like you're a fungible good that could be traded for any-one, or that it wouldn't make a difference if *you* were the one in trouble, because it would matter, but not *that* much..." Crap. What was she trying to say?

He laughed, a deep, warm laugh that resonated through her. "It's okay." He rolled onto his back and tugged her on top of him, dragging her onto his chest, amusement dancing in his eyes. "I know I'm the best lover you've ever had in your bed, and you'd be devastated if you lost me." He took her hand and pressed his lips to her fingertips, mischief dancing in his dark eyes. "You can admit it. I won't use it against you."

Embarrassment flushed her cheeks. "I wouldn't be devastated. I don't need you."

He cocked an eyebrow, making himself look so cute that her heart fluttered. With his mischievous expression, he didn't look like a hardened warrior. He looked like a guy who was flirting with her, and that made her heart tighten. No one had ever flirted with her in her life.

"So, you wouldn't kill to save my life?" he teased.

She was completely flustered. "Of course I would—"

"Of course you would." He grinned and kissed her, a hot, playful kiss that made her giggle as he began to nibble his way along her jaw. "I really appreciate your willingness to kill on my behalf, and I mean that. Any warrior likes to know his partner has his back." He bit her neck lightly, and she couldn't suppress the ridiculously girly squeak in response.

He laughed, and bit her again, his amusement rumbling through her. "But here's the thing, babe." He pulled back to look at her, his face so deadpan that she started giggling.

"Babe?" she repeated. "You're calling a half-demon princess, *babe*?"

"Hell, yeah. Babe translates to 'deliciously sexy goddess that is mine and I like it that way,' so, yeah, *babe.*"

She swallowed, annoyed by the excitement that shot through her at his claim. "I'm not yours."

"As stated by the woman who has my brands on her arms, right? Right. Got it." He kissed her again, before she could argue, but as soon as she started kissing him back, he broke the kiss. "So, as I was saying, I appreciate your willingness to shed blood on my behalf, but you should know that I'm one of the most badass warriors ever to walk the earth. There's no way I could sit back and enjoy a beer while you were doing the killing. I'm a frontline kind of guy. You're not going to kill anything in defense of me, because I'm going to be doing the killing."

She cocked her head. "It's really too bad you don't have any self-esteem, you know?"

"Arrogance is fantastic. It makes every day better." He kissed her again, a playful kiss that quickly turned into so much more. Heat poured into her, escalating as his hands roamed over her body, igniting the nerves on every inch of skin he touched.

She'd never had a man caress her. She'd never experienced foreplay. She'd never known about long, sensual kisses that pulsed deep inside her, awakening the parts of her soul and her femininity that she'd never even realized existed.

"Close your eyes," he whispered, as he caught her around the waist and gently flipped her onto her back on the rough blanket. "Just feel for a moment."

She did as he suggested, tangling her fists in the tattered fabric beside her head as he began to kiss his way down her body. Along her neck. Across her collarbone. Long, sensual strokes of his hands along her sides and over her hips, as his lips pressed kisses over the swell of her breasts. She shifted, her body aching as he slid his hand slowly down her thigh, to the back of her knee, and then clasped the back of her calf, his thumb moving in sensual circles along her skin.

She expected him to part her legs and touch her intimately, but he didn't. His mouth traced sensual designs along her ribs and across her belly, while his hands moved over the curves of her legs, her hips, her arms. His touch was leisurely and deliberate, decadently sensual, and yet, at the same time, there was an innocence, for both of them.

She'd never been touched the way he was touching her, and she was pretty certain it was the first time he'd ever explored a woman's body that way. A first for both of them, a first that took her breath away and made tears burn in her eyes. "It's beautiful, how you touch me," she whispered, almost afraid to say it, to admit how much she liked it.

It scared her to admit it. It made her feel vulnerable.

Gabe, however, eased his way up her body and kissed her gently. "I could get lost in your body for years, and it still wouldn't be long enough to learn all I want to know about it." He searched her face, his hand still sliding over her hip. "For a thousand years, all I cared about was the Order. Everything was a means to that end. I still have those goals, but right now, touching you is simply about this moment. I've never been in the moment before. Not like this. Not simply because it felt so damn good."

She raised her chin, trying to find the willpower not to fall into his arms and just surrender to his strength, shocked by how much she wanted to simply stay there with him, and never move. "We don't have time for this," she said reluctantly, forcing herself to say words she didn't want to say. "People are counting on us."

"I know." He kissed her again, harder this time, deeper, a kiss of possession and ownership, but also a kiss of tenderness and intimacy, a personal kiss, one that was about the two of them, and no one else.

She gasped, shifting as desire began to pulse through her. Not just lust. Something deeper. Something more powerful. Something that seemed to sear her veins, burning through her. "What are you doing?"

"We're about to face a significant opponent." His hand slipped from her hip to her belly. He spread his fingers across the flat of her stomach, and then moved his hand lower, cupping her body where it curved, his fingers lightly resting on the folds of her body, but not invading them. "We need you at full strength." He slipped his fingers inside her, and she gasped, twisting restlessly as sensations flooded her. Heat, passion, need, and something more, something that seemed to pry apart the shields she kept wrapped around her.

She clasped his wrist, trying to still his hand. "It's too much," she gasped. "I can't stay in control—"

"Good." He caught her mouth and kissed her more deeply, shattered the walls she'd lived behind for so long, until there was nothing left protecting her. Her heart, her soul, her very being were exposed and raw, surrendered to Gabe, entrusted to him. She tried to hold on, she tried to keep herself distant, but with each kiss, with each movement of his fingers deep inside her, with each whisper of her name on his lips, she fell harder under his spell, until she was consumed by the sheer power of his presence, his kiss, his power.

"That's my girl," he whispered, as he slid his knee between hers.

She locked her knees behind his back, gasping as he slid inside her, an invasion that was perfect and right...an invasion that seemed to tear apart the walls she held so dear, catapulting her into a free-fall of sensation, need, desire, and emotion. She felt the tears warm on her cheeks, but she had no time to think about them, swept away on the tide of his lovemaking.

He drove deep, again and again, but he never broke the kiss, a sensual, intimate connection that kept her grounded in him, even as sensations were exploding through her body. She wrapped her hands around his neck, holding on desperately to him, afraid to let go, afraid—

"Let yourself go, sweetheart. Just go with it." He unclasped her hands from behind his neck and pinned them above her head, giving her nothing to hold onto, nothing to ground herself in, nothing to anchor her—

You don't need an anchor. Your power is so much more than that. Feel how much you are, Maria. Gabe's voice filled her, rushing through her like a warm, turbulent wind, sweeping aside the noise, the grief, the years of hardness, until there was nothing but him, nothing but her, nothing but the sensation of freedom, of flying, of power, of *more.*

She took a deep breath, and suddenly, the tension left her body. The weight of hundreds of years vanished, and she felt lighter, brighter, joyous. Laughter bubbled up through her, and she tilted her head back, surrendering to the emotions pouring through her.

So beautiful. Gabe's awed voice whispered through her mind, and then he drove deep, a final thrust that tore her from the final, tattered tethers holding her back. She screamed as the orgasm tore through her, throwing her head back as he took her over the precipice of sensation, ecstasy, and illumination.

Maria. Her name tore from his very soul as he bucked against her, the orgasm gripping him as ruthlessly as it had her. Together, they flew, unfettered, free, and exultant, as the orgasm catapulted them from their foundations and sent them spiraling into the unfamiliar, exhilarating rush of the world they'd never experienced.

Chapter Twenty-Five

I T FELT LIKE an eternity before Gabe could think again, before he could summon the energy to move. He was still buried deep inside Maria, his cock still hard for her, despite the fact he'd poured everything he had into her. He'd made love to Maria to empower her, but it had rocked his foundations in a major way.

And he was okay with it.

More than okay.

He always felt strong and powerful. He always knew he could handle anything. But now? He could hear more clearly. His muscles pulsed with energy they'd never had before. He could discern every scent down to its microscopic nuance. He was more than he'd ever been, and it was because of Maria.

"Maria?" He pressed a kiss to her hair, breathing in the faint scent of roses clinging to the strands. How did she smell of roses, when she'd spent her life in the demon world?

"Mmm..." She was nestled against him, tucked in his arms, her face pressed against the curve of his throat. It was intimate perfection, and he tightened his arm around her.

"Even though I won't let you kill for me, I would wipe the earth clean of your enemies to keep you safe." Shit. That wasn't what he'd meant to say. Hell, he didn't even know what he'd meant to say, but that wasn't it. "How are you feeling?" Yeah, that was better.

Maria didn't answer for a long moment.

He frowned, tension suddenly settling in his muscles. He moved fast, faster than he'd intended, rolling on top of her so he could see her face. "You okay?"

She looked up at him, her beautiful blue eyes searching his face. "I've spent my life having sex to power myself, but I've never felt like I do now. I feel energy vibrating through me so intensely, I feel like I could split a boulder in half just by sneezing on it. What happened? Why was it different?"

He grinned, inordinately pleased by her question. He wanted sex with him to be different. He *needed* it to be different. "I used our *sheva* bond to connect us. We merged when we made love. Since we both have demon heritage, we were able to feed off each other's strengths. We took what we needed from each other, and it made us both stronger."

Her eyes widened. "I made you stronger?"

"Yeah."

"But how? I mean, I understand that sex makes *me* stronger, but why did it help you?"

He couldn't stop himself from smoothing a lock of hair off her face. "I'm not sure. I was just trying to strengthen you, but it worked for me, too." He grinned. "Maybe my demon ancestry is lust demon, as well."

Heat flushed her cheeks. "I hate being a lust demon," she said quietly. "I hate having to feed off men for sex."

His amusement faded at the idea of her having sex with anyone else, but he didn't comment. She didn't need shit from him about sleeping with other men right now. She needed to cut herself a break. Instead, he simply said, "I've killed rogue Calydons who were my friends. I've killed women. I've watched good men die. I stood over them, knowing that I caused their deaths, and I took their pain into my heart. I had to do it, to save the innocents they were going to hurt, but it fucking sucks."

She watched him, listening. "It does," she agreed. "I'm sorry you had to do that."

He shrugged. "It's no different from what you've done. We're the same. I killed friends. You did what it took to be

236

able to save the innocents who were counting on you. You're a warrior, Maria. You've spent your life sacrificing yourself to protect the innocents. You've done whatever it took to make that happen. That's admirable as hell. You should be proud of what you've done."

She searched his face, vulnerability etched in her eyes, vulnerability he suspected she'd never shown anyone but him. "You really believe that," she said softly. "That I'm... admirable."

"Admirable?" He snorted. "Fuck that. You almost died saving Sophie, Vlad, and me today. You'd lay down your life for those you protect. You're the hero, sweetheart."

Tears filled her eyes, and she looked away. "I'm not that special."

"You are." He slipped his hand into her hair, palming the back of her head gently, forcing her to look at him. "There are very few warriors with true honor in this world," he said, opening his mind to hers, wanting her to feel the truth of his words. "You're one. You are unique and incredible."

Heat flared in her cheeks, but a small smile played at the corner of her mouth, and he knew she'd heard the truth, that he meant every word. "You're trying to butter me up for something, aren't you?" she said, raising one eyebrow at him. "Spill it, Gabe."

He grinned, and let her change the subject. He knew she'd heard what he'd said, even if she wasn't ready to own it. "I'm not holding any secrets, babe. I need to find Dante and bring him out of the demon world. That's all I need from you."

She nodded, her smile fading as the reality of their situation descended upon them again. "And I need your help with the women."

He frowned at her statement, wanting to understand what it was that drove her, what she was defending. He wasn't deviating from his mission to get Dante, but if these women were in need of protection, he wanted to know about it. "Tell me about the women. What's your role with them?"

She surveyed him for a long moment. "It's surreal to be having this discussion with you. You actually care about what's important to me, don't you?"

"Of course."

"Of course," she echoed softly. "As if the entire world was like you." She traced her fingers over his whiskers, her touch soft and intimate. "A man of such honor," she said softly. "I've never met anyone like you before."

He kissed the tips of her fingers. "Nothing special about me, babe. Just doing my job, which includes the Order, and you. Two jobs now. Tell me about the women."

She watched him kissing her fingers, her features soft. "The demons steal women from the earth realm, and bring them here to be their lovers. Unfortunately, demon semen contains the same toxin that is in their claws, so, over time, they poison their lovers."

His lips stilled on her fingers as an icy cold fury settled inside him. "Do they rape the women?"

"No, no." She shook her head quickly. "The women bond with them. They don't want to leave them." She sighed, the weight heavy in her eyes. "I cleanse the poison from the women. I can keep them alive for a while, but they keep going back until eventually, even I can't save them." She looked at Gabe, sadness etched on her face. "They stay with the demons until they die."

He swore, his grip tightening on her hand. What the fuck? No sex was worth death. "So, it's some kind of psychic control they have over the women?"

"No." Maria shook her head. "I asked my brother about it. He's a lust demon. He said he doesn't do anything. He just craves them, and they crave him." She sighed. "My brother, Damon, is a good guy. He has a good heart. I can see it in his eyes that it tears him apart each time one of his women die, but he can't stop it. Not all demons care, but he does. I...I don't know what it is. Neither does he." She sighed. "Maybe they stay just because demon sex is amazing?" She looked at him, heat flushing her cheeks. "You've had demon sex. Is it addictive? What would you do for more of it? "

"Demon sex? You know damn well I didn't succumb to the demon part of it. I'm too tough for that." He raised his brows. "Sex with you isn't amazing because you're a demon. It's because we're just that damn good together, and you know it. "

She laughed. "It's too bad you're so lacking in self-esteem."

He grinned. "No warrior can afford anything less than arrogance. Otherwise, you lose the first time your ass is on the line." His smile faded as he revisited their discussion. He was in warrior mode, and he wanted to know what he was facing. "So you want to get the women out of here?"

"I wish I could." She sighed. "Most of them don't want to go. But Sophie must leave." Her face fell, and Gabe felt a wave of genuine sadness from her. "She doesn't want to leave me behind, but it's too dangerous for her to stay. The entire demon kingdom is hunting her."

Gabe lightly grasped a strand of her hair and tucked it back away from her face, wanting to connect with her, to ground her over the sudden sadness consuming her at the thought of Sophie leaving. "So you want me to kidnap her and take her out."

Maria bit her lip, but she nodded. "Yes."

He met her gaze. "And what about you?"

"What about me?"

"She seems to think you won't be okay without her here. Is she right?"

Maria shrugged evasively, brushing a piece of lint off his bare shoulder. "I'll be okay—"

"Don't lie. We don't have time."

Maria shifted uncomfortably, all too aware of the ruthless intensity of his question. She bit her lip, not wanting to articulate the depth of pain in her heart, because that would make it too real. "I told you. I'm fine—"

"Maria." His voice was unrelenting. "I need the truth. I need to know what we're dealing with."

She glared at him, chafing under his demands. "Fine. You want to know the truth? The truth is that I'll be devastated when she leaves, but I'll do my best to stay alive. If I die, the women have no one to help them. I owe them, and I will see it through until I die." She bit her lip at the sudden ache in her chest. "A part of my soul will shatter when Sophie leaves," she said quietly. "She's my best friend, my only real friend, and without her, life here is going to feel like an abyss of loneliness."

The words hung out there in the darkness, suspended by the pain in her heart, gaining strength with each moment. Sophie leaving her? How could she do this alone? How—

Gabe sighed, and took her hand, pressing a kiss to her palm. "A heroine who is willing to sacrifice everything for those under her protection."

The reverence in his voice and the feel of his touch somehow stabilized her, catching her before the anguish of losing Sophie could take root. She managed a smile. "Thanks—"

She stopped suddenly, staring at him, realizing that it wasn't just Sophie she was going to lose. Gabe was going to leave as well.

Her heart seemed to freeze in her chest, and she coughed, trying to get air. How could she survive life without Sophie *or* Gabe? He had changed everything for her. He'd redefined what it meant for her to be a lust demon. He'd given her peace, freedom to heal, he'd empowered her, and he'd made her feel cherished and admired as a woman and a warrior. Dear God, how could she possibly go back to frenzied sex with random demons after this?

He narrowed his eyes, searching her face with so much intensity she felt like he was stripping her bare and exposing her soul. "So, you want to stay here for eternity and heal women who get poisoned by their lovers?" he asked.

"Do I *want* to?" His use of that word made her hesitate. No, she didn't *want* to stay here and live this life, especially without Sophie, and without him. "No. What I want to do is go with Sophie..." And with Gabe, not that she would ever admit it, even to herself. "I want to leave the demon world, and live another life, with people who matter to me. I want to breathe fresh air. Feel the sun on my face. Taste fresh fruit. I want to sleep at night without worrying about demons sneaking in, or women dying on my doorstep—"

She stopped suddenly when she saw Gabe staring at her, his eyebrows raised in surprise. Heat flushed her cheeks, and she grimaced, already regretting that she'd said it aloud. She'd heard about the blue skies and warm sun from Sophie and the women, and she'd always dreamed that someday, even for one day, she'd get to see what life was like in the earth realm...but she never articulated those dreams. Ever. They were a fantasy, not a reality. Dreaming of something she could never have made her own life intolerable. She knew that, and yet Gabe had tempted her past her shields.

Hardening her heart, she managed a dismissive shrug. "But I'd never go. If I leave, and there's even one woman left here, then she has no one to save her, so I'll stay. It's what I do."

He nodded, trailing his finger over her breast. "A warrior to the heart," he said softly, unmistakable admiration in his voice.

Sudden tears sprung into her eyes, and she slapped his hand away. "I'm not a warrior. I don't want to do this. I don't want to keep being strong." She sat up, pulling away from him. "You're a warrior because you consciously chose that path. I just...I don't know. This is just my life, and so many times every day, I wish it wasn't. I'm not a heroine! I'm not a warrior! I just—I just have to help them. I'm all they have." She stared at him, tears spilling down her cheeks. "I'm so tired," she whispered. "Every day it gets more difficult to get up. So much death. So much coldness. So much darkness. It never ends. Ever. There is no ending...except death, either for me, or the women."

Gabe gently clasped her wrist and gave a quick tug, pulling her against his chest. She closed her eyes and sank into his embrace, burying her face in his chest while he stroked her hair. "Sometimes," he said, "we're heroes not by choice. I became an Order of the Blade member because my neighbor, who was a Calydon, went rogue and killed my dad, my mother, and my two sisters."

Maria went still, shocked by his story. "Oh, Gabe, I'm so sorry—"

"I attacked him, trying to save my sister, and he threw me across the room. I broke my leg when I hit the wall. I couldn't move as he charged across the room. He grabbed me by my neck, dragged me off the ground, and reared back to slam his axe into my stomach, when Dante showed up, and killed him. My neighbor died just as he shoved his axe into my gut." Gabe's voice was soft, not hard, not cold, and he was rubbing his hands through her hair almost restlessly, as if he was using her to distract himself from the emotions of his memories.

Maria slid her arms around his neck and pulled him close, resting her cheek against his. "So, Dante saved you, and you became an Order of the Blade member, so you could save others."

"Yeah." He nuzzled her cheek. "I didn't have a choice, Maria. There was no other life I could have led after that experience. I didn't choose to become Order of the Blade. That life chose me. Dante became my mentor. Every time I killed a rogue Calydon, I thought of my family, and their deaths, and I remind myself that by taking out the rogue, there are innocents who will wake up tomorrow and get a chance to live another day, a chance my family never had." He held up his hand, his fingers spread wide in invitation.

Silently, she reached up and slid her fingers between his, entangling their hands together. His hand was rough and muscular, dwarfing her hand, but at the same time, his fingers were infinitely gentle as they closed around hers. "How old were you when your family was killed?"

"Seven."

A boy of seven years old, already destined to be a great Order of the Blade member, because of the tragedy that had stolen everything from him. "I guess you didn't have much choice either," she said softly. "Do you ever wish for a different life?"

"The only life I would prefer was one where there was no need for the Order of the Blade, because rogue Calydons no longer exist." His voice was soft, almost a whisper, as if he were sharing a dream so personal he didn't even want to articulate it. "But as long as there is a need, this is what I do."

His whispered confession was just like how she'd told him that she didn't want to live her own life. He did it, but out of duty, and if there was no need for his services, he would be happy. He was so strong, so battle-oriented, so arrogant, and yet, at the same time, she was beginning to see the humanity deep inside, the side of him he kept buried so he could do his job. "I'm not as heroic as you are," she said. "When I dream of the life I want, it's all about me, and sunshine, and love."

"But you have that dream in a world where you aren't needed down here. You wouldn't be in the earth realm if there were women here who needed you, would you?"

"True." She laughed softly. "You have a way of making me sound better than I am."

"You have a way of making yourself sound less than you are."

She sighed, watching his thumb trace circles in her palm. She felt content right now. Peaceful. Whole. Gabe knew who she was, and he was okay with that—

She suddenly felt her forearms burning. She lifted her head to look at the skin on her arm. As she watched, a silver line appeared on her forearm, as if an invisible pen were tracing them. "Look. What did we do?"

"Trust. You told me that you didn't really want to be here. Your deepest secret, right?"

She swallowed, realizing he was right. "I didn't mean to tell you."

He laughed softly. "Doesn't matter. You trusted me enough to tell me, and that was enough." Gabe turned her arm so he could see it, resting his chin on her head as they watched. "I spent my life abhorring the *sheva* destiny," he said. "I despised what it did to Calydons, and I couldn't understand how smart Calydons could get themselves tangled up with *shevas*. When my fellow Order members recently started hooking up with their mates, I was pissed. Really pissed. I felt like they were betraying everything the Order stood for. But lying here, with you in my arms, watching my brand appear on your arm, I feel a sense of absolute contentment, like this is the only possible way my life was supposed to unfold."

Tears filled her eyes at his words. God, all she wanted was to stay there in his arms, and listen to him weave such beautiful words together. She wanted him to make love to her until her soul burst into song, and she wanted to feel the softness of his touch on her skin, leisurely and intimate, just to connect, and not for sex that would sustain her.

She'd never wanted to be anywhere as much as she wanted to be in Gabe's arms, listening to him, feeling his skin against hers...a place that wasn't hers. A place that couldn't ever be hers, because they both had priorities that took precedence.

"You okay, babe?" He lightly pressed a kiss to her head, so gentle that she wanted to cry.

There was no place in her life for crying. Not now. Not ever.

Chapter Twenty-Six

FEELING LIKE SHE was tearing her own heart out, Maria sat up, pulling away from Gabe. "Please don't be nice. I can't get accustomed to having you around. You're making me soft, and I can't do that." She stood up and grabbed her pants. "I have to focus. I have to stay here for these women, I have to get Sophie out of here, and I have to be able to use other men for sex after you leave. I can't be soft. I'm not soft. I'll never be soft! I'll die if I get soft." She knew she was rambling, which was so unlike her, but she couldn't help it. She grabbed her torn bodice, suddenly wishing that for once, just once, she could wear jeans and a sweatshirt. She didn't want to walk around exuding sex all the time...Oh, God. Had she really just thought that? "Damn you!" She threw the bodice at him. "I don't have the luxury of being the woman you make me want to be."

He caught it easily as she stalked over to her small stash of clothes in the corner. She grabbed the sexiest bodice she had, a black one with metal rivets on the breasts. "So, I'm guessing Dante's body is in the Graveyard of the Damned," she said, her hands shaking as she tried to focus on the tasks before them. Focusing on work always made her emotions settle. "Sophie knows that area really well. Tell Vlad to meet us down there. You blood bonded with Dante, right? So you should be able to sense him once we get close. We'll get Dante, and then you guys can take Sophie out—"

She froze when Gabe's hand settled on her bare shoulders, holding her still. He was standing behind her, and she could feel the heat from his body against her back, revealing just how close he was standing.

Scrunching her eyes closed against the feel of his gentle touch, she didn't turn around. She just held the bodice to her chest, the rivets scratching against her bare skin. "What?"

"You can't have sex with other men."

"What?" She whirled around to face him, fury racing through her. "Just because I'm your *sheva*, you think I should die rather than harness sexual energy from other men? Sorry, but I'm not going to sit around and paint my toenails mourning for you after you leave. I have women to save, and that means I need to have sex so—"

"I'll have sex with you."

A part of her wanted to cry out with joy, but she knew better. There was no truth behind that promise. "Really? How are you going to do that from the earth realm? Because we both know that you need to go with Dante back to your Order. Are you going to give up your Order to sit around here and nail me whenever I need it? Doesn't that violate everything that defines you as a man? You can't abandon your mission for me, and I'm not going to walk away from the women here to follow you. There's no way, Gabe. I'm going to have to have sex with other men, and you're going to have to live with it." The words were harsh, but she needed to hear them, and she needed to say them, as a reminder to herself about who she needed to be.

Gabe's eyes darkened, and he went still. He didn't answer, but the muscle in his neck was twitching, a slow, steady beat that was the only indication of how on edge he was.

"See? You can't just declare something and have it be so, right? Life isn't that simple. We both have duties, and we have to remember that." She held the bodice against her chest with her arms, and reached behind her to zip it. When Gabe went to help her zip up, she stepped away from him, refusing his assistance. "Don't you get it? You're going to *leave.* I can't morph into some love-struck, needy, emotionally-sensitive wimp, or else it will be too difficult to go back to who I need to be." She'd never doubted her life, or her choices, or her duties. She'd never yearned for a different life...until now. Until Gabe had shown her there was another way...a way that was so much better.

She wasn't going to lie. Sex with Gabe was amazing. It wasn't a mindless rutting that she had to endure just to fuel herself. It had been a beautiful merging of souls, and she'd loved every second of it. The thought of going back to her life...

No. No. *No.* She had to deal with it. She had to let go of Gabe, and just face her life. Resolutely, she zipped up the bodice, her breasts spilling out of the top so much that her nipples were barely hidden by the black leather. She looked down at her breasts, and, for the first time in her life, she hated them. She hated that she exposed them to the world like that, she hated that she had to put herself on display so that she was always caked in a cloud of lust wherever she went.

She didn't want to be herself anymore.

She didn't want to be herself anymore.

Stricken, she looked up at Gabe. "Damn you," she whispered. "I can't afford this!" She whirled away from him and grabbed a black lace thong and tight leather pants. She yanked them both on, keeping her back to Gabe, who still hadn't said anything. She didn't turn around until she'd strapped on her thigh-high boots and sixteen weapons.

When she finally turned to face him, he was dressed again, his eyes dark, his expression hooded. He looked intense and dangerous, and her heart skipped a beat. He said nothing, but he met her gaze, his expression dark and hard.

There was nothing to say. He didn't want her to sleep with other men. She didn't want to have to. And yet, there was no other choice. This was the life they both had, and neither of them was willing to walk away from the people they'd sworn to protect.

She lifted her chin. "We have a battle to fight."

"I know." His hands flexed, drawing her attention to his

muscular forearms, and the weapons branded on his skin. His feet were spread, his muscles flexed. His black boots were creased and worn, and his eyes were hard and focused. Her heart flipped, and something fluttered in her belly. He was deadly, a warrior so far beyond anyone she'd ever met. This man could most likely slay an entire regiment of demons, all by himself. He was dangerous, deadly, and powerful....and he was on her side.

She was used to seeing powerful males and assessing them as the enemy, but he was different. *This* man was her man, no matter what happened in the future. In every battle, he would be by her side, fighting her battles, slaying her enemies. Against every assailant, he would defend her. Against every foe, he would wield his weapons on her behalf.

Strength rushed through her, an intense, powerful influx of energy. Standing across from him, facing him, realizing that he was her ally, made her stronger than she'd ever been in her life. Sex with him had already empowered her, but his presence magnified her capabilities infinitely.

After being intimate with Gabe, she knew she was strong enough to fend off Lucien without help.

But with Gabe by her side...she knew they could do so much more...like... She blinked as an idea suddenly formed in her mind, a brilliant, overwhelming, masterful idea so outrageous that she'd never even contemplated it before...because she'd never have been able to pull it off.

But with him...and Vlad and Sophie...the impossible might be possible.

Sudden hope leapt through her. Maybe there was a way. Not to keep Gabe, but to at least keep Sophie. If she could make the demon world safe for Sophie, she could stay...but there was only one way to do it.

She'd never be able to do it alone. She'd never be able to do it with Sophie, even if Damon also helped her. But with Gabe, and Vlad, two of the strongest warriors she'd ever encountered? They changed the odds. With them, it was possible...still a long shot, but possible. But if she had more of them? More warriors like them? They had a legitimate shot.

She cocked her head, studying him. "Didn't you mention that the rest of your team is close to the demon world? Near where you came across?"

He narrowed his eyes, studying her carefully. "Yes."

"So, if we could get them across—"

"You want to call them into the demon world, even though we don't have a way to get out at this point?"

"Oh. I hadn't thought of that." When he put it that way, it didn't sound like such a thoughtful, selfless idea. She knew she could never live with trapping more innocents in the hell that was her world. "Never mind. I was just considering my options—"

He still didn't look away. "You want to take down Lucien and Rikker," he said thoughtfully. "You want to become the leader of the demon realm. Then Sophie will be safe, and she can stay with you."

What? How on earth had he come to that conclusion so fast? She didn't even have a plan yet, let alone an idea of how to convince an entire legion of Calydon warriors to fight a battle that wasn't theirs. "What? I have no idea what you're talking about." She quickly turned away and helped herself to a few more weapons.

"You want to attack him, and you assume my need to protect you will result in you being backed up by the entire Order of the Blade team? You plan to manipulate me, and my team, into helping you take down the entire demon leadership?"

She sighed. "And that is why being psychically connected is completely unhelpful for women who want to manipulate their men into doing things that are entirely self-serving," she grumbled, as she picked up another dagger and slid it between her breasts. "But yes, that's what I was thinking. I know, I know, it's against your mission—"

"Instead of trying to manipulate me, ask me."

Something about the tone of his voice caught her attention, and she looked over at him. "Ask you? To trap your team in the underworld to support me on a mission that isn't your battle? Would you say yes?"

His eyes were glittering. "The only way the Order of the

Blade succeeds is because we have absolute faith in each other to back us up. That means absolute trust and honesty. That's how I operate, and I will always be that way with you. No lies. No manipulation. If you want something, ask."

Anger boiled through her. "It's so easy for you to be all high and moral," she snapped. "You have a team that has your back, and you all believe in the same thing. I don't have that luxury—"

He leapt across the cavern and grabbed her upper arms, pinning her against the rock wall. "Ask. Me." His voice was hard, and he sounded pissed.

Maria lifted her chin. "Fine. Will you help me fight Lucien and Rikker so Sophie is safe from them?"

"Yes."

She blinked, startled by his answer. "Yes?"

"You're my mate. Of course I'll stand by you, just as I stand by the Order, and my family. What the hell do you think loyalty means to me? That I'd have sex with you, and then abandon you? You're my soulmate, Maria. *Soulmate.*"

"But your mission for the Order—"

"Isn't compromised by taking a few minutes to shut down Lucien and Rikker."

She laughed softly. "It will take more than a few minutes—"

"It won't. I'm awesome, and so is my team. Shutting down Lucien and Rikker also frees our path to get Dante's body out of here. Once we have his body, it will be difficult to fight freely, because I will need to protect it. So, it's a great plan, and I'm in."

She stared at him, still uncertain how to react. "You mean it?"

"Yeah." He flexed his hands. "Let's do it."

Power rushed through her, and she couldn't help the sudden smile. For the first time in her life, she felt like she had a chance to change things, to make things right, to be strong enough to fight for what matters. "Thank you."

Gabe's face softened. "It's automatic, Maria. Always. Forever. You can count on me."

Tears filled her eyes suddenly. "I don't want—"

"I know," he said gently, sliding his thumb along her jaw. "You don't want to get dependent on me. I get that." He brushed a kiss over the corner of her mouth, and she closed her eyes, breathing in the tenderness. "But here's the thing. I don't know how this is going to work out with us, but the truth is that I could never just walk away and abandon you. You're too deep in my soul. So, it's okay to count on me. I'm here, and I will be here in the future."

She opened her eyes, searching his face. "But how? There's no way to make that work."

He met her gaze. "I don't know," he said softly. "I have no fucking idea." He took her hand and flattened it against his chest. "Do you feel that? You're inextricably entwined in my soul. There's no way to separate us."

"But there's no way to keep us together."

"I know."

Maria took a deep breath, her fingers digging into his chest. She could feel the visceral truth to his words, both that they were connected, but also that he had no idea how to fix it. She wanted answers. She wanted a solution. She wanted to know it was safe to lean on him...but there was no way. But when she was with him, it was impossible to keep herself disentangled from him emotionally. "I don't know how to do this," she whispered.

"Me either." Gabe kissed her gently. "So, let's figure it out as we go along."

She bit her lower lip. "I don't like not having a plan."

"I'm with you, babe, but I have faith." He framed her face with his hands. "We're both incredibly fantastic and amazing. How could we fail?"

She laughed softly. "How indeed, right?"

He grinned. "That's my girl. Now, what's the plan? How are we going to take down these bastards and turn this hellhole into an oasis of peace, love, and sunshine?"

She burst out laughing. "Peace, love, and sunshine? That's not a lofty goal or anything."

"Lofty is good. Keeps everyone on their toes. Now, what

next?"

She realized she felt better. His confidence, his sense of humor, and his affection had taken the edge off her emotions. She smiled at him, lightly tapping her fist on his shoulder as she thought about strategy. "Call Vlad. Tell him and Sophie to meet us—" She thought quickly. "At the southeast ridge of Devil's Canyon one hour after the lava starts flowing." It was dangerous to travel when the lava was moving, but the demons would be less likely to hunt at that hour. It was their best chance to succeed. Besides, it would take her and Gabe at least six hours to get there, which made the timing work out about right.

He didn't move. "Is that where Dante is?"

"No. It's at the place where we found you. We need to get your team over to help us."

He still didn't move. "Can you get them out of the demon world?"

She hesitated. "Yes—"

"Yes?" He raised his eyebrows, and then moved closer to her. She pulled her shoulders back as he took over her space, raising her chin in defiance and refusing to back down. "Sweetheart, you're lying to me. That makes me crazy. Trust me with the truth, okay? I'm on your team, remember? I'm bound to you for all eternity. You don't have to worry about me not liking your idea and taking off. Got it?"

She sighed. "I'm not used to being able to count on anyone unconditionally."

"I know, but you will." He slid his fingers through her hair. "So, I'll ask again. Can we get my team out of the demon world?"

She grimaced. "I'm working on it. I have an idea. I think we can make it work...but I don't know for sure."

He searched her gaze, and she suddenly felt the air between them thicken. "Okay. I trust you."

The moment he said it, her arms began to burn again. She looked down sharply and saw more details of his brand forming on her arm. This time, now that she was facing the reality of him leaving her, the claiming didn't feel so warm and fuzzy.

"Why did that happen? You didn't tell me a secret or give me the power to kill you—"

"The Order is my entire life," he said. "If I fail it, if I trap us all here so we can't get back and Dante can't get back, then I fail. So, yeah, trusting you with the safety of my team and with finding Dante's body and getting him out is trusting you with everything I have." His voice burned through her, and she fisted her hand, overwhelmed by his trust.

She wasn't worth that kind of trust. She was just...her. Ordinary. Regular. To be entrusted with something that meant so much to him... "Don't trust me like that," she whispered. "I'm not that altruistic."

He grinned. "Again, denying how awesome you are. We're going to have to work on that. Let's go."

She didn't move as he headed toward the door, stunned by what had just happened between them. The Order meant that much to him that protecting it could create the bond? She realized then that although she'd known Gabe was a warrior of honor and loyalty, it went far beyond anything she could comprehend. She could never compete with that. Ever. She might be his *sheva,* but she would never be his number one.

She'd known that all along, but he'd made her think there was a chance, that there was hope, that there was a solution she hadn't yet seen. But seeing the line appear on her arm made her fully grasp the truth that she'd been trying to deny. Even though he'd said he'd help her fight Rikker and Lucien, it had been partially because it fit his plans, which he had admitted at the time, but she'd chosen not to really notice.

But now she did. She was his number two. She'd never been anyone's number two before, so that had sounded pretty good to her. But now? She wanted to be his number one, and it wasn't until now that she understood how badly she needed to be his everything. The realization of the truth made the marks on her arm feel like a fake promise that she'd never wanted to be real...until now. "I think I hate you," she said quietly.

"Well, I want to kill every man who has ever touched your body, and every man you're considering letting touch you in the future, so yeah, not exactly a champagne and strawberries kind of mood." He glowered at her, looking so cranky, that she finally burst out laughing, laughter that dissolved the emotions trying to overwhelm her.

"God, we're a pair, aren't we?" Grasping for that relief, she rolled her eyes as she slipped a small, poison-tipped dagger into a pocket over her left breast. "Okay, Mr. Badass. Let's go. If the demons find us before we reach your team, neither of us is going to get what we want." She grabbed a few more weapons and began shoving them into the last pockets of her outfit when Gabe's hand closed around her upper arm.

She looked up at him as she slid the last knife into a pocket sewn into her boot. "What?"

"I wish I could stay for you. I wish I could walk away from my team for you."

The words were so simple, so plain, and yet they were so heartfelt that they made tears burn in her eyes. She nodded once, blinking back the tears that she would never let herself shed. "I appreciate that. Thank you."

She pulled away from him and began walking toward the entrance to the cave. "Let's go."

She didn't look back as she stepped outside, knowing that he would be right behind her, covering her back at all costs, no matter what, for as long as he could.

For as long as he could. Not forever. Just for as long as he could.

Somehow, that no longer felt like enough.

Chapter Twenty-Seven

T HE ACRID SCENT of demon lust jerked Sophie from her sleep. She bolted upright, her heart hammering violently in her chest as she shoved Vlad's arm off her. "Vlad!" she hissed. "Get up! They're here! They're coming for me!"

"What?" He leapt to his feet, awake in an instant, but she was already lurching away from him.

She slammed her hands on the rock wall, trying to find an opening, but there was none. "There's no door! We're trapped!" She whirled around, frantically racing across the cavern. "Can you smell them? They're here! They're coming!" She clawed at the wall, frantic to get through the rock, knowing that they were coming for her, so close, so close, so—

"Sophie." Vlad's hand settled on her shoulder, and she screamed, jerking away before she realized it was just him.

"Can't you feel the taint of evil? Of the darkness?" It was pressing down on her, thicker and thicker. "They're coming! We have to go! Dear God, they're coming for me!" She hammered on the wall with her fists. "Help! We need help! Vlad!" she screamed his name, desperate for him to hear her, to save her, to come—

He grabbed her from behind, his hand covering her mouth. "Sophie," he hissed. "Ssh!"

She fought to get free, terrified of his arms, of being

trapped, of not being able to escape, but he just held her more tightly, drawing her more tightly against his chest. Panic hit her, and she clawed at his arms, desperate. She could feel the heat burning her skin, the air stagnating, the scent of sulfur poisoning her. "No!" She screamed into his hand, writhing desperately to get free, but she was trapped, trapped, *trapped.*

Just like before. It was happening again. They were coming for her, and there was no escape, no hope, no freedom. "No!" She ripped herself free of Vlad's arms and ran for the wall again, clawing at the rock, her fingernails tearing as she tried to get through—

"Sophie!" Vlad grabbed her again. He dragged her against him fiercely, imprisoning her against his chest, trapping her.

"No!" She screamed at him, fighting, clawing, trying to get free.

He swore under his breath, scooped her up, and then suddenly, she was on her back on the floor, pinned beneath his body, her hands trapped above her head. The rock was so hard against her back, digging into her ribs.

"Sophie. Look at me."

The ceiling was rock. The walls were rock. The floor was rock. Dear God, she was already trapped. They'd already gotten her. They'd already won—

"Sophie!" He snapped her name, his voice edged with authority. "Quit fucking around and look at me, or I will cut every primrose in your kingdom and feed them to the damned rats!"

"What?" She stared at him, his threat jerking her out of her panic. "You'd ruin my flowers?"

He stared at her, his eyes dark and penetrating. "No, my little witch, you know I would never do that."

"Your little witch?" His words struck deep, edging past the panic. He called her his little witch only when he was laughing or joking...not when there was danger. "What?"

"That's right. There's no danger right now. It's okay." His voice had softened and gentled, his eyes searching hers.

She stared at him, his face coming into focus. She saw his beautiful eyes, the ones that always made her heart sing...and then she frowned, as his face shifted from the unlined face of a teenager into the hardened face of a man. She blinked. "Vlad?"

He nodded. "I think you were caught in a nightmare."

"A nightmare?" She closed her eyes. "So it's not true, then? No demons? God, I—" But even as she said it, she knew. Suddenly, she knew everything. She remembered everything. She remembered every detail of her life that had been lost to her for so long. She remembered her parents. She remembered falling into the pit. She remembered Vlad reaching for her, his face agonized as her fingers slipped from his. She remembered the moment she'd realized her family had betrayed her, that her world was lost. She remembered her best friend, Vladimir, who had been by her side since they were babies, who had married her when she was sixteen, to save her from her family.

Vlad? Her eyes snapped open.

There he was, lying on top of her, his blue eyes searching her face, his brow furrowed with concern. After almost two centuries, he was there? But how? No. He couldn't be. It was impossible. She remembered him coming through the cavern wall...but she had to have imagined it. Her mind had to be fragmenting, torn apart by the onslaught of memories she'd hidden from for so long. But...he looked real. He felt real, the weight of his body on hers, the feel of his fingers encircling her wrists.

"Vlad?" she whispered, her voice raw. Disbelief clogged her throat. How could he be there? How could he be lying on top of her, after all this time?

"You remember me?" His face softened.

She nodded, unable to breathe, terrified it wasn't real, that he wasn't there. "Yes," she whispered. "But you can't be here. I'm losing my mind, right?"

He smiled, that same beautiful smile that she remembered so well. "No, you're not losing your mind. It's me."

She squeezed her eyes shut, unwilling to look at him, unwilling to fall into the trap. She knew she was dreaming. There was no way he was there. No way that after two hundred years of hell, that her best friend was there with her. "Don't do this to me," she whispered. "I can't handle this."

His fingers loosened around her right wrist, and he gently took her hand. She squeezed her eyes closed even tighter, fighting against the sobs in her throat as he moved her hand to his face. He spread her fingers over his jaw, over the heavy whiskers that pricked her skin. "I'm really here, Sophie."

"No. It's impossible." But even as she said it, she slid her fingers along his jaw, over his cheekbone, across his nose, where her fingers found the bump from when he'd been head-butted by a wild boar. Her lips began to tremble, and she pressed them together. "There's no way—"

He took her hand and pressed a kiss to her palm. "Open your eyes, Sophie. See me."

"No, because you won't be there."

His low chuckle wrapped around her. "Just as stubborn as you always were," he said, the affection in his voice tugging at her heart. "I'm so sorry, babe. I didn't know you were alive. I just found out yesterday. I am a piece of shit bastard fuck up for leaving you here all this time."

A piece of shit bastard fuck up? That was so something he'd say. Reluctantly, terrified that he wouldn't be there, she opened her eyes.

He was there, staring down at her, his face inches from hers. Anguish raked across his face, pain etched deeply in his beautiful blue eyes. Slowly, afraid, so afraid, she placed her palm on his cheek. His skin was warm beneath her touch. Solid. Real. "It's really you?" she whispered. There was such a deluge of memories flooding her brain right now, she could barely think. She didn't know what was real, what wasn't. There were so many pieces, she couldn't even fit them all together, like an onslaught of information paralyzing her brain.

Except for Vlad. He was a solid, real presence, her anchor, just as he'd always been, for her entire life, until her parents had sacrificed her, tearing her from her life, from her world, from her best friend.

He nodded, not taking his gaze off hers. "Yeah."

"*Vlad.*" She flung her arms around his neck with a low cry.

"God, Sophie." His voice was rough and ragged as he pulled her into his arms, burying his face in her hair.

She held him tight, so tight that her arms started to hurt, but she couldn't let go. Suddenly, two hundred years of being strong collapsed, disintegrating into his arms. She cried the tears of terror from when she'd fallen into the pit. The anguish of loneliness before she'd met Maria. The constant fear for the women who were being poisoned. The agonizing depression that would overwhelm her whenever she looked too far ahead in her future, imagining an eternity of hell. All of her emotions swamped her, a ruthless onslaught of pain and fear that she'd kept buried. She'd been so strong for so long...until now. Until she could feel Vlad's arms around her. Until she could breathe in that same woodsy scent she'd always associated with him. Until his body poured warmth into her, everywhere they touched. Until she couldn't be strong anymore. Until it was finally, for the first time, safe to crumble.

"Hey, babe, it's okay. I'm here now." He kissed the top of her head, and then her cheeks, kissing away the tears streaming down her cheeks.

She closed her eyes, lifting her face to his while he kissed her nose, her forehead, his lips so soft and tender. Kind. Gentle. His kiss was surreal, a familiar strength grounding her, dragging her back from the precipice she'd been on for so long.

Still whispering reassurances, he kissed her chin, the tip of her nose, her mouth—

Then he froze, his lips on hers.

She sucked in her breath, shocked by the desperate need that suddenly took root inside her. He'd kissed her a thousand times before, all of them playful and innocent, but this had felt different. Not innocent. Not playful. It felt deep and intimate, burdened by centuries apart, centuries crushed by darkness.

She needed him. She needed her best friend. She needed to connect with him, with her past, with the only person who knew who she'd once been. She needed to feel alive again, like a human being, not a whispered phantom sliding through a life so dark that she tried her best not to feel.

His body was taut, rippling with tension, and he swore under his breath. "I'm sorry. I shouldn't have kissed you—"

"No!" She tightened her arms around his neck as he started to retreat, pulling him down toward her. His mouth slammed onto hers, and she kissed him fiercely, pouring herself into the kiss, desperate for him to kiss her back.

He didn't. He just held himself above her, his body rigid with tension as she kissed him.

Finally, she stopped, an aching loss crushing her chest like a vise. "Why?" she whispered.

"Because I betrayed you." Anguish tore through his voice. "I let you get taken, and I fucked around for two hundred years while you suffered—"

She pressed her fingers to his lips, silencing him. "Shut up," she said, barely able to speak through the tears. "For one minute, for just one stupid minute, get over yourself and look at me. Look at how much I need you right now. I'll be happy to hate you later if you want, but right now, Vlad, I need you to kiss me like your entire world stopped the moment you found me again."

He swore. "It did, Sophie. I never—"

"Then kiss me, you stupid man. Kiss me like you used to. I need that connection again." She framed his face, forcing him to look at her, to see her. "I'm not dead, Vlad. I'm alive. I'm here. I need you—"

He caught her hands, his voice rough. "Sophie. I can't kiss you the way I used to. I used to kiss your forehead because you made me laugh." He grabbed her hand and put it on the front of his jeans. She sucked in her breath at the feel of his erection beneath her palm. "If I kiss you, I'm going to consume you. If I kiss you, I'm not going to stop. I'm strung so tight right now that I can barely think. I thought I'd lost you forever, and suddenly, you're here, in my arms. You're my entire world, and you always have been. Having you back..." He swore, and shook his head. "Jesus, Sophie, I can barely even think around you, but it's not like it used to be." His eyes darkened. "There's nothing innocent or pure about my response when I feel your body against mine. *Nothing.* All I want is to make you mine, to sink my cock into you and cement us together so that nothing can ever tear you away from me again." His voice was tormented, intense with need so raw that her belly tightened. "So, let go of me, let me get up, and you can—"

"*No.*" She kissed him again. Hard. Deep. The kind of kiss that tore every last one of her shields from her soul, exposing her, making her so vulnerable she could barely breathe, but she didn't care. There was nothing to wait for, nothing to look forward to, no stupid morals to try to adhere to. All she had was this moment, with the man she'd lost for the last two hundred years.

He growled low in his chest, a visceral, untamed growl that poured heat through her body, and then he sank his fingers into her hair and kissed her back, a fierce, almost violent claim driven by the darkness in his soul, by a desperation every bit as great as hers.

She knew in that instant, that there was no turning back. Not for them. Not in this moment.

Chapter Twenty-Eight

T HE MOMENT VLAD'S lips descended on Sophie's, his mind stopped functioning. His entire being became a violent, frenzied miasma of desperation and need. He poured himself into his kiss, his entire soul screaming for the woman he'd lost so long ago. His kisses were frantic, beyond his ability to control, desperate to drown them both in the depths of the darkness that had nearly sucked them both in for so long.

Sophie flung her arms around his neck, holding him close, kissing him back with equal passion, her lips searching for his as if she couldn't breathe without his mouth on hers. Need exploded through him, a wild, hungry explosion of craving that tore through him, ripping him from his carefully controlled foundation and plunging him ruthlessly into the swirling whirlwind of *her.*

His hands were possessed, moving of their own accord, over her body, across her hips, under her shirt. He swore as he palmed her belly, the soft skin trembling beneath his touch. He could feel the scar on her hip from when she'd fallen out of the tree when she was eight and landed on a rock.

He rolled her onto her back and pulled her shirt over her head, his lips sinking into the curve of her belly. He kissed the trio of freckles just below her navel, the ones he'd teased her about over the years. Freckles that had once been innocent now seemed to sear his entire body as he pressed his lips to them, his hands sliding along her ribs, to her breasts.

"Oh, God, Vlad." She writhed under him, her fingers delving through his hair as she arched her back, filling his palms with the soft curves of her breasts.

He cupped them, abandoning the freckles to pour kisses over her breasts, to take the rosy buds of her nipples between his teeth. He bit lightly, and grinned when she gasped, his cock throbbing with need for her.

For two hundred years, he'd resented every woman he'd met, because she was alive when Sophie wasn't. To be with her now, basking in every curve of her body was beyond words, more intense than he could even process.

"I need more," he whispered. "I need to taste every inch of your body. I need to learn who you are, who you've become."

She sat up, tugging at his shirt. "Take it off," she demanded.

He grinned at her insistence, and immediately dragged it over his head. "Still bossy," he observed.

"And you love that about me," she retorted, just before she pressed a kiss to his chest, her tongue circling his nipple.

He went still, every nerve ending strung tight, as she worked her way across his torso, her lips and tongue the most decadent temptation he could even conceive of. His muscles were taut, his breathing labored, his focus almost shredded as he tried to hold himself still, letting her take control.

"I like this," she whispered as her fingers closed over the button of his jeans. "You're twice the size you were the last time I saw you, but you still let me boss you around." She unzipped his fly, and he tensed, heat pounding through his cock.

"It's all a façade," he muttered, sliding his fingers through her hair as she pressed a kiss to his belly button, and then lower, following the path of his jeans as she slid them down his hips. "I'm a domineering asshole these days."

"You always were." She tugged his jeans lower, and his cock sprang free. Before he even had time to process that she was seeing his cock for the first time, she wrapped her fingers around it, and pressed her lips to the tip.

"*Hell.*" He gripped her hair, his body rigid as she began to stroke him with her tongue and hand, igniting fires he'd never even conceived of. His cock was so hard it hurt, and every muscle in his body was strained to the limit.

She grinned up at him, light dancing in her eyes. "This is amazing."

It was the sparkle in her eyes that did him in. He hadn't seen that sparkle in so long. He'd never thought he'd see it again. Something inside his chest turned over, and he groaned her name, his throat too tight to speak properly.

Her face softened, and of a single accord, they came together in a kiss that shredded the years they'd been apart, and rebuilt the bond that they'd forged so long ago. With a low growl, he unzipped her jeans and had them off in record time, unable to handle a second more of having fabric between them.

He pulled her onto his lap, and she wrapped her legs around his hips, the kiss still so intimate and powerful that it seemed to infuse sunshine and healing into even the most damaged parts of his soul. "My sweet Sophie," he whispered into the kiss. "I've never stopped loving you."

Before she could answer, he deepened the kiss, too afraid to hear whether she still loved him. How could she? He'd failed her, and he knew it. But right now, he needed her to be loving him the way she was, at least with her kisses and the way her arms were wrapped around his neck so tightly, as if she were terrified that he'd disappear.

He grasped her hips, lifting her just enough for him to adjust the position of his cock, the kiss between them growing in intensity, exploding with two hundred years of loneliness and distance. They moved as one, lowering her onto his erection, and they both gasped as he slid inside her, a perfect coming together that sent fire streaming through his soul.

She went still, her breasts flattened against his chest, her feet locked behind his hips, her lips against his. "This moment," she whispered, against his mouth. "I never dreamed...I never believed..." She looked up at him, tears streaming down her cheeks. "How could I have forgotten you? How could my mind have let you go? My life would have been so much better if I'd had the memories of you to keep me going. How could my brain refuse to hold onto the one person I've always loved with all my heart?"

At her words, he suddenly couldn't breathe. "You still love me? After everything?"

She laughed, a laugh full of tears and disbelief. "God, Vlad, we were teenagers, and our parents had contracted with demons. How on earth could you think I'd be stupid enough to blame you for the fact you couldn't save me? Is that how little you think of me?"

He couldn't talk for a split second, too stunned by her words. She didn't hold him responsible. After two hundred years of tormenting himself, she forgave him. She just...forgave him. He swore under his breath, and kissed her, pouring two hundred years of pain and love into the kiss.

Sophie wrapped her arms around his neck, holding him close as she began to move her hips in a seductive, instinctual pattern that made streaks of desire stream through him. He gripped her hips, holding her securely as he began to move his own hips, driving harder and harder, until it wasn't enough, until he needed more, he needed to be deeper.

He locked his arm around her back and stood up, bracing his legs as she sank deeper onto his cock. She gasped, gripping his shoulders as he drove into her, moving her where he wanted her, his quads straining for balance and power as he thrust again and again, his thumb sliding between her folds, driving her to the edge—

She screamed his name and convulsed in his arms, her fingernails digging into his shoulders. He unleashed his control instantly, and the orgasm seized him, contracting his muscles and pumping his seed into her, again and again, until he'd emptied all he had and all he was into her.

Sophie gasped one final time, and then sank against him, her face pressed into the curve of his neck. Her back was damp with sweat, and her thighs were shaking where they were wrapped around his hips. She'd given him everything, just as he'd given her all he was, until there was nothing left.

Disbelief echoed through him as he sank to the floor, his powerful quads trembling from the intensity of what they'd shared. He leaned back against the wall of the cave and tucked her sideways onto his lap, unwilling to let her soft skin be ravaged by the rock that surrounded them.

Sophie sighed and leaned against him, her cheek against his damp chest, her feet tucked between his thighs. She said nothing, and Vlad rested his head against the wall, his fingers drawing circles on her lower back, still needing to touch her, to feel her, to explore her. "It would never be enough with you," he said softly. "I could make love to you a thousand times, and it would never be enough."

He felt her smile, and she held out her left hand. Her wedding ring was still turbulent and purple, but there were streaks of gold in it now. "It hasn't been gold since the night we got married," she whispered. "As soon as I left you to go home and pack, it turned black."

He slid his fingers between hers, tangling their hands together. His ring matched hers, with tiny, delicate streaks of gold moving between the black and purple.

"The gold is hope," she whispered. "I haven't had hope for a very long time."

Vlad brought her hand to his lips and pressed a kiss to her ring. "Me either." But he did right now. Sophie was alive, in his arms, and she'd given him her trust. "I didn't deserve a second chance, but I swear I won't let you down."

"You didn't let me down before." She sighed, burrowing more deeply against him.

"Except that I didn't look for you. It took me one day to find you once I knew you were alive. If I'd come two hundred years ago—" *Jesus.* The enormity of his failure hit him hard. "One day. *One day* is all it took, and I never tried.*"* Suddenly, he felt like a complete asshole for making love to her. "Shit." He lifted her up and set her on her feet. "I'm such a bastard. I should never have made love to you." Swearing, he stood up, disgusted by what he'd done. "I—"

He stopped when he felt her hands on his back. Gentle hands. Kind hands. "Vlad." Her voice was soft.

He closed his eyes and went still, his entire body vibrating from her touch. "What?"

"I've lived for two hundred years among demons. I've seen horrible things. I know what evil is. I know what it's like to watch people I love die. I was living in terror of being turned into Lucien's concubine." Sophie slid her hand around his waist, holding him. "I know badness, and that's not you. Forgive yourself."

Vlad looked down at her hands clasped around his stomach. He set his hand over hers, engulfing them. He could feel the depth of her words, and he knew she was speaking her truth. It wasn't that she forgave him for failing her. She truly didn't hold him responsible for not saving her, and for not coming after her. "I want you to be angry at me," he said, squeezing her hands. "I need you to be pissed."

Sophie leaned her forehead against his back. "There's no energy in me to be angry," she said, her voice weary. "There's too much real carnage and destruction to waste time dwelling on what might have been. I know that you did everything you could think of, didn't you?"

He closed his eyes, thinking of how he'd clawed his fingers to the bone trying to get through the crevasse after it closed. "My soul died that day when I thought you did," he said quietly.

"I know." She pressed a kiss to his back.

Vlad sighed, trailing his fingers over her forearms "How can you not see my failure to save you as a betrayal? How do you not see the fact I didn't come find you for two hundred years a betrayal?"

She tugged on his waist, and he allowed her to turn him around. She stared up at him, her face soft. "Always trying to be responsible for the world, aren't you? You're the same as you ever were." Her gaze searched his. "This is why I love you, Vlad. You're a hero, aren't you? I bet you've been doing something amazing all this time. What have you been doing for the last two hundred years? Who have you been saving?"

He frowned. "Some kids," he muttered.

"Some kids," she repeated. "How many?"

He shrugged. "I don't know. A thousand? Maybe two."

"Two thousand children?" She smiled, a smile so warm that his heart tightened. "They needed you, didn't they? Was there anyone else to save them?"

He shifted uncomfortably. "No."

"So, you were needed in the earth realm, saving those kids." Sophie smiled at him. "It may damage your male ego to hear this, but I didn't need you for the last two hundred years. I needed to be here with Maria and these women. Maria has become my sister, filling my heart with love, and I've served a higher purpose, helping these women. I was meant to be here, not being some fancy princess in a castle. Do you realize how many women are alive because of me and Maria?" Her face lit up, a glow from within that made his stomach tighten. "I make a difference here. It sucks at times, and it's difficult and scary, but it *matters*. I matter. I do something that matters, and so do you. Neither of us would be who we are today if we hadn't had these paths."

At her words, something inside Vlad began to release, a tension that had been locked around him for so long that it had become a part of him. "But you sounded so lost just a few minutes ago, when you got your memory back."

She smiled, and linked her fingers behind his neck. "It was overwhelming to be deluged with so many memories at once...to be given back the love that had once sustained me. You came back to me when I needed you, Vlad. Don't you understand that?"

The knot in his chest began to loosen even more, and he kissed her. Gently this time. Not the raging, uncontrolled passion of earlier. This was different, even more intimate. It was a kiss with his heart, the blackened, ravaged heart that was starting to beat again for the first time in centuries. He thought back to his visit from the magi, his claim that he hadn't tracked down Vlad because it wasn't time.

Was there truth to that? Was there truth to what Sophie said? That they'd both had roles to play? Women and kids to save?

Her smile faded as he pulled back. "Things aren't okay

here anymore, Vlad. Things have changed. That's why you found me. I need you now."

Adrenaline rushed through him, and his muscles tightened. His vision narrowed to hyper-focus, and he nodded. This was why he'd come. To fight. To stand by her side, and fight. "I'm in. Let's do it. What do you need?"

She hesitated. "We need to somehow neutralize Rikker and Lucien. I don't know any other way."

He studied her. "You want us to take down the demon king and his second-in-command? You do know demons aren't killable, right?"

Sophie sighed and grabbed her jeans. "I am well aware of that, thanks for the insight."

"And they heal almost instantaneously?"

"I know." She pulled on her pants and fastened them, aware that Vlad was watching her with blatant hunger in his eyes. Hunger, and a hint of that same bossiness that used to drive her so insane when they were teenagers.

"And they aren't exactly reasonable," he added.

"Yep. Got that, too." She grabbed her bra and pulled it on, suddenly needing clothing. Vlad made her feel exposed and vulnerable, and she needed to feel strong.

"So, the only option is to get out, right?"

She stopped, looking at him sharply. "Get out? Of the demon kingdom? And what? Leave Maria and the others behind?" The idea was so shocking that she almost couldn't even say it...especially when the wave of almost unbearable longing hit her. God, to be out of this hell, and back in the world of sunshine and flowers? Tears suddenly swam in her eyes, and she had to dig her fingernails into her palms to keep her composure. "I don't want to go back to that life," she lied, her voice stiff with tension. "I don't matter there." That was true. "I matter here. They need me."

"You can't help them if you're dead."

She grabbed his jeans and tossed them at him. They hit him in the chest, and slid down his body when he ignored them. "That's why you're here. To help me figure out how to make this place safe for me."

Vlad sighed. "Soph, this place will never be safe for you, or anyone. It's the demon kingdom."

She set her hands on her hips and glared at him. "So, you're not going to help me? You came all this way, and you're not going to help?"

Anger flashed in his eyes, anger that was laden with such extreme guilt that she almost felt bad for bringing it up...except she was desperate, and she knew Vlad well enough to know that he would never allow her to do anything that he thought could put her at risk...unless she guilted him. "I will help you," he said, his voice low and hard. "You know I will. You got a plan?"

"You can control living matter, right?"

He nodded. "Of course."

"So, they're living, right?"

"I can't hold them for long. They're extremely strong."

Sophie bit her lip, thinking. "There's a part of the kingdom called the Graveyard of the Damned. It's where demon bodies go when the demons finish with them. The bodies are all sealed in rocks. If I dissolve the rocks long enough to make an opening, could you put Rikker and Lucien inside and hold them there until I can close it?"

Vlad studied her, his eyes dark and thoughtful. "Even if that worked, what about the void they leave in the power structure? What about the next demons to take over?"

"They don't want to make me their concubine yet, so we'll deal with that later." She looked at him, hope trying to surge through her. "Could you do that, Vlad? If we worked together?"

He nodded slowly, once, and her heart leapt. "Really?" She could barely whisper the words. Was there really a chance they could do this?

"I don't want you that close to them," Vlad interrupted.

Sophie drew her shoulders back, bristling at the autocratic tone in his voice. "I'm not a teenager anymore, Vlad. You don't get to control me. This is my world, my life, my friends, and I'm going to fight for them. They matter to me, Vlad, in the same way I mattered to you. I can't stand by and leave them to their hell any more than you could. I need your help. Will you help me?"

Vlad swore under his breath. "Jesus, Soph. You're still stubborn as hell."

She grinned. "I know. It's one of my more endearing qualities, right?"

"Yeah, that." He grabbed his jeans. "One condition, princess. If you want me along to trap these fuckers, and to keep you safe, you need to do what I tell you once things get dangerous. And if I tell you to abort, you do it. We find another way."

"The only other way is to leave. Which I won't do. And there's no way out, anyway."

"We aren't demons. We'll be able to get out." Vlad shoved his feet into his jeans. "Agree with me, Soph, or we're heading straight to the barrier where I came across the first time. Your safety comes first."

She lifted her chin, meeting the gaze of the man who'd once been her best friend, her only friend, the only one who'd stood by her. His gaze was like steel, his jaw hard, his muscles taut. There was no softness in him, just the protectiveness that had always driven him. "I'm not the girl I once was," she said softly.

He sighed. "I know. I'm sorry you had to become strong."

"God, I'm not. What woman wants to rely on a man to survive? That's why I ended up down here in the first place. I like being strong. I like being able to fight for those I love." Sophie walked over and poked him in the chest. "You don't get to boss me around anymore, Vlad. You don't get to tell me that I can't endanger myself."

Amusement flickered in his eyes. "I can tell you whatever I want."

The tension vanished from her body, and she grinned. "I don't have to listen."

"You never did." He sighed and pulled his shirt over his head. "Okay, let's go do this, but I promise you that if I think you're in danger, I'm going to haul your ass out of there."

"And I'll stab you in the jugular, render you unconscious,

and do it without you."

With a low growl that was half-laughter, he grabbed her wrist and yanked her over to him. She slammed into his chest, but before she could twist away, he slid his fingers into her hair. "I love you, Sophie. I owe you everything, so I will do everything in my power to give you what you want, I swear."

Her heart ached at the raw honesty in his voice. God, she'd missed him, and his arrogance. "Vlad—"

Before she could answer, he kissed her, a long, sensual kiss that made her almost wish she could be the girl she once was, who'd cared only about her own life, her own future, and her best friend. She wished she could be content to surrender to Vlad's kiss, and never think about all the hell she'd seen in the last two hundred years.

He pulled back, searching her face. "You didn't kiss me back."

She managed a small smile. "If I did, I'm afraid I'd agree to anything you want."

He raised his brows. "Is that so bad?"

"Yes." Sophie pulled back, needing to put distance between them, to find her own footing. She didn't want to be the girl who'd thought marrying Vlad was the only way to ensure her safety. She wanted to be the strong, powerful female she'd become, not the vulnerable girl who hadn't been able to save herself, or anyone who mattered so long ago. "Can you contact Gabe and tell them to meet us near the Graveyard of the Damned?"

He nodded. "He'll be thrilled. He's looking for the physical body of a Calydon, and thinks it's buried there." He cocked an eyebrow. "We can get him out the same way we put Rikker and Lucien in. I owe him."

"Once Rikker and Lucien are gone, I'm happy to help you with anything you want."

"I like the sound of that." Before she could stop him, he grabbed her around the waist and gave her a hard, relentless kiss that didn't cease until she finally melted into him and kissed him back, unable to resist the temptation of his seduction.

He broke the kiss and leaned his forehead against hers. "I can't let you die," he whispered.

"I don't want to," she admitted softly. God, she didn't want to. "I'm scared."

His grip tightened on her waist. "You have to do this?"

"Yes."

"Then we do it." He pulled back, and this time, his eyes were narrowed. He looked intense, like a warrior ready to do whatever it took to make things happen. She shivered, stunned by the change that had come over him. He was lethal, hard, and unyielding...everything she needed, everything that her entire soul burned for. She had gotten strong in the last two hundred years, but so had he. He was a warrior now, not a teenager with big dreams, and he was on her side.

Longing pooled in Sophie's belly, and she took another step back, terrified she was going to walk away from her duty and let Vlad sweep her away, like he'd done before. "We need to go."

He nodded. "We do." He held out his hand. "Let's go."

For a second, she hesitated, afraid of how much she wanted to slide her hand into his. Would that make her too weak to do what she had to do, if she held onto him, like she had when she was younger, a pampered princess who ran away from her troubles?

Vlad's jaw tightened, and he dropped his hand.

Her fingers curled to take his, but it was too late. The chance was gone.

She didn't know how to be with him anymore. He made her want to be small and fragile, depending on him to keep her safe, to hide from life the way she once had. But she didn't want to be that girl anymore. She liked being strong. She liked being the protector of these other women. She liked feeling like she could make a difference, and save herself...but being with Vlad made her want to fall into the girl she'd once been.

Vlad paused in the doorway, his brow furrowing. "Soph—"

"I'm coming." She cut him off, not wanting him to ask questions she couldn't answer for herself. As she squeezed past him, her arm brushed against his stomach. Desire and longing rushed through her, the desire that came directly from the depths of her soul. She glanced up at him, and her heart softened when she saw the pain in his eyes.

So much had passed between them. So much time. So much loss. So much growth.

Was there a way to bridge the gap? She didn't know.

He smiled. "I'll always love you, Soph."

She nodded. "Me, too."

But as they walked out, side by side, she wasn't sure if it was enough anymore.

Chapter Twenty-Nine

THE SILENCE HUNG between them as Vlad and Sophie marched across the barren, acrid lava fields toward the Graveyard of the Damned.

Sophie had been on these fields hundreds of times with only demons for company, and yet, she'd never felt as alone as she did right now, with Vlad beside her. Gone was the attentiveness and the camaraderie. He was focused and vigilant, constantly scanning their surroundings for danger, but she could feel the coolness radiating from him. He'd put distance between them, distance she should be glad of, because it gave her the space to claim her independence. She was glad, but at the same time...she missed him. She didn't want him to be a controlling, inflexible male who decided where she was going to live, but she needed the friendship and bond that had been such a part of her life for so long. "Vlad?"

"What?" He was close behind her, covering her back while she led the way.

"Were you always so much slower than me? I don't remember you being such a slug." She was intentionally ribbing him, trying to rebuild the friendship they had once had, needing that connection with him.

He was silent for a long moment. "What?"

"Slow." She looked back over her shoulder. "You used to be able to keep up with me, but now I have to hold back so you don't get left behind." She raised her brows. "It must be all that muscle weighing you down, huh?"

He stared at her for so long that her heart began to close up. Then, with a completely stoic expression, he said, "I'm letting you win to protect your fragile princess ego."

She smiled then, her heart unfurling. "My princess ego isn't nearly as fragile as your male ego." She gestured at the heavy whiskers on his cheeks. "That unshaven look is all about trying to increase your manliness, isn't it? Just so you know, real men can be clean shaven and still be super hot."

His eyebrows shot up. "My ego is completely intact. I don't shave because I know that if you were to see my face in all its glory, you would be so overwhelmed with my handsomeness that you wouldn't be able to function."

A laugh burst out of her. "You're not so hot, you know."

"So you've always claimed, but we both know you're lying to yourself." He caught up to her, a small smile curving up one corner of his mouth. "You, on the other hand, are just as ravishing as ever. It's irritating and distracting."

She giggled. "Only because you have no self-discipline. You should be man enough to be able to focus even if a thousand women ran naked and screaming past you."

His eyes darkened. "Sweetheart, a thousand women could be doing naked yoga all around me, and it wouldn't distract me in the slightest. You, however, are a different story." He caught her wrist and pulled her back toward him. "All it takes is one glimpse of you, and I can't even think."

She caught her breath, her heart pounding as he slid his hands through her hair. "Don't blame me for your lack of discipline—"

"It's all your fault," he whispered, as he bent his head. "One taste of you, and I'm completely lost." He brushed his lips over hers, a feathery-light kiss that made butterflies take flight in her stomach.

She wrapped her fingers around his wrists, her breath shuddering. "If you're so vulnerable to my awesomeness, then you probably shouldn't kiss me—"

"Probably not," he agreed, and then he angled his head

and claimed her mouth.

His mouth on hers was like instant fire. Maybe it was because the silence between them had hurt so much and made her miss him. Maybe it was because they were venturing deeper into the lava fields, and her adrenaline was racing. Maybe it was simply because their brief banter had touched a part of her that hadn't been alive in so long, the light-hearted, happy heart that he'd kept alive during her childhood. Maybe it was because he'd never left her heart in all those years, and it had taken a burning lava field to make her remember.

"Sophie." He whispered her name into the kiss, his fingers tightening in her hair. His touch was sensual and warm, familiar, and, at the same time, wildly new.

"Kiss me, Vlad. Kiss me like I've always wanted you to." She didn't even know what she meant by that, but as soon as she said it, Vlad groaned low in his throat, and deepened the kiss. It was sensual, intimate, and intoxicating, so hot that fire seemed to sear her veins.

She melted into him, her breasts pressed across the hardness of his chest. His arms wrapped around her, enfolding her in the strength and size of his body as he deepened the kiss. His tongue slid across hers, tempting, teasing, seducing.

Heat poured through her belly, and she couldn't keep herself from whimpering as her fingers gripped the front of his shirt, trying to hold him closer, as if somehow, if she held tightly enough, she could keep him from ever leaving her again...

The moment she thought about losing him, she tensed, terrified at the depth of her desire to never have to live without him again. The need for him ran so deeply in her soul, that he was entangled hopelessly inside her, which meant he could trap her if she wasn't strong enough to stay on her own path. But she wanted him. She didn't want to be alone again...but she had so much to do here with Maria and the other women.

"God, I want to rip your clothes off again." With a low growl, Vlad nipped the side of her neck playfully, jerking her away from her thoughts. "How much time do we have until we have to meet Gabe and Maria? Enough to throw you down on some rocks and show you exactly how intact my male ego is?"

She burst out laughing, unable to resist his playful tone. "I love rocks, but being thrown down on them so you can prove your virility isn't exactly my greatest romantic fantasy. They're kinda hard, and all."

"Hard?" He raised his brows. "You don't like hard? 'Cause I got hard."

She smacked him in the chest, still laughing. "How can you make me laugh right now? We're on our way to the Graveyard of the Damned, for heaven's sake. It's not a time for laughing or kissing."

His smile faded. "It's always the right time for laughing and kissing. We both know that."

She draped her arms over his shoulders, cocking an eyebrow at him. "Is it, really? How do you figure that?" She couldn't believe how good it felt to be playful with him again. Being with him made her think of the bubbling streams they'd played in, of the laughter, of the secrets they'd shared, not the hell that was her actual life.

"You want to know why right now is the best time to laugh?" He studied her, twirling a lock of her hair around his index finger. "The way I see it, when you've been through hell for centuries, when something good happens, you hold onto it with everything you have." His smile faded. "We both know that this could end at any second. We've lived that. So, we take what we can get."

Some of her happiness faded at the reminder of how fleeting the moment was. "It will end."

"It will, yes," he agreed, "but maybe we can make the next moment worth living, too." He kissed her forehead. "And then the one after that, and the one after that, finding the meaning in each one."

She closed her eyes and inhaled deeply, breathing in the sensation of his lips on her forehead. "When did you become so philosophical?"

"When I had to figure out a way to make myself face every day for the last two hundred years since you died."

Her heart turned over, and she opened her eyes to look at

him. His eyes were intense blue, the same blue from their youth. "I'm sorry you suffered like that."

He shrugged. "It makes me appreciate this moment in a way I never could have."

She smiled. "Me, too, I guess."

He smiled back at her, and her heart skipped. She traced her fingers over his lips. "When you smile like that, you look like the boy I once knew."

His eyebrows went up. "What do I look like when I'm not smiling?"

"A man twisted by his pain."

His expression cooled. "Yeah, well, you always knew me well." A loud explosion made them both start, and they spun toward the lava fields. In the distance, a spiral of steam was rising, shooting out of the rocks.

"It happens all the time," she said. "It's not a big deal, unless you're standing right over the spot. The heat would incinerate us almost instantly, but if you're listening carefully, you can hear the air beneath the rock right before it explodes."

He looked over at her. "How much time have you spent down here?"

She shrugged, and gestured to the lava fields. "Somewhere in there is the key to freeing demons from their realm. The magic was trapped in a stone, and every night, Rikker and his team take me down there to hunt for the jewel that will free them. I love going down there and being so close to all the jewels..." Her voice faded as she recalled her last hunt, when Rikker had felt her hair.

Vlad glanced at her. "What is it?"

"I was just remembering that the last time we were down there, Rikker was able to touch me. Barely, for a split second, but it still happened." She shivered at the memory, at the moment she'd realized she was no longer safe. "Was it you? Was it your arrival that changed me?"

"I don't know." He frowned, running his fingers through his hair as he scanned the lava fields. "But I'll tell you that I don't like that you've lost your defenses. We need to get it back."

"I didn't know how to make it happen before, and I don't know why it stopped." Suddenly restless, she began to walk again, the heat from the lava burning through the bottoms of her boots. She was sweating now, her hair damp from the steam rising thicker and thicker around them. The talk about Rikker had been a visceral reminder of the danger she was in. They didn't have time to kiss. They had to get to the Graveyard of the Damned by the time Rikker and Lucien tracked her down. "I'm not going to lie, though, I wish I could still dissolve to get away from them. It made me safe."

"Didn't you dissolve on purpose when you merged with the rock that was blocking your underground safe house?" He fell in beside her, their boots crunching on the gravelly rock as they walked.

"Yes, but that's different. It's not really a dissolution, so much as a merging with the rocks." She glanced across the landscape, noting the position of the light. The lava would stop flowing soon, and the nightly search for the jewels would begin. The demons would be appearing soon. "When the demons tried to touch me, I just dissolved on my own. I didn't even have to see them coming. My body did it automatically." She glanced at Vlad's hand, remembering how good it felt to be touched by him. Would she trade being able to touch him, with the safety of dissolving? God, she didn't know. Being touched by him was a gift that made her soul cry out, but was it worth her life? Her freedom?

"So, rocks can make you dissolve?" Vlad leapt up on a rock beside her as they moved swiftly north, heading toward the rendezvous point where they were going to meet up with Gabe and Maria.

"Yes." Sophie frowned, thinking about his question. "Actually, Rikker and Lucien both used jewels to keep me corporeal as well..." She looked at Vlad. "Do you think the minerals are the key, somehow?"

"Sounds like it." He stopped and faced her. "Can you dissolve right now? Not to go into a rock, but just to dissolve?"

She closed her eyes and concentrated on her ring finger, where the dissolution always began, but there wasn't so much as a tingle. She sighed and opened her eyes. "No, but I've never been able to do so. When demons tried to touch me, it was pure instinct."

Vlad walked a short distance away and picked up a rock. "This time, I want you to focus on getting into this rock as quickly as possible. If you can dissolve by directing your energy toward a rock, even if you're not touching it, then at least it's a way to escape if they come after you."

Hope leapt through her. If she could still escape the demons like that, it would change everything. "Oh, good idea." She nodded and closed her eyes. Instinctively, she reached out for the rock on a metaphysical level, connecting with its energy. The warmth of the stone surrounded her, pouring strength and energy into her. She opened herself to it, picturing her body merging with it, as she always did when she was hunting in the Graveyard of the Damned with Rikker. She felt the particles of her body separate, and she sped through the air, streaking toward the rock.

She plunged into it, pouring warmth into the stone, and accepting the same from the rock. It felt so good to be merged with the stone, to feel the strength of the solid mineral fusing with her cells.

Vlad's voice penetrated her oasis. "Reform, Soph."

For a split second, she felt her body hesitate, unwilling to venture back into the grittiness of the demon world. She could stay in the rock forever, and no one would ever find her...

"Sophie!" This time, his voice jerked her out of her safe haven.

She immediately withdrew from the rock, taking her human form again. She was standing in front of Vlad, who was still holding the rock. "It didn't want to let me go." She didn't like that she hadn't wanted to leave the rock. She'd never had trouble leaving a rock before. It was almost as if it hadn't wanted to let her go...or that she hadn't wanted to leave it. Fear gripped her as she looked at the rock. Rocks had always been her salvation, but suddenly, it looked different, almost like a threat. "That has never happened before. I'm not sure I would have come out if you hadn't called me."

Vlad frowned, and turned the rock over in his hands. "Is this stone different from others?"

"It felt good, but nothing alarming." Despite the heat from the steam, she was suddenly cold. She hugged herself, but even that didn't stop the shiver. "What if that's changing, too? What if something is happening to my connection with the stones?"

Vlad studied the rock. "There's no living matter in there. I don't feel any magic." He tossed the rock aside, and it landed with a jarring clunk that made Sophie start, as if she'd felt the impact.

He frowned. "You felt that?"

"Yes."

"That's not usual?"

"Never." Sophie shivered again. "Get another rock. Try again. I need to see if it's just me, or if it's that particular rock."

Vlad picked up another stone, this one smaller, and a much darker shade of gray. It was clearly made of a different mineral than the one they'd just tried. "I'll call you out if you get stuck."

Sophie took a deep breath. "You better." She met his gaze once, and she saw the steely determination in his eyes, his absolute commitment to make sure she was safe. It should make her feel better, but she knew that all his determination and skills hadn't been enough before when the demons had taken her.

As if reading her mind, he scowled. "I'm not a kid anymore, Soph. I've spent the last two hundred years rescuing people, and I'm really good at it. There's no chance I won't get you out. No. Fucking. Chance." His voice was hard, low, and focused, his body tense.

He was no longer a gangly, well-meaning teenager. He'd become a hardened, dangerous warrior, with two hundred years of grit to build on. Tension eased from her body, and she nodded. "Okay."

"Okay." He held up the rock. "Do it."

She immediately closed her eyes and focused on the rock. Again, it called to her, a beautiful song of warmth and music that filled her body with a sense of completeness. It summoned her, and she went, effortlessly abandoning her human form and merging with the rock. The droplets of her being settled among all the particles that created the rock, weaving in and out of them. It was perfection, and beauty, and she sighed as her entire soul seemed to settle. She was tired now, sleepy, and she began to relax—

"Sophie!" Vlad's shout jerked her out of her peacefulness.

She focused on him, using him as her anchor to get her out of the rock...but nothing happened. Panic hit her hard, and she started to fight in earnest, trying to separate herself from the rock, but it gripped her more tightly, clouding her mind, making it difficult to concentrate, to remember what she was fighting against...

"Sophie!" Again, Vlad's voice penetrated the rock. "Get the hell out of there *now.*"

His voice felt distant, and the urgency washed over her, unable to grip her. She shut him out, focusing on merging with the rock, knowing that he couldn't get her. Sudden fear gripped her, and she realized she was never going to leave that rock.

Ever. *Vlad. Help!*

Chapter Thirty

S UDDENLY, HER ENTIRE being screamed with pain. She felt as if her very body was being torn apart, ripped out of the rock. She fought against it, trying to stay where she was, but she was dragged ruthlessly from her oasis, pried free with unstoppable force. She held on as long as she could, and then she was torn from the rock and out into the air. For a split second, she hovered in the air, disoriented and confused, trying to get her bearing.

"Sophie. Come back to me." Vlad's gentle voice penetrated her mind, and suddenly he came into focus. He was standing in front of her, his index finger extended toward her. She felt the warmth of his energy surge through her, and he began to bring the particles of her body together, reconnecting them.

Vlad. She immediately focused on his touch, using his energy to rebuild her body. Working together, it took only a moment, and then she was standing in front of him again, her body solid, corporeal, and aching. Her legs trembled, and suddenly they gave out.

Vlad caught her instantly, sweeping her up into his arms. "Shit, Sophie. What the hell just happened? Could you hear me when you were in there?"

She rested her head on his shoulder, every muscle in her body shaking. "I heard you yell a couple times, but it was really far away. I couldn't really process it."

"I had to pull you out of there."

"I know. I felt it." She closed her eyes, trying to finish rebuilding her body, but her mind felt sluggish, as if it didn't want to rebuild her. "I never would have left that time. It was like a drug, trapping me." She began to shiver again, a bone deep shuddering she couldn't stop. "This has never happened to me. Ever. The rocks are a part of me, but never a trap." She looked over Vlad's shoulder at the vast expanse of rocks surrounding them, and fear shuddered through her. Suddenly, every rock was a potential death trap. Without Vlad pulling her out, she would still be in there, with no way out. "It's like they're trying to trap me." But even as she said it, she realized that wasn't true. She was hiding in them, like she used to when she was little.

Dismay filled her at the realization. After all this time, she was still the terrified little girl who would always choose to hide instead of fight?

Vlad swore. "We need to get you out of here." He turned and started walking again, moving fast, and keeping her in his arms, making sure not to brush even her arm against any rocks. He was heading in the opposite direction, away from the Graveyard of the Damned.

Alarm raced through her. "You mean out of the demon realm? No!" She hit his arm, trying to get him to let go of her. "Stop it! You don't get to make that decision!"

He didn't even slow down, or appear to notice her struggle. "It's not safe for you, Sophie. Something's happening to you, and there's no way for you to stay safe. You have to leave."

Irritation flooded her, a need to find her strength again. She pushed against him. "Put me down."

He kept walking. "I don't think it's a good idea for you to touch any rocks right now."

"Put me down! I'm not going to be carried like some weak victim!" She shoved at his chest. "I can't be so weak that I can't even walk, Vlad."

Swearing, he stopped, searching her face. "I barely got

you out of there, Soph. I don't know if I can do it again."

"We'll stop it before it gets that far. I let myself merge with the rock. Standing on it is different. I'll be fine."

He didn't stop walking. "What if you're wrong? What if I put you down, and you get sucked into the rocks, and I can't get you out? What then?"

The raw terror in his voice made her heart turn over. "Vlad." She touched his face. "Listen to me." She spoke gently, trying to get past his fear.

He stopped walking and closed his eyes, his arms still tight around her. "What?"

"We'll never make it back there before they find us. You can't protect me by spiriting me away from the threat. It didn't work last time, and it won't work now. We need to know what I'm capable of. We need to know how bad it is. Put me down, and let's deal with this now." She didn't want to be afraid anymore. She didn't want to hide. She *couldn't* be that girl she'd once been. Not anymore. She realized suddenly that all her dissolving over the years to hide from the demons had been just another form of being a victim, hiding, unwilling to fight for herself.

God. She was weak. All this time, she'd thought she was strong, and she wasn't. "Please," she whispered. "I don't want to run away anymore." Her fear would have trapped her in that rock forever. *Forever.* She couldn't live like that anymore. She just couldn't. Hiding had become the enemy, not her salvation. She didn't want to live in fear. She wanted to feel strong, powerful, and brave.

For a long moment, he didn't move. His muscles trembled where they held her, and his jaw ticked. Finally, he opened his eyes. His eyes were blazing with emotion, but he said nothing.

His face rigid with emotion, he loosened his grip on her arms, allowing her to slide down his body toward the rocks. Her feet touched, and he held her still, the toes of her boots brushing the rocks. "You good?"

She nodded. "Yep."

Slowly, he released her, but still kept his hand on her waist. "Still okay?"

"Yes." She could feel the call of the rocks through the soles of her boots even though she wasn't even reaching out to them. It wasn't a siren call, but she could feel their presence, as if they were alive. She'd always been able to initiate that connection, but she'd also been able to turn it off...but she couldn't anymore. "But stay close."

"You got it." Grimly, he put his hand on her back as they began to walk again, this time back toward the Graveyard of the Damned. Her back was warm where he was touching her, and she knew he was sending energy through her body, strengthening her cells and her physical being, giving her a shield of sorts. "I've changed my mind, Soph. I don't think you should use dissolution into rocks to escape from demons."

She managed a strangled laugh. "You think? I don't know. It seems to be going pretty well, and all."

He shot her an amused look. "Yeah, true, but I feel like it might hurt a demon's ego not to be able to catch you. It's kind of mean, you know?"

Her arm brushed against a rock, and her entire body tingled. She quickly jumped to the side, pressing herself more tightly against Vlad and his radiating energy. "Well, I wouldn't want to impinge upon any demon ego, so maybe I'll lay off the rock bonding for a while."

"Excellent. So glad our demon etiquette is on the same page."

Their tense humorous exchange faded as they walked, until the only sound was the thudding of their boots on the rocky terrain...until Vlad suddenly stopped. She sensed it at the same moment he did, and together they turned, looking out across the lava fields. In the far distance, she saw shadows moving, a line of heavily muscled males steadily winding their way down the trail. "Demons," she whispered. "They're out for the hunt."

Chapter Thirty-One

VLAD SWORE AND moved her back from the edge, into the shadows. "If we can see them, they can see us."

She shivered at the thought. "There's a pathway through the cliffs up ahead. We can cut through there and get on the other side..." As she said it, she realized that the crevice was narrow. There was no way for her to squeeze through it without touching the sides. She wasn't sure she wanted to do that right now. She was so used to weaving in and out of rocks without thought, that without that ability, suddenly, she didn't even know which way to go anymore. "Too narrow. I don't want to be that close to the rocks."

"I agree. We'll go around." Vlad tugged her further back into the shadows. "Let's go."

Sophie bit her lip, staying close to Vlad as they moved through the shadows, hugging the base of a high cliff. "We're not that far from Gabe and Maria," she said, "but we need to go around the rim of the lava fields. I don't know how we can do it without being seen."

"I can redirect their attention if necessary."

"For how long?"

"We'll see."

Sophie swallowed, her heart starting to pound. She felt as if all their escape routes were closing in around them, one by one.

Vlad gently squeezed her wrist. "Soph. You do realize that you have to leave the demon world, don't you?"

She sighed. "Vlad, this is an old topic now. I can't—"

"You have to."

She glanced over her shoulder at the demons. There were at least twenty of them, steadily marching across the lava fields. She could hear their low chant now, the one they always did when marching. That had been her life for so long, marching with the demons every night to search for the stone that would free them. It hadn't felt so terrible, but now that she remembered her past and had Vlad back, the darkness of life in the demon realm felt glaring and almost overwhelming. She couldn't deny that she didn't want to live this life anymore. She wanted to go back to a place where the sun warmed her skin, and people had a chance to be free. She wanted a second chance at a life with Vlad. "A part of me wants to leave," she said quietly. "But I will never be happy knowing that I abandoned Maria and the other women. I can't live with that."

Vlad swore. "I get that, Soph, but you literally have no way to stay safe here, even if we take down Lucien and Rikker. There will always be more demons."

Resolution flooded her. "There has to be a way. We could figure it out—"

Vlad stopped and turned to face her. His eyes were dark and tormented, his muscles tense. "Sophie. I would do anything for you. You know that, right?"

She nodded, tension gripping her. Was he going to tell her he couldn't stay in the demon world with her? Was he going to leave without her? She lifted her chin, trying to steel herself against the words she knew were coming, but tears still burned in her eyes. As important as Maria and the women were to her, she didn't know if she could handle losing Vlad again. He'd been a part of her soul since she was a baby.

She knew suddenly why she'd forgotten about her previous life when she'd fallen into the demon world. It hadn't been because of her parents' betrayal. It was because she'd been unable to cope with the loss of Vlad. Losing Vlad again would be like severing her own heart in half and throwing the good part away. *Don't make me choose*, she whispered silently, desperately.

He took her hands, his touch warm around her fingers. "Soph."

She took a shaky breath and looked at him. Her throat was tight, and she felt like darkness was crushing down on her, because she knew she wouldn't leave with him. As much as she loved him, as much as every piece of her soul cried out with longing to leave this hellhole and go to the earth realm with him, she knew she could never abandon Maria and the others. She would let him go. "What?"

He brought her hands to his mouth and pressed a tender kiss to each of her palms. "Since the day we met, I've loved you. I loved you when you got angry. I loved you when you were scared. I loved you when you were brave. And I loved you when I thought I'd lost you." His dark eyes fixed on hers. "For the last two hundred years, since I lost you, I've been a bitter, angry bastard trying to survive one minute at a time. I forgot what it felt like to smile, or to care about anything, even whether I lived another day."

She couldn't keep the tears from sliding down her cheeks. How could she live without this? Without him? When she hadn't remembered what she was missing, it had been easy. But now?

He wrapped his hands around hers, sandwiching her hands between his. "Finding you has brought light back into my life, and back into my soul. I can hear my heart beating again, and I can feel my own life force again, instead of stumbling around numbly. You know why that is?"

She shrugged, emotions strung too tight to talk.

"Because I am deeply, passionately, completely in love with you." His face softened. "I've always loved you, but it was a different kind of love than it is now. Back then, it was between kids, best friends. Now, it's the kind of love that makes this matter." He pressed a kiss to her wedding ring. "You're my woman, not just my best friend, though it's that, too. I love you, Soph, and I'll love you until the last breath I take."

His beautiful, heartfelt words made her want to fall into his arms and cry until she had no more tears left to fall. It was all she could do to make herself simply stand there, and wait for him to finish, to break her heart.

"But—"

The "but." She'd known it was coming, but just hearing that word made a sharp stab of pain pierce her heart.

Danger glittered in his eyes. "That also means I am fiercely protective of you. I failed you once, and I won't fail you again."

She tensed at the look on his face, and she knew what he was saying. "You're planning to force me to leave?"

Regret flickered across his face. "If you stay here, you won't survive, and we both know it. You won't do Maria and those women any good if you die. Staying doesn't fix that problem."

She lifted her chin. "I will not leave—"

"You will."

Anger surged through her. They'd had this discussion before, but she could feel the difference. He wasn't being theoretical. He meant it, one hundred percent. He wasn't going to give her an option. "You don't get it, Vlad. I'm not a sheltered teenager anymore afraid to go against the rules. You don't get to decide my life. No one does. Only me." She had to make him understand that she couldn't run away anymore. She had to face that which scared her, or she would crumble in fear for the rest of her life.

His eyes narrowed, but he didn't back down. "When I married you, I gave you an oath to keep you safe, and I will do that."

"I don't want to be safe," she retorted. "I want to live! I want to matter!"

"You do matter. To me."

"That's not enough!"

Her words pierced through the air, and she saw the shocked look on his face, the flash of raw hurt that flooded his eyes. She immediately grimaced. "I didn't mean it like that—"

"You did." His expression cooled, and she felt the sudden distance between them. It was as if the air cooled off, and the warmth that had been surrounding her vanished. "I get it. I fucked you over, and you've shut it down between us."

Regret flooded her. "Don't be an ass, Vlad. I'm not shutting you out. It's just that I have a life here that matters, people who count on me—"

"Don't be an *ass*?" He turned to face her. "You don't get it, do you? I love you, Sophie. I don't just sort of love you. My entire soul burns for you. There's no halfway with me. I get that you have forged your own life and your independence while you were down here. I respect that. I even admire it. But there's no way I can handle being with you, knowing that you're halfway out the door, looking for something else, something that *will* be enough. It ripped my soul in half when I lost you, but *I* remembered you. I lived with that pain every single day. I loved you too much to forget."

She blinked. "I forgot you because it hurt too much to lose you, not because I *didn't* love you—"

He didn't let her finish. "You won't leave without the women? Then I'll find a way to get them the hell out so you'll leave, but then I'll let you go, so you can find a life that *is* enough, since I'm not." He looked down at his wedding ring, which was still black. "Bound forever," he said softly. "Fuck forever."

He turned and began to walk away, his boots crunching on the rocky terrain.

Sophie stared after him, her heart tearing apart. "I love you," she whispered, her words drifting unheard into the air. She watched his broad shoulders and his strong back as he walked away from her. She could call him back. She could run after him, grab his wrist, and yank him toward her, shouting at him until he understood how much she loved him.

But the words stuck in her throat, held in place by fear. Fear of losing who she was to the man who'd once consumed her world. Fear of attaching to him again, after she'd already lost. She realized then, that despite her claim that she forgave him for not saving her, a deeper part of her hadn't forgotten that moment when she'd fallen, reaching for his hand, only to have her fingers slide through his. Logically, yes, she knew he hadn't failed her or betrayed her, but deep inside her soul was a primal fear coiled inside her, a raw terror that if she turned her heart over to him, he would shatter it again.

It made no sense. She knew that. But there was no way for her to ignore the piercing fear gripping her so fiercely. Over and over her mind replayed that moment when he'd reached for her, and her fingers had slipped from his. That moment when she'd realized that he couldn't save her. That moment when she'd realized how wrong she'd been to think that turning herself over to him in marriage would save her. That moment when she'd realized what a fool she'd been for not being prepared to save herself.

And now...she'd thought she'd become strong, but her experience with that rock made her realize that she was no more capable of saving herself than she had been before. She was still afraid. Still vulnerable. Still ready to run and hide. And Vlad brought that out in her. She loved him so much, she wanted to lean on him, to let him be strong. Her love for him, and his love for her, made her weak and afraid.

She realized his questions about how she could forgive him for not saving her was more on point than she'd realized. Intellectually, of course she didn't blame him. But on a visceral level, deep in her soul, she'd shattered when she'd lost him, when her fingers had slid out of his and she'd plummeted down into the crevasse of hell. She'd broken so badly that her memories had vanished. She'd lost her entire life and her entire past, simply because the loss of Vlad had been too much for her to handle.

Standing there, watching him walk away, made pieces of her heart shrivel. Her entire soul cried out for him with the same intensity it ever had, but now there was a deep, paralyzing fear of opening herself up to him again. The truth was that he wasn't the superhero she'd always thought he was when they were kids. He was a man. An insanely badass warrior, but a man, nonetheless. It was possible he would fail to keep her alive. It was possible he could get killed. Fear gripped her, a terror of believing in him again...and having it all go to hell. "I can't do it," she whispered. "I can't do it again."

Vlad turned around to face her. He was almost twenty yards away, but she could still see the emptiness of his expression. "I know. I won't make you." He held out his hand. "Let's go."

She tried to take a deep breath, but she could barely breathe. She felt like she was losing him all over again, facing the same loss that she was trying to protect against. "Vlad—"

He walked over to her. "Tell me about the women."

"But—" She wanted to talk about them, about him, about the terror hammering at her so violently.

"We need to focus, Soph. Getting all the women out is going to be a logistical nightmare, so I need information. Talk to me."

He was so cold now. So focused. "Did I hurt you that much?" she whispered. "When I said you weren't enough just now?"

Pain flickered across his face, but it was gone almost instantly. "You can't help how you feel. I get it, but at the same time, I can't turn off how I feel either. I can feel the distance between us. I can feel your distrust." He brushed his fingers along her jaw. "I will always be there to protect you and support you, but I can't stand here and love you when you will never let me in."

She clasped his wrist. "I do love you—"

"I know." He pressed a kiss to her knuckles. "But not the way I love you. It's okay. You have a right to love however you need to love." He took a deep breath. "I had it all built up in my mind over the last two centuries, how great we were together, how intense our bond was. I created this vision of you, of us, of what we had. I never took into account that we were teenagers back then, and it was not the same kind of love that happens between adults who've been through hell and back. My love held onto a past that's gone. Yours moved onto a new life. I will have to find a way to live with that."

Tears filled her eyes. A part of her wanted to beg him not to give up on her, to fight for her, to find a way to drag her out of her hell of fear...but she was too scared to even say that. She wanted to hide from what he awoke in her, from the fear of losing him, Maria, the women, the only life she'd ever really known. She knew now why she'd hidden in the rock. She didn't want to face the amount of loss that was coming her way. "I'm not a warrior," she whispered. "I'm not brave. I don't want to face this."

He sighed and took her face in his hands, his gaze searching hers. "I love you, Soph, but you need to understand something."

She lifted her chin. "What?"

"You got through two hundred years in the demon world without me. You're stronger than you think you are. Don't forget that."

Tears blurred her eyesight. She didn't feel strong right now. She felt fragmented and lost. "Vlad—" She stopped when she heard a distant shout.

They both looked across the lava fields, and she saw the demons were closer now, still marching in formation.

"We don't have time for this, Soph," Vlad said softly. "We'll be out of time much too soon. Where are the women located?"

"They're all spread out." She wiped the back of her wrist over her cheek, trying to destroy the tears threatening to take her down. "And they have demon blood in them. And Maria is half-demon. It's impossible to get them across the border, unless we find the cursed jewels, but then it will free all the demons, and that's not exactly a great idea."

He ignored her protest. "How many women are there?"

"Right now there are only eleven of them, but not all of them want to leave. Only Lucien's castoffs want to go." What if Vlad could figure out a way to get them out? Would she make them all leave, or leave behind those who wanted to stay? And if they stayed behind, could she leave, knowing that they would die without her and Maria?

"Why don't they want to leave?"

She sighed. "They say they can feel the emptiness of their demon's souls, the aching loneliness that beats at them. They want to save them, to somehow bring humanity back to them." She glanced at him. "They believe in the demons. They believe redemption is possible...except for a few, like Lucien."

He watched her. "Do you believe redemption is possible for them?"

She thought of Rikker, of that one moment where she'd seen that flash of humanity on his face...before he'd reverted to his caveman ways and decided to claim her. She thought of Maria's brother, Damon, and the love he had for his sister. "I don't know. Maybe, I guess, for some of them."

Vlad raised his brows. "So, these women are willing to risk death for the one they love? They'd refuse to give up on the one they love until the very end, even if failure means death and suffering? To them, a shitty ending isn't enough reason not to give everything they have on the chance of saving the one they love? Is that what you're saying?"

She jerked her gaze to him and saw the challenge in his eyes. Irritation bristled through her. "So, you're calling me out because I'm not willing to risk having my heart shattered by you again?" At his non-committal shrug, anger rushed through her. "I'm sorry I can't be stronger," she snapped. "I'm sorry that I can't handle going through it again. I'm not some super-strong warrior. I'm just me!"

"Shit, Soph. When are you going to realize that that's enough?" His fingers drifted through her hair, a soft touch that made longing pulse through her, but neither of them made a move to close the distance between them. "I have a question for you. What if you told them that you and Maria were leaving, and it was their choice to stay or go with you? What if they choose to stay?"

She grimaced as he voiced the question she'd already thought of. "If they stay, they'll need healing—"

He swore in frustration. "Why is it your responsibility to sacrifice yourself to save people who have made the choice to risk themselves?"

"Because I can make a difference—"

"So, they have a right to keep you from happiness because they're making a choice that could kill them? Is that your job?

To sacrifice yourself to save women who choose to endanger themselves?" He softened his voice. "Don't you get it, Soph? You don't need to be a hero to matter. You don't need to save all these people to matter," he said softly. "You matter just by being you."

Tears burned her eyes again, and she turned away, feeling as if the foundation she'd built her life and identity on was trembling beneath her feet. "Damn you, Vlad. I—"

"Quiet." His hand went over her mouth, and he looked past her, his face rigid.

She froze, her heart pounding at the sudden tension coiled in his body. "What is it?" she whispered.

His answer was a faint murmur in her ear, so quiet that she could barely hear it. "The demons. They've changed direction."

She turned around and looked out across the lava field, searching for the demons, but they weren't where they'd been before. She scanned quickly, and saw them moving swiftly toward the south. They were dark now, almost shadows, in the form they took when they were on the hunt. Fear gripped her when she realized what direction they were heading in. "That's where Maria and Gabe are," she whispered. "Do you think they found them? Is that why they're going that way?"

"Shit, I hope not." Vlad swore under his breath. "I'll tell Gabe to be on the alert, but we need to get there first." He grabbed her hand and started to sprint along the path, but she stopped.

"No. This way." She spun around and raced toward the narrow passageway that she'd discounted only moments ago. Fear for Maria pounded fiercely through her, and she knew that passageway was their only chance.

"It's too narrow—"

"I don't care." She plunged into the passageway, but just as the rocks touched her arms, Vlad's hand settled on the back of her neck. His power plunged through her, holding the particles of her body together, fighting the call of the rocks.

"Got you." His voice was grim and hard, and his energy was so strong that it hurt to breathe. She glanced back at him, but he wasn't looking at her. He was looking past her, searching for threats. The wall she'd created between them was still there, and he wasn't going to bring it down again.

Maybe they could get through this passageway, maybe they could get to Maria and Gabe in time, but then what? She didn't even know. But she had no time to figure it out.

Time was up. The battle was upon them.

Chapter Thirty-Two

*M*ARIA. *DO YOU see any demons yet?* Gabe was directly behind Maria as they were scaling a steep cliff. It was a sheer rock face, but she was ascending it with swift agility worthy of any Calydon warrior. Vlad had contacted them to report that he and Sophie had seen demons heading their way, but so far, none had appeared.

No. Do you?

No— The weapons in his arms started to burn fiercely in warning. Swearing, he stopped and turned his head, scanning the vast barren landscape. The shadows were long and dark, and spirals of smoke arose from the Graveyard of the Damned, where lava was flowing thick and heavy. The air smelled of sulfur and rot, and it was a battle for his lungs to glean enough oxygen from the air. *Maria, wait.*

She stopped and looked around, scanning as carefully as he was. *Maybe Vlad was wrong about where they were headed. Maybe they aren't tracking us. But we need to keep going. We're meeting Sophie and Vlad soon.*

Gabe still didn't move. His weapons felt like they were on fire, vibrating in his forearms. *Something's hunting us.* He flexed his hands, ready to call out his weapons. He didn't want to do it too early, however, because the crack and flash of black light would pinpoint their location to anyone coming after them.

Really? Then we need to get to the top of the cliff. Maria dug her fingers into the almost invisible crevices in the rock, her muscles flexing as she hauled herself up the sheer rock face. *We can't fight down here. It's too narrow.*

Gabe leapt up on the wall, ascending rapidly as he followed her, realizing she was correct. They were hanging by their fingertips on the side of a steep precipice. There was no way they could fight in this position. *Let's go.*

Just as he reached her, the back of his neck prickled with sudden awareness. The threat was close. Dangerously close. He let go of the wall with his right hand, swinging his arm free as he dangled from the sheer rock face, held in place only by his boots wedged in the crevice, and his left hand locked in a crack in the rock. He reached out with his preternatural senses, scanning their surroundings for body heat, an energy signature, a ripple in the atmosphere, for *anything* that was off...but he couldn't sense anything.

But his weapons continued to burn. Shit. He was out of his element here. It was different enough from the earth realm that he didn't know exactly what he was looking for, or what to attune to. But there was something. *Be careful.*

Seriously, Gabe? You think I need instructions on how to navigate the demon world without getting killed? She laughed, sounding amused. *Trust me, I know every danger in this place, and every trick to staying alive. And that includes getting to the top of the cliff because neither of us can fight from this position. So climb, Blade Boy.*

He glanced up at Maria. She was ascending quickly, with astounding grace, the muscles in her legs flexing as she climbed. She moved like a wild cat, agile and predatory, the weapons strapped to her body glinting in the dim light. Heat raced through him, a possessive, sensual fire. That was his woman, a fucking badass who ruled the demon world. *Jesus, woman. You're hot.*

She laughed, a delightful, happy sound that made him grin. She looked down at him, her eyes dancing. *No one has ever flirted with me before. I think I like it.*

Only from me.

You're the only one who's sane enough around me to be able to flirt, so you have no competition. Her gaze flicked past him to the ground. *Hurry.*

Gabe followed her gaze past his boots, and then swore when he saw shadows emerging from a crevice at the bottom of the cliff. They moved swiftly, taking the shape of men, and he realized they were demons, shrouded in darkness, heading straight for the bottom of the cliff. At least twenty of them. *Shit.*

He swore and began to haul ass up the cliff. He had no chance of defeating twenty demons if he had to use one of his hands and both feet to keep from plummeting a thousand feet to the rock below. He was damn good, but one-handed was going to be a challenge he didn't feel like taking on if he could avoid it.

Maria was moving fast, as fast as he was, but the demons were moving faster, ascending the rock with alarming speed. *Why are they after you?*

I don't know. She sounded grim. *Usually they leave me alone. Lucien might have sent them to retrieve me.*

Lucien? The leader of this shithole?

Yes, he decided to claim me, but gave me up when Sophie offered herself as a substitute. Since neither of us held to the bargain, he's probably pretty pissed.

White hot rage shot through Gabe. *He wants to mate with you?*

It's more like fuck me until I die from his poisonous semen, but sure, you can call it mating if that makes it more palatable for you to handle.

Gabe swore as his vision actually turned red for a split second, and his muscles clenched. *Jesus, woman. Don't you know Calydons have jealousy issues? I can't handle shit like that.*

She looked back at him, her eyes wide with surprise. "You're jealous?"

"Fuck yeah. You're my woman."

Her face softened, and she smiled. "When Lucien said I

was his woman, I wanted to kill him. When you say that, it feels different. Nice. Autocratic, possessive, and not acceptable, but also, nice."

"It doesn't feel nice," he growled, "so drop the subject."

Her eyebrows went up. "It doesn't feel nice to say I'm your woman?"

"No." He glared at her, still climbing fast. "It pisses me off to be thinking about some asshole making the moves on you when there are demons hunting us. We're in the middle of a battle zone, and I'm thinking about sex. This is why I was celibate for so long. So I could focus. *Jesus.*"

She grinned. "I think about sex all the time, and I've managed to stay alive, so it's not the end of the world."

She looked so amused and pleased that some of his irritation faded. "You're crazy, woman."

Her smile widened. "Thanks." Her gaze flicked past him, and she wrinkled her nose. "I finally meet a guy who noticed I'm more than boobs, and I don't even get a chance to tease him about it. Life is just so unfair."

Gabe actually found himself chuckling as he followed her gaze and glanced over his shoulder at the ground below. He narrowed his gaze when he saw the demons were only two hundred feet below them, and moving quickly. He and Maria were still too far from the top. At the speed the demons were ascending, there was no way they were going to reach the top before the demons were upon them.

He was damn good with his weapons, but demons were tricky, especially in that many numbers, and the stakes were much higher now that he had a *sheva* to protect. He wasn't used to going into battle without his team, and he didn't like this situation. This was why the Order needed to be rebuilt. There was no way he should have had to make this trip alone. His team should have been all over getting Dante back...not that it mattered. Right now, they had to deal with the situation, not waste time whining over shit that couldn't be changed.

He glanced at Maria, who was climbing again, the muscles in her legs flexing as she raced up the cliff, moving fast...but not fast enough. Shit. *Vlad? You nearby?* He shared his location with the warrior.

Vlad responded almost immediately. *Sophie says we're about twenty minutes from there. Why?*

We got trouble. Gabe dug deeper, channeling more strength into his muscles. He began to gain on Maria, but the demons were still gaining on him.

We're coming. We'll be there in twenty.

Make it two, or we're all fucked. The demons were now only a hundred and fifty feet behind. Their muscles were cut and hard, their gazes fixed on him and Maria. They looked like men, in their leather pants and boots, but their eyes were black pits of hunger, devoid of humanity, devoid of emotions. They weren't like rogue Calydons, who were enraged. These were like automatons, predators caught in the thrall of the hunt, focused on nothing else but their prey.

He glanced at the top of the cliff, quickly calculating if they could make it.

They couldn't.

He was going to have to fight. *Keep going, Maria. I'll hold them off.*

She stopped immediately and looked down at him. *What? No! Keep going, Gabe.*

Fuck, Maria. Keep moving!

Not until you do.

We won't make it. You get to the top, and fight from there. He hauled himself up another ten feet, onto a ledge that was less than five inches deep, and a foot wide. He braced himself on it, his back against the cliff, then called out his weapons. The crack and flash of black light ignited the darkness, and he felt the mountain shudder under the force of it.

He immediately hurled both weapons, in a one-two hit that decapitated the two lead demons. They fell off the cliff with screams of agony while he recalled his weapons. They hurtled back to him with blinding speed, and the moment he caught them, he threw them again. He lined up his shots this time, and one of his swords cut through three demons in a row—

Until the fourth one caught it, snatching it out of the air.

Fuck. He tried to call it back, but the demon's fist closed around it, his body jerking as he fought the axe's attempts to return to Gabe.

His other hook sword slammed back into his hand just as the lead demon reached Gabe. He swung hard, slamming his blade into the demon's chest as another one leaped up onto the ledge. They swarmed him like locusts, biting, slicing, and clawing. He swung hard and fast, moving with lightning efficiency, but there were too many, too fast. They moved like Calydons, every bit as fast, agile, and deadly, except their only weapons were their claws, their teeth, the sheer force of their strength—

A demon slammed its claws around Gabe's throat and slammed him up against the wall. Gabe swung hard with his hook sword, slicing through the demon's torso, but it didn't move. Its eyes darkened and it pressed its claws into Gabe's chest. *Jesus*. It was going to tear his heart out! Gabe struck again, but the demon didn't seem to feel it. He couldn't get the angle to decapitate it, and nothing else seemed to be slowing it down. The other demons surged past him, heading after Maria.

Shit! He glanced up, his gut clenching when he saw her surrounded by demons, fighting desperately. Blood was pouring from her shoulder, and her cheek, but she was heavily armed, fighting with impressive skill that would have kicked ass in any other situation. There were just too many demons, and the fact they were hanging on the side of a cliff meant both he and Maria had only one arm free to fight with. "Hey!" he shouted, trying to draw their attention. "Come after me, you dumb fucks—"

At that moment, one of the demons hit her hard, slamming his fist into the side of her head.

She swayed, and then fell, free-falling straight down toward him.

"Maria!" With a roar of fury, Gabe hurled the nearest demon aside and lunged forward. "Grab my hand!"

She shook her head, as if to clear it, then reached out as she dropped past. They grabbed each other, and he braced himself as he jerked her to a stop. "Come on, babe." He hauled her up onto his ledge. She flashed a grin at him, but the demons were on them before they could recover.

Gabe struck hard and fast with his weapon, as she did the same with hers, but he knew they were outmatched. They wouldn't last three minutes, let alone twenty. There simply wasn't enough maneuvering room, and the demons were so much more agile on the cliff.

"Look!" Maria suddenly shouted, pointing across the darkened sky. Swooping across the sky was a demon, its black, feathered wings flapping slowly as it raced toward them.

He recognized it instantly. It was her brother, the bastard who'd tried to kill them when they'd first arrived. Son of a bitch. They didn't have time to deal with an overprotective brother right now.

Maria threw her arms around Gabe's neck and wrapped her legs around his waist. "Jump," she shouted. "*Jump!*"

It was a thousand foot drop onto solid rock, with demons swarming below them. It was suicide.

A demon slammed its claw into his back, and he stumbled, almost losing his grip on the cliff.

Gabe. Trust me. Jump. Maria tightened her arms and legs around him, no longer fighting the demons. Just holding onto him.

He didn't have his team with him. He didn't even have a partner. All he had was Maria, and they were outmatched.

This was her world. The one she'd survived in for centuries.

Swearing, he wrapped his arms around her. *I will be incredibly pissed if we die.*

We won't.

Okay. He tightened his grip on her...and jumped.

Chapter Thirty-Three

THE MOMENT THEY emerged from the passage-way between the cliffs, Sophie could hear the sounds of battle. The scent of sulfur burned her nose, and she knew the demons were close. Fear leapt through her as a sudden wave of heat hit her. The warmth was coming through the rock wall in front of them, and she recognized it as the dark energy that demons sometimes exuded during intense battles. "They're on the other side of that! Maria!" She broke into a run, sprinting alongside the base of the cliff, panic hammering at her.

"Shit, Soph." Vlad hissed. "Keep quiet! We don't want to alert the demons we're here."

She ignored him, scrambling over the rocks. "It will take us twenty minutes to get around it. Hurry!" They were so close, and yet she couldn't get through. "Run!" She scrambled over the rocks. Urgency coursed through her, and sweat was beading on her forehead. "What did Gabe say? Are they still alive?"

"Yeah. He said they need us *now.*" Vlad was moving swiftly, keeping pace with her easily as they raced down the narrow path winding along the cliff side.

"Dammit! I knew we shouldn't have split up." Panic was hammering at her chest. "What if something happens to her? What if—"

Vlad caught her arm and spun her around toward him. "Hey."

"Let me go!" She tried to get free. "We don't have time—"

He ignored her. "Listen to me, Soph. You can't help them if you're panicking. You have to keep your head clear."

She grabbed his fingers, trying to pry his immovable hand off her arm. "Let me go! We don't have time for some meditative moment to get me in touch with my inner self. Maria is being attacked by *demons*!"

Vlad was infuriatingly calm. "Maria's half demon, and Gabe's a Calydon. Together, they're absolute badasses."

"But the demons outnumber them—"

He nodded. "I know. So, we need to focus. Twenty minutes is going to be too late."

Her heart seemed to freeze in her chest. *"What?"*

"We have about two minutes." He pointed at the cliff. "Get us through it."

"Get us *through* the rock wall?" She stared at him. "But—"

Vlad raised his brows. "Do you happen to know anyone else who can take us through rocks?"

"Shut up. Of course I can do it, but I can't go through solid rock quickly. It would take us forever, and I don't even know if I can trust myself with rock right now—"

"So, what *could* you do?" His voice was steady, calming her just enough to realize the enormity of the situation. Maria was in trouble, and needed help. Twenty minutes would be too late. Was Vlad right? Was there something she could do?

"Could you widen a passageway that was already there?" he asked. "Would that be faster?"

"Yes, but there's no passage. It's solid." Even as she said it, however, she spun around to face the rocks, scanning them quickly for any kind of crack. Her heart sank. "Nothing."

Vlad pointed at the ground. "Isn't that hell hound droppings?"

She looked down. "Yes—" She spun toward the cliff again, her nose burning from the scent of sulfur from the battle. "They travel through cracks in the rock. There has to be something here."

In unison, she and Vlad raced to the wall. They both set their hands on it and began running their palms over the rock. It felt impenetrable, but she knew it couldn't be. There had to be a sliver, a crack, something tiny that she could slide into—

Then she felt it, a cool wind that brushed over her fingertips. "Here!" She pressed her hands to the crack, pouring her energy into the rock. It began to shift immediately, the molecules drifting to the side to widen the passageway—

"What the hell is that?"

The sudden tension in Vlad's voice made her turn. She followed his gaze, and she saw a dark shadow racing across the sky. A winged demon. Fear knifed through her. "A demon. Only a few of them have wings." Her heart began to pound as it headed right toward them.

Its wings were massive, flapping in a slow, unhurried rhythm that propelled it forward with blinding speed. It was in full beast form, with no human features at all. Just a scaled body and face, like a dragon born from hell itself. It was still too far away to see the details, but its horns were more curved than most, and the sheer size of its body was apparent. "Oh, God," she whispered. "It could be Lucien."

"Lucien? Fuck." Vlad grasped her arm and jerked her back against the cliff. "Stay still," he said. "I'll divert his attention." He pointed his finger to the other side of the lava fields.

The approaching winged beast swung to the right, hovering as it stared in the direction that Vlad had just pointed to. The moment it went still, she was able to see it clearly, and she knew. There was no mistaking the shape of its horns and the sheer size of its body. "It's him," she whispered, stunned. "It's Lucien. He never comes down to the lava fields. *Ever.* Why is he here?"

Vlad grabbed her and shoved her behind a rocky outcropping. "Stay low." He crouched beside her, his index finger still extended, as he tried to direct Lucien's attention away from them with his magic.

For a long moment, Lucien hovered in place, searching the far cliffs. "It's working," she whispered.

But even as she said it, Lucien turned his head and looked

directly toward them.

Sophie sucked in her breath, flattening herself against the rock. Her fingers dug into the rock, and she wanted to dissolve into it, even at the risk of losing herself in it, but to transform the rock required a burst of energy, which Lucien would be looking for. It would bring him right toward her, not to mention the problem of being stuck in it. Fear hammered at her. "We don't have any weapons."

Vlad crouched down beside her, and she felt a pulse of energy from him as he began to amass his power. "He's made of living matter," he whispered. "I should have been able to hold him, but he broke through it too easily—"

There was a victorious roar, and suddenly Lucien landed in front of them, hitting the ground so hard that the rocky ledge shuddered beneath him.

Sophie yelped and scrambled to her feet. Vlad leapt up, grabbed her wrist, and thrust her behind the rock, back out onto the ledge they'd just been on. He followed quickly, keeping his body between her and Lucien as they scrambled to get out in the open.

Lucien followed them, his clawed feet digging into the rock. His face was dark with fury, his claws extended, his horns curving back from his head. Up close, she realized that his face still had remnants of his human form, just enough that she could make out the same cheekbones, the same eyes, the same forehead, almost as if his human face had been transplanted directly into the beast's visage, merging the two together. The effect was terrifying. "You ran from me." He didn't even look at Vlad. His entire focus was on Sophie.

Dear God. What chance did they have? They could never fight him. "Lucien—"

"She is mine." Vlad stepped in front of Lucien, his hands flexing by his sides. His face was stoic, and power radiated off him so fiercely she could see the air undulating.

"Yours?" Lucien turned his attention to Vlad. "Who the fuck are you?"

"Her husband."

Her husband. The words were so possessive, spoken like a

man who would never, ever relinquish his woman. She'd thought it would scare her, but it didn't. It made strength pour through her, as if she could feed upon Vlad's power and make it her own.

Lucien shrugged. "I don't care." He dismissed Vlad, and raked his gaze over Sophie. "You made a bargain, Sophie. You cannot walk away." He held out his clawed hand. "You will come to me now."

His command seemed to thunder through her head, and Sophie gasped, pressing her fingers to her forehead, fighting against the sudden compulsion to walk toward him. "He's doing something to me, Vlad," she whispered. "I can't—" She took a step toward the demon.

Vlad's hand clamped around her wrist, jerking her to a stop. "You made a deal with him?"

"Yes, to save Maria, but I didn't mean it." She tugged against his grip, trying to get free, trying to get to Lucien. Dear God. What kind of power did he have over her? "Vlad—"

He jerked her against his side, and locked his arm around her waist. "Mine." He shot the single word at Lucien, no longer bothering with an explanation.

Lucien, however, was staring at Sophie, shock on his face. "You're holding form."

Too late, Sophie realized that she'd just revealed herself. She was pressed up against Vlad, touching from shoulder to hip, and she was staying corporeal. "It's because he's not a demon," she snapped, forcing bravado and hostility into her voice.

"You fucking bitch." Lucien lunged across the ledge, his claws outstretched—

Vlad pointed his finger and Lucien was thrown backwards, slamming into the cliff. He roared with fury, twisting violently as he fought to get free of Vlad's hold. The cliff cracked, and pebbles began to roll down, showering over the ledge. "I can't hold him," Vlad muttered, sweat beading on his temple. "He's strong as hell. Can you bring the rocks down on him? Bury him?"

Sophie glanced up at the rocky cliff. "I'll try." Fear flickered through her at the thought of connecting with the rock, but she shoved it aside. She had no time to be afraid. She raced over to the wall and placed her bare hands on the rock. The moment she made contact with it, she felt the call of the minerals, trying to drag her into it. Without Vlad to anchor her, she felt herself tumbling into the rock, trying to hide from Lucien, the way she'd dissolved so many times in the past. Panicked, she jerked her hands off the wall.

"Soph! I can't hold him! Bury him!" Vlad's voice was tight, and she glanced over at him. He was down on his knees, his palm outstretched toward Lucien, who was still pinned against the cliff above her head. Lucien was struggling violently, crashing against the cliff and sending rock fragments down upon them as he fought.

"I can't! The rock is trying to take me!"

"You can do it." Vlad's muscles were visibly shaking with the effort of containing Lucien's power. "You don't need to run away anymore, Soph. Do it."

"I—" She glanced up at Lucien again, fear hammering at her. He was a terrifying beast, so powerful and strong that she knew she had no chance against him. No chance to fight. No chance to run. No chance to survive him.

"Sophie! Now!"

Vlad's voice ripped through her, and she jerked her gaze off Lucien. She focused on the rock wall. "I can do this," she whispered to herself. "*I can do this.*" She took a deep breath and set her hands on the rock again. Instantly, she began to dissolve, merging with the rock. "No, dammit!" She jerked her hands off again, sweat beading down her back. She needed to manipulate the rock, not dissolve into it, but she couldn't. All her body would let her do was hide.

"Sophie!" Vlad's anguished cry made her turn, but just as she did, pain shot through her shoulders, and she was jerked off the ground as Lucien snatched her in his claws. She screamed and twisted around, but within a split second, they were a hundred feet in the air, racing back across the lava fields. She twisted around, trying to look behind her. Vlad on his knees, his palms outstretched toward her, his face stark with horror as Lucien sped away, rising higher and higher. She felt Vlad's energy pulling on her, but Lucien was stronger, so much stronger.

She reached toward Vlad, her fingertips stretched toward him just as they had been so long ago. And just like before, she was torn away from, their outstretched hands nothing more than a silent call for a rescue that would never come. All she could see was his anguished face, the horror in his blue eyes as she got further way. "Vlad." The wind tore his name from her, dissolving it in the air.

Tears filled her eyes, and within seconds, Vlad was swallowed up by the rocky terrain, a speck of dust in a barren wasteland of hell.

Chapter Thirty-Four

THE AIR RUSHED up at Gabe and Maria with violent fury, whipping past them just as Vlad's anguished cry rent the air. Gabe swore, almost doubling over at the intensity of Vlad's pain. Jesus. Something horrible had just happened to Vlad, something unbearable, so devastating that his anguish flooded Gabe, crushing him with grief.

Swearing, Gabe had to block his connection with Vlad so he could focus, knowing he and Maria would both die if he couldn't control their fall. His heart thundering for Vlad's suffering, Gabe pulled Maria more tightly against him, fighting to balance them. They plummeted past demons, their poisoned claws ripping at their flesh as they fell. His blood was searing through his body, burning with the toxins, and he could feel the heat rising from Maria's flesh as her body fought the toxins as well.

Swearing, he looked down at the ground rushing up at them. It was solid rock. He was very, very good, but landing a thousand-foot drop onto solid rock was outside his skillset. *What's the plan now, sweetheart?*

Damon.

The nice guy who almost killed Vlad and me not so long ago? Not liking that plan, babe—

Suddenly, arms slammed around them, jerking them to the

side. Gabe swore, tightening his grip on Maria as they were ripped sideways, speeding across the sky. He glanced up, and saw they were in the arms of a massive dragon-like beast, with clawed arms, a scaly body, massive wings lined with spikes....and her brother's face. Shit. This was not what he'd been thinking of when he'd been wishing for a little backup.

He flexed his hand, preparing to call out his weapon if he needed to.

"Let go of him, Maria." Damon snarled, his voice rough and animalistic. "Let him fall."

Gabe tensed, scanning the underside of the beast's chest for a vulnerable spot to hit when they were closer to the ground. No way was he letting the demon take him wherever he was planning to go.

"No," Maria snapped at the demon. "Gabe's with me." Her arms tightened around him. "He's my chosen, Damon."

Her chosen? Gabe had no idea what it meant, but the claim of ownership was unmistakable. He wouldn't have thought demons were human enough to honor something like that, but he felt the immediate shift in Damon's body, the protectiveness that surged around both Maria and Gabe. Damon's arms tightened around them both, even as he unleashed a litany of curses which made it apparent just how irritated he was by that news.

Well aware of the conflict surging through Maria's brother, Gabe continued to watch him carefully, scanning the tightly overlaid scales for an opening. *Chosen? Is that like a soulmate in demon lingo?*

It's more like I've decided you're going to be my only sex toy until I've exhausted your resources and you die in my arms in the throes of ecstasy.

Her voice was light, but he felt the weight behind her words. It *was* like a soulmate. Son of a bitch. She'd chosen him, just as he'd chosen her. His cock tightened, despite the fact that they were a thousand feet above the earth, their fate in the hands of a possessive dragon-beast who wanted to drop him on his ass. *Damn, woman. You have a way with words.*

"He's a human." Damon was still flying with numbing

speed. "He isn't worthy."

"He's not human. He's an immortal warrior, and he stays sane when we have sex." Maria's voice was becoming labored. "Take us to the fourth ridge."

"Sane? You're kidding." Damon looked down at him, shock etched on his features. "How?"

Gabe shrugged, grimacing as the poison began to settle in his bones. "Just a badass kind of guy I guess."

Damon continued to stare at him, and Gabe stared back. "I'm a Calydon," he said, his voice low. "Descended from demons. Not entirely human."

"Half human, and half demon?" Damon asked with a frown. "Like Maria?"

Gabę glanced at Maria, who was still locked around him. "I guess." He frowned when he saw her looking at her forearms, her brow furrowed. "What?"

"More lines. A lot more."

He swore. "I trusted you with my life when you told me to jump, and I did." Son of a bitch. "There's only one left. The transference of my weapon."

She held up her arm, and he saw the lines of his weapons appearing on her arm. Possessiveness roared through him, a visceral, instinctive surge of power. She was almost completely bound to him. *His.* To claim. To protect. To serve. To honor.

Her gaze snapped to his. *Not yours. I'll never belong to any man.*

Need poured through him, a need to drag her into his arms and pour his seed into her, to mark her as his. His cock got hard, and he swore, jerking his gaze off hers. This was not the time. *Not the fucking time.* He was a thousand feet in the air, for hell's sake, in the middle of demon hell...but son of a bitch. The physical need to claim her was insane. He suddenly wondered how the bloody hell his teammates had stayed sane after bonding with their women. Her presence was almost overwhelming, plunging ruthlessly into every crevice of his being, and they weren't even fully bonded.

He could taste her. He could smell her. He could hear the

beat of her heart, the air whispering through her lungs with each breath, the fear thundering through her.

It was the fear that got him. He jerked his gaze back to her. *You're afraid.*

She lifted her chin, her hair whipping past her face as they shot through the air. *I'm not afraid.*

Something inside him softened, and he suddenly wanted to slide his hand gently along her jaw, offering comfort and solace, things he'd never even thought of before this moment. *I swear I will protect you with my life.*

She met his gaze. *What about Dante? What about the Order? What if you have to choose? Has that changed? Who would you choose?*

You. It was the first thought that went through his mind, but he shut it down before she could hear it. For the first time, fear ripped through him. Fear that he really *would* put her first. Fear that this woman, this courageous, amazing woman would rip him away from his duties, from his oath to protect the *entire fucking world*. He suddenly realized that he hadn't reopened communication with Vlad. He'd been so consumed with that bond that he'd forgotten his own teammate. Jesus. This wasn't him. This wasn't how he was supposed to live his life! Swearing, he opened his mind to Vlad. *Where are you? We're coming.*

Vlad's anguish flooded him so hard that even Maria flinched. *He got her. He fucking got her.*

Sophie? Who got her? Gabe brought Maria into the communication, so she could hear.

Lucien. He took her. Jesus, Gabe.

"Sophie!" Maria's grief tore through Gabe so hard that his breath caught. She. He needed to shield themselves from their pain so he could think, but he needed to maintain communication. *Where are you? We'll come to you.*

Apparently on the other side of a rock wall from you. Fuck, Gabe. He swore again, anguish raw in his voice.

"Damon!" Maria shouted at her brother. "Lucien got Sophie. We have to turn around!"

"Sophie?" Damon swore, and immediately began to fly in

an arc, turning them back toward where they'd come. "Where?"

"On the other side of the cliff. Vlad's there. He saw it."

Gabe expected Damon to protest being asked to team up with Vlad, just as he'd told Maria to drop him, but he didn't. He just sped across the sky, his urgency evident in every line of his body. Gabe realized then that like his sister, Damon's loyalty ran deep. He might be a demon, but there was more to him as well. Sophie was in his circle of protection, and that made his decision to help her automatic. Damn. He respected that. He wouldn't have thought there was anything about demons to respect, but Damon had just made it onto the list.

Maria pointed at the rocks. "There!"

"I see him." Damon tucked his wings and dove toward the cliff.

Vlad leapt to his feet, and held up his hand. Instantly, Gabe felt the push of his magic, shoving them back. *It's us, Vlad! Let us land!*

Instantly, Vlad dropped his hand, and sank to his knees. His palms were braced on the cliff, and his head was down, as if he were fighting to breathe. He was a man broken, and the sight made Gabe's blood congeal.

That was his ultimate nightmare, to lose who he was because of a woman. The sight of Vlad on his knees drove terror right into the depths of his soul.

Never. He could never go there. *Never.*

Chapter Thirty-Five

DAMON SLOWED JUST before landing, setting both Maria and Gabe on their feet. As they landed, Vlad looked up. Gabe swore when he saw the anguish in his eyes. Not just anguish. Gabe knew he was seeing the death of a man's soul. Gabe stopped in shock, too stunned to move.

The only time he'd seen that kind of anguish was when his Order of the Blade teammate, Ian Fitzgerald, had lost his *sheva*. Ian had almost died from the grief, but since she'd been his *sheva*, it was understandable. Vlad, however, wasn't a Calydon. There was no fated bond between him and Sophie, and yet, he could feel that Vlad's grief was almost overwhelming, so brutal that even Gabe could barely focus through it, even though he was feeling it only second-hand.

That was why he could never finish the bond with Maria. That was why he'd stayed celibate his whole life. Who could afford to let someone drag them down like that?

Maria raced over to Vlad and fell to her knees in front of him. She grabbed his shoulders. "Where did he take her? We have to find her now."

Vlad looked up at her, his face a barren wasteland. "She stayed corporeal," he whispered, his voice hoarse with raw anguish. "She has no defenses. He knew it. You should have seen his face when he realized she could stay corporeal. I couldn't stop him." He held up his hand. "I couldn't do it. I gave it everything I had, and it wasn't enough to hold him."

Gabe tried to harden himself as he listened to the conversation between Vlad and Maria. He fucking *tried*. He tried to tell himself he was there for Dante, and for the Order. He tried to remove himself emotionally. He tried to stay focused on the oath that had driven him his entire life. He tried, but he couldn't shield himself from their grief. It was too deep, too visceral, too real.

Beside him, Damon shifted into human form, his body lean and muscular. He strode over to Vlad and crouched beside his sister. "Which way?"

Vlad pointed silently, and everyone turned around to look where he was pointing. Maria slowly stood up, her face ashen. "He's taking her to the Temple of the Sun."

Damon swore violently.

Vlad stared at her. "What's the Temple of the Sun?"

"It's..." Maria looked at her brother, and the pain in her eyes seemed to plunge right into Gabe's soul. Without a word, he walked over to her and slid his arm around her waist, pressing a kiss to her temple. There was literally no way he could stand there and pretend none of this mattered. He just couldn't.

Maria leaned into him, her body shaking and cold.

"It's a place he takes women when he needs to break their will," Damon said. "It's a place of seduction. No woman has a chance. It's an ancient temple of sorts. Most demons don't use it, because it sucks the will out of the woman. It destroys who she is, until there is nothing left but a soulless body to fuck."

Vlad looked like he was going to pass out, and Gabe instinctively reached out, clamping his hand around the other man's arm. "We'll get her."

"How?" Vlad sounded strangled. "It's too late."

"No, it's not." Maria leaned into Gabe. "The temple closes at sunset. Until then, we can get in."

Gabe looked up at the sky, which was actually an endless cavern. "There's no sun here."

"It's a volcano that erupts in one hundred year cycles. The light from the lava is considered our sun." She gestured to the lava fields. "That's what this is from."

"Hundred year cycle?" Vlad looked at her. "What does that mean?"

"It means that in forty-five minutes, it will stop erupting for the next hundred years." She looked at him. "Sophie will be sealed in the temple with Lucien until the next cycle begins."

"You mean, she'll be trapped in there with him for a hundred years?" Vlad swore and stumbled to his feet. "We have to get her. We have to go now. Where is it?"

But neither Maria nor Damon moved. "It's protected by a thousand demons." Maria looked at her brother. "We can't get past them."

"Fuck that." Vlad shook his head, pacing the small cliff. "We're going in there."

"We *can't*." Tears glistened in Maria's eyes. "It's impossible. We'll die instantly." She pressed her hand to her heart and walked away from them. "Lucien never would have tried for her if she hadn't offered herself to save me." She looked at her brother. "It's my fault, Damon. *My fault.* Sophie's going to go through hell because she was willing to be my friend."

Gabe's hands balled into fists as she looked at her brother. He didn't want her looking to Damon for comfort. He wanted her looking at *him.* "Where is this place?"

"On the other side of the Graveyard of the Damned," Damon said.

"The Graveyard of the Damned?" Where Dante's body was buried? Gabe stiffened, his adrenaline surging. They were that close to his leader? Not that he could bring himself to care. He was too consumed by the emotions of the trio on the ledge with him. But shit, he had to try to stay focused. Dante was about protecting the entire world. Sophie was one woman. One woman wasn't his priority. The world was. But he couldn't do it. He couldn't find that place anymore, that one that let him sacrifice one to save thousands. Jesus. He was losing everything that defined him.

Helplessly, he looked at the others for help, but no one was paying any attention to him.

Damon focused on his sister. "Maria, you can't punish yourself. Sophie would never change it. You know she wouldn't."

"I should have forced her away from me," she snapped. "I was too selfish. I needed her as my friend. I needed her, and I knew it was dangerous." She spun away from them and walked to the edge of the cliff, staring across the wasteland. "I'm so sorry, Soph. Dear God, I'm so sorry." She dropped to her knees and bowed her head, tears falling silently down her cheeks.

Damon swore and ran his hand through his hair. "I can call some demons to help—"

"They won't come," Maria whispered. "They can't afford to piss off Lucien. You know that. You're the only one willing to stand up to him. We'd need an army, anyway. A few demons wouldn't do it."

Vlad raised his head to look at Gabe. "Call them."

Gabe frowned, trying to clear his head enough to focus. All he cared about was Maria, and the pain crushing her. His entire being was calling to her, needing to heal her, to take away her pain, to protect her. "Call who?" he asked blankly.

"Your team. The Order of the Blade." Vlad surged to his feet, his muscles taut. "I'll bring them across—"

"To rescue Sophie?" Gabe blinked as Maria and Damon spun toward him. "The Order's mission is to protect against rogue Calydons," he said automatically. "I can't bring them here to get Sophie. We don't do that—"

"Don't *do* that?" Vlad surged to his feet. "Are you fucking kidding me? That's the Order you're trying so hard to preserve? It's some bullshit group of losers who won't use their power to help a woman who needs them?"

"Gabe." Maria stared at him. "You said you would call them for me."

"I know, but—" His voice faded. How could he explain it? In that moment with her, he'd wanted to give her the world. He truly had. He'd meant it at the time, but when faced with actually making that choice, the reality of it struck him hard and brutally. It was against his oath. It was against the oath of every one of his teammates. It violated everything they had sworn their loyalty to.

But even as he thought it, Gabe shifted uncomfortably, tormented by the look on Maria's face. For a split second, he imagined calling them across and asking them to help. Hope leapt through him, a raw, visceral hope of making a difference, of helping these women who had fought like hell to survive against all odds, of helping the woman his soul burned for.

But then he thought of his team, the one that had been assembled centuries ago for the sole purpose of hunting rogue Calydons, a team that was fracturing even as he stood there, not going after Dante. "They wouldn't do it," he said, unable to keep the regret out of his voice. He knew he shouldn't feel regret, because helping Sophie violated everything the Order was about, but he couldn't help it. In this moment, in this crazy, brutal moment, he didn't want the Order to be about hunting rogues. He wanted it to be about helping those who needed help, regardless of where the threat was coming from.

He'd lived for the Order his whole life. He'd believed in their mission with every fiber of his soul. He *was* the Order. And yet, standing there, looking at three people who'd lost someone they loved, he didn't give a shit about the Order's mission. He just cared about the people who mattered.

Swearing, he clasped his hands on his head, trying to get a handle on the battle raging within him. "If we bring them across," he gritted out, "they're more likely to string me up for mutiny than to help. For thousands of years, the Order has refused to be swayed from their path. All they do is protect from rogue Calydons. That's it. And even with focusing all our efforts there, many people still die." He looked at Maria, needing her to understand. "They're sworn to their oath. They can't deviate. They won't deviate."

"You have." Maria's voice was quiet, but strong. Unwavering.

He stiffened. "What? In what way?"

"Because you came down here for Dante, and you haven't done a damned thing to look for him." She walked over to him and stood in front of him, staring up at him. "You've taken care of me. You've helped Sophie and Vlad."

He closed his eyes, realizing what she said was true. He'd completely abandoned his oath. Guilt tore through him, a wrenching, brutal guilt. "Maria—"

"I saw the look on your face when we said the temple was in the Graveyard of the Damned. I saw you remember Dante. You'd forgotten about him, hadn't you?" She touched his arm, and he opened his eyes to look at her. "Gabe, I love your loyalty to the Order. I love that it drives you, but there's more to life than blind loyalty. Did you ever think that the Order is dying because the oath you take has sucked the life out of it? That it's time to become more?"

He fisted his hands. "Dante believed—"

"Dante's gone. It's not his Order anymore. It's yours. The world is different than it was two thousand years ago when he began." She touched his arm. "Call them. For me, Gabe. For Sophie."

Gabe ground his jaw. "I can't—"

"You care." Vlad was the one who spoke, and Gabe looked over at the other man, whose face was so haunted and stark. "I can feel it inside you, Gabe. You care about more than the Order. You care about Maria. Fuck, you love her, don't you?" At his words, Maria sucked in her breath, but Vlad didn't stop. He just walked over to Gabe, still talking. "You're too fucking afraid to admit it, aren't you? Afraid it makes you weak? Afraid that caring about anything other than your work makes you a pathetic piece of shit."

Gabe stiffened, his jaw tightening. "You know nothing about the Order—"

"Yes, I do." Vlad's voice was hard. "I was there when you guys tried to kill a rogue Calydon because he'd lost his shit. I stopped you, and let the rogue go, because it's bullshit to kill people just because you think it's right. My parents tried to kill me to save their kingdom, and Sophie's parents sacrificed her to save theirs. And you know what? Both those kingdoms were gone a decade later, reduced to a bunch of rubble. Why?" His words were hard, full of venom. "Because they didn't rule with love. They ruled out of duty, and made choices for the greater good, but the greater fucking good starts with love and loyalty to those closest to you. Without it, the entire thing crumbles." He stopped in front of Gabe. "It just fucking crumbles, like their kingdoms. Like your precious Order. The minute you start sacrificing innocents for the greater good, it breaks down the fabric of your humanity. Doesn't it?" He slammed his palm over Gabe's heart. "Do you feel that? Your heart is beating for the first time in your life, because in this hellhole, you've let yourself care. You've let it become personal, and *that's how you win*."

At Vlad's words, images began tumbling through Gabe's mind. Not images of all the rogues the Order had killed, but images of the carnage that was always left behind. Of his family, decimated by the rogue that had stolen his world. Of Ian, crushed under the weight of losing his *sheva*. Of his teammates who had broken the rules and bonded with their *shevas*, and yet had managed not to go rogue. Of Quinn Masters, their interim leader, insisting that rogues could be redeemed, despite centuries of evidence to the contrary.

What if the foundation of the Order's mission had been wrong? What if, after all these centuries, they'd been *wrong*? Killing people who didn't need to be killed? Not seeing that there was another way? Not understanding that the old way didn't work?

Suddenly, he couldn't breathe. He sank down to his knees, gasping for breath as images and memories assaulted him. He gripped his forehead, trying to make it stop, trying to make it end, trying to get back to the place where his brain worked, where everything made sense.

Everything started to spin violently. Gritting his teeth, he bowed his head and dug his fingers into the rock, fighting for balance. He closed his eyes, pain searing through his chest, when he felt Maria kneel beside him. He didn't open his eyes, but he tensed, viscerally aware of her as she wrapped her arms around his shoulders and put her cheek next to his. "Gabe." Her voice was a whisper, a beautiful, amazing sound that made his entire body go still.

He waited.

"I love you, too."

He scrunched his eyes shut, unable to breathe.

"I love you because of your honor, but I also love you because you gave it all up to save my life. No one has ever done that for me. No one has ever cared about *me* the way you do." She slid her fingers between his, and he opened his eyes, staring down at their entwined hands. Her fingers were so much smaller than his, her skin lighter than his. Feminine. And yet, the hands of a warrior.

He felt the warmth of her love wash over him, filling him with a sense of wholeness he'd never felt before, even after he'd won a battle and saved hundreds. Nothing had filled him the way this moment had. Ever. "I gave my life to the Order," he said, his voice raw. "I believed we were doing the right thing. How can my life be wrong?"

"It's not wrong," she said gently. "You saved many lives, and every life saved matters. But maybe it's time to expand. Maybe Dante died because it was time for a new future, one that was different than the one he could give you. Maybe he died because he knew it was time."

Gabe thought back to the night of Dante's death, to that moment when they all relived it. Dante had sacrificed himself, not fighting back to defend himself against the assailant who had killed him. At the time, they'd thought it was for the greater good, but maybe...maybe...it had been because he'd known it was time to make the others step up.

"He came back to us once," he said. "Through Quinn's *sheva*. He said there was a new future, that it was our turn. We thought it was because of the enemy we were fighting at the time..." His words faded. Could it have been more? Was Maria right? Dante's message through Quinn's *sheva* had been one of acceptance of her, not criticism that they'd let a *sheva* into their midst. He thought of how Thano and Zach had left the Order. He thought of how every current Order member except him and Thano had taken on a *sheva*. He thought of the fact that they'd added only one new Order member in hundreds of years. The way they were doing it was failing. He'd known that, but he'd thought that survival meant anchoring to the past. What if he was wrong? What if survival of the Order meant using the past as a building block toward an evolved future, instead of using the past to trap them?

Son of a bitch.

Son of a bitch.

His head snapped up, and he looked at Maria. "If the Order is no longer solely about rogues, where does that leave it? What's next?"

She smiled. "Sophie's next. After that?" She framed his face with her hands. "After that, the future is unwritten. You get to write it. You and your team."

A new future? One without Dante and his legend? Swearing, Gabe looked across the lava fields toward the Graveyard of the Damned. *Give me a sign, Dante. Show me the path.*

He waited...but nothing happened. No answers were offered by their leader.

Vlad crouched beside him. "Gabe, I get that you have issues. I'm down with that, because I have a shitload of baggage. I respect you and I consider you a friend, but if you don't pull your shit together and haul ass with me to get your team, I will personally fuck up every mission you go on for the rest of your damned life."

Gabe looked up sharply into Vlad's grim face, and something inside him released. A tension that he'd been holding inside him his entire life. He grinned, a shit-eating grin that seemed to light up from within. "Let's go, buddy."

Vlad blinked in stunned shock, and then he let out a whoop of victory. "Fuck, yeah!" He jumped to his feet. "Damon! Can you carry all of us? We need your speed."

"Yeah, no problem." As Damon shifted into full beast form, Gabe looked at Maria, who was still crouched in front of him.

She smiled, a smile that danced inside his heart. "Thank you," she said.

He shook his head. "No. Thank *you.*" He shackled her wrist and pulled her close, sliding his hand behind her neck while he kissed her. Not a kiss to claim. Not a kiss to infuse her with his power. A kiss that was so much more than sex, power, or lust. It was a kiss from the heart that she'd just awakened.

"Let's go!" Vlad shouted. "Now!"

Maria grinned. "I've been wanting to crush Lucien forever. I'm so excited."

Gabe laughed as he grabbed her hand and stood up. "You're so bloodthirsty. I love it." They ran over to Damon, and he tossed Maria on the beast's back, before climbing up behind her. He wrapped his arms around her waist, and leaned on her shoulder as she locked her arms around Vlad, who was already on board.

As Damon began to flap his wings, Gabe took a deep breath. *Maria.*

She looked over her shoulder at him, her eyebrows raised. *What?*

He wanted to say it. He wanted to tell her that Vlad was right. He wanted to give her those three words that she'd offered him. But they stuck in his throat. To admit he loved her was making a promise of forever, a promise of his heart, a promise of his entire loyalty. How could he do that? How could he offer his forever, when his entire world had been the Order? He didn't know what was next. He didn't know the future. He couldn't make promises anymore about whose side he was on, because he didn't even know what that meant anymore. *Never mind.*

Her smile softened. *I love you, too, Gabe. You don't need to say it. It's okay.*

It wasn't okay. He knew it wasn't. Maria deserved more. She deserved the words.

But he couldn't make them come. He felt them in his heart. He knew they were true. But to say them to her would be to make a promise that he wasn't sure he could keep. What if he really had to choose between her and the Order someday? Could he do it? What kind of man was he really, when all his years of battle and honor had been stripped away?

He didn't even know anymore.

Chapter Thirty-Six

L UCIEN'S CLAWS WERE so painfully tight around Sophie's shoulders that she had to bite her lip to keep the tears at bay. The wind from his wings was brutal, ripping at her clothes, making her hair slash across her face. She glanced down, and then had to shut her eyes when she saw how high they were. She squeezed her eyes shut, fighting against the dizziness. "Where are you taking me?"

"Shut up, bitch. You've lost the right to talk to me."

She flinched at his brutal tone, fear hammering at her. She wanted to dissolve. She wanted to hide. Right now, she would have no problem with any instinct to hide and retreat. She didn't want to be brave and fight him. She wanted to simply be gone.

But she couldn't. Her body was completely corporeal, and nothing she tried made it dissolve. She was trapped in her own body. Trapped in his claws. Trapped in the sky, far away from any rocks. Vlad couldn't fly. His magic wasn't strong enough to stop Lucien. Just like before, so many years ago, she had nothing to save herself with, but this time, she couldn't even dissolve. She had nothing.

"Temple of the Sun."

At his words, fear shot down her spine, paralyzing her with terror.

Lucien laughed, a harsh, brutal sound that made the hair

on the back of her neck stand up. "That's right, bitch. You're mine for a hundred years. You'll be nothing but a mindless wench, and Maria won't be around to heal you. You'll just rot away with my cock in you, and you'll love every second of it."

Dear God. She couldn't let him take her there. No one would be able to reach her. There would be no way out. Ever. She turned her head and saw the mountain in the distance, the one that housed the Temple. It was harsh and arid, a mountain of burned out lava so dead that nothing could live there, not even demon hounds. Lava poured out of the top of the mountain, trickling down the sides of it, the bright orange glow casting a haunting hue on the surrounding fields.

There was no way she could go in there. *No way.*

She looked down at the ground again, and this time, she didn't flinch. They were hundreds of feet in the air. If she fell, she would die. It wasn't her first choice for escape, but it was better than what he had in mind. There was no way she was going to let him take her.

She looked up, scanning the underside of Lucien's chest, looking for a vulnerability, a spot she could strike to take him down. His scales were thick and hard, glistening with the reflection of the lava. She set her hand on his chest, and could feel the energy of his heart. She'd never have an opportunity like this again. Once he landed, she'd never get close enough, but right now, while he was flying and she was hanging in his claws, he was vulnerable. One strike there wouldn't kill him, but it would slow him down. All she needed was enough time to hit the ground before he recovered.

She reached down and grabbed one of Maria's knives that was still strapped to her calf. She pulled it free, and wrapped her hand around it. Her heart was pounding. Power filled her, the raw, bold power of taking control of her own future. No more being the victim. She angled her body and drew her arm back, summoning all her strength into her arm. "Good-bye, Vlad. I love you—"

Vlad. Her heart seemed to shatter as she thought of him, and her arm fell to her side as the agony of losing him again hit her. Not just him. Maria as well. Right then, in that moment, she knew that they were on the ground, desperately trying to figure out how to get her. But they couldn't. It was too late. The temple was surrounded. It was too far away. She would be lost long before they could ever get there.

She had to act now. She had to. She tightened her fingers on the dagger and raised her arm again, but Vlad's face kept flashing through her mind. His horror as Lucien tore her out of his hands. His anguish as she'd fallen into the pit the first time. His smile when she'd remembered him in the cave. The way he made her laugh. If she let herself die now, they had no chance. If she ran away because she was too scared of what was to come, they had no chance. If she stayed alive, if she was brave enough to face what might come, they had a chance.

She closed her eyes, her fingers tight around the handle of her dagger. Was she strong enough to face what might come, for the chance of seeing Vlad and Maria again? She wasn't. She wasn't. But somewhere deep inside her, another voice whispered to her. *Fight, Sophie, fight. You can do it.*

Vlad had believed she could save herself, but he'd been wrong. She hadn't. She wasn't a hero. She was just *her*.

"I have to do this," she whispered. "I *have* to." But her arm didn't move. The dagger felt like a lead weight in her hand. If she stabbed Lucien right now, and fell to her death, she'd be running away, just like she had every time she'd dissolved over the last two hundred years. Just like she had when she'd rejected Vlad's love.

She looked up at Lucien, and the raw, brutal lines of his face. The demon king. Unstoppable. Undefeatable. A hundred years in the temple with him would be hell. She knew that. But would it be worse to plummet to her death, knowing that she hadn't given it every last effort to survive and to stay alive long enough for Vlad and Maria to find her? To give herself a chance for the life she'd never fought for? What if there was a way out? What if Vlad was right that they could do it? What if there were answers she'd never thought of, because she'd been too busy running away and hiding?

Dammit. She didn't want to run away anymore. She didn't

want to give up. She wanted a chance with Vlad. She wanted a chance to get Maria and the others out. She didn't want this to all end badly.

She knew she couldn't defeat Lucien alone, but she knew Maria and Vlad wouldn't give up. They would fight for her. Together, could they do it? Together, could they find a way? She looked down at the dagger in her hand, one of the ones Maria had successfully used for so long to keep herself safe. The dagger wasn't about weakness. The dagger was about one little sliver of metal, and the power it could wield if used the right way.

Sophie tightened her fingers around it as determination flooded her. Screw running away. Screw letting Lucien win. She was tired of hiding. She was tired of not being worthy of Maria and Vlad. Vlad was right. Hiding away and healing didn't save anyone. It just prolonged their misery.

She wanted victory, and it was time. Maybe not to win, but at least to fight until the very bitter end. With one last glance at Lucien's chest, Sophie slid the dagger in the waist-band of her jeans.

She might die. She might face an even worse fate. But that was okay, because, for the first time in her life, she was going to stand and fight until there was nothing left at all.

But even as she hung there in Lucien's claws, watching the Temple of the Sun getting closer and closer, she knew that if Maria and Vlad didn't get to her in time, all the bravado in the world wasn't going to save her.

She could choose to stay alive, but she couldn't defeat Lucien herself. She needed their help, and she knew she needed it soon.

MARIA HUNCHED LOW on her brother's back, shielded between Vlad and Gabe, as Damon tore through the tunnels, heading toward the cavern where Vlad and Gabe had crossed over from the earth realm. His wings shattered the rock walls of the tunnels, leaving behind a carnage of rubble. The sound was deafening, and Damon's body shuddered from the impact each time he tore out another section of the wall. Maria knew that any demon could track them given the sound of their passage, but she also knew it didn't matter.

They had no time to be quiet. No time to be careful. No time to do anything but move as fast as they possibly could. *Please stay safe, Sophie. We're coming.* She sent the message out, but she knew her friend would never hear it.

Gabe's arms tightened around her, and sudden tears threatened. Maria bit her lip, fighting off the tears. *Don't be nice,* she snapped. *I can't be weak. I have to focus.*

Loving her doesn't make you weak.

Tears spilled out. *If I'm so upset I can't focus, then, yes, it does.* She scrunched her eyes shut. *God, Gabe, I'm so scared for her. She's not just my best friend. She's my sister, a part of my heart. What if—*

No. Gabe's fingers tightened around her hips. *No what if's. Focus on solutions. The Order is unstoppable, and Kane can teleport. Once they're across, Kane can get us there in a split second—*

But what if they won't help? What if you're right?

They'll help. Gabe's voice was low and hard, so steady that some of Maria's panic eased.

She twisted around to look at him, keeping low so her head didn't crack against the ceiling of the tunnel. *How can you be so sure? You said before that they wouldn't.*

Gabe's face was determined. *Because I won't let you down.*

Maria's heart seemed to come to life at the absolute conviction in his tone and on his face. She knew he meant it. His commitment to her was absolute. Not because of sex. Not because of the *sheva* bond. But because he had the purest, most beautiful heart in the world, and he'd given it to her. Tension left her body, replaced by hope. *Thank you.*

He smiled. *You're welcome. I think you'll like them.*

They're a bunch of arrogant badasses that are too focused to be sucked into your sex demon lure. You'll be able to be yourself around them.

She stared at him, stunned by his comment, both that he'd even thought of the fact she'd already been preparing to deal with the lust issue, and also by the hope that it might be true. *Really?*

Really.

"Two minutes," Damon said, interrupting them. "But I can sense demons approaching. We won't have much time."

Gabe squeezed Maria's waist. "You ready, sweetheart?"

Sweetheart. He'd called her sweetheart? *I'm so not a sweetheart type, Gabe. I'm too...me...to be sweet anything.*

He pressed a kiss to the side of her neck just behind her ear. *You're wrong, Maria. So wrong.* He kissed her again, a tender, gentle kiss that made her believe that he meant it. This time, when the tears filled her eyes, it wasn't grief or sadness. It was the softening of a heart that had worked so diligently and so long to be hard.

LUCIEN DROPPED SOPHIE on the edge of the cliff. She gasped and grabbed a rock outcropping, trying to keep herself from falling. The moment she grabbed the rock, she felt it calling to her. For a split second, she considered dissolving into the rock, but the pull was so great she knew she'd never get out. It would trap her forever...and she would never have a chance to be with Vlad or see Maria.

She had to stay alive for them, because she knew they were coming for her.

Lucien landed next to her and grabbed her wrist, dragging her away from the rock as he shifted into his human form. "You fucking lied to me. All this time, you fucking *lied.*"

She scrambled to her feet, trying to stay up as he yanked her along the precipice. Above them, the sky was bright orange, and lava flowed past them. She realized they were on the top of the volcano that housed the Temple of the Sun.

They were too close.

She pulled back, trying to get free, but he jerked her against him.

Her body slammed into his naked chest, and she gasped at the shock that flooded her. He was pure energy, almost crackling with it. "You can't escape," he snarled. "Look behind you."

He jerked her around so she was facing down the mountain. Below them, as far as she could see, were demons, pacing in the shadows. As her eyes adjusted, she realized that they were all around them, just outside the circle of Lucien's energy, as if they'd parted just enough to allow their king to land. Her heart stuttered with fear as she realized they were completely surrounded, that the mountain was literally coated with demons.

Not the demons she knew, like Rikker and Damon. These were mindless automatons, barely evolved beasts whose only job was to fight and protect. These demons didn't trap women and take lovers. They weren't even capable of hunting for jewels. They were the lowest, basest form of demon existence, deformed, mindless beasts whose only job was to protect the light that warmed their kingdom.

One of them wandered close, and she caught a glimpse of its deformed, ghastly face before it slid back into the darkness. Revulsion made her shudder, and she realized suddenly the true impact of severing the barrier between the worlds. It wouldn't just free Lucien and Rikker. It would also unleash this army into the earth realm, to prey upon every innocent they found. How long could the earth realm survive the barrier being down? Weeks? Days? Hours? Dear God. No matter what the cost, that magical barrier had to remain intact.

And how on earth could Maria and Vlad possibly rescue her from this throng of demons?

They had no chance. They'd be killed.

She couldn't let them take the risk...but how could she stop them? Even if she dissolved into a rock, they wouldn't know that, and they would still come for her...and they would die.

Damn. The die had been cast. They would come, which meant she had to do *something* to give them all a chance to survive.

Chapter Thirty-Seven

D AMON HADN'T EVEN completely landed in the cavern when Vlad launched himself off him and sprinted across the rocks toward the wall he and Gabe had originally come through. Gabe swore, leaping off Damon as he followed Vlad. Now that he'd committed, he was in full battle mode, wasting no time.

Vlad slammed his hands against the rock, and Gabe felt the rush of energy as Vlad reached out in search of living matter. Almost instantly, Vlad swore. "They're not there. We're too late. They've left. It's just fish and plant life in that pond now."

The anguish in Vlad's voice made Gabe tense, and he took a deep breath, forcing the emotions out of him. He might have told Maria that loving Sophie didn't make her weak, but she was right that panic got them nowhere. "Let me check."

Gabe pressed his hands against the rock wall and closed his eyes, reaching out across the barrier telepathically, searching for his team. *Gideon. Quinn. Elijah. Are any of you there?*

For a long, agonizing moment, there was silence.

Quinn! I need your help! Come on! He shoved every last bit of energy into his communication, but he knew he wasn't breaching the barrier, even psychically. "Shit! I can't penetrate the barrier that separates the worlds."

"I can." Vlad stood up. "Let's do it together. Use your

psychic connection to your team, and I'll use my energy to cross the barrier."

Rightness poured through Gabe at the suggestion. It was natural and right to be working as a team. Vlad's power was different than a Calydon's, but just as penetrating. He immediately connected with Vlad telepathically. *Okay, so, I'm going to reach out telepathically, and you're going to use your energy to cross the border?*

Yep.

Gabe closed his eyes and opened his mind, pouring his energy into his mental bond with his team, and drawing Vlad into the connection at the same moment. The men's minds merged, and Gabe felt a rush of massive power flooding him. For a split second, he lost focus, stunned by the sheer force of Vlad's power, but, he regrouped almost instantly, tightening the bond between them. He wove layers of connection between them, like a thousand invisible filaments threaded into a brilliant tapestry of power. *Do it.*

Vlad immediately shifted their focus toward the wall. Gabe felt the rush of power as Vlad thrust his energy into the barrier. It held for a moment, resisting Gabe's demon energy. Gabe renewed his push, joining his power with Vlad's. The barrier resisted, blocking Gabe's demon heritage, but Vlad's power was surreal, shoving past the barrier and taking Gabe's psychic energy with him. With a loud pop that nearly shattered his eardrums, suddenly, they were through.

Gabe thrust his telepathic energy outward, racing through the water toward the shore above, Vlad's consciousness still wrapped tightly around his. His telepathic energy shot out of the surface and he flooded it in all directions. *Quinn! Gideon!*

Where the hell have you been? Zach's voice filled his mind. *What the fuck is going on?*

Astonishment flooded Gabe at the sound of his longtime teammate, the one he'd grown up with, who had abandoned the Order to guard a South American jungle. *Zach? What are you doing here?*

You were trapped in the demon world. What the hell was I going to do? Get a Brazilian suntan while you were rotting away?

A Brazilian suntan might have been out of the question, but I still think you should give the Brazilian wax a try and spare all of us, Thano chimed in.

Thano! Elation rushed through Gabe. Son of a bitch. They had the whole team. *You're back.*

Just to save your ass. These other old guys can't figure out how to cross the barrier. They needed someone who has the ability to problem-solve and look at life from a new perspective. So, yeah, we all know that's me.

Who else is there? Gabe asked.

Everyone, Thano answered. *I brought Rohan and his team, because they can't live without my wit and charm now. Even Dante's son is here, but honestly, that kid's a problem. Not going to lie.*

Gabe grinned. *We've got a situation. I need your help.*

Of course you do. Everyone needs a piece of Thano. What's up?

Not just your help. Everyone's. I need you guys to come across the barrier and take down a demon king.

There was silence from his team.

Cross the barrier? Quinn Masters, their interim leader, finally asked.

Take down a demon king? Gideon sounded cautious. *Why?*

Gabe swore under his breath. *I'll explain when you get here.*

Again, silence, and he knew they were discussing his request.

Just out of curiosity, Thano asked. *If we cross, are we going to be trapped there?*

Gabe looked at Vlad. *Maybe.*

Our mission is to protect the earth realm, Quinn said. *To protect innocents from rogue Calydons. Crossing the barrier to attack a demon king who can't even get to the earth realm isn't our problem.*

It needs to be. Gabe glanced at Maria, whose face was pale. He realized she was listening to the conversation.

Why? That was Kane Santiago.

His entire damned team was there. If they agreed to help, they could do it. Gabe looked around the cavern, at Vlad's anguished face, at Maria's stricken one, and at Damon, whose wings were bloodied and damaged from flying through the narrow tunnels. There was no rogue Calydon to defend against. There was no greater good to preserve and protect. There was simply one woman who they all loved. One woman who had spent her life saving others. How did he make his team understand? *He has kidnapped a woman. My* sheva's *sister. She's...* He paused, trying to think of a way that would make his team value Sophie's safety on behalf of the greater good.

Your sheva? *When did that happen?* Ian asked. Ian Fitzgerald, who'd lost his *sheva* multiple times. If anyone would understand the bond Gabe had with Maria, his need to help her, Ian would.

Gabe glanced at Maria. She was pacing behind him, daggers clenched in her fists, her body lean and muscular. But her face was pale, almost ashen, and he could feel the fear emanating from her. She was both a warrior and a woman, strong and vulnerable. She was everything. *It just happened,* he said, even as he wondered how on earth it *had* happened. He'd done everything in his life to resist his *sheva,* and yet Maria had broken through his barriers almost instantly. *You'll like her.*

Maria glanced at him, and a small smile curved the corner of her mouth.

I'm sure I will. Ian sounded pleased. *Congrats, Gabe. Glad to hear you've come over to the dark side.*

Gabe focused on Ian. *Her sister Sophie has been kidnapped, Ian. We need to help her.*

I'm in. Ian didn't hesitate. *How do we get across?*

Gabe grinned. *Come to the bottom of the pool, and my partner, Vlad, will pull you across the barrier. But we need everyone else, too.*

Fuck, Gabe. That was Quinn. *We're all that's left of the Order. If we get trapped there, fighting a battle that's not ours, then the entire earth realm is unprotected. You're asking us to risk our oath for a single innocent.*

Hey. Maria interrupted. *She has the most beautiful, purest, kindest heart, and the world will be a darker place without her.*

I'm sorry for your pain. Quinn's voice softened. *As Gabe's soulmate, we honor you, but you ask us for more than we can give.*

Fuck that! Maria snapped. *You can give it! You're just afraid.*

And blind as to what really matters, Vlad added. *Do you guys really think that running around taking out the occasional rogue is the way to save the world? How's that been working out for you?*

Ryland Samuels, the most dangerous and deadly Order member responded instantly. *Who the fuck are you?*

Vladimir Hawkings. I fucked up one of your missions with Dante a few years back. Sorry and all that shit, but this is important.

Gabe suddenly felt Ian's presence on the other side of the wall. His teammate had swum to the bottom of the pool, and was directly across the barrier from them. Hope shot through him. "Vlad? You feel that?"

"Yep." Vlad focused his energy on Ian, and Gabe felt a shocking, violent tear as Ian's body was pulled toward them. For a split second, there was a massive resistance, and then suddenly Ian was dragged through the wall, landing on his knees in the cavern.

For a moment, Ian didn't move, and then he looked up. His blond hair was short, and his muscles were cut and lean. He stood up quickly, his gaze landing first on Damon, who was still standing in beast form. Ian instantly called out his weapons with a crack and a flash of black light, but Maria and Gabe simultaneously leapt in front of him. "No!" Gabe held up his hands. "He's on our side."

Ian's mouth dropped open. "He's a *demon.*"

"Yeah, and a good guy, so back off." Gabe decided now might not be the most appropriate moment to mention that Damon had almost killed him upon his arrival. He held out his hand, and Ian grabbed it, then they thudded their fists on each other's backs. "Thanks for coming," Gabe said.

Ian shrugged. "It's automatic." He then turned to face Maria, and went down on one knee. He bowed his head. "My name is Ian Fitzgerald, and I welcome you to our world."

Gabe's chest tightened at the show of loyalty, and he glanced at Maria. Shock was etched on her face, and there were tears glistening in her eyes. She glanced at Gabe, then back at Ian. "I'm half demon," she said. "Lust demon."

Ian nodded. "I can tell." He grinned. "Good thing your mate is a Calydon, huh? Gabe can handle the lust and the demon."

She stared at him. "That's it? You don't care?"

Ian rose to his feet. "Care about what? That you carry the same heritage and lust that every Calydon I work with deals with? Just makes you one of us." He saluted her. "I'm just glad you're strong enough to handle an Order member as a mate. Not every female would be." He winked at her, and then held out his hand to Vlad. "Ian Fitzgerald. You're Gabe's new teammate?"

Vlad shook his hand. "Vladimir Hawkings. We need to get the others across now."

"Two minutes," Damon said. "There's a team of demons less than two minutes from here, and they aren't as charming as I am..." He paused and cocked his head, then he swore. "It's the warrior demons. They're fiends. Shit."

Gabe swore and reached out with his mind again to his team. Vlad was still holding the bridge across the barrier. *A team of demons is headed this way. Get the fuck down here, and we'll figure out the details later.*

Quinn swore. *Shit, Gabe.*

I'm calling in my blood oath as an Order member. I need you guys. Now. Gabe had never called in his oath. He'd never invoked his right as an Order member to ask for help. No one ever had, in the history of the Order, at least that he knew of. But it was always there, always an option, one that no one ever took, because to invoke that oath, meant that the Order had to come to their aid, no matter what the risk, no matter what the consequences. The Order wasn't about blind risks. The Order was about strategic strikes, planned threat management, and efficient use of resources, none of which applied here.

There was silence from the team.

A silence that stretched out.

"What are they doing?" Vlad asked. "What the hell?"

"They're discussing." Gabe looked back at Ian. "We're fucked if they don't come."

Ian shrugged, twirling his double spiked flail in circles. "They'll come."

Gabe felt the ground beneath his feet begin to tremble, and the acrid smell of sulfur began to drift into the room. Swearing, he called out his weapons and faced the door. *They're coming. I need you guys. We can't do this alone.*

More silence, then Vlad came to stand next to him. Ian moved up beside him, and so did Maria. The five of them facing down the open door. Gabe tried one last time. *The kidnapped woman is Vlad's soulmate. He's my partner. We've blood bonded. I owe him, and you guys do too. What would you do if your* shevas *were kidnapped?* It wasn't an argument he'd ever thought he'd use on the Order of the Blade, who used to kill *shevas* to protect the Order. But now, it was different. Now, he understood, and so did they.

A loud rumble began to echo down the hall, the sounds of boots hitting the ground.

"Five seconds." Damon said.

Five seconds, Gabe told his team.

There was a low curse from someone, Gabe couldn't tell who, and then Quinn replied. *We're in. Bring us over.*

At that second, demons burst through the door of the cavern, howling like creatures of the darkest night, striking fast and furious. They were more like deformed beasts than men. They were massive, lethal instruments of death. He'd seen beasts like this before, creatures designed only to kill, to fight until death. Jesus. What the hell were they? Gabe swore and leapt forward into the fray. "Bring my team across, Vlad!"

Gabe and the others charged into the fray, swinging hard, while Vlad sprinted over to the wall. He was vaguely aware of

Vlad slamming his hands onto the wall, but then a demon leapt toward Maria, and all that mattered was saving her. Gabe hit it hard, his blade slicing clean through, but before he could recover, another demon leapt on his back. Ian shouted and slammed his flail into its head, ripping it off Gabe's back. But even as they fought, more demons came in, and he knew they were outmatched—

Then suddenly, a gleaming machete sliced through the air, decapitating a demon that was lunging at Gabe. Ryland Samuels leapt forward, unleashing a battle cry that rent the air as he tore into the battle, moving with blinding speed. And then Thano came charging up, riding his black horse, Apollo. Ian was there, and Gideon, and Quinn...

Within seconds, the demons were down, their decapitated bodies littered across the cell. Gabe looked around at his team. Not one of them had been cut or hurt, or even broken a sweat. Even Thano had brought across his new team of Order members, all of their faces hidden behind hoods.

They were all there, all together, just like it had once been. Fuck, it felt good. His gaze settled on Zach, who was holding a glowing fireball in his hand. "You got your fire back."

Zach grinned. "Yeah. Love will do that for a guy, right?" His smile faded. "What now?"

Gabe sheathed his weapons in his arms. "Now we go get a girl."

Chapter Thirty-Eight

L UCIEN SHOVED SOPHIE up the mountain, his jaw hard and tight. Sophie moved slowly, frantically trying to figure out some solution that wouldn't result in everyone she loved, including herself, dying—

She suddenly realized that it had gotten darker. She glanced at the lava pouring down the mountainside, and realized that it had slowed. There was less of it. The volcano was going dormant...which meant the temple's entrance would be closing soon—

"In here." Lucien caught her arm, dragging her to a stop in front of an opening in the mountain. Above the entrance, the stones were arranged in a spiral that culminated in a massive rock in the middle. On the center stone was the carving of a winged demon with a scaled body, massive claws, and deadly fangs. Its eyes were made of a stone that appeared to be glowing red, giving it a chilling, live visage. Ancient words were carved into the header stone, words she knew would translate to Temple of the Sun.

She stopped, digging her feet into the ground. She knew she couldn't go in there. Once a woman entered, she lost her identity and her mind. There would be no going back, no survival, nothing.

Lucien's claws dug into her arm, and he jerked her off her feet and threw her toward the entrance. She hit the wall, but her body sank into the stone instead of bouncing off it—

"No!" Lucien roared with fury and leapt across the clearing. He snatched her off the ground, ripping her body out of the stone that it had already started to merge with. Pain ripped through her, and she had to stifle a scream as Lucien threw her over his shoulder.

"No fucking rocks for you." He strode across the entrance. The shadows fell over her, and she gasped, reaching out toward the rocks outside the cavern, trying to get her hands on them. She dropped all her shields, opening her mind to the stone, to merge with it. It didn't even matter now if she was stuck in the rock forever. It was better than being in the temple with Lucien—

Except her body didn't dissolve.

She didn't merge with the rock.

She had *nothing*.

Horrified, she realized that Lucien's body was somehow acting as a buffer between her and the stones. Frantic, she lunged upward and grabbed the rocky threshold above her head. Her fingers slipped across the rock, but it felt dead, empty. She couldn't access them, even when she was touching them. Her fingernails scraped against the rock, and they were past it...

Inside the temple.

URGENCY COURSED THROUGH Vlad as Gabe greeted his team. "Who can fly?" Vlad asked. "We need to move fast."

A tall, dangerous looking Calydon looked over at him. Vlad's connection with Gabe gave Vlad instant knowledge of who it was, and he tensed. Ryland Samuels was as dangerous and unpredictable as they came, as close to full demon as any of them had ever been. Vlad tensed, half-expecting him to hurl the machete in his hand at him. But Ryland simply nodded. "I can. I can carry about half the team."

"I can take the rest," Damon said.

"Apollo and I are good," Thano said, patting the neck of his massive horse.

"I can teleport," Kane said, "but it can get ugly if I don't know where I'm going. We should fly if we can."

"We'll fly, then." Vlad divided up the team, putting himself with Gabe, Maria, Ian, and three others on Damon's back, while Ryland shifted into a massive, winged dragon that looked suspiciously similar to Damon's demon beast. He saw a few Order members notice the similarity, but no one commented as they leapt on his back.

Within a split second, they were all loaded up. Vlad leaned forward over Damon's neck, with Maria's arms around his waist, and Gabe behind her. "Haul ass, buddy."

"You got it." Damon took off instantly, streaking through the tunnels at blinding speed. The screech of his wings as he shattered the walls of the tunnel was deafening. Ryland's wings were even wider, so he followed with an equally resounding roar of stone being torn apart. Behind them, Thano and Apollo followed, the horse and rider galloping easily through the tunnel that the dragons had widened. As fast as the beasts were flying, Thano's horse had no trouble keeping up, his strong legs moving so fast they were almost invisible.

Within moments, they had burst out of the tunnel, and were streaking across the lava fields, Apollo galloping through the air as if it were solid ground.

Vlad swore as he saw that it was almost dark, and the orange glow of the distant mountain had faded significantly. "Hurry!"

Damon surged forward with a massive effort, flying through the air so fast that the wind bit at Vlad's skin, and yet still, the light continued to fade, darker and darker—

"There!" Maria pointed ahead of them. "That's the Temple! That opening in the north side!"

Vlad saw the dark shadows on the side of the mountain, and narrowed his eyes. "I don't see them," he yelled over the wind.

"They must be inside already," Maria said, horror etched

in her voice. "Oh, God. We're too late!"

"No!" Vlad leaned forward and extended his hand, reaching out with his magic, searching for Sophie, but the moment he opened his senses, he was blasted by a tsunami of living matter. The mountain was teeming with it. Swearing, he looked more closely, and saw that the shadows on the mountain were moving. "Demons," he said. "They're all over the place." All down the side of the mountain, and clustered around the entrance.

"So, we go prepared to fight." Gabe gestured at Ryland, and his teammates on the dragon's back, indicating the mountain ahead. He opened a communication link that Vlad could hear. *When we land, Vlad, Maria, Damon, and I will try to get through the entrance. The rest of you will cover our backs, and try to keep it clear so we can get out.*

There was instant assent from every Order member.

The plan was in place.

Would it work?

It had to.

Vlad bent low over Damon's neck, holding out his hand as he reached out with his magic, scanning the demons clustered around the entrance. They were packed in, an impenetrable force blocking the entrance. He kept his link open with the other Order members, showing them what he found.

The night exploded with multiple flashes of black light, and the ear-splitting crack of weapons being called out. Vlad narrowed his eyes, focusing his energy on the demons, directing their attention away from the sky, toward the bottom of the mountain, hoping to give the rescue team a chance to arrive unnoticed. They resisted him, and he swore.

Let me help. Like they'd done before, Gabe connected his energy with Vlad's. The rush of power was blinding, and Vlad thrust it at the demons, hurtling them backwards. They flew up into the air, crashing into each other as they tumbled down the mountain, creating an opening just in front of the cavern's entrance.

Damon swept low, and four of his passengers leapt to the ground, landing on their feet with weapons out. Thano and

Apollo landed easily, charging directly into the battle. Gabe, Vlad, and Maria stayed on his back as Damon careened through the open door. Behind them, Ryland landed, and there was a resounding battle cry as the Calydons launched themselves at the demons.

The tunnel narrowed, and Damon tucked his wings as they all crouched low on his neck, straining to see in the darkness as he sped around a corner—

Lucien exploded out of the darkness with a roar of fury, his wing smashing into Damon before they could stop. Damon grunted with pain, crashing to the ground, as Vlad, Gabe, and Maria leapt off his back.

Vlad had barely landed when Lucien attacked again, slamming his tail into Maria and flinging her across the room.

"Piece of shit!" Gabe launched himself at him, slashing with blinding fury as Lucien lunged for Maria.

Vlad saw Sophie behind Lucien. She was strung up by her wrists, suspended from the ceiling by a rope, so she wasn't touching any rocks. She appeared to be unconscious, hanging limply. "Sophie!" Terror knifed his heart, and he lunged for her—

"No!" Gabe bellowed at him. "Stop Lucien!"

Vlad didn't even hear him. He just raced across the floor and swept Sophie up in his arms. She was dead weight in his arms, her eyes closed, and her body limp. *Jesus.* He was too late. "Sophie—"

Lucien's tail smashed into him, ripping him away from Sophie and slamming him against the wall. Pain shot through him, and for a split second, he couldn't move, immobilized by the blast of pain beyond anything he'd ever experienced.

He tried to breathe, but he couldn't get any air. His arms and legs were numb. He couldn't feel them. The pain in his back was blinding, and he realized he'd been impaled on something, something laced with demon poison. He tried to use his magic to lift himself off the rock, but the pain was too great. He couldn't move. He couldn't save himself. He turned his head, and saw Sophie dangling limply. *Gabe. Help her.*

But even as he said it, Gabe shouted with fury, and then he

was thrown past Vlad, slamming into the wall beside him. His head hit first, and he didn't move.

They were all down.

MARIA STRUGGLED TO her feet as Lucien whirled toward her. Gabe and Vlad were unmoving on the other side of the cavern, and Sophie appeared to be unconscious. Damon was also out, crumpled in his dragon form. A single blow from Lucien was all it had taken to knock them all down. *A single blow.*

She'd known he was powerful, but she'd had no idea he was like this. Now, everyone she loved, everyone who mattered to her was at risk, exposed to danger because she'd been selfish enough to befriend Sophie. *Gabe. Can you hear me?*

Lucien ignored them all as he swung toward her, his face stretched and deformed. He grinned, his half-human face grotesque. "And so I have both of you for a hundred years."

Maria could feel the poison from the earlier demon attack still coursing through her veins, burning her. They had all been running on adrenaline, but it was getting more difficult to hold it off. She needed to heal.

Lucien smiled. "I can feel your need for sex." He moved closer, stalking her. "Your body won't let you turn down sex, not when it will die without it. You will fuck me without me even having to try, because I'm all you have, lust demon."

Sweat beaded on Maria's brow as she glanced at Gabe again. He still wasn't moving. She knew the poison was in his body as well, eating away at him, leaving him weakened for his battle against Lucien.

She pulled out a knife and held it up, trying to keep her hands from shaking. "Never." *Gabe. Wake up.*

Maria. His voice was groggy in her mind. *Call my weapon.*

She backed up as Lucien neared, still holding her dagger between them. *What? That will finish the* sheva *bond. We can't risk it.*

It's the only way.

It won't help. She backed up further, trying to edge toward the entrance. If only she could pull him back toward the front of the cavern, away from her friends, toward the other Order members.

Gabe laughed softly. *As spoken by someone who has no concept of the strength of the* sheva *bond.*

Won't it kill us? Isn't that the destiny? That you'll lose me, and then go rogue, and then I'll have to kill you to stop you?

Yes.

Tears filled her eyes at the thought of him dying. *But—*

Going rogue to save you is the only way I'll be strong enough. Do it now, Maria.

But if you die—

It will be worth it to save you.

The tears spilled out at his words. *You'd die to save me?*

Fuck yeah. I love you, woman. And I expect your love for me to haul me back from insanity, just like it's done for my teammates. Got it?

She looked across the cavern at him. His eyes were closed, and he was unmoving. He looked dead, and she could feel the weakness of his body. *You love me?* She whispered it, unable to believe it.

Damn right, I do. I thought I was coming here for Dante, but I think Dante sent me here to find you. He wanted me to become the man that you have made me become, one that has taught me a different way to be, a different vision of the future, of the Order, of myself. He opened his eyes and met her gaze. *You matter, Maria. Just because you're you. So, call my damn weapon and let's kick his ass.*

Maria looked back at Lucien, who was grinning at her, the lascivious, disgusting smile of a predator who was certain he had no enemies. "You bastard." She reared back and hurled her dagger at him, unleashing it with all the speed she could muster.

His speed hampered by ego, he didn't react in time, and the blade plunged straight into his chest. "Bitch!" He ripped it out and lunged at her, his claws reaching for her throat.

Gabe bellowed through her mind. *Do it!*

She stood tall and held up her hand, not flinching as Lucien lunged at her. She just opened her mind to the man she loved and called him to her. There was a loud crack and a flash of black light, and then his hook sword appeared in her hand. Power flooded her, and she felt Gabe's roar of possessiveness and triumph. His strength surged through her, and she felt Gabe's entire soul settle onto hers, mingling, becoming one, claiming her, granting her his protection for eternity. *Maria.* His voice filled her, wrapping around her like a shield that wove through every cell in her body. *My forever.*

It felt right. More than right. It felt like the home, the connection, the love, that she'd been searching for her entire life. *I love you, Gabe.* Then, she looked up at Lucien, gripped Gabe's weapon, and swung hard, throwing all her weight behind it as it sank into his chest, right where his heart was, if the organ that beat in his chest could be called a heart.

He stumbled to a stop, gasping as he clutched the sword. Smoke poured out of the wound, and he went down onto his knees. "Bitch—" He fell forward, lunging at her with surreal speed, catching her just as she scrambled again. His claw raked across her chest, and she gasped as she felt his claw pierce her heart, plunging demon toxin straight into her bloodstream.

Pain shot through her and she gasped, gripping her chest as she rolled away from him, her body burning instantly as the poison flooded her system. It was too much. Too much, too fast. She knew she had no chance to heal it. It was over. She'd failed. They'd all failed.

Gabe. I'm sorry.

FURY ERUPTED THROUGH Gabe, a blinding, white rage that exploded through him. *Maria!* The room was swathed in red light, and he leapt to his feet, screaming with rage, with loss, with anguish. His woman was dying! He'd lost her! "Maria!" His tormented cry tore through him, eviscerating him with blinding agony.

"You bastard!" He had to kill. He had to destroy. The fucker had to die! A roar of brutal fury tore from his throat as he leapt up, his body so charged with energy that he was already running by the time he landed. Greedily, he burned through the rage, channeling it into his body. The poison that had been killing him was incinerated almost instantly, destroyed by the raging power within him, a power focused on only one thing.

Kill.

Kill.

Kill.

His weapons clenched in his fist, he charged across the room and leapt on Lucien's back, ripping the demon king away from Maria. Lucien twisted and turned, trying to dislodge Gabe, but the superhuman strength pouring through Gabe gave him a grip the demon couldn't break. He hurled Lucien to the ground so hard that the entire mountain shook, and rocks crumbled down from the ceiling.

The bastard wouldn't stay down, leaping to his feet and ripping Gabe off him. Gabe catapulted through the air, but landed easily on his feet, sprinting back toward the demon instantly.

Black, noxious blood flowed down Lucien's chest, but he moved easily, not even hampered by the blow Maria had dealt him. *Maria!* Panic streaked through him and he spun around, searching for her.

She was down on the ground at the far side of the cavern, not moving. "Maria!" Anguish tore through him and he raced across the cavern, falling down to his knees beside her. He sheathed his weapons and pulled her into his arms, his skin burning at the feel of her tainted skin. She was being poisoned, and she needed to heal. Without hesitating, he kissed her, pouring his energy into her, feeding her every bit of himself that he could—

"She's mine!" Lucien grabbed Gabe by the head and

wrenched him sideways, almost breaking his neck.

White hot rage wiped out his concern for Maria, replaced by a frenzied need to stop the monster that had hurt his woman. "Fucking demon!" Gabe called out his weapons with a crack and a flash of black light, and lunged at Lucien, slashing harder and faster than he'd ever fought in his life. "You die now!" His blades moved too fast for even him to see, but the demon moved faster, avoiding every blow.

Son of a bitch. What the hell?

Gabe. Quinn's voice brushed across his mind. *The light is almost gone. The mountain's going to close in less than a minute. You need to get out now.*

The red-hot fury blasting through Gabe's mind obliterated Quinn's comment before it could register. All he could think of was destroying the man who'd attacked his *sheva*. "You piece of shit!"

Gabe! Quinn tried to reach him again. *Can you hear me?*

Gabe slammed up his mental shields, blocking the irritating distraction. All he could see was Lucien. Every cell in Gabe's body was focused on destroying the monster that had attacked his woman. He lunged again, fighting, fighting, fighting, moving faster and faster, but still Lucien evaded him, taunting, and laughing.

He would win this.

He. Would. Win.

Chapter Thirty-Nine

GABE'S FURY BURNED through Vlad, leaping across their blood bond like a poison threatening to consume him. Vlad dragged it into his body, pulling on Gabe's power and harnessing it. The Calydon's rage exploded through Vlad, ripping him out of his lethargy. Vlad immediately channeled it, shoving the energy into his own cells and fueling his magic.

Using Gabe's power to augment his, Vlad flicked his hand at himself. His body shot up into the air, freeing itself from the stake that had trapped him. He landed hard, gasping for breath as Damon finally lifted his head, his head bloodied and raw.

Vlad! The voice of Quinn Masters, the interim leader of the Order blasted through his head. *You have forty-five seconds of light left. Get the hell out! I can't reach Gabe!*

"Gabe! Let's go!" Vlad lurched to his feet, trying to get his bearings. Gabe was in a battle with Lucien, distracting the demon. "Get Maria," he shouted to Damon. "We have less than forty seconds!" He sprinted across the cavern toward Sophie, who was still dangling from the ceiling.

"Got it!" Damon shifted back to human form, and raced toward his sister, ducking past the battling warriors.

Vlad swept Maria's abandoned dagger off the ground and slashed the ropes holding Sophie. She fell into his arms, and he pulled her against him. Her body was warm, and he could feel the pulsing of her heart.

She was still alive. Son of a bitch. He wasn't too late this time. *He wasn't too late.* He pulled her against his chest, pouring his energy into her as he sprinted for the opening to the tunnel that led outside.

Thirty-five seconds! Quinn shouted.

Damon scooped up Maria, and sprinted toward him. "Get on! We'll never make it running!" He shifted back into dragon form as he ran, keeping his wings tucked so they didn't get caught up in the battle between Gabe and Lucien.

As Damon neared, Vlad prepared to leap onto his back. "Gabe! Let's go!"

But the Calydon didn't even look over. Vlad paused. "Gabe! Come on! We have the women! We need to go!"

Gabe roared with fury and lunged at Lucien, not even responding to Vlad. It was then that Vlad realized that the Calydon's eyes were glowing red. Son of a bitch. He'd gone rogue, just like that crazed Calydon that the Order had been hunting so long ago when Vlad had first encountered them.

"Shit." Damon was also watching Gabe. "They don't come back from that. Poor bastard."

Vlad remembered all too clearly why the Order had been hunting the rogue that day. They'd claimed he couldn't be saved. That he was irredeemable. Lost forever. His own kind, his own brothers, had been so certain he was lost forever, that they'd been willing to kill him instead of trying to save him. Vlad was the one who had let the rogue go, and he'd never found out what had happened.

Thirty seconds! Quinn warned.

Gabe's rogue, he shot back. *What do I do?*

Quinn unleashed a string of epithets. *Is it the* sheva *bond? Is that why?*

Vlad glanced over at Maria, and saw the detailed outlines on her forearms that were a perfect replica of Gabe's weapons. *I think so. How do we bring him back?* He didn't ask if they could. This was Gabe. A good man. An honorable man. Vlad hadn't given up on a stranger so long ago, and he sure as hell wasn't going to give up on the Calydon who'd risked everything to save the woman Vlad loved. He expected Quinn to tell him Gabe was lost, but the Calydon surprised him.

Bring him out with you. We'll deal with him out here. You have twenty seconds. Get out now!

"Come on, Gabe!" Damon shouted. "We need to go!"

But the Calydon just kept fighting, slashing violently.

"Fuck. We need to get him."

Damon swore. "If we grab him, Lucien will see we're leaving. We'll never get out. Sophie and Maria will die in here, at his mercy."

Vlad went cold at the idea of Sophie becoming Lucien's plaything. "Fuck. No. We can't do that." He needed to get her out of there, now, but his feet were welded to the ground, watching the man who had somehow become his best friend fight a battle he'd never win. He couldn't leave Gabe behind, but he couldn't let Sophie get trapped in there either. He looked at Damon, desperate. "What do we do?"

Determination flooded Damon's face. "He intentionally sacrificed himself to save Maria. We honor that sacrifice. We leave. I'd give my life for my sister in an instant. If you then decided to risk her life just to save me, after I'd already offered my life for hers, I'd be furious. It's about her safety, not mine, and not Gabe's. He made the choice to sacrifice himself to keep her safe, and we honor that choice by getting her out of here. If they both die, then what's the fucking point of Gabe's sacrifice? Let's go."

But still, Vlad couldn't tear himself away. *Gabe. Look at me. Maria needs you.*

The Calydon didn't even glance over. He was completely consumed by the rogue haze, utterly focused on the battle. *Shit.*

"Vlad." Sophie's voice caught his attention, and his gaze snapped to hers. His heart seemed to stutter when he saw her looking at him, awake, conscious, and lucid. His arm tightened around her, and suddenly, he could barely breathe. How could he have considered risking her to save Gabe? Damon was right. Gabe had made the choice. He'd violated every rule of the Order and chosen to sacrifice himself to save one, which meant if he died, the hundreds of lives he would have saved in the future would have no one to protect them.

Gabe had made the ultimate sacrifice, the one Vlad had thought no Order member would ever make.

"He sacrificed himself to save her," she whispered. "And she did the same for him. That's true love. We can't let them die."

Vlad stared at Sophie. He'd expected her to say that because of their sacrifices, they needed to honor Gabe's decision to sacrifice himself. Her need to preserve that love felt so much more right, so much better. It felt like the only decision that they could make.

Vlad looked back at Gabe, at the man who'd abandoned his quest for Dante to save Sophie. An Order member who'd violated all that drove him, for the good of one. Not for the good of all. For the good of one, *Vlad's* one, Sophie.

Gabe had sacrificed himself, and his own true love, to save the woman Vlad loved. He'd finally absolved himself of the guilt of failing to save her so long ago by saving her today, but he hadn't done it by himself. He'd needed Damon. He'd needed Maria. He'd needed Gabe, and the entire damn Order.

For the first time in his life he understood what the greater good really meant. It hadn't been what his parents thought it was, sacrificing their children to preserve the safety of the kingdom. It also hadn't meant what the Order had believed for so long, that it was right to kill one person to save others. What the greater good meant was that one person alone couldn't make a difference. That was why he hadn't saved Sophie before, because he tried to do it all by himself. The greater good meant pulling together across boundaries to defeat an enemy or save a loved one with team effort, creating loyalties that bonded souls, hearts, and minds.

He looked down at Sophie, still in his arms, understanding, for the first time, what she had meant when she told him again and again how important it was to her to be there to save the other women. For the first time in his life, he understood the power of knowing that he could make a difference to someone else.

Yeah, he'd saved all those kids, but he'd done it for selfish reasons, to distract himself from the guilt and self-hate that had driven him for so long. This was different. This was channeling all his energy into something good, for the sake of accomplishing something that helped someone else, not himself. He grinned at Sophie, his heart light for the first time in maybe his entire life. "You're right. We're not leaving here without him."

Sophie beamed at him, her face lighting up, and he knew in that moment that he'd finally learned what it meant to truly live. He reached out with his mind to the Order leader fighting so valiantly outside to keep their exit available. *Quinn. I'm sending Damon and the women out. Cover them. I'm going to stay and try to get Gabe.*

Fierce determination flooded over their connection. *Don't you dare let him die. He's one of us.*

I know. Vlad looked down at Sophie. "I love you, Soph. I free you. Go live your life the way you deserve." He then handed her to Damon. "Get them out. I'm going to help Gabe."

Damon swore and took Sophie. "You won't make it. There's not enough time."

"I'm going to try." He turned away, and then Sophie caught his wrist. He looked back at her, his heart tightening. "You aren't beholden to me anymore, Soph. I let you go."

"I don't want you to let me go. I love you. You matter. You are enough." She tightened her grip on his hand. "Together, Vlad. We do this together."

He blanched when he realized what she was saying. "You want to stay here? No. Your safety is all that matters."

"No, it's not. Standing together with those you love matters. You won't make it out without me." She twisted out of Damon's grasp, landing on her knees. "I can help. I can hold the doorway open. I can give you more time."

Fifteen seconds! I don't see Damon or the women!

Swearing, Vlad looked at Maria and Damon, and then back at Gabe...and then at Sophie, the woman he'd spent his life trying to protect. "I can't let you stay here—"

"I'm not a princess anymore, Vlad. I'm a warrior, and we

can do this together." She met his gaze, and he finally understood what she'd meant when she said that simply being his protected woman wouldn't be enough. Not when there were people she loved that needed help. He got it, because he was standing in a cavern, ready to sacrifice himself for a Calydon he would have disdained only days before.

This was what drove her, and this was what made her the woman he loved. He had two choices, to accept her as she was and allow her to be the woman she wanted to be, or to try to destroy it so she would live a safe, small life devoid of danger. He knew there was no choice. "I love you, babe. I loved you as a wimpy princess, and I love you even more as a badass warrior."

Five seconds! What the fuck are you guys doing in there?

"Well, shit. If you guys are staying, then we are too." Damon set Maria down beside Sophie. "Let's fucking kick his ass, Vlad."

He grinned, and looked down at Sophie. "You got this."

She nodded. "I know. I'll hold the doorway open as long as I can."

It's closing! Where the fuck are you guys?

Sophie slammed her hands onto the rock and thrust all her power into it. The mountain shuddered, lurching so violently that Vlad had to brace himself to keep from falling. The rocks behind her convulsed like a raging river, an earthquake ripping a trail back toward the entrance. Her hands dissolved and became one with the ground, but the rest of her body didn't disappear. She held her form, controlling the rock, using it, not hiding.

Shit. It's holding. Quinn sounded shocked. *What did you do?*

It's Sophie. She's strong as hell. Vlad couldn't keep the pride out of his voice, and he knew Sophie heard it when she looked up at him and smiled.

"I'm never hiding again," she said, her voice tense with the effort of controlling the stones. "Now go get him."

Vlad kissed her hard, and then he and Damon turned to face the battle. Lucien had Gabe pinned up against the far wall, laughing as he easily ducked the warrior's blows. Gabe was still moving with lightning speed, but Vlad could see the strain on the warrior's face, and knew he would soon be out of energy. "How do we stop him?" he asked Damon, not taking his eyes off the battle. "How do you kill a demon?"

Damon was watching the battle intently, tracking every move of the demon king. "You don't."

"So, then, what do we do?" Vlad studied Lucien's moves, noting which way he ducked to evade Gabe's blows, assimilating data as fast as he could. He knew they would have one chance to take him down, one moment to act. Any mistake, and they'd fail.

"We trap him in the temple, then you get the hell back to the earth realm before he gets out," Damon said, beginning to circle around the battling duo that had forgotten about them. "The temple won't hold him a hundred years, but it'll hold him for a few hours."

Vlad began to move in the opposite direction, flanking the battling warriors. "He'll hunt you down when he gets out if you stay in the demon realm."

"I know, but I can't cross over." He looked over at Vlad. "She's my sister. She's all I have. She's worth it."

Respect rushed through Vlad, and he knew this was the kind of leader that his parents had never been. Loyalty. Courage. Honor. Everything he'd never associated with a demon before. They both knew that Damon would be fucked once Lucien got out, because he would be the only one left to blame. "She's lucky to have you."

"Hey, guys." Sophie's voice was strained. "I know I'm a badass and everything, but I can't hold this temple open forever."

Vlad glanced over at her, and opened his palm toward her, thrusting his magic into her. She connected with it, and the mountain shook again as she renewed her hit. "Can you do that to Maria? She's in trouble. Give her life force?"

Vlad and Damon both looked at Maria. Her skin was pale, and she was barely breathing. Swearing, Vlad pointed his index finger at her and poured living energy into her. For a moment, nothing happened, and then she coughed, sucking her breath. Her eyes slitted open, glancing at him, and then slithering to Gabe. "Gabe." Her voice was a raw whisper.

Her voice was low and weak, dying out long before it reached the one who'd gone rogue for her. Damon swore. "She needs to heal, and Gabe's the only one who can save her. Let's go."

"You bet." Together, they stepped forward, man and demon. Vlad flung out his hands, catching Lucien off guard. His power ripped the demon off his feet and slammed him against the wall, impaling him on the same stones that had trapped Vlad. He hadn't even landed when Damon leapt forward, howling with rage as he shifted into dragon form. He swooped down and attacked Lucien, who screamed and ripped himself free, diving at the smaller dragon.

Vlad focused his energy on Lucien, merging his mind with the demon king's cells. He flicked his finger, and jerked the demon back, slamming him against the wall again. The moment he hit, Damon tore into him, his claws and teeth ripping at the thick, impenetrable scales. Once again, Lucien recovered almost immediately and lunged at Damon, screaming with fury, his face twisted and deformed as the demons battled.

Vlad narrowed his eyes, summoning more energy, realizing he had to hit Lucien hard enough to stun him—

A movement out of the corner of his eye caught Vlad's attention, and he glanced to his right just as Gabe turned toward him, his eyes glowing hellishly red. Vlad swore. "I'm not the enemy, buddy. It's Lucien—"

Before he even finished, Gabe unleashed an unearthly howl of crazed fury and launched himself at Vlad, his hook sword streaking through the air right at him. Vlad swore and threw himself sideways, barely evading the gleaming blade. As he rolled away, he saw Lucien strike Damon, throwing the smaller demon against a rocky outcropping. Vlad extended his hand toward Lucien, trying to drag the demon king backwards away from Damon, but before he got a good grip on him, Gabe struck again, his blade glancing off Vlad's right shoulder.

"A little help, big guy," Damon shouted.

"Trying!" Vlad held out his left hand, trying to hold Gabe back, but he couldn't control both Lucien and Gabe at the same time, and both assailants ripped out of his grasp. Vlad rolled to the left, evading Gabe only because the Calydon was moving too fast to be able to change direction. "Gabe! Maria's dying! She needs you!"

But Gabe didn't even slow down. He just whirled toward Vlad, and he saw in his eyes an absolute commitment to death. In that second, he understood why the Order had killed so many rogues over the centuries. In that second, there was nothing left of the man he knew, just an insane, crazed predator who was about to destroy everything that he'd sacrificed himself to save.

Chapter Forty

"**M**ARIA!"
Sophie's voice forced its way into Maria's foggy consciousness, and she forced her eyes open, trying to respond to the urgency in her friend's voice. She blinked several times trying to focus, but her eyes hurt, her body hurt, even her blood hurt.

"Maria! Wake up!"

The urgency in Sophie's voice jerked Maria out of her daze. This time she forced her eyes to stay open as she sought to find the source of Sophie's voice. She found her several feet away, her hands buried in the rock floor of the cavern. Sweat was dripping down her temples and matting her hair, and her arms were shaking. Alarm leapt through Maria. "Soph?"

"You have to get Gabe back on track. We can't win without him." Sophie twisted around to look behind her.

Gabe! The events of the last two minutes came rushing back into Maria's mind. She jerked her gaze off Sophie and gasped when she saw the battle raging in the cavern. Lucien had Damon pinned against the wall, and Vlad was fighting for his life against an enraged Gabe.

"Gabe!" She choked out his name, trying to get to her knees, but her legs and arms were too weak to hold her up. She collapsed, unable to do anything but watch the man she loved descend into a madness that would destroy them all.

The *sheva* destiny commanded that she kill him, but she didn't really care what destiny wanted her to do. She'd been given so little in her life, so little human connection, so little emotional support to keep her going. There was no way in hell she was going to kill the man who'd showed her what it felt like to be truly loved.

Gabe. Even as she called out to him, she felt the weakness of her voice, and knew that she'd never reach him that way. She didn't have the strength even to hold a psychic connection across the frenetic vibrations of his rogue mind. So instead she opened her heart to him. She poured her love for him into their connection, flooding the fragile filaments with all the warmth, all the love, all the passion she'd stored so deeply inside her soul for so long. She gave him the anguish of a lifetime of having to have sex with demons she hated. She showed him her sleepless nights, wondering how she would spend eternity in the hell that her life had become. She shared with him her fear over what would happen if she ever lost Sophie, the one friend who kept her going, and how that fear had eased when she'd met him.

She offered him all the vulnerability, the softness, the fragility that she had kept buried so deeply her whole life. She gave it to him, and offered it into his safekeeping. She tore down the shields that had kept her safe. She let him see the truth of what she was, a warrior who hid the softness of her heart behind a dozen weapons in black leather.

He hesitated, a hitch in his gait in his pursuit of Vlad.

Maria didn't take her eyes off him. She just kept pouring her love out to him. She let him feel her pain, both in her heart and in her body. She showed him the poison coursing through her veins. She invited him into her searing agony as it ate away at each healthy cell. She showed him that unless he came back to her, she would die of both the broken body and a shattered heart. She let herself stop being strong for the first time in her life, and turned herself over to the safekeeping of the man destined to be her strength. Allowing herself to be weak was by far the most difficult thing she had ever done in her life, but at the same time she'd never felt so liberated as she had in that moment.

She relaxed, and finally allowed herself to be who she truly was: strong, vulnerable, and utterly in love with the man who loved her for who she was.

Gabe suddenly whirled around and faced her. The red faded from his eyes, and her heart leapt as they became brown again. A deep, vibrant joy filled her, a joy that was woven with love, hope, and everything that made life worth living. Love had broken through the fate that was supposed to take him. Not daggers. Not violence. Not sex. Just love, the most powerful weapon of all. His voice filled her mind, and his healing energy flooded her, making her lungs expand with sudden fierceness. *You stay alive for me, sweetheart. You got that?*

Welcome back, Gabe. Take me away from this, okay?

He blew her a kiss, and then spun back to Vlad. The two warriors exchanged glances, and then, as a unit, they raced toward Lucien and Damon. With a victorious battle cry, they leapt into the fray, both warriors moving faster than she'd ever seen. Vlad flicked his hand, and Lucien flew back against the wall, pinned there as Damon and Gabe attacked the demon before he could break free. They were holding him in place, but he wasn't weakening. If they tried to make a break for the entrance, Lucien would come after them. They needed more strength.

Desperate, she looked over at Sophie. "Can you help them?"

"Can't." Sophie was drenched in sweat, and her whole body was shaking. "I can't hold this much longer. In another minute we're all going to be trapped in here. You have to do it."

"Me?" Maria's first response was negative. She needed sex in order to heal. But as she looked back at the battle, her heart filled as she saw the three warriors fighting side by side against an enemy that no one had ever dared take on before. How could she lie here and let them lose, just because she hadn't had sex? Surely there was more to her than that, wasn't there?

There had to be. Gabe had already broken one rule by staying sane when they had sex. Why couldn't she break other ones? For heaven's sake, this was demon poison, and she was half demon, right? Why couldn't she take that demon toxin and use it? The moment she thought it, rightness poured through her, and she knew it would work. She'd spent her life hating that she was a demon, despising and fearing that side of her, but two of the three warriors fighting Lucien had demon blood running through their veins, and that hadn't stopped them from being heroes.

She took a deep breath, and opened her mind to her demon side. The moment she did so, power roared through her. The demon toxin that had been poisoning her suddenly pulsed with power that flowed into every cell.

She leapt to her feet, stunned by how strong she felt. She reached behind her back and pulled out the dagger that she used for healing, the one that had sliced her palm so many times so she could heal. It was a dagger of power, of love, of goodness...everything that Lucien wasn't.

Clenching the dagger in her fist, she walked into the middle of the cavern, standing behind the wall of warriors. "Lucien!" she shouted.

The demon king's eyes met hers. They were twisted and black, consumed with a vile hatred of them all. For the first time in her life, she didn't feel violated by facing down a demon. She didn't feel lust. She just felt steady, strong, and powerful. "This is for all the women I've had to heal because of you." She pressed a kiss to the flat of the blade, a kiss not of sex, but of love, of kindness, of gentleness, all the things she'd never been allowed to be, all the things that Gabe brought into her life. "Let this be your poison." Then, she hurled the blade, with pinpoint accuracy and blinding speed.

It reached Lucien just as he began to react, but it was too late for him, much, much too late. The small, gleaming blade plunged into his head, right between his eyes. For a split second, there was no reaction, then gold smoke began to rise from his head, pouring out of it like a geyser unleashed after centuries of inactivity. He screamed, his head rolling back in agony as the gold steam continued to pour out of his forehead.

Love was poisoning him, and it was beautiful. *Gabe. Stop.*

Two simple words, whispered silently into the mind of a powerful warrior, and it was enough. Gabe halted mid-blow, his hook sword in his hand. He held up his hand, and Damon and Vlad stopped as well.

"Let him go, Vlad," she said.

Vlad didn't hesitate. In a show of absolute faith, he lowered his hand. Lucien crashed to the ground, still screaming and writhing as the gold smoke continued to pour from his head. He didn't go after the warriors. He didn't go after the women. He was too consumed by his pain to do anything but fight for his own survival.

Gabe looked over at her, and grinned. "Nice job, Maria."

She grinned. "Back at ya, big guy."

"We have to go," Sophie shouted. "I can't hold it open any longer! It's closing!" As she spoke, she jerked her hands out of the floor of the cavern and lurched to her feet. "Now!"

Damon shifted instantly into dragon form, Gabe and Vlad leaping on his back even as he took shape. Damon tore across the cavern, and Maria held up her hand as he sped by. Gabe caught her wrist, his hand secure and strong around her as they raced past, pulling her easily up in front of him. Vlad caught Sophie at the same moment, hauling her in front of him as Damon hurtled past. The rocks started shifting, falling down around them as Damon raced through the tunnel.

Maria and the others bent low, hanging on tight as Damon careened around corners, his wings ripping out walls as he shot through it. "Faster!" Sophie yelled. "It's closing!"

Up ahead, Maria could see the opening of the cave...and it was shrinking. "We're never going to get there—"

Suddenly, Gabe's teammates appeared in the opening, using their bodies to hold up the rock that was trying to close. Quinn appeared first, slamming his hands into the ceiling, his feet braced in the rubble. Then Ryland leapt in beside him, bracing his shoulders against the wall as his boots dug into the ground, sliding as he fought against the sheer force of the earth. Suddenly, others joined them. Ian Fitzgerald. Rohan, in his black hooded robe. Behind them, Maria could see the other warriors still fighting, trying to protect the opening from the demon guards.

The mountain screamed in protest, pressing down against them, trying to smash the warriors who were fighting back, willing to sacrifice themselves for their teammate, and three strangers they didn't even know. Tears filled her eyes at the show of loyalty, how all these people had come together to fight for one goal, to fight a single enemy.

"Hurry!" Quinn yelled, his feet sliding as the mountain continued to press down on them. But even the ceiling was coming down now. It was too much.

"Kane!" Gabe shouted. "Come get us!"

Kane appeared in the doorway. His shoulder was bloodied, and his left arm was hanging limply by his side. Maria had only a split second to register his presence, and then he was gone, vanishing literally into thin air.

A millisecond later, he appeared in front of her, astride Damon's neck. Then, her body felt like it was being torn into a million pieces, and the world felt like it was falling away. She locked her arms desperately around Gabe's waist, fighting against the nausea as the world seemed to vanish completely.

Then, suddenly, she was reforming outside the entrance of the temple, still on Damon's back as her brother and the rest of his riders became corporeal again. Around them, battle was raging, screams of demons, the shouts of the Order.

But before the others could leap onto Damon's back to escape, she saw a man, a demon, rise from the masses of demons, shoulders above the rest, his eyes boring right down onto hers.

Rikker.

Chapter Forty-One

"RIKKER." MARIA'S WHISPER of horror made Sophie look up. She froze when she saw Rikker standing on a rock in the middle of the battle, watching her.

She gripped Gabe, and he followed her glance, swearing. "Who the hell's that?"

"Rikker."

The demon held up his hand, and instantly, the demons stopped fighting.

Showing surreal discipline, the moment the demons stopped, the entire Order did as well. They were bloodied and beaten, but their weapons were clenched tight in their fists, their bodies ready for more.

"On one knee." Rikker's voice bellowed across the battle-field, and Sophie tensed as all the demons around them went down on one knee, as far as she could see.

Gabe swore under his breath, his hand tight around the handle of his weapon, but he made no move either. Every Ca-lydon waited, the only sound the heavy breathing as they fought to get their breath back. Apollo stood still, awaiting a command from his rider.

Rikker raised his arms. "Salute Maria Souvaine. She has defeated the demon king," he announced. "She is our new queen."

Maria tensed, tightening her grip on the dagger. "Don't believe them," she whispered to Gabe. "It's a trick."

Then Rikker himself went down on one knee, bowing his head. "We pledge our allegiance to the new queen," he said, his voice resonating across the battlefield so loudly that no one could miss it. "There will be peace in the demon kingdom for a fortnight, at which time a challenge may be issued."

"Oh, God," Sophie whispered. "It's legit. He's following protocol. You defeated Lucien. You really are the queen."

Rikker bowed his head, and the entire demon army did the same.

Maria stared at the army of demons all on their knees around her. The only ones still standing were the Order members, who still had their weapons out, prepared to fight if necessary. She couldn't believe it, but it was true. She was the queen. Somehow, she'd become the top of the food chain in a hell that had marginalized her, and all females, since the beginning of time.

Adrenaline rushed through her, and she suddenly grinned. "Hot damn," she whispered. "This is awesome." She raised her voice. "Sophie, Damon, and the entire Order of the Blade are my special guests," she announced. "They are under my protection, and the protection of the entire demon kingdom. None of them are to be harmed." She paused. "Every female in this kingdom is to be considered free to make her own choices, to leave whenever she wants."

Rikker's eyes flashed, but every demon, including him, murmured assent.

God, it was surreal.

Sophie looked back at her, a look of equal shock on her face. "Okay, so this feels weird, doesn't it?"

Maria grinned. "Totally. Girl power, right? Should I order them to start belly dancing or something?"

Sophie didn't smile. "What happens in two weeks? When your position can be challenged?"

Determination flooded Maria. "I'll fight them off. You remember the legacy of the half-demon princess? It's me, Sophie. I'm the queen that the legacy was about. It's my job to be here and fight—" But even as she said the words, she felt Gabe's arms tighten around her waist.

Gabe. He wouldn't stay. He had a mission to defend. An oath to uphold. She closed her eyes, sudden grief washing over her. *You're going to leave, aren't you?* she asked him.

No.

She twisted around in his arms and looked at him. "What?"

His face was deadly serious, but his eyes were soft. "I love you, Maria. I came back for you. That's my mission. You're my mission. You've given me perspective. I'll stay here with you and rule the demon world with you, if that's what you want."

Tears suddenly filled her eyes, and Maria's heart swelled. "You'd stay here for me?"

"Every day of my life." He caught her chin with his fingers. *I love you, Maria. There is no end to that. Do you understand?*

She nodded, and suddenly, she didn't want to be a demon queen. She didn't want to fight daily battles to keep demons from killing each other. She wanted to be with Gabe, in the earth realm, fighting to protect an already good place. She wanted more...but how could she leave? There was no way—

"Permission to approach?" Rikker called out, his voice taut.

Maria turned back to him, and nodded. "Permission granted."

The demon army parted, and Rikker jumped off the rock and strode toward them. The Calydons moved tightly around Maria, protecting her, making her heart tighten again. As Gabe's *sheva*, they'd accepted her as one of their own, affording her the same protections as they'd give their own teammates, even though she was half-demon, derived of the very things that they'd fought against for centuries.

Rikker came to a stop in front of her, looking up at her, still on Damon's back. "A word with you and Sophie."

Maria glanced at Sophie, who nodded.

In unison, the two women slid to the ground, and Maria

had to hide a smile at how quickly Gabe and Vlad moved in behind them, crowding their women's backs. Damon shifted back into human form, and the other Order members formed a tight circle around them, creating a physical shield between the group and the demon army.

Rikker glanced at Gabe and Vlad, and the others. "Just the women."

"No." Vlad and Gabe spoke in unison, and Sophie and Maria exchanged amused smiles.

"They're with us," Maria said. "They stay."

Rikker narrowed his eyes, but acknowledged her command with a silent nod. "The others need to move the perimeter back."

Maria raised her brows at Gabe. He ground his jaw, but nodded at the rest of the Order. Quinn held up his hand, and the Order enlarged the circle, stepping back and forcing the demon army away. When they were a good twenty-yards away, Rikker turned toward them. His gaze settled on Sophie, and for a split second, Maria saw an agonizing expression of sadness and loss cross his face. She jerked back in surprise, and heard Sophie suck in her breath. Had Rikker loved Sophie all this time? It seemed impossible, and yet the expression in his eyes was so raw and visceral that there was no way to fake it.

He pried his gaze off Sophie and looked at Maria. "I have a deal to offer you," he said, his voice so low that she had to strain to hear it.

Maria frowned. "What kind of deal?"

"The only one of you who can leave the demon realm is Sophie. Everyone else, including Vlad, has enough demon blood that they won't get across. Everyone is stuck here for eternity."

Maria's heart fell, and she closed her eyes for a moment. She didn't want to believe his words, but she knew the truth too well. She and Damon had tried for centuries to get out, and they never could. The Order had come here to help them, and now they were trapped? "My fault," she whispered, looking at Gabe. *I'm so sorry.*

He met her gaze, his face gentle. *Everything we do is our choice. We knew it was a possibility. No regrets. Ever.*

"There is a possible solution," Rikker said.

Maria frowned. "What is it?"

Rikker looked over his shoulder at the demons, and then put his hand over a metal pendant around his throat. He jerked it off, breaking the chain, then flicked a latch to open it. The gold opened, revealing a small, black stone.

"Oh, my God." Sophie sucked in her breath. "*Oh, my God.*"

Maria looked sharply at her friend. "What is it?"

"It's the stone with the curse. He found it." Sophie's face was ashen. "You've had it all this time."

Maria tensed, and around her, the entire Order did the same. Every one of them knew what would happen if the barrier between the worlds was broken, and the demons were unleashed into the earth realm.

"I did." Rikker looked at Sophie. "You never knew. It was so close to you all this time, but you never knew. It was damned difficult to conceal it from you. You're very good."

"Why?" Sophie whispered. "Why didn't you use it? Or tell Lucien?"

"Because Lucien is a scourge that almost destroyed the demon kingdom. Unleashing him upon the earth realm would be the end of existence." Rikker's fist closed over the pendant. "Keeping the stone to myself was the only way to protect the earth realm."

Maria's jaw dropped as she stared at him. "I don't understand. You don't want the demons to cross over?"

"You're him," Damon said suddenly. "You're the one who was left behind. It's true, then. The rumors are true."

Rikker looked past her at Damon and nodded. "I'm the one."

"The one who was left behind? What are you talking about?" Maria looked between her brother and Rikker, and suddenly she knew. "You were left here by the woman who created the curse, weren't you? It's your job to make sure the stone is never found. You're the protector of the earth realm."

"I am." Rikker was looking at Sophie now, his gaze once again wrought with pain, before he schooled his features into a cool mask. He looked back at Maria. "I am bound here to this stone for eternity. It is my job to protect it, and I can do that best as the leader of the demon realm. Let me defeat you, Maria, and I will open the barrier so you and your team can get through. Then it will be sealed forever."

Maria's heart started pounding so hard she could barely think. "I can leave? We can leave? What about Damon?"

Rikker's gaze flicked to her brother. "He's a full demon. No demon can be allowed to leave. Ever."

Maria looked back at her brother, and her heart tightened. "I won't leave without him."

"No." Damon spoke up. "I won't let you stay for me." He turned toward her. "You have a chance for a real life outside of here," he said, taking her hands. "Take it. Gabe's worthy of you. You deserve him. The earth realm needs you."

Tears filled her eyes. "I won't leave you—"

"Leave me." Damon brushed a finger over her cheek, wiping away the tears. "I've never seen my strong sister cry," he said softly. "Emotion looks beautiful on you."

Maria wiped the back of her hand across her cheek, her heart breaking. "I can't leave—"

"I'll send all the women with you," Rikker said.

"And if the demons pull anyone else over in the future, you'll send them back?" Sophie added. "If not, Maria will return and claim her place. You have to protect the women, Rikker."

He met Sophie's gaze. "For you, Sophie, anything." His voice was soft, a heartbroken caress across her cheek, and Maria knew then that she was right. Rikker had fallen in love with Sophie. "I'm sorry I lost it that day when I heard Lucien had touched you. I was absolutely fucking terrified for your safety, and I didn't know how else to protect you." He went down on one knee and bowed his head. "Forgive me."

Sophie looked at Maria, then back at Rikker. "I forgive you," she said softly, "if you promise to protect the women."

He looked up. "I promise."

Sophie looked at Maria, her eyes bright with tears. "That's it then. No reason for us to stay. It's time to go, Maria."

Maria looked at her brother, standing there so silently. "I can't—"

"You can't stay in this hellhole for me," he said. "Come on. I'll give you a ride." He shifted into dragon form, offering himself to her for one final flight.

Maria looked at Gabe, who was standing beside her. *I can't leave him, Gabe. He's my family.*

I know. He wasn't looking at her.

Something in his tone caught her attention, and she looked at him more sharply. *What are you thinking?*

You know what I'm thinking. He cut her off then, and she knew it was so none of the other Calydons could hear their conversation. Her heart began to pound. Was he really thinking of smuggling her brother across the border? It was impossible. The Order was founded to fight the very thing that Damon was. How could Gabe go against it for her? For her brother? He wouldn't really...would he? *Gabe?*

But he wasn't looking at her. "Is Dante Sinclair's body in the Graveyard of the Damned?" he asked.

Rikker looked at him. "Yes."

Every member of the Order of the Blade went still, their bodies rigid. She could feel the tension pouring through them, the shocked disbelief.

"Can we take it home with us?"

Rikker frowned. "I don't know how you would move it—"

"I can move it," Vlad interrupted. "I can do it."

The mountain shook suddenly, and they all looked up at it. Steam was rising from the top, golden steam. "He'll break through soon," Rikker said. "You guys need to be gone before then so I can deal with him. We'll stop by the Graveyard on the way." He snapped his fingers, and several of the demon army stood up and shifted into winged dragon beasts.

Maria gaped at them, shocked by the extent of Rikker's control over them. "Why are they obeying you?"

"Because I was Lucien's second in command, and now they believe I'm yours. Whatever command I give, they assume it comes from you, since you're standing here." He looked at her. "You're a hell of a lot easier to deal with than he is."

Maria managed a smile. "You know, if you'd come clean a few centuries ago, we could have defeated him."

"No." Rikker looked at the rest of the Order. "We needed everyone. This was our only opportunity." The mountain shook again, and he nodded at the dragons waiting. "Let's go."

Maria glanced at Gabe, who nodded. Silently, she hopped up onto her brother's back, and he did the same. Sophie and Vlad also joined them, and the others spread out between Ryland, and the other demons. Thano, as before, rode solo on Apollo, the two of them moving with such grace it was as if they were a single unit, instead of horse and rider.

Within moments, they were all airborne, soaring high above the land that had been her home since she had first come into creation, the only living child of a demon and human woman who had been dragged across the barrier.

She belonged here...and she also belonged in the earth realm...with the man she loved, and her best friend.

Gabe wrapped his arms around her waist and rested his chin on her shoulder, as she surveyed the barren, blackened landscape that was all she knew. *I'm scared to leave. Sad, too.*

I know. But we'll come back.

She twisted around to look at him. *How? Lucien will be out and he'll—*

Rikker will need our help sometimes, and we'll come. He squeezed her arms more tightly. "There are more people for you to save, sweetheart. The ones here are safe now. There are others who need you." He pressed a kiss to the side of her neck. "Including me."

She smiled and leaned back against his chest. "I need you, too." *And Damon.*

He said nothing, but he squeezed her more tightly around the waist. She bit her lower lip, knowing that Damon would refuse to cross, and Rikker would refuse to let him go. But how could she leave Damon behind to be targeted by Lucien when he got out? He wouldn't stop until Damon was dead, and no one would be able to stop him. Rikker would have more power than Lucien, once he became king, and he would control the demon army, but she had no doubt that Lucien wouldn't stop until he destroyed Damon, who wouldn't have the protection of being king.

Ryland pulled up beside them, Rikker on his back. The demon pointed down below, to a sea of black rocks. "Dante's body is in there." The mountain they'd just left behind rumbled, and he looked over his shoulder. "You have two minutes, and then you're out of time."

Damon dove straight down toward the rocks, the other Order members right behind him. The moment Damon landed, Gabe was off his back, his entire body tense.

This was it, Maria realized. She looked at the man she loved, and realized that she was hoping with all her heart that he got what he'd come for—

He looked at her then, and smiled. *I already got what I came for, sweetheart. You.*

Her heart tightened, and she smiled. *You've gotten soft, warrior.*

I know. It's exactly how it should be.

And she could tell he meant it. Her warrior had become soft for her, and he wouldn't want it any other way. She felt the same way, about him, and about herself. He'd given her softness, and she would always love him for that.

Always.

VLAD FELT THE tension of the Order members as he stepped down off Damon. They were on edge. Their weapons were sheathed, but their energy was pulsing as they waited. He recognized all of them except for Rohan and his team, and a new Calydon named Levi, from the time in the Oregon high desert when he'd done his best to destroy all they stood for, including their leader...the same leader he was going to retrieve for them now.

Rikker strode over to a spot in the rocks, and Sophie knelt down. Vlad couldn't help but smile as she put her hands on the rocks without hesitation. In that cavern, fighting for the lives of those she loved, she'd found her strength. He knew she would never live in fear again, and never rely on anyone to be her strength...and that was the way it should be. They were equals now, and he knew that when they returned to the earth realm, they would find a future together to make a difference, taking down bad guys or helping those in need, in whatever form they found them.

His heart turned over, and he knew that she'd helped him find himself, and what he was meant for.

"Here?" Sophie pressed her hands on the stone. "Vlad? Can you feel him?"

Vlad made his way across the stone, aware of the gaze of every Order member on him. He crouched beside Sophie. "I love you, Sophie."

She looked at him, her face softening into a beautiful smile. "I love you too, Vlad. Thanks for coming to get me."

He grinned. "My pleasure."

"One minute," Rikker snapped, his voice taut as he moved away from them.

Vlad's smile faded, and he held out his hand over the rock, reaching through the layers for living matter. Since Dante had been of demon descent, Vlad knew that he could never fully die. If his body was there, it would still respond to Vlad's magic...

He felt it. A thudding pulse of energy so strong it startled him. Dante wasn't simply a shell of his existence. His life force was strong, preserving his body. "He's here. I can get him."

The Order shifted, muttering under their breath. Ryland went down on his knees beside him, pressing his palms into the rock. "Is he alive? Is his soul there?" His voice was raw and harsh, on edge.

"I don't know about his soul, but his body is still living." Vlad looked at Sophie, knowing that she was waiting for him to give the command to open the rocks, to free the leader who had made the Order into everything Vlad didn't believe in. He looked up at the team standing around him. "Are you sure you guys want this? I think you guys are finally headed in the right direction. You don't need him anymore."

The mood shifted, the tension escalating.

"Open it," Ryland ordered. "Get him out."

Vlad looked at Gabe, waiting.

After a long moment, Gabe nodded. "Do it."

Swearing, Vlad nodded. *I owe you, buddy, but just so you know, I think you're the leader that the Order needs, not Dante.* When Gabe didn't respond, Vlad nodded at Sophie. "Open it up."

Immediately, she pressed her hands to the rock, and it dissolved instantly beneath her hands, but she didn't dissolve with it. She stayed corporeal, with visible ease, and Vlad's chest thudded with pride. "Love you, babe."

She grinned at him. "Get Dante, Vlad. We have about five seconds."

He took one last look at Gabe, whose face was expressionless, then held out his hand. His energy surged into the darkness that Sophie had opened, wrapping around the Calydon buried so deeply beneath the surface. He flicked his finger, drawing it upward, until he was able to lift it through the opening.

Shock reverberated through the Order as the inert body of a heavily muscled man in jeans, heavy boots and a black tee shirt appeared, hovering above the rocks. His hair was short, his face clean-shaven, his forearms branded with a spear. His body was slightly translucent, held together only by Vlad's magic.

"Son of a bitch," Ryland muttered, his jaw slack. "He looks exactly the same."

"Dad?" The youngest Calydon, one he didn't recognize, stumbled forward, going down on his knees.

"His soul's not there, Drew. It's just his body right now." But even Quinn's voice was rough.

"Time's up." Rikker said. "We have to go now."

Not a single Order member moved until Vlad was back on

Damon's back, and had Dante's body hovering in the air beside him. Gabe and the two women got on board with him, and then Damon took off.

The others were right beside him, in a tight formation. There was a crack and a flash of black light as all the Order members called out their weapons, ready to defend their fallen leader. To his surprise, Vlad felt his throat tighten at the show of such loyalty. For Gabe to defend someone so completely...for the rest of the Order, who'd risked everything to help their own, to stand by Dante...it meant something. Maybe there was more to Dante than Vlad had been willing to see. Maybe there was more to the Order than he'd been able to see.

Sophie looked back at him and smiled, her eyes full of joy. "It's so beautiful to see them, isn't it?"

He glanced around at the Order, all of them so majestic and silently proud as they escorted their leader. "Yeah," he said. "It is—"

Just then, the mountain behind them exploded, and Rikker shouted. "Lucien's out! Go!"

Chapter Forty-Two

GABE TWISTED AROUND on Damon's back, scanning the mountain behind them as Damon took off through the air. Behind him, the mountain literally exploded, shattering into millions of fragments of dirt, dust, and rock. With a piercing scream, Lucien ripped through the carnage, his wings beating fiercely as he took to the air, hovering in place as he scanned for them.

Gabe saw the moment that Lucien saw them. He unleashed a howl of fury and took off, moving with mind-numbing speed.

"Fuck." Rikker was beside them. "We'll never make it—"

"I can get us there. I've been both places." Kane spoke up. "I can take us in two trips." He urged his mount toward Damon. "Dante first." He reached over with his hand, and Gabe locked onto his wrist. "Everyone else touch him!" Gabe held Maria tightly as she locked her fingers around Gabe's arm. Vlad and Sophie did the same, and then he shifted Dante so the warrior was against Kane's chest.

Kane swore, his face shocked as Dante drifted close. "Jesus," he whispered. "It's really him." Two other flying demons came close, and their riders, one of which was Rikker, also clasped Kane's arm. "Okay, let's go!"

In an instant, Kane disappeared, and Gabe felt the familiar sensation of the world falling away, and his body disintegrating. Within a split second, his body was reforming in the same cavern that they'd arrived in such a short time ago. Kane vanished almost instantly, and Rikker sprinted toward the wall of the cavern. "Over here, now!"

Gabe grabbed Maria's arm and pulled her toward the wall of the cave. Maria shot him a worried look, but he couldn't risk reassuring her. "Damon," he snapped, just as the demon was shifting back to human form and facing the doorway to the tunnels that Lucien would be coming through. "I need you back here by the wall by Maria. Lucien will be coming straight for her, since she was the one who defeated him, which makes her the current queen. He must kill her before she leaves, so you need to protect her."

Damon spun around, his face hard and determined. He nodded once, and sprinted across the cavern, taking up a protective stance in front of Maria. Vlad and Sophie were already by the wall, along with Dante, Quinn, Ian, and Elijah, all of whom had their weapons out, and their backs around Vlad, Sophie and Dante, providing a protective shield.

Gabe moved up beside Vlad and Rikker. "What do we need to do?"

Rikker already had the amulet open, and the stone in the palm of his hand. He placed it on the wall, closed his eyes, and began a low chant of words that Gabe had never heard, and didn't understand. As he did so, Gabe felt his skin prickle, and heat began to pour out of the wall, as if life itself was flooding from the earth realm into the demon realm.

Kane reappeared with the rest of the crew, including Thano astride his majestic horse. Apollo had to duck his head to keep from hitting the ceiling, and he tossed his head restlessly, prancing in small circles, as if even he understood the threat that was hunting them so fiercely.

"It's open." Rikker stepped back. "Can you get them through?" he said to Vlad.

"It'll take too long to get them through solid rock." He looked at Sophie. "Can you make the wall thinner?"

"Of course." She raced over to the wall and placed her hands on the rock. Instantly, the wall shimmered and became translucent. Gabe could see the water from the pool, and even the plants and animals. Stunned, he put his hand up, but there was some sort of invisible barrier there that kept him from going through.

Vlad jerked his head at Quinn. "Go."

"Dante first."

"No, because Sophie needs to hold it open, and I'm not leaving until she is over, so go!"

There was a loud crash and the rocks began to fall from the wall. Lucien had entered the tunnels.

Quinn swore and sprinted right at the wall. He leapt at it, and Vlad flicked his finger, throwing him through the opening. On his heels were the others, racing across. Apollo leapt through, and Vlad had no trouble sending both of them across, until the only ones left were Gabe, Vlad, Sophie, Maria, Dante, and Damon. The mountain was shaking violently now, and Gabe knew they had only moments until before Lucien would be upon them.

Rikker faced Maria. "It's time." He pulled out a dagger much like Maria's. "Give me permission to go against the rules and challenge you before the fortnight is up."

Maria faced him, and pulled out her own dagger. "I give you permission, on the condition that you keep your promise to protect the women. If you break this promise, my permission is revoked, and I will come back and hunt you down."

"Agreed."

The thundering roar became louder. "I give you permission."

"Queen Maria, I hereby challenge you for leadership of the demon realm."

"I accept your challenge." She braced her feet and faced him.

Gabe glanced at the doorway, and Damon moved closer, using his body to shield his sister. Rikker slashed once with the dagger. Maria didn't react, and let him knock the dagger out of her hand. It clattered to the floor. "Oops," she said. "You win." She gave him a long look. And then went down on one knee. "I pledge my fealty to the new king of the demon realm."

Damon dropped to one knee. "Me, too, now get the hell out of here—"

At that moment, the rock wall exploded outward. Rikker spun toward the carnage. Gabe and Maria instantly launched themselves at Damon, throwing him back toward the opening Sophie was holding. Vlad flicked his hand to thrust them through, and then he, Sophie and Dante came after them.

Gabe looked back just as Lucien appeared in the doorway to the cavern, and then the wall reformed, and all vision was cut off.

The rest of the Order were all waiting in the bottom of the pool, weapons out, every single one of them aware that Rikker had the stone. If Lucien figured it out, or if Rikker hadn't had time to redo the curse, at any second the bottom of the pool could collapse into the demon realm, the barrier severed forever.

They waited, using their preternatural powers to hold their breath for an extended time. The seconds ticked by ominously. Then the seconds became minutes. No sound came from the other side. No ripples broke the water. Just silence. Finally, Gabe looked over at Vlad. *What do you think?*

Vlad held out his hand toward the wall. *I can feel living matter. They're there, on the other side, but the barrier is solid at the moment. It feels exactly how it did the first time we went through.*

Damon spoke. *Lucien can't challenge Rikker for a fortnight. That will give Rikker time to figure out how to manage the situation. If he hasn't come across now, we're safe for two weeks.*

Gabe looked at Damon in surprise. *You can hear us? I thought only Calydons were telepathic.*

He shrugged. *I can hear you.* But then he turned to Vlad. *Send me back over. I shouldn't be here.*

No! Maria grabbed his arm. *Stay here—*

No. Damon pulled his arm away. *Demons can't cross over. It's never happened. You know what I am, Maria. I'm not a half-demon. I'm the full deal. I'm too dangerous—*

Gabe swam over to him and put his hands on Damon's shoulders. *You're loyal, honorable, and a hell of a warrior. You're dangerous as hell, and we need that on our team. I brought you over on purpose, because we need you. Join the Order, Damon.*

What the hell? Quinn swam over. *He's a full demon! Vlad, send him back!*

Ryland and Kane were floating nearby. *We're both half-demon,* Ryland said. *And every Calydon has demon blood. Maybe it's okay. We could use some help.*

Damon looked over at Ryland and Kane, and emotion flashed across his face, so stark and vulnerable that Gabe's throat tightened. *You guys want me? In the Order?*

Yeah. It's about time someone was scarier than I am. Ryland grinned. *But if you fuck up, I'll kill you, and we'll send you back to the demon realm.*

Damon met his gaze. *Promise?*

Fuck yeah.

Damon drew his shoulders back. *Then yeah, I'm in.*

Gabe didn't even look over at Quinn, their interim leader, for approval. He just pointed upward. *Let's surface.*

Ryland looked at Vlad. *Can I escort Dante?*

Vlad nodded. *He's fully corporeal now. You don't need me.* He flicked his hand, sending Dante's inert form through the water to Ryland. Shock flashed across Ryland's face, and he wrapped his hand around Dante's wrist. The rest of the Order immediately surrounded him, and as a unit, they began to swim to the surface, escorting their leader.

Damon waited beside Maria, looking toward the surface, such hope and awe on his face that Gabe felt himself smile. *Go ahead, Damon. It's your world now, too.*

Damon flashed a grin at him that looked so much younger and boyish than he'd ever looked, then he kicked hard, shooting toward the surface, leaving only Vlad, Sophie, Gabe, and Maria behind.

Gabe looked over at Maria, who was also looking toward the surface. Her face was pale, and she caught Gabe's arm, slowing him down so the others moved ahead. *I'm not sure I belong up there, Gabe.*

He took her hands in his and pressed a kiss to each one. *You're half human, sweetheart, and you're all mine. That world up there needs you.*

But I'm a demon—

You're a healer. You're a warrior. You're a best friend. You're a sister. All amazing things that we need in the earth realm. He slipped his hand behind her hair. *And most of all, I need you. You're my world. My life. My future. Hell, you're even my moral conscience. I'll be by your side at all times.*

She searched his face, but before she could answer, Sophie swam over and threw her arms around Maria's shoulders, hugging her tightly. Gabe could see the tension on Sophie's face, and knew she was also nervous about returning to the world she had left behind.

Maria saw Sophie's expression, and then smiled, sliding her hand into Sophie's and nodding. Sophie grinned back, two sisters of solidarity. Gabe was damned glad they'd been able to bring them both over.

Gabe grinned at Vlad, who was behind Sophie. Vlad grinned back, and set his hand on Gabe's shoulder. *We got damned lucky that these women agreed to keep us around.*

Gabe's smile widened. *That we did.*

The women began to swim toward the surface, still holding hands. Vlad and Gabe caught up to them, each of them taking the free hand of their woman. Gabe looked over at Vlad. *Hey.*

Vlad glanced his way. *What?*

You looking for a job?

What do you need?

Want to join the Order?

Vlad's eyebrows shot up. *It's just for Calydons and, apparently, demons.*

You have my blood now. That's close enough. Gabe hesitated. *You taught me a lot about how to be a warrior, Vlad. I was so obsessed with mindlessly following my oath that I never thought about what being a hero or a protector really meant. I get it now. The Order needs your insight. We need you.* His gaze moved to Maria. *And you.*

Her eyes widened. *Has there ever been a female Order of the Blade member?*

Nope.

She laughed then, a laugh that filled his heart with joy. *I can't think of anything more fantastic than having a demon queen become an Order of the Blade member. The irony is a beautiful thing. I'm in.*

Gabe grinned as they neared the surface. He didn't know what the future would hold for them on the surface, but he had a feeling that the rest of his team was going to give him a fair amount of shit about bringing a demon, a demon queen, and a non-Calydon into the Order...but he was ready.

He knew what his team needed, and he was going to make sure they understood.

The Order had changed now, and it had changed for the better.

Chapter Forty-Three

THE WARMTH OF the sun on her face was amazing. Sophie closed her eyes and lifted her face to the sky, holding her palms upward. She breathed deeply, inhaling air so fresh and so clean that she felt as if her entire body was being cleansed simply by the act of breathing. The grass was fresh and soft against her bare feet. She buried her toes in the dirt, awed by how it crumbled beneath her toes.

She was home.

Well, not back in her kingdom, but after a lifetime in the demon realm, anywhere on earth was home...especially if Vlad was there.

"Hey, babe."

She smiled as she felt him nuzzle the side of her neck, his arms sliding around her waist as he crouched behind her. She leaned back against him, resting against his chest. "Any sign of Dante's soul yet?"

"No, but they're taking turns guarding his body. They all believe he'll return to claim it. The body is in perfect condition, as if he's been asleep this whole time." Vlad rested his chin on her shoulder. "You sure you don't want to join us? Gabe said you were invited to join the Order."

"No. I want my freedom. The last thing I want is to sign my soul away to anyone's cause. I want to find my own path now." Sophie looked across the grassy clearing to where the Order members were preparing the induction ceremony for Maria, Vlad, and Damon. A few of the *shevas* were there, and a few of them were being inducted as well. Once the decision had been made to allow Maria to join the Order, apparently, some of the *shevas* had demanded their right to join.

Women joining the Order. It was amazing and right. Sophie loved it, and she was so proud of Maria for being the one to break through. She couldn't imagine any Calydon being any more capable than Maria.

Damon was standing with Ryland, and the warriors were in deep discussion. From what she understood of Ryland, he would be the perfect mentor for a demon. "I can't believe they agreed for all of you to join the Order."

"How could they not? We're amazing." Vlad lightly bit her shoulder, not bothering to acknowledge the long night of debate that had ensued before Gabe had triumphed. Thano, Ryland, and Ian had agreed with him from the start, which had helped wear down the others. "So, I have a question for you."

"What is it?"

He released her and walked around her until he was facing her. He went down on one knee and took her hand. "When we were married so long ago, we were both teenagers. I had no understanding of what it meant to be a husband. I had no understanding of how amazing you were, and what a great future you had ahead of you. I didn't know what teamwork meant, or equality, or partnership. I understand that now, and you're the one who taught it to me." He rubbed his thumb over the ring that was shining gold on her finger. "Sophie," he said, looking right at her.

Her heart started to pound, and her fingers tightened around his. "Yes?"

"I want another chance to do it right. To be the husband and partner that you deserve." He opened her fingers and pressed something cold into her palm, covering it with his hand. "Will you give me another chance, Sophie? Will you marry me again? Renew our vows? Commit to a new future together? I understand if you don't want to. I understand if you want your space, but—"

"Yes." She answered before he could continue, pulling his hand to her heart. "I never stopped loving you, Vlad. We both had to grow to become the people we were meant to be, but we grew together. You make me better, you make me happy, and you enrich my life. I would love nothing more than to marry you again, and be your wife, and your partner, and your best friend." As she said the words, her heart seemed to swell with warmth, pouring emotions into her that she had shut down for so long. She knew this was where she was meant to be, with the man who had been her best friend for so very long. "I love you, Vladimir, and I will always love you."

He grinned, a huge, happy smile that reached his eyes, chasing away the shadows that had been there for so long. Silently, he moved his hand away from hers, and she looked down to see that he had placed in her hand the most beautiful ring she'd ever seen. It was gold, like her other one, but this one had the most extraordinary blue stone shimmering in the setting. The stone hummed with energy, and she instantly recognized that it was from the demon realm, the place that had been her home for so long. "You stole this?"

"I brought it over for you," he clarified. "I would never steal. I'm not that kind of guy." At her deadpan expression, they both suddenly burst into laughter. "Yeah, well," he admitted, "I might have pilfered it from that home you had underground where you and Maria ditched me and Gabe. I knew you would want something from there, and a stone was the only thing that seemed right." He picked it up and angled it toward the sun. "It looks like fire, the same one that kept the light going in the demon realm. You can feel the energy of the demon realm in it." He slid it on her finger. "Home on your hand, just like before." He pressed a kiss to her wedding ring, and the ring he'd just given her. "You will always be part of both worlds, Sophie."

Tears filled her eyes at the thoughtfulness of his gesture, and her heart felt like it was going to explode with love. She clasped her hands behind his neck and smiled at him, smiling with all of her heart, all of her soul, and all the happiness she hadn't felt in so long. "I love you, Vlad. Always and forever. I promise not to forget you ever again."

He grinned and pressed a kiss to the underside of her wrist. "And I promise that if you ever fall into a crevasse that leads to the demon realm again, I will hunt for you from that instant until I find you again, and then I will stand by your side while you kick ass."

"A perfect team."

He nodded. "A perfect team." He grinned and leaned over to kiss her, but just as his lips touched hers, Gabe shouted his name.

Vlad pulled back, his eyes bright with anticipation. "It's time to become an Order member."

She smiled, so proud that her throat was tight. "They're lucky to have you. As am I."

"Back at ya, babe." He kissed her once, hard, and then stood up, turning to face the world that had become his.

GABE STOOD BESIDE Thano and Apollo, watching as the Order made their final preparations for the induction ceremony. Maria was standing beside Quinn, wearing black jeans, a leather jacket, and hiking boots. Her tee shirt was white, and her hair was in a ponytail. He grinned, thinking about how excited she'd been that morning, when they'd slipped away from the rest of the Order and set a small bonfire in the woods. Once it had been burning brightly, she had tossed her red bodice, her leather pants, her stiletto boots, and her red lace bra into the flames. The moment her old clothes had disintegrated into ash, his brave, tough warrior had collapsed to her knees and cried.

He would never forget that moment when she'd let go of the past, of the woman she'd had to be for so long. Her new acceptance of her demon heritage had made her stronger, but the part of her that was a lust demon would always be a part of who she was. Now that she had Gabe, however, he was able to satisfy her, and there was no longer any need for her to incite lust wherever she went. She had finally been able to give that up, and be the woman she wanted to be, a woman who focused on justice, healing, and making the world a better place.

She glanced up at him and caught him watching her. A huge smile broke over her face and she lifted her arm just enough so that he could see the dagger she had tucked under her arm. He'd counted this morning when she got dressed. She had seventeen weapons on her body, and she'd loved strapping on every single one of them. His warrior, his woman, his world, his *sheva*.

"You love her, don't you?" Thano asked quietly.

"Yeah. I do. She's my world."

Thano cocked his head at him. "I have to admit, you are the one guy who I thought would never go down that road. I'm kind of impressed that you have the flexibility to admit you were wrong, and to go in some new directions."

Gabe looked over at the younger Calydon. "Are you talking about Maria, or are you referring to the Order?"

"Both." Thano was quiet for a moment, watching the Order members milling around and preparing for the ceremony. Rohan was standing at the edge, his arms folded over his chest. His hood was up, shrouding his face, and he was keeping his distance from the rest of the team, just enough to give the message that he was not a part of the group. "I miss you guys," he said quietly.

Gabe looked up at Thano. "After this, are you leaving with Rohan again?"

Thano nodded. "The Order of the Blade has a mission, and its new direction is exactly what needs to happen. You've done good, Gabe, and the team was right to make you the new interim leader until Dante returns."

Gabe stood taller at the reminder of what had happened earlier in the day, when the Order had gotten together and asked the weapons who the new leader should be. Every weapon placed at Gabe's feet stayed visible, and the ones placed at the feet of the other members faded almost instantly. The weapons had chosen Gabe as the new leader, even after he'd brought a demon across the barrier. "Maria is the one who made me see the right path. It's all her."

"Then keep her." Apollo stomped his front foot restlessly, and Thano stroked his sleek neck. "You guys are in good shape. You've got a demon on board to train, and some new team members. You don't need me, but Rohan does."

Gabe looked over at him. "Why? What's going on with you guys?"

Thano was quiet for a long moment before he finally spoke. "We're no longer Order of the Blade."

Gabe raised his brows, aware that Rohan was one of the very first Order of the Blade members, before he'd broken off with Dante many centuries ago. He'd reappeared only a few months ago, when the Order had run into him and his hooded team. He'd still technically been Order of the Blade at that time, though what he'd been doing all that time, no one knew. "He's not Order? And you? What are you guys?"

Thano looked over at him. "We're still Order. But it's no longer about rogue Calydons." He gestured to his horse's neck, to the inky blackness. As if on command, Apollo tucked one front leg back and bowed low, his muzzle almost touching the earth. At the same time, Thano bowed low, sweeping his arm out wide. "Welcome, my friend, to the Order of the Night."

ABOUT THE AUTHOR

Hailed by J.R. Ward as a "paranormal star, "*New York Times* and *USA Today* bestselling author Stephanie Rowe is the author of more than forty-five novels, and she's a four-time nominee for the RITA® award, the highest award in romance fiction.

For a complete booklist, visit:
www.stephanierowe.com

Keep up with the latest Stephanie Rowe news on Facebook at
www.facebook.com/StephanieRoweBooks

On Twitter at StephanieRowe2

Or by signing up for her private newsletter at:
http://stephanierowe.com/connect.php

ALSO BY STEPHANIE ROWE

CONTEMPORARY ROMANCE

BIRCH CROSSING SERIES
Unexpectedly Mine
Accidentally Mine
Unintentionally Mine
Irresistibly Mine
Mistakenly Mine (2017)

WYOMING REBELS SERIES
A Real Cowboy Never Says No
A Real Cowboy Knows How to Kiss
A Real Cowboy Rides a Motorcycle
A Real Cowboy Never Walks Away
A Real Cowboy Loves Forever (2017)

MYSTIC ISLAND SERIES
Wrapped Up In You

PARANORMAL ROMANCE

HEART OF THE SHIFTER SERIES
Dark Wolf Rising
Dark Wolf Unbound
Dark Wolf Untamed (Coming Soon!)

SHADOW GUARDIAN SERIES
Leopard's Kiss

ORDER OF THE BLADE SERIES
Darkness Awakened
Darkness Seduced
Darkness Surrendered
Forever in Darkness
Darkness Reborn
Darkness Arisen
Darkness Unleashed
Inferno of Darkness
Darkness Possessed
Shadows of Darkness
Hunt the Darkness (2017)

ORDER OF THE NIGHT SERIES
(An Order of the Blade spinoff)
Book one coming in 2017

NIGHTHUNTER SERIES
Not Quite Dead

ROMANTIC SUSPENSE

ALASKA HEAT SERIES
Ice
Chill
Ghost

YOUNG ADULT

ONCE UPON AN ENDING SERIES
The Fake Boyfriend Experiment
Ice Cream, Jealousy & Other Dating Tips
The Truth About Thongs
How to Date a Bad Boy
Pedicures Don't Like Dirt
Geeks Can Be Hot

CPSIA information can be obtained
at www.ICGtesting.com
Printed in the USA
FSHW02n0632231018
53220FS